Ghost Wolf

Brandon Chen

Ghost Wolf

Formatting by Rik - Wild Seas Formatting

Table of Contents

Behind Silver Bars

The massive gates to the arena groaned as they swung open, and the sun's beaming light shined into Yuri's turquoise eyes. The young man brushed his flowing black hair from his face as he sauntered onto a dirt battleground, surrounded by large grandstands filled with affluent citizens and nobles alike. They cheered like barbarians, their formality absent in the coliseum.

Yuri, dressed in the tattered clothes of a street rat, pressed the soles of his bare feet onto the scorching dirt, his skin tingling from the heat. Dirt and grime was smeared across his ripped clothing, from his grey shirt to his torn pants.

Yuri felt the puzzled looks of countless nobles burning into him. After all, what was a boy from the slums doing in Horux's Noble Arena?

The Noble Arena was a coliseum that hosted an annual competition between the various Houses of the nobles. Each House chose a fighter that would participate in the brawl and battle for their faction's honor. It was typical that most noble Houses opted to hire professional fighters, trained warriors, or skilled heroes to fight on their behalf. But the group that Yuri represented picked a destitute boy from the grim corners of the ghetto.

Yuri scanned the crowd and eventually caught sight of his best friend, Asmund, of the Wolf Noble House. The boy brushed his curly blonde hair from his sky-blue eyes. He wore vermillion garments coupled with golden necklaces that dangled to his chest, flaunting his wealth.

It was Asmund's father, Beo, who'd enlisted Yuri for this prestigious contest. The winning House of the competition was awarded tremendous amounts of gold, wealth that each faction wanted in their treasury. Many were bewildered by the noble's choice of Yuri as the Wolf House's champion, but Beo seemed confident in Yuri's skill.

The other four combatants were all shirtless, revealing their rippling muscles and toned bodies. They all had their eyes trained on Yuri, whom they believed to be the weakest of the brawlers. It was clear that their plan was to eliminate the young man first.

Yuri licked his bottom lip and smirked at his opponents. He cracked his neck and hopped about, trying to get his blood circulating. Any ordinary boy would've been nervous in his current situation, being thrust into an arena against experienced warriors. However, he didn't feel anything but the electrifying sensation of adrenaline channeling through his veins, filling him with excitement. He slammed his fist against the palm of his other hand, a smile spreading across his face. *I'm ready.*

The announcer's voice reverberated through the stadium: "Hello, ladies and gentlemen! We've gathered today to witness the annual battle in the Noble Arena of Horux! We have our five contestants, each representing their Noble House! Now, brawlers, you were frisked before you entered the arena, and you know that you will fight using only your body. As this is a friendly match, murder is prohibited. You are to battle until there is only one man left standing! The winning House of today's event will receive three tons of gold and the victorious champion will be invited to dine at Horux's palace with the royal family!"

Yuri blinked, his arms drooping to his side. Suddenly, the roars of the crowd became muffled. He found himself staring at the king, who was seated on the far side of the stadium beside his beautiful daughter. *The winner gets to have dinner with the royal family?* He looked to the graceful princess, whose beauty mesmerized him in an instant. It took all of his willpower to pry his gaze from the highborn woman and turn his attention back to the overly-confident fighters before him. The boy's hands balled into tight fists at his side, his knuckles cracking. His eagerness for victory was now enhanced tenfold.

"Get ready!"

Yuri acknowledged his first target, the man to his right that was nearest to him. The opponent was about fifty meters away, so it would take a brief sprint to reach him. Yuri knew that he would have to knock that man out quickly before the other three fighters reached him. Would he get there fast enough?

"Go!"

"Get them, Yuri!" Asmund called out, his voice somehow standing out amongst the countless cries and shouts that shook the stadium.

Yuri dug the tip of his right foot into the ground and took off, racing across the arena with incredible speed. The wind pounded into his face, blowing back his hair, but his confident gaze stayed locked on its target. The crowd watched in awe as the young man reached his opponent in six seconds, moving at such a fast pace that it didn't seem like he would stop. And he didn't.

The stunned man stood, stupefied by the boy's sprinting speed. Yuri leapt forward and clobbered the man across the cheek, sending the brawler spinning to the ground. The opponent was unconscious before he struck the dirt. Yuri skidded to a stop, turning to see that another participant was quickly approaching him from behind. *That's one down.*

The street boy swung his body around, bringing his leg upward and kicking the man right in the throat. A gasp escaped the man's lips, but Yuri couldn't afford to give him a moment to catch his breath. He grabbed his enemy by the head and relentlessly smashed his knee into the fighter's skull. The crowd roared at the resounding crack that split air. *That's two.*

Yuri released his fallen opponent and allowed the limp man to collapse to the sandy ground, blood streaming from a massive gash on his head. The boy turned around and received a solid

3

punch to his face, sending him staggering backward. He twitched his aching nose and ignored his spinning vision. He'd taken plenty of punches before; this was nothing. *But wow, this guy really knows how to punch.* He glared at his next foe, a bulky man of massive proportions.

Yuri shot forward and unleashed a barrage of fast punches that pounded against the man's forearms, which he held up to protect his face from the oncoming flurry of blows. Yuri brought his knee upward and sank it straight into the man's genitals. The color drained from the man's face as he exhaled painfully through his mouth. His arms instinctively lowered to protect his private area, leaving most of his body open to attack. Yuri launched a powerful blow into the brawler's cheek, driving him straight to the ground. *And there goes three — one left.*

The boy waved his aching fist in the air, wincing at the bleeding cuts on his knuckles. At that moment, he received yet another punch to his face, sending him staggering sideways. Yuri groaned, the metallic taste of blood flooding into his mouth. He eyed his last enemy, the final obstacle standing between him and his dinner with the princess. Not to mention winning honor and riches for his best friend's House.

Yuri shook his head, trying to clear his dizziness. The corners of his vision were already starting to blur after receiving such a fierce strike to the face. "Yeah, that's a nasty punch," he spat, watching as his enemy bounced back and forth, patiently waiting for Yuri to make his next move. *It doesn't matter though, I've probably been in more fights than you can even dream of.*

Yuri brought his right leg in a sweeping kick that rushed upward towards the man's ribcage. The brawler swept his arm to the side, perfectly prepared to block the attack. *You're finished.* Yuri halted himself and brought his leg back, swinging his entire body in a spin so that his kick cut around from the left instead of the right. Shock and disbelief registered on the fighter's face as Yuri's heel cracked straight into the unprotected side of his face, sending him crashing to the dirt ground.

Like a starving wolf, Yuri pounced on his prey, sitting on his opponent's stomach as he mercilessly rained a bombardment of heavy blows on the man's face. Blood splattered onto the dirt around him and Yuri felt the warm liquid sticking to his stinging knuckles.

Realizing that his opponent was unconscious, the boy lowered his hands to his side. Gasping as he staggered to his feet, he towered triumphantly over the defeated participants. A prolonged silence dragged out as the spectators stared at the arena's champion.

An uproar of mixed reactions suddenly erupted from the crowd. Some were angry that Yuri had won, believing that he'd used cheap tricks to win. Some were surprised, for they didn't expect a young man from the slums to be able to compete against experienced warriors that had participated in real wars. And the rest were of Asmund's Noble House, overjoyed that their chosen participant was victorious.

Yuri could feel the ground beneath him quaking from the roaring cheers and he turned to look at Asmund, who grinned like a child on his birthday. The victor chuckled and then turned his gaze to the princess. Now, he was finally going to have the chance to talk to her.

***

"Ow, ow, ow," Yuri grumbled as one of Asmund's servants pressed a bag of cold ice to his swollen eye. He snatched the bag away from the woman, who retreated several steps. She seemed startled. "I can do it myself." The boy sat on the edge of a large bed, wincing as he watched Asmund pace back and forth excitedly.

"I can't believe you won that!" Asmund exclaimed, throwing his arms into the air. "That was incredible. I mean, I know that you said that you were really good at fighting, but I didn't know you were *that* good! Outstanding, and the fact that you just took those punches and kept standing … I would've been knocked out from the first one!"

"That's why you wouldn't last a day in Horux's slums," Yuri said, laughing. He lowered the bag of ice from his eye and pointed to his face. "Let's forget the arena for a second and focus on the important issue here. How am I going to fix this eye before my date with the princess?"

"You realize that it isn't a date, right?" Asmund said, folding his arms as he smirked at his injured friend. A small smile crossed his lips as he looked at Yuri's swollen face. "The king is going to be there, along with dozens of knights, so you won't have any private time to enchant her. I doubt you'll even get the chance to hold her hand."

"Who knows? I'm a sneaky guy. I'm sure that I'll figure something out." Yuri winked. "Don't underestimate a thief. I've been stealing my whole life, especially the hearts of fair maidens. My charm will indefinitely claim her love."

"What charm?" the noble jested.

"Oh, shut it."

The door opened and Yuri turned to find Beo sauntering into the room. The noble was dressed in a fancy black suit tailored from the most expensive cloth in Horux. He had a rose tucked into his front pocket and wore a buttoned white shirt underneath the jacket. Tapping his ebony leather boots on the marble floor, the handsome man smiled charmingly at the two boys. He ran his hand over his slicked-back dark hair. His brown eyes drifted over Asmund and rested on Yuri. "I'm impressed that you won, Yuri," Beo said with a grin. "Those were highly talented warriors that you were facing. Most of the nobles bet that you would be the first one to be knocked out of the competition."

Yuri smirked, pointing to his chest with his thumb. "Those warriors might have been on the battlefield once or twice before … but I'm on it every day." He lowered his hand and grabbed his ice pack, pressing it back to his stinging eye. "Those brawlers did hit hard. But in terms of agility, they were lacking."

"Hm, it would seem that the Lower District sure has trained you to become quite the fighter," Beo said observantly. "No one from our Noble House had ever seen you in action before, so it was quite the delightful surprise that you were able to single-handedly defeat the rest of the participants. Even the king himself was impressed with your talent."

"Did the princess say anything?"

"Not that I am aware," Beo said, raising his eyebrow.

"Yuri's got a little crush," Asmund said to his father.

"Quiet," Yuri muttered, his face beginning to turn beet-red. His face became even hotter when Beo burst out in merry laughter. "H-Hey! Princess Violet is one of the most stunning women in all of Horux," he grumbled. "Either way, I don't stand a chance if I don't get rid of this swollen eye."

"I know a relatively skilled magician in the marketplace that can fix you up quickly. She's expensive, since she uses magic to heal her patients, but I'll cover the expenses. It's the least that I can do after today's victory," Beo said, walking over to a wooden table that had several sheets of paper stacked beside a quill and ink. The noble dipped the quill in the small container of ink and began to scribble on a piece of parchment. "Go and see her first thing tomorrow morning. If you hand her this, she'll heal anything you present to her." Beo held out the note to Yuri.

The boy took the piece of paper and put it in his pocket, nodding thanks to Beo. "I appreciate it."

"It's no problem. The king will send a messenger to let you know when your dinner with the royal family is scheduled," Beo said. "We have a celebratory feast planned for tonight. Will you stay? The cooks are making exquisite dishes that I know you'll love."

"No, sorry," Yuri said, standing up. He bowed his head in apology to the noble. "I should go home tonight. I haven't seen my family in several days, but I'll make sure to come by tomorrow."

"I can give you your portion of the earnings then." Beo smiled.

Yuri shook his head. "I don't need the money. It's fine."

The noble blinked, surprised that the poverty-stricken boy was rejecting such a generous offer of wealth. "But with the gold you could—" Beo met Yuri's gaze and sighed. "Okay, I understand. Perhaps we can talk about this later." He reached into his pocket and pulled out a small pouch that jingled with gold coins. It was probably enough to buy food for Yuri's family for an entire week. "At least take this. Since you won't be having dinner with us, you might as well grab something to eat on your way home."

Yuri stared at the pouch for a moment and accepted it, knowing that Beo's House was now rich beyond belief from the tournament winnings. The boy tucked the money into his pocket. "Thanks." He grinned at Asmund. "I'll catch up with you tomorrow then?"

Asmund smirked, raising his hand as he bumped his forearm against Yuri's, forming a X with their arms. That was their sign of friendship. "Sounds good. Give Terias my regards."

Minutes later, Yuri was strolling down the cobblestone path that left Asmund's mansion. The manor's front yard was the size of the entire street that Yuri lived on, a street that was home to five hundred people. But here, all this fresh grass was used for nothing but show.

Yuri narrowed his eyes, playing with the pouch of coins in his pocket. The luxurious lifestyle that all of the nobles lived was extremely unfair. He knew that. Many of the inhabitants of the Horux's Lower District loathed Yuri, for his connection with Asmund's family allowed him to benefit from a few of the luxuries that the nobles enjoyed daily.

In fact, Beo and Asmund both regularly offered Yuri money to help him and his family get by. Taking the bag of money from his pocket, the boy tossed the jingling pouch into the air and caught it. Most of the time, he rejected their generosity. Although, there were always exceptions.

***

Beo lumbered through the dark corridors of Horux's abandoned jail, located two thousand feet beneath the city. The noble held a luminous torch, its vibrant light combating the blackness that swallowed the catacombs. Trudging forward, his heavy footsteps echoed loudly through the empty halls. Behind him, he dragged a heavy sack, soaked with blood.

He finally halted at a gigantic cell with hundreds of silver bars that touched down from the high ceiling. Reaching into his bag, he pulled out a slab of raw, bloody meat. He tossed it into the cell, watching as the bait slapped onto the stone ground.

"Come out, Faelen," Beo called out, his expression stern as he gazed into the darkness before him. He reached out and used his torch to light a small brazier beside the cell, illuminating the area. "There's no need to be shy, it's only me."

"*Filthy noble,*" a deep voice growled. A monstrous creature, with fur the color of night, emerged from the shadows. It stood ten feet tall, towering over Beo. Its snout and face were like that of a wolf, but it stood upright on two legs like a human. The beast bared its dagger-like set of teeth, which were capable of biting the limbs clean off of any beast. Its claws were so sharp that they could shred most metals to pieces. "If it weren't for these silver bars, I'd be gnawing on your cracked skull right now."

"That's why you're in a cell, werewolf," Beo said, standing inches from the silver bars. "You'd better watch your tongue around your master, otherwise I'll have to punish you. How long have you been isolated in this cell? Two centuries now?"

"How dare you call yourself my master? Do you know who I am?" Faelen roared, lashing out at Beo. The very moment that his claws touched the silver bars, a surge of agonizing pain detonated through his body. The palms of the werewolf's hands, which had briefly grazed the metal, were burning as if they had just been dipped in scorching lava. Doubling over in pain, Faelen darted an irate glare at the noble, his red eyes flashing with rage. "When I escape this accursed chamber, I'll infect everyone in Horux. Everyone you know will die, including that pampered son of yours. I'll rip him to shreds and devour him right before your eyes. You'll see. All of you pathetic humans will finally become the beasts that you've feared for so long."

"Today's generation has only heard of werewolves in stories. Besides me, no one has even seen one. In fact, you're the last of your kind," Beo said calmly, his words striking a blow to Faelen's heart. "You're an endangered species, which is the only reason I'm still keeping you alive. That, and ensuring your survival has been a family tradition for generations."

Faelen slammed his hands on the floor cracking the stone with his tremendous power. "I can't wait to snuff the lights from your eyes when I escape, you bastard." The werewolf watched as Beo turned and walked away. It was only seconds before the beast saw the flickering light of the noble's torch vanish. He lowered his head, grabbing the slab of meat on the ground and raising it to his mouth. Swallowing the food in a single gulp, he plopped himself back onto the ground, smirking. "I know you're there, skulking in the darkness. Does Beo know that you followed him into his secret catacombs?"

A man walked from the darkness, stepping into the brazier's light before the ferocious beast. He had hidden in the shadows, skillfully avoiding Beo's line of vision. The stranger trembled slightly, and Faelen could sense visceral fear shredding this man apart. His face was completely blanched, his skin nearly the color of snow. His brown hair was long and bundled up into a bun, and he wore ebony leather armor that was hidden behind a black cloak. His dark brown eyes stared at the werewolf, his powerful gaze unwavering even though he was absolutely terrified of the creature.

Without a word, he bolted in the opposite direction, fading into the darkness.

***

The man, Archerus, held his hand tightly over his mouth, muffling his heavy breathing. He could feel his heart pounding in his chest and sweat streaking down his face. The werewolf's wrathful roars shook the ground beneath him as he snuck away. Archerus wanted to break into a sprint and get the hell out of the catacombs as soon as possible, but by doing so he would run straight into Beo, who was still unaware of his presence.

It took him thirty minutes to blindly navigate his way through the thick darkness, finally reaching an abandoned cave in the ominous forest just outside of Horux.

Archerus stumbled out of the grotto, immediately crumpling to his knees. The moonlight made the perspiration on his face glisten. He panted, shaking his head in disbelief.

To think that such a monstrous beast really existed. Archerus had heard tales that werewolves once wandered the forest outside of Horux. However, he'd never thought that such rumors could be true. Many nobles noticed that Beo went for a midnight walk every night for the past decade, journeying outside of Horux's walls and into the eerie forest. Archerus had merely followed Beo out of curiosity. He never expected to find a creature of myth!

I have to tell the townsfolk. They need to know of the beast's existence! Beo will surely be condemned for his treachery.

Archerus sprinted through the forest in the direction of Horux. The trees around him were all dead and leafless, with drooping branches and bark the color of burned charcoal. Black ravens with gleaming red eyes rested upon the branches of these trees, watching Archerus as he dashed towards Horux with haste. His eyes were wide and his arms flailed, as if he were running away from a beast.

Watching him from the shadows was a silent man, shrouded in a black cloak. The mysterious figure turned his head toward the cave from whence Archerus had come, eying the entrance to Horux's secret underground catacombs. A small smile split across the man's lips before he turned away and began to walk deeper into the forest.

Alone with the Moon

Cool mead trickled into Yuri's mouth, tickling his throat with its bitter taste. Smacking his lips, he set his mug down on the table of the pub. Fast fiddle music fused together with the boisterous sounds of singing drunkards and laughing fools to create a cacophony of sound that hurt Yuri's eardrums. He sighed and lowered his head. After spending several days with Asmund's polite family, returning to a chaotic environment such as this was unsettling.

Yuri spun a gold coin on the table and leaned his face against his palm, pressing his elbow against the hard wood of the table. He bit his lower lip, watching as the coin spun. *I'll get used to it again, I always do.*

There was a loud bang at the entrance of the tavern and the entire building suddenly went silent. Yuri's coin clattered to the table's surface.

All of the drunken men and women in the pub stared at an exhausted stranger that was doubled over, gasping for air. The man wore a black cloak that curled around his body, covering his leather armor. His long hair was undone, causing it to cascade over his face. "Listen to me!" he panted, even though he already had the attention of everyone in the tavern. "Werewolves ... they aren't just myths. They really do exist, there is one underneath the city ... I saw it!"

A chorus of laughter arose from a crowd of drunks near the tavern's entrance. The stranger stared at the nearby group of guffawing men, shocked that they did not believe him. "Beo, the noble, is the one that has the beast locked up! Please, you must believe me! We are living so close to an infectious creature that could turn us all into abominations if it is let loose!"

"Aren't you a bit old to be believing tales of werewolves, Archerus?" said a man standing in the tavern's main doorway. The newcomer was clad in shining metal armor that covered him from neck to toe. His helmet was gripped in his right gauntlet, resting at his side. A red cape streamed down his back, grazing the wooden floor of the pub. Over his iron chest plate was a dark-blue tabard, bearing the majestic insignia of a white wolf woven into the fine fabric.

Yuri took another swig of his mead as he watched the knight. The tabard that the warrior wore was a sign that he worked directly for the king of Horux, it was only worn by the city's greatest warriors. Yuri tapped his chin, feeling that he recognized this man from somewhere. *That's it! He's the stern man that was standing next to Princess Violet during the arena match.* Yuri narrowed his eyes. *So, what's he doing here? We're in Horux's Lower District. No one here likes members of the upper class.*

"I'm telling you the truth," Archerus insisted, turning to face the knight. "It is so like you to make judgments before you see the proof, Senna."

"You won't be showing any proof because werewolves *do not exist.* Now, silence. I am not here for you," Senna growled, pushing Archerus aside like an unwanted toy as he entered the silent pub. Three armed guards, men that also worked for the king, clanked through the doorway behind their superior officer.

The royal knight's gaze met Yuri's, sending a subtle chill creeping through his skin. "I'm here for today's champion, Yuri."

"Yuri?" Archerus grumbled, watching as the three soldiers walked past him. "You care nothing for the wellbeing of the people if you let something like this slide, Senna! A vicious beast lives beneath the streets of Horux. I can show you, the entrance to the catacombs that confine the monster is in the forest just outside the city. All I need is a moment of your time and—"

"Enough of this!" Senna boomed, darting Archerus a glare from across the tavern. The warrior's commanding voice froze everyone in the pub. The man cleared his throat and nodded to the musicians. "Go on."

The music started to play once more and the conversations continued, sending the inn diving back into its former chaos.

Senna walked to Yuri's table and bobbed his head in acknowledgement. He pulled out a letter that was marked with the red ink of the royal seal, holding it out to the boy. "This letter is directly from the king, inviting you to the palace tomorrow night. Please follow the instructions carefully and do not be late."

Yuri examined the knight closely, looking him up and down. Taking the letter, he slid it into his pocket and nodded thanks to the warrior. "Thank you."

"Do not thank me," Senna said, a hint of hostility in his voice. "I'm surprised that a weakling like you managed to win the Nobles' Tournament this year. Normally there are more talented participants, but this event was especially disappointing. A boy from the slums, defeating famed war heroes? What a disgrace they are, since they managed to lose so easily to someone like you."

The corners of Yuri's lips curved into an arrogant smirk. "Oh? You think you can do better?"

Senna's eyes flashed with confidence as he glared down at Yuri. "Not just better, boy. I could erase you from the face of Terrador if I wanted."

"Well, let's see you try." Yuri grinned.

"Sir!"

Senna turned around at the voice of one of his henchmen. He saw that Archerus had bumped into a man, causing him to slam into an entire group of people that were drinking at a table. Within seconds, a massive brawl broke out as the drinkers started to punish the clumsy man. Individuals were rapidly taking sides and soon the pub became a war zone. "Calm things down in here," he commanded his three soldiers, who immediately rushed to try and break up fights. "As for you—" he began, but found that Yuri had already disappeared in the chaos. The knight scowled in annoyance as he stormed towards the entrance of the pub. "Damn it!"

Senna used his heavy gauntlets to shove people out of the way, sending them sprawling onto the ground, as he marched towards his target. Finally reaching Archerus, who had defeated three men already, Senna gripped his metal helmet in his hand. The knight bashed Archerus across the skull with the helmet, knocking the man out instantly. The cloaked man hit the ground with a powerful thud, his eyes rolling back. "Wrong time to start a fight," Senna snarled, dragging Archerus out of the tavern by his hood. "This time, I'm putting you behind bars."

***

Yuri sauntered through the streets of the Lower District as he munched on an apple. He yawned, exhausted after everything that had happened during the day. At least he'd managed to slip out of that bar fight before things got too messy.

Yuri suddenly stopped walking, his eyes fixed on the cobblestone street before him. That man in the bar had mentioned Beo. He'd said that the noble had a werewolf locked up ... underneath the streets of Horux? The boy's features contorted into a puzzled frown. He had realized that Beo left his mansion every night at around midnight with a sack slung over his shoulder. *What if...?*

"Bang!"

Yuri snapped back to reality, finding three thugs trundling from a shadowy alleyway. The man in the middle had his fingers pointed like a pistol and he blew on the tip of his index finger as if the gun were real. "How fares your journey back from your masters, slave boy?"

"Don't call me that," Yuri grumbled. "Just because I have a highborn friend does not mean that I am his slave."

"It doesn't? But you're always off running errands for them, like a lap dog. Fine, I won't call you a slave then. What are you then, a gladiator?" The boy hurled a piece of parchment onto the ground. Written on the paper was news of Yuri's victory in the Nobles' Tournament. "The title doesn't matter, Yuri. You're still a part of their damned world."

"We're all citizens of Horux, Terias," Yuri growled, storming forward towards the three thugs. He thrust his face inches from Terias's, his unwavering glare burning into the shifting eyes of the young man. "I come from the same background as you. I'm poor, desperate, and I have a family to feed, so don't you dare go off calling me one of the nobles, because if I were then I wouldn't have to return to this hell every damned night to see your repulsive face."

One of Terias's friends reached out and grabbed Yuri's shoulder, but the boy twisted the man's wrist abruptly, and a slight gasp escaped the thug's lips. Yuri smashed his fist into the man's face, causing a spurt of blood to spray onto his knuckles as the enemy struck the ground. The boy turned, but was too late to avoid a heavy strike from Terias's other companion. A powerful punch struck Yuri straight across the cheek, causing him to stagger backwards slightly. Compared to the blows he'd received earlier in the day, it was like being struck by a child.

Yuri rotated his body and leapt into the air, spinning twice with blinding speed. He cracked a heavy kick across the man's face, causing the thug to spiral to the ground. Yuri landed gracefully after the strike and turned to glance at Terias from the corner of his eye. "You aren't going to attack me?"

Terias clenched his jaw and glanced away, clearly irritated. "What's the point? We both know what the outcome of the fight would be."

17

"You're right," Yuri said, tossing his apple into the air. Catching it, he swiftly took a bite out of the fruit and shrugged as he walked past Terias. "You can thank yourself for making me this strong. After ten years of getting the living crap beaten out of me every day, I've finally learned how to defend myself. I could even say that I'm one of Horux's greatest fighters."

Terias glared at Yuri from over his shoulder, watching as the boy walked away. "One of these days, your arrogance will get the best of you, Yuri."

"Maybe so, but I'll deal with that problem when the time comes," Yuri called without looking back. "Also, if you and your friends bother to assault me again I won't just leave you idiots with a couple of bruises. I'll start breaking bones."

Terias broke his gaze from Yuri and knelt to tend to his friends. He lowered his head and sighed, staring at the bruised visage of one of his unconscious companions.

Terias had abused Yuri since they were children. Yuri had always been alone, lacking friends while Terias was the popular one. A group of boys would descend upon Yuri, in the same alleyway every day, and unleash barrages of punches upon the young boy. At one point, they beat Yuri so badly that he almost died. Regardless of that, Yuri always returned to the same alleyway at the same time each day, because it was how he got home after school. He could have decided to take an alternate route, but he never did. Instead, he stood up to Terias and his cronies, enduring relentless abuse every day. That is ... until one day he decided to fight back.

At first, Yuri was only able to land a couple punches before he was knocked out. But as the weeks went on, Yuri was soon able to beat up one of the five boys that would ambush him. Months went by, and eventually Yuri was able to take down all five. Then Terias decided to bring more of his friends to ambush Yuri in the alleys. By the time he was eighteen, Yuri was able to beat up over thirty of Terias's thugs effortlessly. Through experience, perseverance, and endurance, Yuri managed to become one of Horux's most skilled fighters.

Terias bit his lower lip. "You damned freak ... why did you keep coming back every day? Did you enjoy getting hit?" *Every time I saw you coming back to the alleyway ... all I would see is that stupid, arrogant look of confidence in your eyes! That expression ... even though you're getting the crap beaten out of you, you still think you're better than me!*

Isn't that right, Yuri?

***

Yuri's hands were jammed deep into his pockets as he strolled down the narrow alleyway that led to his home. Leaning against the stone walls of the passage were several homeless people that were either sleeping or dead from starvation. Walking past them, Yuri's expression did not change. He kept his eyes forward. He knew that if he ever failed to bring home food for his family then they would all end up like these poor souls on the streets.

The boy looked up and saw an open window on the building to his right, three stories above the ground. Running forward, he pounced towards the wall on his right. He slammed the front of his right foot against the hard stone, pressing his boots against the building. He leapt to the left building and then back to the right. Lashing out with his hands, he used his fingers like talons and latched onto a windowsill. Yuri began to haul himself upward, scaling the side of the building with ease until he reached the open window of his home.

He dragged himself up, pressing his toes into the windowsill. He stepped down into a tiny room where his family lived. It was tough for three people to sleep and eat in a room that was smaller than a servant's bathroom in Asmund's mansion.

A single candle, placed below the window, illuminated the room. There was a bucket in the corner where waste was stored. Positioned on the floor beside each other were two mattresses, both caked in dirt. Yuri's mother and young brother shared one of them while Yuri took the other.

Yuri reached into his pocket and pulled out his pouch of gold coins. "I'm home," he whispered, smiling warmly at his mother and young brother.

His brother was asleep, which was expected of an eight-year-old child at two in the morning. He had short black hair and wore some of Yuri's old clothes, since their family could not afford to buy his brother his own set of garments.

Yuri's mother, on the other hand, was completely awake. She sat on Yuri's bed in her ragged dress, which was now tinted black despite its original white color. Her dark hair was greasy, for she was in great need of a bath, and her hazel eyes watched Yuri as a panther would its prey. The patient woman sat on her knees, her hands folded before her. "Where have you been, Yuri?"

"I left you enough money to—"

"I don't care about that," Yuri's mother snapped, standing up. "What's that on your face? Another beating?"

"No, I participated in the Nobles' Tournament," Yuri murmured, turning his head from his mother so that she would no longer have to look at his swollen eye. "I won."

"Y-You did?" The tone in her voice changed completely from anger to that of surprise. "Then that means you must have—"

"Money? Yeah, this should be enough to feed us for a week," Yuri said, holding out the bag of coins. He tossed it to his mother, who caught it. Instead of being gleeful, her countenance reflected disappointment and shock.

"You won the Nobles' Tournament ... and all you got was enough food to feed us for a week? You should've been granted enough wealth to buy a home in the Upper District! How is this possible? As the victor of a prestigious competition, you should be awarded much more than just this! Is that bastard Beo hoarding all of the winnings for himself? If that's so, I'll—"

"You'll do what, Mom?" Yuri said, watching his mother. His expression was apathetic. He'd known that this would be her reaction. "You'll do nothing. It's not Beo's fault that we didn't get a lot of money from the tournament. He offered me half of the winnings, which would be more than enough to buy a mansion in the noble sector."

Yuri's mother's face was filled with dismay as she stared at her son. Her hands trembled and she dropped the pouch of money on the mattress. "You ... you rejected his offer?"

"Yes," Yuri replied.

Her face turned red with rage as she lashed out and struck Yuri across the face. The sound was loud enough to wake up Yuri's brother, Han, who sat up and rubbed his eyes. "What's going on?" he murmured.

"We live in an absolute shit hole, Yuri! We are one of the most desperate families in Horux, barely scraping by with enough food to eat. We're unhygienic and we don't even have the money to afford medicine when we get ill. I can't believe that you have the audacity to turn down any amount of money. Money that could change our lives. Do you not care about us?" Yuri's mother was practically screaming.

"M-Mom...," Han croaked out, watching his mother with wide eyes.

"Shut up and go to sleep!" she barked angrily, her eyes still on Yuri.

"Don't talk to him like that," Yuri snarled. "The reason that I didn't accept the money is because I don't want to earn wealth through my connection to the nobles. There are thousands of people in the Lower District who are just as unfortunate as us. They don't have the same opportunity that I do, to come home with money to feed you and Han. And if either you or Han ever got sick … I know that Asmund would give the money to—"

"You're denying wealth … because you think that we don't deserve it?" His mother brought her hand back, about to strike Yuri once more. But Yuri grabbed her wrist before she could hit him. The woman's eyes went wide with disbelief, her hand shaking as she attempted to overpower Yuri, but to no avail. "You dare—"

"I'm the reason we have this home," Yuri declared, squeezing his mother's wrist, inflicting slight pain. "I'm the reason food is put on the table and that we are clothed. I am the reason that our family is still alive. Do you think that your job sweeping crap off the streets is enough to pay for anything? Without me, you and Han would both be on the streets or *dead*." His gaze was cold, striking visceral fear into the heart of his mother. "The only reason I don't shatter the bones in your wrist right now is because of my respect for you as a member of my family. If you were anyone else, I wouldn't hesitate."

Yuri released his mother's wrist and leapt out of the window behind him. His hands latched onto the edge of the tiled rooftop of the building on the other side of the alleyway. He grunted as he pulled himself onto the roof and turned to glance at his mother over his shoulder, watching her from the corner of his eye.

"Where are you going?" his mother demanded, rushing to the window.

"Out. Use the money I gave you to buy food for you and Han," Yuri said, dashing away along the rooftops. He'd taken a few gold coins for himself, and they jingled like bells in his pockets as he ran.

The boy's shoes thumped loudly against the tiled material of each roof as he leapt from building to building with no real destination. Regardless, he had no intention of stopping. He marveled at the full moon, which beamed its luminous light down on the sleeping city.

Slowing to a stop, Yuri realized that he'd reached Horux's docks, which housed dozens of monstrously large ships. His heart pounded from the brisk run as he gazed upon the glistening seawater, the moonlight delicately reflecting off the ocean's surface.

Yuri plopped down at the edge of the building with his legs dangling off the roof. "Sometimes I don't know what to do," he murmured. "I know that it's best for Mom and Han if I just take the money that Beo offered me. But ... it's unfair to everyone else. People like Terias don't have the chance to get money like I do." He groaned, looking up at the shining moon, as if it would offer him guidance. "I would never let anything bad happen to Mom or Han. I can provide what we need to survive, but do we need more than that?"

Silence.

"Maybe Mom is right and I should accept the offer ... for the good of our family. Han deserves to get an education, and I don't remember the last time that I saw Mom smile. She tried to hit me today and I said some awful things to her ... damn it. I just wish—" Yuri swallowed hard, wiping moisture from his eyes. "I just wish that you were here, Dad. You'd know what to do. You always did."

Fellowship

"**O**i, wake up. You're going to fall off the roof. From this height, you'll go splat as soon as you hit the ground. Hey, are you listening to me?" an echoing voice called to Yuri.

The boy's eyes groggily cracked open, spotting Terias hovering over him with his hands on his hips. Yuri blinked several times and rubbed the crust from his eyes with the back of his hand, yawning. He dragged his legs off the side of the roof and rolled over, laying his stomach on the hard tiles. "Eh? What are you doing up here, Terias?" he groaned, stretching himself out like a cat.

"I saw your ass drooping off the side of the building from the streets," Terias grumbled, folding his arms. "I came to make sure that you didn't fall off and break all your damned bones, that's all." He was about to walk away when his stomach began to howl like a whimpering hound. The young man's hand went to his belly and he grimaced, the features of his face scrunching up in pain.

"Hungry?" Yuri said, pushing himself to his feet. He brushed some dust off his clothing and reached into his pocket, pulling out a few golden coins. "I have enough to grab some grub. Anyway, I was heading to the market. Do you want to come?"

"Huh? I don't have the money to go there!"

"I'll pay for you, idiot."

"I don't want your pity!"

"It's not pity," Yuri said with a shrug. "It's me thanking you for waking me up before I shattered my back. If you're not hungry then don't accept." Without warning, he started to jog along the rooftops once again, his shoes tapping against the tiles. He smiled as he heard the noisy footsteps of Terias behind him. Yuri was actually surprised that Terias was willing to tag along for breakfast. Ordinarily, his dislike of Yuri would've steered him away, regardless of the offer of free food. *He must be really hungry then.*

After fifteen minutes of hopping from rooftop to rooftop, the two young men returned to the streets and walked the rest of the way to the marketplace.

The market was located between the Upper and Lower Districts and was open to people of all socioeconomic classes. It was probably the busiest area of Horux, for traders from around the city would gather in this massive plaza to barter and sell their products.

Yuri raised his eyebrows and whistled as they walked into the market, impressed with how many people there were today. "It usually isn't this packed. Is there a celebration today?"

"Who knows?" Terias mumbled, still holding his stomach. His face was weary and there were heavy bags underneath his eyes, clearly the result of sleep deprivation. "I've never been here before."

"Yeah? It's a pretty nice place if you're looking for random stuff to buy," Yuri said. "Plenty of food as well." He reached into his pocket and flicked a golden coin through the air in Terias's direction. He caught the money cautiously with both hands, as if it were a fragile egg that would shatter if he weren't too careful. "Get something for yourself. There's a lot of choices to pick from."

Terias's face drained of color and he blinked several times, shocked that Yuri had just given him a gold coin. This was worth at least a thousand copper coins and could buy him several meals. "T-Thanks," he muttered, averting his gaze.

"What was that?" Yuri said.

"Nothing," Terias snapped, sliding the coin into his pocket.

"What were you doing near the docks so early anyway?" Yuri asked, holding up his hand to shield his eyes from the sun's dazzling beams. "Don't you live on the other side of town?"

"I work there," Terias murmured with a shrug.

"Really? Do they not pay you or—"

"Of course they pay me, you idiot!"

"I was just wondering! It doesn't make sense that you look like you haven't eaten or slept in days!" Yuri replied angrily, but the frustration left his face within seconds. Terias was glaring at the ground, his hands balled into tight fists at his side. He was clearly angry about something. *It's probably not smart to press the issue.* "Hey, stop being a wimp and tell me what's wrong." *That was subtle.*

"A wimp," Terias murmured. His eyebrows were knit together and he clenched his teeth so tight that Yuri thought they would fall out. He closed his eyes and began to move away, shaking his head to himself. "Don't worry about me." Within moments, the marketplace's gigantic crowd swallowed him and he disappeared from view.

Yuri put his hands on his hips, watching the place where Terias had vanished. "What's his deal?"

"Healing! Healing! You have an illness? I can cure it! You have a wound? I can mend it!" an elderly woman called out. "Come here today to get all of your physical ailments miraculously healed by my magic and ancient remedies!" Her voice wasn't exactly loud, compared to the hundreds of other merchants that were screaming and hollering like a bunch of irate protesters. But for some reason, she stood out for Yuri, and before he knew it, he was standing at the entrance of her little white tent.

The decrepit woman was dressed in a long black shroud that covered her entire body. Her grey hair was bundled up into a ponytail, which was not a style that elderly women in Horux typically adopted. The healer's aged face was filled with more wrinkles than Yuri had ever seen on a person before, making her look ancient. *How old is this lady? Two hundred?*

"Oh my, it looks like you have quite the bruise there. Did you get into a fight recently?" the woman said, pointing to the boy's face with a doddering finger.

Yuri pouted, narrowing his eyes. "You could say that. I don't know if you're the right person, but I figured that I'd ask. I have a letter that I'm supposed to give to a particular healer." The boy reached into his pocket and pulled out the parchment of signed paper that Beo had given him. He held it out to the healer. "I was wondering if that was you."

"Well, it must be your lucky day! You've found me!" the old woman threw her hands into the air excitedly and snatched the piece of parchment, stuffing it into her pocket. *She sure has a lot of energy for her age.* The healer pointed to a table inside of her tent and smiled at Yuri. "Lie down on the table and I'll make those bruises disappear. Once I'm done healing you, there won't be a scratch on your body!"

Yuri chuckled nervously as he obeyed the lady, sprawling himself out on the table. He exhaled, listening to the bustle of the populated marketplace. "So, um, what's with all of the people today?"

"Well," the elderly woman said, sliding white gloves onto her hands, "I believe that the princess has decided to come down to the marketplace today. Of course, she's escorted by a dozen royal knights and is being protected by at least a hundred different magical enchantments granted by talented mages. Tough luck to the thousands of young men looking to charm her and win her favor." She placed her hands on Yuri's warm cheeks, chilling his skin with her freezing-cold gloves.

"Wait, what?" Yuri exclaimed, not hearing past the healer's first sentence. He was about to lean forward but the woman was surprisingly strong. She clamped her hands tightly on the boy's cheeks and pinned him down on the table. "Ow, ow, ow!"

"Stay still, otherwise you're not going to be healed!" the mender exclaimed. "Are you one of those unfortunate chaps that wants to charm the damsel?"

"Huh? I don't know what you're talking about," Yuri said, folding his arms over his chest.

"Your heart is racing, your face is red, and your right leg is twitching uncontrollably; you're like an excited child on its birthday. I don't understand how you kids can keep falling for people that you've never met before. That isn't true love, is it? It's just you finding someone attractive," the woman said, her chilling hands suddenly feeling warm on Yuri's cheeks. A tingling sensation began to surge from his face throughout his body, but he hardly noticed, being invested in his conversation with the old lady. "So, tell me, why her? She is beautiful, but there are plenty of enchanting girls in Horux. What makes you want her?"

Yuri blinked several times, looking up at the elderly woman. "I suppose it's because I find Princess Violet to be very … mysterious."

"Mysterious?"

"Yeah, mysterious," Yuri said with a slight smile. "No one knows what she's like since she's always stashed away in the royal castle. I've always wondered so many things about her. What she thinks like, sounds like, acts like, looks like up-close … I don't know. There's just something about the princess that makes me want to get to know her. Besides," Yuri's expression softened as he spoke, "I can tell that she's lonely."

"How can you tell that?"

"I was in the Nobles' Tournament yesterday," Yuri said, chuckling wearily. "That's where I got all of these bruises. I saw the princess there, and she was absolutely gorgeous. But there was a look on her face that told me that she felt alone. Even though people constantly surround her, I'm not sure if she regards any of them as true friends."

The woman looked down at Yuri pitifully. "But how do you recognize the look of loneliness?"

"When I was younger, that was the look I used to wear." The healer lifted her hands from Yuri's face and smiled slightly. "All finished," she said, handing Yuri a mirror. The boy's mouth dropped open in awe as he looked at his face, which didn't have a single scratch on it.

"Whoa, ma'am! You really can use magic. I heard that there weren't many mages in Escalon, let alone in Horux. How does your magic work?" Yuri asked, dragging the tips of his fingers across his smooth, unmarked skin.

The boy knew little about magic, but he did realize it was rare. Certain individuals were born with magical energy locked up in their bodies, waiting to break out. There were a variety of methods to awaken this magic, though most people lived their lives without ever bringing their talents to fruition. He'd read that on the continent, Dastia, mages inscribed permanent tattoos into their flesh using enchanted ink. The tattoos activated the magic and allowed individuals to utilize their powers. If this healer was from Dastia, she was hiding her tattoo.

"I got my magic from a pill many decades ago, given to me by a talented alchemist," the old woman said. "Now I am capable of healing most wounds and illnesses, though I do feel awfully tired afterwards. Using magic takes a huge toll on me these days. I used to have little trouble with healing mere scratches and bruises." The healer plopped herself down in a chair, exhaling.

Yuri lowered the mirror and got off the table, smiling thankfully at the healer. "Well, I appreciate you fixing me up. Thank you."

"You're probably going to dash after your beloved princess now, aren't you?"

"If I can manage to push past the horde of charming men that you mentioned, then yes." Yuri ran his hand through his hair, chuckling. "Otherwise, I'll still have my chance later on. Apparently, I'm to dine with the royal family tonight!"

"Really? My, that must mean that you were victorious in the Nobles' Tournament!" the woman exclaimed, her eyes twinkling with excitement. "To think that I would be healing the bruises of such a skilled warrior! That is interesting, that they are hosting the dinner the day after your battle, though. Do they not give you any time to rest?"

"I don't know," Yuri said with a shrug. "The letter that was delivered to me yesterday told me that I should be at the palace tonight. Anyway, I ought to get going now. I have a lot of errands to run today. Thanks so much for fixing me up!" he said, reaching into his pocket to dig for some gold coins to tip the healer, but the elderly woman shook her head.

"Don't worry about it. Use that money to get yourself some food. You look famished," the healer said.

Yuri smirked, shrugging. "All right. Hopefully we will cross paths again," he called, waving to the magical mender as he walked out of the tent and into the relentless torrent of the marketplace's aggressive shoppers.

Being swept up like a child trapped in churning rapids, Yuri was shoved about as he attempted to locate the princess. But there were just too many people. Hundreds of faces filled the plaza and he couldn't recognize the one that mattered most to him. Wincing, he exhaled. *Maybe I should just go and get some food.*

"Out of the way!" a recognizable voice, filled with assertion and authority, boomed. Senna!

Yuri turned and found the gigantic knight's helmet peeking over the heads of the townsfolk as he shoved them aside, clearing a way for the princess. Around the powerful warrior were a dozen other soldiers, clad in spotless armor that was clearly just polished. These men were just as large as Senna, if not larger, and they towered over the rest of the civilians, who gaped in awe at the massive humans. Their heavy armor clanked as they stomped forward. Dozens of young men, holding boxes of expensive chocolates and bouquets of roses, were being shoved aside by the great knights.

"Senna!" Yuri exclaimed, stumbling in the warrior's path.

"You...," Senna growled, glaring at the young man through his visor. "You disappeared last night."

"Yeah, I guess so," Yuri said, scratching the back of his neck. He could feel the eyes of many spectators burning into him. The marketplace had suddenly fallen silent. He bit his lower lip, feeling uneasy at the attention that he was getting. "What happened to that rowdy guy? You two seemed acquainted somehow."

"The fool that was spewing nonsense about a werewolf? His name is Archerus. He used to be one of the king's best knights, before he went insane. He's been obsessing over werewolves a lot recently, always claiming that the beasts still exist. Now he believes he actually saw one, the maniac. Right now, he's locked away," Senna said, tilting his head to the side with a questioning look. "So, why have you stopped me? Is there something you want?"

"I'm here to meet the princess."

"You'll see her tonight. Why do you need to meet her now?" Senna snapped.

"Why do I need a reason to want to meet her?" Yuri retorted.

"Because right now we're in a public area surrounded by hundreds of people! This is simply not a safe place to—"

"Now, now, Senna! Who is this person that wants to meet me? The two of you seem to know each other well. You're bickering like siblings," a gentle voice said. The charming men that surrounded the squadron of knights all gasped when they realized that it was the princess that had spoken. "It can't hurt for us to exchange a few words, no?"

"I-I suppose not," Senna murmured, bowing his head a bit. "Yuri and I are acquaintances, nothing more. The king assigned me to give him the invitation to have dinner with your family tonight. That was the first time that we met."

"Is that so? Well, step aside, Senna. Let me see the mighty champion of the Nobles' Tournament for myself," Princess Violet said from behind Senna. The knight obeyed, gliding to the side.

Yuri's eyes widened as he gazed upon Horux's gorgeous princess, who was even more stunning up close. Her skin was so fair that it looked like it had never been marked in her entire life, and her brunette hair was perfectly straightened and quite long, cascading down to her lower back. Dangling from her neck was a golden locket, which rested just above her breasts. The princess wore a long dress rimmed with gold, its hem brushing diamond slippers that gleamed like starlight. Her attire was the same violet color as her irises. *I've never seen eyes like those. How beautiful.*

Everything about Princess Violet seemed so clean, pure, and affluent.

Yuri swallowed back his nervousness, realizing that he had been speechlessly staring at the princess. He saw that the townsfolk around him were actually all on one knee, bowing before the highborn woman. Yuri, Violet, and the knights were the only ones in the marketplace that were still standing. Gazing over the crowds of groveling civilians, Yuri felt heat rising to his face. He quickly scrambled to one of the obeisant men, who was holding a bouquet of roses, and swiftly plucked out a flower.

"H-Hey!" the man exclaimed, darting Yuri a hostile glare. But he quickly lowered his head again, realizing that he couldn't act rashly in the princess's presence.

"What are you doing?" Senna whispered crossly to Yuri.

Yuri stumbled over to the surprised princess and dropped to one knee, as if he were about to propose. He bowed his head like the rest of the townsfolk and held the rose out to her. "For you, milady," he said, with more confidence than he actually felt.

Senna narrowed his eyes, about to burst out laughing, until he turned and saw that Princess Violet was giggling. The knight raised an eyebrow, surprised that Yuri's foolish action had produced any positive reaction at all.

"That's cute," Princess Violet said, gently taking the rose by the stem. She twirled it in her hands, holding it close to her chest. "Yuri, is it? You fought valiantly in yesterday's tournament. Though I am afraid that I'd never heard of you prior to yesterday's event. Where did you receive your training?"

"I trained myself, Your Highness," Yuri said, his gaze still trained on the ground.

"Is that so? Impressive. Well, I look forward to seeing you at dinner. Perhaps you'll tell me more of how you've become such a grand fighter," Violet said with a smile. "Are you in need of attire for tonight? If so, I can—"

"Stop!" a man screamed in the crowd.

Yuri turned his head and saw that Terias was leaping over the ocean of bowing civilians with a large sack of fruit slung over his shoulder. Chasing him was a fruit merchant that was wearing a white apron and wielding a broom. *That idiot is going to steal right now?*

The knights immediately took up formation around Violet, shielding her from sight. Senna glanced at Yuri. "Would you mind—"

"Already on it," Yuri said, bolting after Terias. "Stay down!" he boomed to the civilians that were still groveling on the ground. If they stood up, he would lose sight of Terias. He grunted, accidently bumping into the fruit merchant, knocking the man to the ground. The young man blinked and reached into his pocket, pulling out the rest of his coins. *You need that money to eat!* Yuri tossed the currency to the stunned merchant. "That's for the fruit." *Idiot. Idiot. Idiot.*

Yuri broke into a dash once again, sprinting through the streets of Horux. However, he'd already lost sight of Terias, and was blindly searching the city for the thief.

Journeying deeper into the Lower District, Yuri found himself near home. Slowing to a stop, he took a moment to catch his breath after nearly an hour of running through the streets. He wandered toward the alleyway near his house, and surely enough, Terias was there. The thief was sitting on the ground, his face ghostly pale. Lying several feet away was a corpse, an ill-fated woman that had tragically died of starvation.

Yuri's nose twitched as he caught a whiff of the pungent scent of human excrement that was dumped on the streets. Or perhaps it was the rotting corpse that was lying in alleyway. The young man was purposely loud as he walked forward so that Terias would know he was approaching. But he didn't even look up from the cadaver.

"Hey," Yuri said, his jammed hands deep into his pockets. He stopped beside Terias. "What are you thinking? I gave you money to buy yourself food, so why did you need to go ahead and steal? And if you're going to steal, why would you do it while the princess and the king's royal knights are in the marketplace? If one of them wanted to, they could've shot you with an arrow. What would your family think if they heard that you got killed doing something dumb like stealing a sack of apples?"

"They're dead," Terias murmured quietly, his sorrowful gaze staring at the ground.

"Huh?"

"*I said they're dead, damn it!*" Terias boomed, glaring at Yuri, causing the boy to stagger backwards in surprise. The distraught man reached up and put his head in his hands, sobbing. "Just when I got a job at the docks. My damned boss wasn't listening to me … he only pays me enough money to feed one person. So, I gave my portions to my family. I've been starving myself so that they could live … but it didn't do shit!" he roared, his lips quivering. "One by one, the members of my family dropped dead, and I couldn't do a damned thing. At this rate ... I'll be joining them soon."

"Terias, why didn't you tell me? I can help, I didn't—"

"And then I heard all of this bullshit about you turning down an offer from Asmund and Beo. They offered you half of the damned winnings of the tournament, Yuri! That's a fortune; it's enough to buy a home in the Upper District. You're poor as hell, just like the rest of us, and yet you had the nerve to *reject their offer?*" Terias yelled, pushing himself to his feet. He rotated his body, preparing to throw a punch right at Yuri. "Everyone in the Lower District would murder *anyone* for that kind of money!"

Yuri grunted, tilting his head to the side as Terias launched a quick jab straight for his face. "Terias, if I knew that your family was suffering so much, I would've taken the money to help you out. I didn't—"

"You didn't what? Think that we were in anguish?" Terias barked, unleashing a barrage of rapid punches at Yuri. "Everyone in the Lower District is suffering, you damned idiot!"

Yuri weaved around the attacks with ease, pitifully watching the enraged man as he flailed his arms about. Ducking, Yuri elegantly knocked out Terias's legs with a sweeping kick.

Terias grunted, immediately losing his foothold. He fell backwards and slammed onto his back, the wind forced from his lungs. He coughed several times, gasping for air. Wincing, he stared up at the afternoon sky as tears filled his eyes. Within moments, they were streaking down his cheeks and dripping onto the cobblestone ground. "Everyone is suffering, Yuri. Everyone."

Yuri bit his lower lip. Terias was right. Everyone was suffering, his family included. *Don't you care about us?* His mother's words echoed continuously in his mind and he closed his eyes, exhaling shakily through his nose. "I'm sorry, Terias," he said quietly.

35

"Shut up." Terias sniffed and reached up, wiping the salty tears from his moist face. "I can't wait until that smelly merchant gets his ass over here and cuts me into little bits. End my misery."

"He's not coming," Yuri said. "I gave him the rest of my money to pay for the fruit you stole."

"You did *what?*"

"You heard me."

Terias leaned forward a bit, enough so that he could stare straight at Yuri, gawking in disbelief. That was when a smile cracked across his chapped lips and he crashed back onto the ground, shaking his head. "I have never met a bigger dumbass than you." He began to chuckle and that gentle laughter soon turned into a boisterous guffaw that shattered the silence of the alleyway. "I cannot believe you, Yuri. Do you not give a single crap about the wellbeing of yourself or your family? You need that money."

"Of course, I do," Yuri said with a shrug. "But that doesn't mean I'm going to sit back and watch you get executed for stealing a couple of lousy apples."

"Huh," Terias murmured, covering his eyes with the back of his hand. "Why are you doing this? You're helping me even though all I ever do is cause you trouble. Don't you remember the countless times I beat the crap out of you? Back when you were weak, sometimes I was almost sure that you wouldn't get back up. And I was okay with that … you never opening your eyes again. But you always did."

"Yeah," Yuri said as he took several steps backward and leaned against the wall of the alleyway. "There are a lot of things that I still want to see and do in this world, like marry a princess. I can't die so early."

"Ha, still going on about that nonsense? You're too ambitious." Terias laughed. "You have a dinner with her tonight too, right? Word spreads fast."

"Yeah, I do."

"So, what the hell are you doing here with me while I'm sulking?" Terias said. "Better start getting ready, you're only going to have one chance to impress the girl of your dreams."

***

"I'm surprised to hear that you and Terias are finally starting to get along," Asmund said, with one leg crossed over the other as he sat in a chair. The ostentatiously dressed noble was wearing a bright red shirt, made of the finest material and perfectly-fitted ebony pants. He sank his teeth into a juicy peach and nodded to Yuri, who was having his measurements taken for the clothing that he would need for the royal dinner. "What was it that you wanted to talk about?"

"Don't worry about it now, that can wait until we are alone," Yuri said. "Also, I appreciate your help with my attire. It would be a riot if I appeared at tonight's dinner dressed like a street rat."

"It's no problem. You're practically my brother. I want the best for you and this is a big night! We're finally going to see if you really are as charming as you boldly claim to be!" Asmund exclaimed, raising his peach into the air as if making a toast. He made eye contact with the servant, who had just finished taking the rest of Yuri's measurements. The servant dipped his head respectfully and hastily fled the room. Unfolding his legs, Asmund shot Yuri a sly smile. "All right then, let's hear it. We're alone now."

Yuri sighed, scratching the back of his neck. "Fine. Just ... no matter how this sounds, know that I mean no disrespect."

"Of course," Asmund said, his eyebrows knitting together, now realizing the seriousness of the matter. He had been expecting a jest from his friend, but Yuri's tone and countenance said otherwise.

"Yesterday as I was walking home from your house, I stopped by a bar to have a pint. Several minutes later, a man named Archerus staggered into the tavern, making claims that he'd seen a … werewolf, underneath Horux. He said that there was an entrance to some catacombs in the forest outside of the city. Look, I know how this sounds—" Yuri said.

"Werewolves? And here I thought it was going to be something serious like your mum's gotten ill!" Asmund let out a great sigh of relief, falling back into his chair with one hand on his belly, as if he were stuffed after a great meal. "Werewolves are just myths that circulate around these parts. They've been extinct for centuries. You realize that if they really did still exist, we would've seen them by now. Horux takes up most of the peninsula in southern Escalon. Those beasts hunger for flesh; they wouldn't be able to resist a place like Horux, which is full of juicy humans."

"I'm being serious, though, Asmund," Yuri insisted, shaking his head. "Archerus mentioned your father and said that Beo was the one who had the beast captive and—"

"You believe that fool? He's just some insane freak spitting out nonsense and you're letting it get to your head. Not once have I heard my father say a word about werewolves. I haven't heard of these underground catacombs before, either. I doubt anyone has!" Asmund exclaimed, his eyes narrowing. "Just because some random man at a bar starts accusing my father of treachery doesn't mean that you should believe him."

"I don't," Yuri grumbled. "But my gut is telling me that it's worth checking out. Can't we just find out if there are secret catacombs underneath Horux? If there aren't, then we'll just denounce Archerus as insane and leave it at that." He rubbed the back of his neck and sighed. "He even offered to lead us directly to the werewolf, which means that he really believed he saw one."

"So that's why you're interested in this man's nonsense," Asmund said.

Yuri nodded. *That and the puzzling fact that Beo leaves Horux every night at midnight.*

The noble tossed his peach high into the air, his eyes trained on the ceiling. Catching the fruit, Asmund shrugged. "If you could prove to me that the catacombs are indeed real, then I'd investigate the issue further with you. However, as it is, I see no reason to—"

"No reason to what?" Beo said, suddenly opening the door to Asmund's room. The man peeked his head inside and blinked rapidly, realizing that he'd disturbed an important conversation from the shocked stares that he received from both his son and Yuri. "Did I interrupt something?"

"No reason to believe this ... claim that there are catacombs that run underneath Horux," Asmund said, his eyes darting from his father to Yuri. "Er, Yuri ran into some maniac at a bar that claimed there are secret passageways under the city. Is that true?"

Yuri exhaled with relief at the fact that Asmund did not make any mention of werewolves. But the boy watched Beo, and immediately saw the man's face pale at his son's question. His right eye twitched. "Of course not," he said, opening the door fully as he walked into the room. "There were never plans in the original architecture of the city for any catacombs. I believe that I have a map of the city on me. One moment," he said, reaching to pull out a piece of parchment that was tucked into the back of his pants. He placed the map on a table and unfurled it, revealing that it was indeed a detailed map of Horux.

Yuri raised his eyebrows. *How convenient that he has a map....*

Tracing his finger along the map, Beo smiled. "You can see that there are no entrances to catacombs of any sort throughout the city. Feel free to take a thorough look." The noble turned his head and glanced at Yuri. "Might I ask the name of the man who told you this?"

"I ... didn't catch it. He was just some drunk guy that was yelling gibberish at the bar," Yuri lied. He watched as Beo simply nodded and turned to the door.

"All right, well, it's best not to believe random twaddle that drunken fools in bars spout. I figured that you'd know that already, Yuri," Beo said as he walked towards the doorway. He glanced at Yuri over his shoulder, winking. "I came to check on how you guys were doing with the measurements, but it looks like they finished all of that already. Tonight is a big night, Yuri. Are you excited?"

"Very much so, sir," Yuri said politely with a nod of his head.

"Good. Well, enjoy yourselves, you two. You still have a couple hours until Yuri's clothes are ready, so feel free to relax here," Beo said, closing the door of Asmund's room behind him, leaving the two friends in silence.

"Well, the proof is right here," Asmund said, pointing to the map. "There are no marked entrances to catacombs of any sort. I can't even see a legitimate place where they could put—"

"The whole point is that the catacombs are a secret," Yuri said. He sighed and shook his head, staring at the map, unconvinced. There was something off about Beo's reaction, which only piqued Yuri's curiosity. In order to find out if these catacombs really did exist, Yuri knew that he would have to find Archerus and ask the man himself. Senna had mentioned that the criminal was locked away, meaning that he was most likely located in Horux's jail, a tower located in the Lower District. "How much time do we have until the clothes arrive?"

"Around four hours, why?"

"Perfect, I'll be right back!" Yuri exclaimed, bolting out of the room.

"Eh? Where are you going?" Asmund called after him. But his friend was already too far away to hear him. Slumping back into his chair, he shook his head and sighed. "Once that idiot sets his mind to something there's no stopping him, is there?"

Treachery

Archerus pressed his back against the cold walls of his cell. His bare feet trembled on the freezing stone floor. The man stared across the chamber at the iron bars that confined him to this claustrophobic room, his dark hair sweeping down near his steadfast eyes. The sound of tapping boots echoed through the hallway outside of his cell and Archerus watched as a soldier, clad in clanking metal armor, stepped before him.

The guard held up his torch and illuminated the cell, which was dark even though it was still only afternoon. Stepping beside the soldier was a noble that Archerus recognized well. Smirking, the man called out to the highborn visitor. "It's been a while, Beo. You're looking well."

"I could say the opposite for you," Beo said, his stern gaze burning into the criminal. He nodded to the guard and the soldier marched away. The noble waited until the man had left, closing the door at the end of the hallway behind him. The two acquaintances were locked in darkness as they stared at each other. "It would seem that you've been following me. Usually I am able to detect when I have a stalker at that time of night, but for some reason I failed to notice you."

Archerus smirked. "I have been skulking in the shadows since I was a young boy. There was no way that you could detect me, even with your level of skill."

"That may be so," Beo said, folding his arms over his chest. "My only concern now is what to do with you. You've seen too much. Is there any way that I can keep you quiet?"

"You know that's impossible without using magic to silence my tongue," Archerus grumbled, slowly pushing himself to his feet. Swaying slightly, he walked towards Beo until only the cell's iron bars separated the two men. Glaring at the noble through the gaps in the metal, Archerus chuckled softly. "Even if you did do that, I would figure a way to dispel that magic. Your sinister secret will reach the ears of the civilians, you can count on that."

"Your selflessness will be your downfall," Beo snarled, sliding his hands into his pockets. "As a member of the king's counsel, I could have you executed if I wanted. That would surely silence you for good, wouldn't it?"

Archerus winced at the sound of that. He scowled, his eyebrows furling together as he clenched his jaw. "If you're going to kill me, fine. But I want to know something. Why the hell are you guarding that accursed beast? It's sealed away, meaning that you know of how dangerous the werewolf is. Neither of us wants it rampaging around, but one day those bars will shatter and it will escape. What will you do then?"

"I can only hope that such an occurrence does not happen during my lifetime," Beo said coldly. His harsh words caused Archerus's face to turn red with fury. "In my family, it is my duty to preserve the werewolf, nothing more. As long as it is alive and locked away, my job is complete. And when it finally is my time to pass, the responsibility of preserving the beast will be handed down to my son."

"You're locking away a disease that has the power to affect the entire human race. It must be destroyed, not contained!" Archerus barked, grabbing the bars of the cell tightly, as if he were about to pry them apart. His knuckles turned ghostly white as he squeezed the metal fiercely. "Think about what you're doing."

Beo shrugged and began to walk away, his hands buried deep in the pockets of his expensive clothing. "It is not my place to decide whether or not the werewolf deserves to live or die. I am just a man that is following the tradition that is passed down through generations within my clan. Enjoy your final days, Archerus. They are numbered."

"This isn't you, Beo. The great man I knew would never corruptly use his power to eradicate his enemies!" Archerus shouted after the noble.

"Is that so?" Beo said to the trapped man, stopping in his tracks. "Who do you think it was that advised the king to have you discharged from the royal knights?"

Archerus's eyes widened in shock, his lips trembling. He yanked hard on the iron bars, wrathfully roaring like an untamed beast trapped in its cage. "You bastard!" he bellowed.

Beo laughed softly, turning to face Archerus. "I've known that you've been keeping your eye on me for a while, Archerus. I saw that you suspected my involvement with werewolves years ago. But you made it so easy to get rid of you, once you started prattling to your fellow knights, telling tales of the forgotten beasts and how you believed them to be real. Even better, now you've claimed that I'm involved with them. Who would believe nonsense like that?" He tilted his head back slightly and inhaled deeply through his nostrils, his eyes closed. "I thought that once you were discharged from the royal knights, you would give up your foolish hobby of chasing fairy tales. But you didn't, isn't that right? You've conducted research on werewolves. I stopped by your house on the way here and found two Phoenix Hearts, one for you and one for your wife, I assume."

"If you've done anything to her—"

"Your wife and the Phoenix Hearts have been left untouched. Don't worry, I am not as malicious as you think," Beo said, his eyes opening. "I do not take pride in using my political power to have you discharged, nor do I want to have you executed. However, I am committed to preserving the werewolf no matter what the cost. It took me a while to figure out that you were the one who tried to warn the townsfolk of the werewolf. But after asking around, I now realize that I am not surprised at all that you were the one who followed me into the catacombs. It must be hard to always be deemed insane, to have no one believe you. I pity you, Archerus, I really do."

Archerus watched as Beo turned around and walked away, until eventually, like the guard, he left the hallway. Trapped in silence, the distraught man slunk back into the darkness of his cell. He looked down at a small spot of light that was beaming on the stone floor. Walking to the wall of his cell, he gazed through the window of his chamber, looking over the city in the distance.

Archerus's cell was located high in Horux's jail tower, so he could see much of the city from his vantage point. He reached out and gently touched the warm metal bars on the window and sighed, wishing that he could escape. That was when a young man popped his head in the window. "Hey," the person said.

Archerus yelped with surprise, immediately losing his balance and falling onto his back. His heart pounded rapidly as he stared at the dark-haired man in his window with disbelief. "H-How did you get there? This cell is a hundred floors above ground!"

"I climbed," the stranger said simply.

Archerus blinked, recognizing the person. It was that young man that he had seen at the tavern, the one that Senna had confronted. "It's not possible for someone to simply scale the side of this tower!"

"Well, I did it," the man said. "It was a lot harder than most things I've climbed, and I'm actually worried about getting back down. That's going to be challenging."

"R-Right. So, who are you and how did you find my cell?"

"I'm Yuri. As for how I found your cell, I've been locked up in this tower a couple times when I got caught stealing. I know that recent criminals get put into cells higher on the tower, so I just climbed up and started checking each room until I found you."

Archerus winced. *That must've taken hours!*

45

"Okay, enough with your questions. The whole reason I climbed this damned building was to get mine answered," the young man said, holding onto the iron bars. "I've been here long enough to have heard the majority of your conversation with Beo. I can't believe that he's kept a secret like that locked away for so long," he grumbled. "At any rate, I expect that you don't want to get executed, right? To avoid that, we're going to need to prove that you're not crazy, like everyone thinks you are. I'm willing to help you."

"Y-You are?"

"Yeah, it's disconcerting to know that there is a werewolf living beneath the city streets," Yuri said. "I've read stories of them. When they're in their beast form, they rampage and slay anything in sight. If that werewolf that Beo is housing ever got loose, Horux would be doomed. It's dangerous to have a creature like that living in such close proximity to a populated city. So first, I need you to tell me how you found out about the underground catacombs."

"Okay," Archerus said. He figured that he had nothing to lose by telling this boy everything. The way things were currently going, he would be executed. Trusting Yuri was his only chance at survival. "Within the royal library is a manuscript, created by the original architects that planned the building of Horux. It is the only copy in existence, and it shows where the entrance of the catacombs is, for there is only one."

"Only one entrance?"

"Yes, I believe that the original architects built the catacombs specifically to jail the werewolf," Archerus murmured. "There is more detail in the book when you find it. The only problem is that the library, where the manuscript is, is inside the palace, where the royal family lives. No offense, but it will be extremely difficult to infiltrate the castle and get into the library."

"Do you happen to remember the exact name of the book?"

"*The Inception of Horux,*" Archerus said with a puzzled look. "But how are you—"

"Don't worry about the details, I'll get you out of here," Yuri said with a grin. The boy ducked from the window and began to descend the tower. "Sit tight, old man, you'll be free in no time."

***

Later that night, Yuri was back in Asmund's room, putting on his new linens. His dark blue shirt was of the finest quality and had golden buttons running through the center of the garment. His ebony pants were perfectly fitted, from the waist down to his polished leather shoes.

The young man gazed at a full-length mirror and raised his eyebrows, realizing that this was probably the fanciest he would ever dress. Bathed, and with his hair done by Asmund's stylists, he looked more handsome than ever before. Yuri smiled confidently at the mirror and turned to Asmund. "Thanks for letting me borrow these clothes," he said thankfully.

"You can keep them," Asmund said with a smile. "They're fitted for you anyway. I'm sure that someday you're going to need to wear those again. They're yours."

"Really? Are you sure?"

"Of course." Asmund chuckled. "It's almost time for you to head over to the royal palace. You know how to get there? Sorry that I won't be there to hold your hand the whole way," he joked, leading Yuri out of the room.

The two friends laughed with each other as they made their way to the front door of the mansion. Yuri glanced over his shoulder and saw that Beo was standing at the top of the stairway that led to the building's second floor, watching the two boys. Swallowing hard, Yuri averted his gaze, unable to look at him. *He's been lying about the catacombs, the werewolf, everything. To think that he'd have a man, like Archerus, executed just to preserve his secret ... that's unbelievable.* He bit his lower lip. *Then again, if he were caught housing a werewolf, then he would surely be punished as well. He's only trying to avoid his own persecution.*

Yuri looked to Asmund, who was grinning at him as they talked. *But if I expose Beo ... what will happen to him? Will I be dooming Asmund's father to his demise?* He shook his head, trying to clear his mind of the guilt that he felt. *No, this isn't just about Asmund or Beo! This is about the safety of everyone in Horux. This is about protecting defenseless citizens like Han and Mom.*

"Yuri, you better be off," Beo called with a gentle smile. "The royal family is waiting."

Yuri swallowed hard and nodded. *Without Beo, I wouldn't even be going to this dinner tonight. It's difficult to turn against someone that has granted me so many opportunities.* He turned away, watching as one of Asmund's servants opened the door for him. *But I need to think of the wellbeing of everyone in Horux. We can't live safely if there is a dangerous beast under us.*

He waved to Asmund and Beo as he departed their mansion, following the main path that ran through the Noble District and eventually led to the royal palace. As his shoes tapped against the cobblestone pathway, Yuri bit his lower lip gently. He was nervous — not just because he was about to meet the princess once more, but because he had to figure out a way to sneak into the library and get the manuscript that Archerus had told him about. If he managed to steal the book, he could prove to Asmund and the citizens of Horux that the catacombs really did exist. *It'll be fine. All I have to do is find a moment to slip from the guards' vision and I'll get the book.*

Yuri spotted the palace, a massive castle with several towers connected by a gigantic wall of white stone. The tops of the towers were pointed like spikes, piercing the night sky. Each tower had dozens of orange-tinted windows. An impenetrable wall of steel surrounded the beautiful fortress. Yuri's path brought him to a large gate that loomed at least twenty feet over him.

Standing before the closed gate was Senna, who wasn't dressed in his knightly uniform, for once. Instead, he was wearing a black suit with a white undershirt. Even though he was dressed for a special occasion, his heavy two-handed sword was still sheathed at his side. He nodded to Yuri as the boy approached, and waved to two guards that were standing on top of the walls. "You're on time. I didn't expect that from you."

"You hardly know me," Yuri said with a raised eyebrow, stopping beside Senna. A grinding noise split the silence as the gate slowly groaned open. Inside was a squadron of soldiers that were fully armed and, unlike Senna, were dressed in their armor. "Is this a royal dinner, or are we preparing for a war?"

"A hilarious jibe," Senna muttered sarcastically as he began to pat Yuri down to ensure that he was unarmed. After confirming that Yuri was clean, he walked through the gateway and motioned for the young man to follow him. "These guards will be our escorts. I'm sure that you understand certain precautions must be taken when allowing a stranger to dine with the royal family. Especially when that stranger happens to be a random boy from the Lower District."

"Right," Yuri said with a roll of his eyes as he sauntered behind Senna. The guards filed behind him, stalking the party of two from several meters back. The boy's nose twitched, irritated at the noise of clanking metal behind him.

He gazed upon the marvelous lawn before him, which was filled with elegant bushes that had been trimmed in the shape of various creatures. His eyes locked onto one plant in particular that looked like a ferocious wolf. "Hopefully you don't stay grumpy the entire night, Senna. I was hoping to enjoy my dinner without receiving a glare or scowl from you each minute."

"I'm not grumpy," Senna murmured, not bothering to turn back to acknowledge Yuri. "I simply do not understand why a rat from the slums is being granted the chance to dine with the royal family when most of the nobles have yet to enjoy such a luxury. You are neither intelligent nor skilled. You're just … average."

"I'd like to think that I have some degree of skill—"

"You don't."

"All right then."

The two men walked in silence the rest of the way as they approached the royal palace, which looked even larger up close. Yuri whistled as he tilted his head back, gazing up at the towering citadel before him. He felt like an ant entering a giant's home.

The golden door to the castle was open, with two guards positioned at the entrance. But as Yuri and Senna entered the citadel and walked down a wide hallway, he saw that there were actually dozens of guards on both sides of the passageway. They were all completely still, frozen like figurines. They didn't even glance at Yuri as he strolled past them.

"BOO!" Yuri yelped suddenly at one of the soldiers, and frowned when the guard didn't budge. He turned to Senna, who was glaring at him disapprovingly. "I've never seen statues that look so realistic before," he quipped, pointing to the expressionless warrior.

"Stop being so childish," Senna grumbled, storming on.

Yuri followed the knight through several hallways, making so many turns that eventually the boy had no idea where he was. Each hallway was designed similarly; the only differences were the various paintings on the walls. Some had sculptures of famous historical figures of Horux positioned upon bronze pedestals, leaning against the walls of special halls. Eventually, Senna came to a door where two more soldiers were assigned, each holding iron pikes that were pointed at the ceiling.

Senna turned to the squadron of soldiers that marched behind Yuri and nodded to them. With that signal, they quickly created a formation around the doorway, boxing Senna and Yuri in. "The dining hall is right through this door. Make sure that you bow properly to the royal family upon entering. You know how to do that much at least, right?"

"To some extent," Yuri said with a half-smile.

Senna groaned and shook his head. "Just do as I do." He reached forward and grasped the handles of the door and pulled, revealing the incredible dining hall of the royal palace.

A lengthy table ran through the center of the room, as long as the alleyway by Yuri's home. It was adorned with a white table cloth and golden silverware that gleamed with luxury. The goblets, spoons, forks, and plates ... all of it was solid gold, and there were enough utensils set out to feed at least fifty people. The red chairs were cushioned to look as comfortable as clouds. Standing around the perimeter of the room were several armed knights that were dressed in suits, like Senna. The dining hall had two other entrances, one each to the right and left of the table. Yuri expected that one of them led to the kitchen where the food was being prepared.

At the end of the table was Horux's beloved king, who was seated on a black chair instead of red. Yuri was actually surprised that the ruler's seat looked just as comfortable as the others. He had expected the leader to be seated on a throne of gold that was covered in brightly colored pillows, but then realized how ridiculous that might look in reality.

The king had a head of curly brown hair, and a well-groomed mustache that, to Yuri, looked like there was a squirrel above his lip. Resting on his head was his grand crown, which was golden and had dozens of glittering jewels embedded in the metal. The ruler wore a dark blue robe over his expensive black linens, which was made of the finest material in all of Terrador — abyssalite.

Abyssalite was one of the world's hardest metals, and was extremely expensive because it was also very light. The metal could be fabricated into cloth that functioned as armor. While the king looked like he was wearing elegant attire, he was also wearing the world's toughest body armor. Yuri wasn't sure whether or not the king always wore abyssalite garments, or if he was just wearing it because tonight they had a guest from the Lower District.

The queen, who sat to the king's right, looked incredibly young for her age. Supposedly, she was around the age of fifty, but she still looked like she was in her late twenties. Unlike Violet, she had straightened hair the color of night. However, her eyes were the same violet color as her daughter's.

On the king's left was the striking Princess Violet, whose beauty was without equal. Her hair was entwined with violet flowers and twisted into a complex braid that dangled to her lower neck. She was wearing a gorgeous blue dress that was the same color as the clear skies of a summer day. *Violet looks absolutely stunning.*

The young woman saw that Yuri had stepped into the room. Her lips curved into a welcoming smile and she nodded to her side, indicating that he should sit beside her. Yuri certainly had no objections there.

Yuri was about to walk to his seat beside Violet, but halted when he saw that Senna was bowing deeply in veneration for the royal family. The guest mirrored the knight's posture, copying him precisely. As the two men rose up, they took their positions. Yuri plopped down gently on the seat beside Violet while Senna joined his fellow knights around the perimeter of the room.

"Welcome to the royal palace, Yuri," the king said with a gentle smile. "It is rare to see such a young champion win the Nobles' Tournament. I must congratulate you on your victory. I am sure that Beo and his family have awarded you quite handsomely for your efforts. They are a very generous House."

"It is an honor to meet you, Your Majesty," Yuri said with a polite nod of his head to the king. He smiled. "Beo has indeed proposed to grant me half of the tournament winnings, a very generous offer. However, I told him that I did not require such a fortune."

That statement took everyone in the entire room by surprise, sweeping the welcoming looks right off their faces. Now they all just gawked at him with disbelief. Even the king's mouth had dropped open at Yuri's words. But soon he was grinning, intrigued by Yuri's decision.

"Why is it that you denied such an offer?" the queen asked curiously. "I was told that your family is enduring a ... difficult economic situation. Would the wealth from the tournament not help lift you from the clutches of poverty?"

"My Queen!" the king said, giving her a disapproving glare.

"I mean no disrespect, of course!" the queen exclaimed, her countenance now expressing fear that she had insulted her guest. "I was simply curious. I tried to phrase my words as politely as possible."

Yuri chuckled awkwardly, scratching the back of his neck. "Ah, yes. Everyone seems to be quite confused by my decision. Well—" The boy was interrupted when the door on the right side of the room flew open. A dozen chefs barged into the room with golden plates covered by silver domes. They set the food down in the center of the table and swiftly removed the covers in unison, revealing a collection of foods emitting incredible aromas that gradually filled the room. For some of the dishes, the chefs had taken simple foods like pork and prepared them in an ostentatious fashion through decoration, such as placing an apple in the center of a ring of rare clams. The other dishes that were served were exotic, such as the wolf steak. Yuri had never heard of a person that ate wolf.

"You may finish what you were saying after we eat!" the king said with a hearty laugh. He clapped his hands together and then extended his arms outward. "Tonight's dinner is a grand meal, Yuri! Feel free to eat as much as you like. If there is a special request that you'd like to make, ask away! I'm sure the chefs can make something to your liking."

Yuri swallowed hard, his mouth watering as he gazed upon the platters of food before him. This was enough food to feed every person on his street for a week! "I-I think I'll be fine, Your Majesty. I appreciate your generosity, and I must thank you for inviting me to tonight's meal. All of the food looks delectable."

The chefs, who were standing in a line at the door to the kitchen, all bowed in unison. They smiled graciously at Yuri's compliment, and then filed out of the room together.

"Don't be afraid to dig in!" the king said with a grin.

The dinner went a lot smoother than Yuri had thought it would. At first, he was very reserved around the king, queen, and princess. He tried to be as polite as he could around the royal family, in his attempt to impress them. But as he continued to eat, drink, and talk, soon the layers of his façade were peeled back and his true, goofy self was revealed. Within an hour, Yuri was telling the royal family stories of what his life was like in the Lower District.

"But even though Terias used to always beat me up and put me down when we were younger, I knew that holding a grudge against him wouldn't accomplish anything," Yuri said, telling of his rocky relationship with the bully. "Recently the two of us have been getting along, though. I'd like to think that he's finally accepted me as a friend." He shrugged and lifted his goblet of red wine to his lips, allowing the expensive liquid to trickle into his mouth and tickle his tongue. The sweet taste filled his mouth and he exhaled as he set down his goblet, feeling slightly tipsy. But that was nothing compared to the king and queen, who were already inebriated.

"That's incredible how the hardship that Terias put you through was what transformed you into such a skilled fighter!" the king said, waving his cup around, causing the wine to slosh around in the chalice. Luckily, nothing spilled out. "After tonight, you must go home and thank him! He indirectly granted you the power to win the Nobles' Tournament!"

"You are such a great boy, Yuri! Selfless, talented, and handsome! Not to mention, you aren't greedy like most of the nobles and princes these days," the queen slurred. She gave a sly smile to Violet. "Perhaps Violet should consider you as a potential husband! I'd prefer if you married her over the rest of these unworthy chumps!"

"Mother!" Princess Violet exclaimed, blushing profusely.

Yuri met the princess's gaze and chuckled warmly. *By the gods, she's cute.* He took another bite of his wolf steak and swallowed. "Given the chance, Your Highness, I would take her hand in a heartbeat. But I do worry what people would think of a highborn princess being engaged to a lowly street rat." He grinned at Violet. "Regardless of what the future holds, any man given the chance to marry Princess Violet would surely be the luckiest man in all of Terrador."

The princess bit her lower lip in embarrassment and averted her gaze from Yuri. "Oh, stop it!"

Yuri laughed and then looked to the king. "Excuse me, milord! Er, I may require a trip to the bathroom."

"Ah, yes! The door across the room there," the king said, pointing to the door on the opposite side of the room from the kitchen. "Just continue down to the end of the hallway. There is a bathroom on the right side."

"Milord, shall I go with him?" Senna said, taking a step forward.

"Why? I'm sure the man can piss on his own," the king said, waving his hand as he let out a boisterous laugh that filled the dining hall.

"Your Majesty, I beg you to reconsider your decision! He is a *guest* and therefore must be watched at all times. Perhaps I should—"

"Senna, let him be. He's only making a quick trip to the bathroom," the queen assured the knight.

Yuri almost wanted to laugh. Never in his wildest dreams did he ever see himself enjoying a dinner with the drunken king and queen of Horux. This was outstanding.

Standing up from the dinner table, Yuri gave another bow of respect to the royal family before he departed from the room. He shot the princess a charming smile just as he left, receiving yet another embarrassed blush from her.

The young man started off walking down the hallway, but then broke into a dash. Now was his chance to find the library, but he didn't have much time before the royal family would expect his return. Well, maybe the king and queen wouldn't notice; they were too drunk. But Senna and Princess Violet definitely would notice his disappearance.

Yuri rapidly opened the doors to random rooms in a desperate attempt to find the royal library. He opened door after door, only to be disappointed again and again. How many rooms were in this castle? The deeper that Yuri journeyed into the building, the more he realized that he would need more than just a couple minutes to find the library. It might not even be positioned close to the dining hall.

"Damn, damn, damn!" Yuri swore to himself as he shut yet another door. He suddenly heard footsteps tapping on the carpeted floor on the far side of the hallway that he was currently in. Swallowing hard, he picked a random door and opened it, entering a room of pitch-blackness.

"Hm?" Yuri heard someone say in the hallway. "I could've sworn I heard someone talking here." The boy blinked. *Is that Beo? What is he doing here?* As one of the king's personal advisors, he was given free access to the royal palace, so it actually made sense that he was on castle grounds. However, tonight he had a night off, since the king was dining with Yuri. There was no real reason for him to be here.

The young man waited until Beo's footsteps faded away. Cautiously reaching out, he gently grasped the doorknob before him and twisted slowly, making little noise. Sneaking back into the hallway, Yuri began to stealthily creep down the passage after Beo. *Why am I following Beo right now? This is dumb. I should head back to dinner. I've been gone for way too long.*

After following Beo for several minutes, Yuri watched as the noble opened the door to a grand room. The royal library. *No way.* The boy quickly flitted forward and slipped through the entrance after Beo, just before the door fully closed. He stepped silently into a gigantic room that was nearly the size of half of Horux's marketplace. This library surely had the capacity to house hundreds of thousands of books. Now that he was here, he realized that it would be impossible for him to find the manuscript that he needed without the help of one of the royal librarians. *I'm done for.*

There were thousands of bookshelves that towered a hundred feet high, making Yuri feel puny in comparison. Scrolls and books alike were crammed onto these shelves, and each shelf was marked with a specific label. Not that those labels would help, Yuri had no idea what they meant.

The young man saw that Beo was skimming his index finger along the spines of several books, as if he were searching for a specific title in this mess of tomes. He still had not spotted Yuri, and the boy wanted to keep it that way.

Yuri stealthily crept down another hallway of bookshelves, directly behind Beo. He reached out and pulled two books from the shelf in front of him, revealing a hole that he could use to spy on the suspicious noble. Watching the patrician, Yuri narrowed his eyes when he saw that the man plucked out a book and tucked it underneath his arm. The young man spotted the spine of the book as Beo strolled past him. *The Inception of Horux.*

Yuri's eyes widened. That was the book that he needed! Could it be that Beo wanted to make sure that no one found out about the catacombs, like Archerus had? *Damn it, he's going to get rid of the book! If he does that, he'll be eradicating all proof that the catacombs of Horux really exist. What do I do?*

The door to the library swung open and Yuri's heart leapt a beat. He carefully pulled out another couple of books from the shelves, widening his peephole. He saw that Senna had entered the library, accompanied by several other armed knights. Yuri watched as Beo suddenly panicked and secretly slid the book underneath the shelf that he had taken the manuscript from. He pushed the book deep enough that it was impossible to see with a casual glance at the shelf.

"Lord Beo, I was unaware that you were in the castle today. My apologies if I have disturbed you," Senna said, nodding respectfully.

Beo rose to his feet and brushed some dust off his hands, turning to face the knight, who had just missed the noble's hiding of the book. "Oh, you didn't disturb me. I was just doing some studying. I thought that I would come by the dinner table later on to see how Yuri was getting along with the royal family. How is the boy?"

"He's actually gone missing," Senna murmured. "I don't know what the fool is doing. He said he was going to the bathroom, but he wasn't there when I checked. I'd like to think that he just got lost, but then he would've eventually run into a squadron of soldiers. In that case, they would've just led him back to the dining hall."

"Is that so?" Beo said with a frown. "All right, let's go look for him. I'm sure that he's just lost, as you said."

Yuri smiled slightly and watched as the noble left the library with the knight, leaving the library in silence. He scampered around to the bookshelf where Beo had hid *The Inception of Horux* and quickly pulled out the manuscript. He began to aggressively flip through the pages, scanning the book rapidly for the map. He blinked, reaching a page with a sketched design of a cage, built to contain a werewolf. Swallowing hard, Yuri shook his head as he continued to turn the pages. "The original architects really did build the catacombs to trap a werewolf," he whispered to himself.

After a minute of skimming the book, Yuri finally found a page with a map of Horux and a highlighted entrance to its catacombs. The only entrance was outside of the city deep within the woods, disguised as an ominous cave. Yuri smiled to himself, satisfied that he had found the book. He tore the map from the book and rolled up the piece of paper. Tucking the parchment into his pants, the boy slid the book back under the shelf, and turned to find a man watching him from several meters away.

The bald man was wearing a white robe that draped down to his feet, covering his sandals. He had circular beads around his neck and looked more like a priest than anything else, but Yuri knew that he was one of the librarians that worked in the royal library. The stranger held a book in his hand and frowned, his gaze burning into Yuri. "What are you doing here?" he demanded.

"U-Uh … look, I—"

"He's with me," a familiar voice called from the entrance to the library.

Yuri turned around to find Princess Violet standing in the doorway. His eyebrows shot up with surprise, for he hadn't heard her open the door. Maybe it was because the librarian had terrified him. Either way, the boy was relieved to see her and strode towards the princess. He glanced over his shoulder and saw that the librarian had simply bowed and turned away, continuing on with his business without pressing the young man further.

"Sorry, I got lost," Yuri murmured to the princess.

"I'm pretty sure we both know that's not true," Violet said with a raised eyebrow, her arms folded over her chest as if she were a disappointed mother scolding her child. *Did she follow me?* "What are you up to?"

"I'm not up to anything!"

"I'm not drunk like my mother and father, Yuri," the princess said with a roll of her eyes. "I'm not gullible either, and I just saw you flip through a book like a mad man and then tuck a page into your pants."

Yuri groaned. "Oh, you saw that. Okay, I know how this looks, but I'm not a bad guy. I'm just trying to do the right thing and—"

"I get it," Princess Violet said abruptly, taking Yuri by surprise. "I don't think you're a bad person. I just want you to tell me what you're up to, why you're sneaking around the castle and ripping pages out of a random book in the library. And be honest."

Yuri looked into the young woman's eyes and sighed, nodding his head. And he did it, he was completely honest with the princess. Even though he didn't really know Violet all that well from the brief conversation that they had at dinner, Yuri felt like he could trust her. He did not hesitate to tell her everything about Beo, Archerus, and the werewolf underneath Horux.

Violet's eyes were wide with incredulity at the tale that she was hearing, but she also could hear the sincerity in Yuri's voice. He was genuinely concerned for the people of Horux. "So, you have the proof that the catacombs do exist. Now what?"

"I need to confirm whether or not the werewolf is down there," Yuri said. "I'll depart Horux tonight and—" His heart skipped a beat as he saw the door to the library creak open.

"I left something—" Beo said, walking into the room. His eyes went wide with surprise upon seeing the princess, and his face paled slightly as he spotted Yuri as well. No doubt, he was nervous that the two of them were standing around the area where he had hidden *The Inception of Horux.* "Ah, Yuri! What in the gods are you doing in the library? Senna said that you were going to the bathroom and you had gotten lost."

"U-Uh...." Yuri was having trouble coming up with an excuse for stumbling into the library.

"Well, Yuri was lost and looking for the bathroom originally," Princess Violet chimed in, smiling at Beo. "But I found him and told him that I would show him the library, since he mentioned to me that he likes to read."

Beo raised his eyebrows and he relaxed, exhaling softly. "Ah. Well, the two of you ought to get back to dinner. It was rude of you to leave the king and queen at the table alone! Yuri, I thought you knew better than to do something like that."

"A-Ah, yes. Well, I figured that this was my only chance to check out the library, so I tagged along," Yuri said, taking Violet by the hand and leading her towards the door, wanting to leave as quickly as possible. "We'll head back to dinner right now!"

**

As soon as Beo saw that Yuri and the princess were out of sight, he went to retrieve *The Inception of Horux*. Pulling the manuscript from underneath the bookshelf, he sighed with relief. If he could destroy the book, then all proof of Horux's catacombs' existence would be gone. No one would be able to discover Faelen after Archerus's execution, unless someone manually searched the forest outside of Horux for the entrance to the catacombs.

Beo flipped through the book, frowning. There was a page missing. Heat rose to his face and his hands trembled so much that he almost dropped the book. Swallowing hard, he frantically tore his way through the pages of the book, searching even harder for the detailed map of Horux. *It was here just minutes ago!*

"Are you looking for a specific page in that book?" a librarian called, walking over.

Beo blinked, looking at the man. "Yes, why?"

"The boy that was with the princess ripped a page out just before he left. I saw him do it. Maybe that is the page that you're looking for?" the librarian said with a raised eyebrow.

The noble gawked at the man. The book slipped from his numb hands, thumping on the rug. Beo stumbled backwards as if inebriated, his head spinning. *Yuri ... has the page?* It all made sense. Yuri had made direct contact with Archerus at some bar, and that crazy bastard had been the only one to know about Beo's secret. "Damn it!" he boomed aloud, storming from the library like an angry giant. *With that page, he has the proof that the underground catacombs exist! He could ruin me! But he won't take the page straight to the authorities, no. Yuri will go to the catacombs first to confirm that Archerus told him the truth.* It was starting to seem that Archerus was not the only one that needed to be executed.

***

Yuri turned to the princess as they walked in silence through the hallways of the castle. "I can't go back to the dinner," he said suddenly. "I need to go and make sure there really is a werewolf under the city. It won't be long before Beo figures out that I'm in possession of the book's map. Who knows what he'll do to try and cover up the evidence of the beast. I'll bring Asmund with me and together we'll be able to prove that there really is a beast under the city."

"Can I do anything to help?" Princess Violet asked.

"Give the king and queen my apologies for leaving the dinner at such short notice. I really did enjoy my time with them," Yuri said, biting his lower lip as he looked at the princess. "You're royalty, so I can't bring you with me. It's too dangerous. But hopefully ... you'll let me return to this castle and tell you tonight's story." He grinned. "I'd love to see you again."

"I'll want to hear every detail," Violet said, returning his smile. She waved him off. "You'd better hurry and go, before Beo catches up to you."

Yuri nodded, and turned down a familiar corridor that he knew led to the exit from the castle. He briskly jogged, eager to make his way to Asmund's house as quickly as possible. "Yuri!" The young man abruptly halted and glanced over his shoulder at Violet. "I hope that you'll come back to the castle. I enjoyed your company tonight. I know my parents did too."

Yuri grinned from ear to ear, his heart fluttering at Violet's flattering words. "I promise I will."

Chasing Fairy Tales

"This can't—" Asmund shook his head in disbelief as he stared at the map. "Wow, you were telling the truth. This map is signed by one of the original architects of Horux! The catacombs really do exist. So, what about this werewolf?" He looked at Yuri. The two boys were standing on the lawn outside of Asmund's mansion.

"That's what we're going to find out," Yuri said, staring into Asmund's eyes with a look of resolution. "Come with me. I'm going to the catacombs right now to find out if that beast really is there."

"But—"

"Don't you find it weird that your father just lied to us like that?" Yuri said, shaking his head. "He told us that the catacombs don't exist, but it's right here! Not to mention, I saw him trying to hide the book in the royal library so that no one else would get their hands on this map. It looks like he was trying to destroy the evidence of the catacombs' existence. There's no doubt that he's going to figure out that this map is missing soon, so we don't have a lot of time before he tries to hide the werewolf somehow. Are you with me or not?"

Asmund hesitated for a moment, looking at his friend. He let out an exasperated sigh and shrugged. "I have nothing else to do tonight, I suppose. Damn, I really don't want to go out into those woods. People say the forest is haunted, you know."

"We aren't children anymore, Asmund," Yuri said with a scoff, raising his forearm to the air.

Asmund bumped his arm against Yuri's, smirking. "Yeah, but we're still chasing fairy tales."

***

The two young men made their way through Horux, traveling for about an hour through the Upper and Lower Districts to get to the front gate of the city. At first, the guards barraged Yuri with questions, for they wondered why he wanted to leave the city in the middle of the night. But once Asmund spoke up, the soldiers let the two boys leave Horux without any more trouble. They were clearly not willing to argue with a noble.

This was the first time that Yuri had ever left Horux's walls. Setting his boots down on the soft dirt, he saw a long stone road before him that supposedly led to mainland Escalon. Surrounding the road was the haunted forest that many people feared. Countless horrors and ominous creatures were said to dwell amongst the dead trees of the woods.

The blackened trunks and slender branches of each tree looked like giant ebony hands of the undead, prying their way from the earth. There was an abnormal aura that surrounded this forest, one that left Yuri uneasy. It felt as if he were stepping onto a burial ground where thousands had perished. But he knew that he couldn't let these feelings of discomfort turn him back.

Yuri sympathetically looked to Asmund, who was already trembling in fear. The noble had never left Horux, either. In fact, he'd never really journeyed deep into the Lower District before, so this was a big step out of the highborn boy's comfort zone. His eyes darted about at the slightest of movements. As a breeze blew through the forest, gently swaying the branches of the trees, Asmund flinched.

"Come on, let's go," Yuri said, with as much confidence as he could muster.

The two boys trudged through the forest, swallowed by the painful quiet. The silence dragged on; the only sounds that could be heard were those of the howling winds and the snapping branches. The full moon illuminated the forest, casting its luminous light across the desolate land.

Asmund was clearly on edge. His eyes shifted left and right, as if he were expecting to be ambushed at any moment. At the slightest of sounds, he would jump like a startled pup. The boy's teeth were chattering, and he rubbed his index fingers against his thumbs with such force that the outer layer of skin at the tips of his fingers began to peel off.

Yuri had his eyes glued to the map in his hands, navigating through the hushed woods. The dead silence did not bother him as much as the malevolence that he felt radiating through the forest.

Asmund felt the disconcerting sensation that they were being watched as they sneaked onward. Occasionally, he would turn around to see if they really were being stalked, but nothing was ever there.

"There it is," Yuri said, pointing to a small cave that was lodged in the earth at the bottom of a cliff. The cavern was dark, and currents of cold air drifted from the mysterious grotto. Swallowing hard, he stepped to the mouth of the cave with Asmund close by his side. "Do you have a match?"

"Y-Yeah," Asmund murmured, reaching into his pocket. He handed Yuri a box of matches with quivering hands. "Can't I just stay out here?"

"Trust me, you don't want to stand out here alone."

"Good point," Asmund grumbled. "Why did I agree to come here again?"

"Don't worry, we're just going to check it out quickly," Yuri promised his friend. He lit a match, slightly illuminating the darkness with the tiny flame. He saw that there was a torch conveniently placed on the wall, secured on a sconce. *Beo probably uses this every night to get into the catacombs.*

Yuri used the matches to light the torch, which immediately sent the shadows scattering before its blazing light. He peered into the chilling cave and saw that deeper into the cavern was a stone stairway winding downward into the supposed catacombs. He exchanged glances with Asmund and the two boys nodded, progressing into the darkness.

The silence in the cave was even worse than out in the forest. Here there was absolutely no sound besides the echoing footsteps of the two young men. Yuri could swear that he could hear his own anxious heartbeat, which was racing. He had no idea what to expect from the mysterious catacombs. No one, besides Beo, had been here for years.

Yuri and Asmund stepped down onto a stone floor, staring at a narrow tunnel that led into a sheet of blackness. The ceiling was only six feet high, and the passageway was so narrow that Yuri felt claustrophobic just looking at the path ahead. He swallowed back his discomfort, wiping a bead of sweat on his brow with the back of his hand.

The tunnel before him branched off into various pathways. There were so many alternate routes that Yuri knew that it would be impossible for them to find a werewolf in a place like this — until he heard a sound, one that did not come from the two boys. It sounded like a heavy thump, as if a giant had just bashed its skull against one of the walls. The vibration of the thump rumbled through the floor, pulsating up through the soles of Yuri's feet.

"D-Did you hear that?" Asmund whispered, grabbing onto the back of Yuri's shirt, peeping over the boy's shoulder. The noble was more terrified than he had ever been in his life. More than anything, he just wanted to turn back and forget this whole venture.

"Yeah," Yuri affirmed, slowly walking in the direction of the sound. There was another thump. And another. Soon, it was occurring at intervals of about three seconds. *If I just follow the vibrations and the sound, I can find the source. It has to be the werewolf. That's the only living thing down here that could be making that noise.*

Right? He bit his lower lip. In reality, he had no idea what was down here in the catacombs. There could be other creatures lurking in these tunnels.

"*I can smell you … children,*" a low, rumbling voice growled.

Yuri heard shuffling behind him and turned to find that Asmund had already broken into a sprint, dashing up the stone stairway of the cavern as he fled the area in terror. "Asmu—" he began but gulped back his words and shook his head. He had to continue onward. At least Asmund had stayed long enough to confirm that there was something down here in the catacombs. Now it was only a matter of finding out what that "something" was.

He pushed on, following the mysterious thumps that trembled through the catacombs. His breathing was heavy, and his clammy hands gripped the handle of the torch so tightly that he thought his knuckles might pop off. The beastly voice came again.

"Come closer so that I may see you. It has been a long time since I have seen someone other than Beo. But surely you must be one of his servants. You have his scent clinging to your clothes," the voice snarled. "Come now, speak your name."

Yuri turned around a corner and found himself standing in a long corridor that led to a cell at the end of the tunnel. The ceiling in this particular passage was much higher than the others. Peering down the corridor, Yuri saw that the cell had silver bars. Past the metal, all that he could see was a sheet of impenetrable darkness, until a pair of glowing red eyes suddenly beamed from the shadows. The young man's eyes widened as he felt curiosity drawing him towards the cell, his heart pounding so rapidly that he thought it would burst through his ribcage. A low chuckle came from the other side of the silver bars. Soon Yuri found himself staring in awe at an enormous hairy beast that towered over him. The ferocious creature would've had no problem ripping him into pieces.

"You seem scared, little boy," the werewolf spoke, revealing its teeth, which were sharper than honed swords. The beast's mouth curved into a smirk as it gazed down at the trembling visitor. "What are you doing so far from home?"

"You're real...," Yuri said in trepidation, shaking his head. He wished that this were a mirage, that his eyes were playing tricks on him. But the details of this horrific monstrosity were too realistic to be deemed a mere illusion.

Seeing the beast in person was completely different from hearing about the creature in stories. This werewolf was terror incarnate in every aspect of its physical being. Its claws could shred a person to pieces while its teeth could gnaw straight through a human skull. The monster's legs were surely strong enough to propel the beast faster than the swiftest horse, and its bulky arms were proof of its supernatural strength. The werewolf was a killing machine, and every part of its body was perfect for hunting almost any prey. If this monstrosity were ever let loose, the people of Horux wouldn't stand a chance. "And you can talk?"

"Yes, all werewolves were human once," the beast spoke. "Now, tell me your name."

"Y-Yuri," the boy croaked out.

"I am Faelen. I expect that you have come here of your own accord, for if you came in Beo's stead, he would surely have sent you with food," the werewolf grumbled. "Not to mention that I can smell him approaching."

"He's coming?" Yuri exclaimed, turning to glance over his shoulder.

"Free me and I will make sure that he brings no harm to you."

Yuri shook his head, averting his gaze when the werewolf let out a ferocious snarl that shook the floor of the catacombs. He quickly retreated from the corridor, breaking into a sprint as he raced for the exit of the underground tunnels. The once-silent crypts were now filled with the wrathful roars of the irate werewolf. Yuri wanted to escape the catacombs as quickly as possible. More than anything, after this terrifying experience, he just wanted to return to his family.

Dashing up the winding stairway, Yuri finally staggered back to the shadowy cave. He leaned forward, panting in a desperate attempt to catch his breath. His torch had just blown out and his eyes still hadn't fully adjusted to the darkness. He glanced up and saw that there was a silhouette of a man standing in the entrance of the cave, one too tall to be Asmund.

"It looks like you found out about my little secret," the man said, taking a step backward so that he was in the moonlight. It was Beo. He reached to his side, grasping the bronze hilt of a sheathed sword. He ripped the weapon from its holder and pointed its tip at Yuri, who stood frozen in place. "I'm sorry, but I can't have you telling anyone about this place."

Yuri bit his lower lip, clutching the blown-out torch in his hands and still breathing heavily. Exhaling through his nose, he attempted to calm himself despite the precarious situation. "Why are you keeping a beast like that hidden away underneath a populated city? Are you insane? If he gets loose ... all of Horux would collapse!"

"It is simply my duty," Beo said, charging at the boy. "I don't expect a lowlife like you to understand!"

Yuri grunted and hopped to the side as the noble jabbed outwards with his sword, tearing through the air with his blade. Beo winced, realizing that his agile opponent had avoided his attack and turned his sword sideways, aiming to decapitate his enemy with a swift stroke. But Yuri reacted perfectly, dropping to the ground to dodge the swiping blow.

Yuri gripped his torch tightly with both hands and swung his weapon hard, slamming it against Beo's leg with such force that the man immediately lost his foothold and crumpled to the ground. Slamming hard against the stone floor, the noble tried to recover, but Yuri was already upon him before he could move. The warrior smashed his torch down on Beo's wrist with tremendous force, forcing him to release his grip on his sword.

Beo cried out in agony, clutching his broken wrist. He watched in horror as Yuri brought the torch crashing downwards several more times, barraging the defenseless noble with a flurry of heavy strikes. By the time the young man was finished, Beo could hardly move his bruised body. The noble was barely conscious as he watched Yuri toss his torch to the ground and heard it clatter across the stone floor. Yuri reached over and picked up Beo's sword.

"Your duty should be to preserve the wellbeing of your family," Yuri said, moving to Beo. He unstrapped the sheath and took it, sliding the noble's sword into its holder. The boy gave the man one final look of pity before turning to run away, gripping his new sword. "By preserving a beast like that, you're doing just the opposite."

***

Beo groaned and leaned his head back against the floor of the cave, closing his eyes as tears flooded out, tiny droplets streaking down his cheeks. He lay there, unmoving, and unwilling to get back up. "I know," he whispered sorrowfully to himself. *But the responsibility of being Faelen's warden has been passed down through my clan for generations. I have no choice in the matter.*

After several minutes of silence, Beo heard footsteps echoing at the mouth of the cave. His eyes cracked open, expecting to find Yuri walking back to him. Instead, he was surprised to see a mysterious figure, wearing a black cloak, walking towards him. The man's identity was concealed in shadow cast by the cowl of his hood.

"Who are—"

Beo's words were cut off as a sword slammed into his chest, pinning him against the ground. Blood splattered on the stone and he gasped, his vision blurring as agony took hold of his body. Then he was still.

Silence seized the night once more as the cloaked stranger ripped his blade from the man's body and continued onward into the darkness. The blackness swallowed him as he descended into the catacombs, but he had no need for light. The darkness was where he found comfort; it was where his purpose for existence was forged.

The figure ambled patiently through the narrow tunnels of Horux's catacombs, following the sound of Faelen's furious roars, until he was walking down a long corridor towards the werewolf's cage.

Faelen eyed the newcomer curiously and he sniffed the air. "I smell the blood of Beo on you. You killed him?" he said in a surprised tone, standing tall. "Who are you?"

The man chuckled gently as he reached up and pulled back his hood, revealing his face. He was bald, and had a small, diamond-shaped tattoo seared into his forehead. His eyes were violet, and gleamed so brightly that they shined through the darkness like two miniature suns. "My name is Junko," he replied, a wicked grin spreading across his lips. "I've come to offer you a proposition that you cannot refuse."

Faelen narrowed his eyes. "How so?"

"I work for an organization known as the Bounts. Our goal is to dominate Terrador, and I am interested in recruiting you. You're strong, stronger than any ordinary man-beast. I will free you from this cell on the condition that you join my cause and infect all of Horux," Junko said with a sadistic laugh, "bringing anarchy to Escalon's civilizations."

Faelen's eyes widened with surprise. "You want me to turn all of the humans into werewolves?"

"Did I stutter?" Junko said with a slight tilt of his head. "Yes, I want you to turn them all into hungry beasts. I've done my share of studying werewolves. I know that newly infected werewolves enter a *berserk* phase where they will slaughter anything that isn't one of their kind. They lose all sight of whatever humanity they once had and are completely swallowed by the monster that they've become. Their human rationality is replaced with beastly instinct, and it just so happens that their instinct is to follow a pack leader." The Bount pointed his index finger at Faelen and licked his lower lip. "That's where you come in. You will become the pack leader of Horux and will lead the werewolves across Escalon, where you will conquer the rest of the continent in the name of the Bounts."

Faelen raised his eyebrows in surprise, slightly amused at the elaborate plan that Junko had devised. It was a lot to accomplish in exchange for freedom. But after centuries of being stuck behind these silver bars, he was desperate.

"If you don't accept my offer, you'll be stuck here until you starve to death, since I've killed the only man with the key to this cage. No one else in Horux has the strength to tear these bars apart as I do," Junko said. "Or that dark-haired child that was just here will bring back a mob of soldiers that will personally execute you. Either fate is not favorable to you."

"I'll do it," Faelen growled. "Just get me out of here."

Junko smiled at the werewolf. "If you try to betray me, wolf, understand that I will annihilate you without remorse. I don't have time for silly games."

Faelen snorted. "I always honor my accords."

The Bount reached outwards and grasped the silver bars. His muscles bulged as he pried them apart with ease, bending the creaking metal with brute strength until there was a wide enough opening for Faelen to fit through.

The beast leapt through the aperture, adrenaline surging through his veins, filling his body with newfound energy. He bared his fangs and laughed boisterously. "At last … freedom!" he declared exultantly.

"Once you've secured control of Horux and the werewolves, I will return with your next set of instructions. For now, welcome to the Bounts," Junko said, watching as the beast began to charge through the catacombs, searching for the exit. The Bount smirked, feeling the murderous aura radiating from the monster. "And enjoy your vengeance."

The Vile Taste of Vengeance

Guard Thompson stood watching the unmoving forest from the city walls. He yawned, tired of staring at the same dead woods every night. His eyes felt heavy, and his grip on his iron pike loosened as he felt drowsiness overcoming him. That was when he suddenly heard a rustling sound before him, like a gentle breeze stirring the slender branches of the ebony trees. The soldier snapped to attention as he spotted a black blur scampering across the forest, dashing forth with such speed and agility that the man couldn't tell what it was.

The guard's eyes widened with fear as he took a step backward, reaching to his pockets to pull out some matches. The black blur shot from the forest, rushing towards the base of Horux's outer walls. Whatever it was, it was approaching the city!

Guard Thompson's heart pounded rapidly as he quickly struck the match, creating a tiny fire that he used to light a large torch behind him. It ignited instantly, and the man grabbed the torch, visceral fear and panic seizing control of his mind. He began to sprint along the wall's walkway, making his way towards a giant, unlit, brazier.

Scraping sounds shattered the silent night, and the soldier glanced over his shoulder to find a massive beast vaulting over the side of the wall, landing heavily on the walkway behind him. Guard Thompson's eyes widened in terror as he scrambled forth, realizing the beast that he was dealing with. A werewolf.

There was no way that he could outrun such an agile beast. Knowing this, the guard pulled back his arm and hurled his torch at the brazier. The brazier burst into flames, filling the night with its brilliant flash. Upon seeing the light, other guards around the perimeter of Horux's walls began to light their own braziers, warning that there was a dangerous threat invading Horux.

Before Guard Thompson was able to smile at his own successful throw, he felt a sharp pain in the side of his neck. His eyes bulged with horror as he turned to find that the werewolf was already upon him, sinking its sharp teeth deep into his flesh. Warm blood poured from his gushing wound as he collapsed forward, screaming in anguish. But the beast did not finish him off. Instead, it simply rose to its feet and let out a nefarious chuckle.

"Be honored. You are my first victim."

***

Archerus stood in his quiet cell, watching the luminous moon in the distance through the bars of his window. His arms were folded over his chest as he watched the city. Then he suddenly spotted one of the braziers being lit on Horux's outer walls. Frowning, he put his face closer to the window to get a better look. Within minutes, all of the braziers on the walls were aflame, illuminating the dark night. That could only mean that there was an invasion of some sort, but there had not been an incursion into Horux in decades.

Suddenly Yuri popped his head in his window and the man yelped, completely startled by the boy's sudden appearance. He leapt back and then raised his eyebrows when he recognized that it was only the boy. "You climbed up this tower again? Impressive."

"You were right about the werewolf," Yuri said, gripping the metal bars with one hand. Strapped to his back was the sword that he had stolen from Beo. "I explored the catacombs with Asmund and found the beast."

"That's Beo's sword that you have," Archerus said observantly. "Did you—"

"No, I didn't." Yuri shook his head. "Look, I don't have much time. Beo is still alive and once he comes back to the city he's going to—" He was interrupted by a loud howl that shattered the night, instilling terror in his heart. *That can't be….* The boy could also see the look of fear fixed on Archerus's face, for he too recognized the origins of that cry.

"Yuri, behind you!" Archerus yelled.

Yuri glanced over his shoulder and spotted a werewolf leaping over the rooftops of nearby buildings, quickly converging on his position. Suddenly the beast slammed its hind legs into the top of the roof, smashing the floor beneath its feet as it propelled itself hundreds of feet into the air. Like an unstoppable bullet, it soared straight for Yuri, its crazed eyes lacking humanity.

Yuri grunted and shifted his body to swing out of the way as the werewolf plowed straight through the wall of Archerus's cell, sending bricks of stone flying in all directions. A cloud of dust swept around the area and Yuri gasped, his right hand grabbing onto a piece of the fractured wall, his body dangling from side of the tower. *That was too close.*

"Yuri! Your sword!" Archerus shouted, rushing to the hole in the wall.

The young man reached to his back, pulling his sword from its strap. He hurled it up to the prisoner, who grabbed the weapon and whirled around to confront the invading beast.

Yuri hauled himself up into Archerus's cell and saw that the werewolf was on the far side of the prison's hallway, having smashed directly through the iron bars that had kept Archerus captive. The beast was on the ground, dazed, but was beginning to stir. But Archerus was not going to give the monster any time to recover.

The brave man charged forth, jamming his sword downward into the werewolf's throat, pinning the creature to the ground. Blood spewed from its wound and a sickening, gurgling noise emerged from the creature before it went completely still.

Yuri stared aghast at the slain werewolf. His bottom lip quivered, his stomach beginning to churn at the sick murder he had just witnessed. But he clenched his jaw tightly, biting back whatever fear he had. This werewolf was not Faelen … that meant that this was someone that had been infected. Beo must've released Faelen from his prison. "That bastard … how could he do this?"

Archerus tore the sword from the werewolf's corpse and slammed it back into its sheath, handing the weapon back to Yuri. The former prisoner walked to the gaping hole in the tower's side, gazing over the city, which had already descended into chaos. Shrill screams of agony echoed through the night, coming from all directions, forming a dissonance of anguished cries mixed with the dreadful roars of newly infected werewolves. "Horux is beyond saving, we need to leave. To escape this city alive, we'll need to board the boats. Running into the forest will be impossible since the werewolves have already overtaken the area near the gates. We would never make it out," Archerus said, his face composed despite the precarious situation. "The only issue is that the docks are in the Lower District. The infection spreads quickly and I expect by the time we get to the docks either it will be full of panicking citizens trying to escape or it will be overrun by the beasts."

"There are more boats behind the royal castle," Yuri said, swallowing hard. "I can get us aboard. I'm somewhat acquainted with the royal family. I'm sure that they would let us on. But I need to find my family first."

"As do I," Archerus said, turning to Yuri. "We should gather our families and meet at the docks behind the royal castle. If you can indeed get us on a boat, then hopefully we'll all get out of this mess in one piece." He walked over to the werewolf's corpse and bent down, picking up a sword that was sheathed at the creature's side. It looked like this monster was a guard before he had been transformed.

The man pulled the sword from its sheath and tested its balance, tossing the weapon from hand to hand. With a fluent whirl, he slid the blade back into its holder. Yuri watched him with admiration. He seemed so calm and relaxed, completely different from when he had been screaming in the pub the previous night.

"I'll meet you there," Yuri said with a nod, beginning to make his way towards the stairs that led down the tower.

"Yuri," Archerus called the boy, who halted. "If you do end up encountering werewolves, know that they can only infect you with a bite. That's how they insert their saliva into your bloodstream. A slash from their claws can certainly rip you in half, but it won't transform you into one of them. Understand? Avoid getting bitten at all costs."

"I understand," Yuri said.

"Then good luck to you," Archerus said with a weary smile. "And thank you for your help."

***

Yuri dashed through the chaotic streets of Horux. Survivors were either running in terror or attempting to fend off the ferocious beasts, which only resulted in their inevitable deaths. The boy quickly made his way into an alleyway, trying to keep himself hidden. That was when he remembered that Faelen had been able to smell him from an extreme distance. It didn't matter if they couldn't see him. These werewolves had enhanced senses, and they would find him.

The man glanced up and exhaled. Maybe it would be better to take the high ground. If he was going to be hunted down regardless, it was probably better if he was harder to reach.

Yuri ran three steps up the side of a wall and lashed outwards with his arms, grabbing onto a windowsill. He hauled himself upward and glanced through the window, only to find that there was a werewolf inside. The beast was gnawing on the mutilated corpse of a woman. The monster turned its head and met Yuri's eyes with its beastly gaze, opening its mouth and allowing the limp body to fall from its mouth to the wooden floor.

Panic usurped Yuri's mind and he used his upper strength to leap upwards, grabbing the edge of the roof with his hands. He groaned as he pulled himself upward, breathing heavily. A moment after, the werewolf's claw smashed through the window beneath him, sending glass spraying into the alleyway.

Yuri rolled onto the tiled rooftop and reached for the sword on his back, grabbing its handle tightly. He tore the weapon from its sheath and watched in anticipation as the werewolf's claws slammed into the side of the roof, digging into the clay tiles. The young man grunted as he ripped his sword sideways, cutting off one of the beast's hands. The beast let out an enraged roar that pierced Yuri's eardrums, causing him to stumble backwards as the werewolf leapt onto the roof, snarling angrily, blood spewing from the hemorrhaging stub of his right claw.

The werewolf pounced forward with incredible speed, moving faster than any opponent Yuri had ever encountered. But he anticipated that the beast would leap and had already rolled to the side. The monster smashed into the tiles where Yuri had been only a moment before, snorting as its eyes watched its prey roll away. As soon as Yuri rotated to his feet, his sword came swiping diagonally upwards. The silver blade shredded straight across the creature's chest, causing blood to fountain out of the beast.

Yuri winced, realizing that such an attack was surely not enough to kill the beast. However, as he watched, he saw that the werewolf collapsed to the roof, writhing in pain. It began to convulse as smoke drifted from the slash wound, as if its flesh were smoldering. *Silver must be what weakens a werewolf. That's why Faelen was trapped behind those silver bars!*

The young man realized that this was his chance to finish the monster, and he let out a loud cry as he hacked the beast's head clean off its body with a tremendous swing.

A pool of crimson liquid formed beneath the beast, running through the cracks of the rooftop tiles. Yuri collapsed to his knees, staring at the werewolf that he had slain. This was the first life that he'd ever taken. He gulped, staring at the corpse of the monster in disgust. Even though it looked like he'd murdered an abomination, he knew that this being had been human only an hour before. Shaking his head, Yuri pushed his distraught thoughts from his mind. *I did this in self-defense. This is no time to be sulking. I need to get home. Mom and Han are in danger!*

Yuri looked to the streets and watched the carnage as dozens of werewolves descended from other rooftops upon helpless civilians, slaughtering or infecting them. The werewolves scampered towards crowds of fleeing people, but Yuri noticed they weren't attacking each other.

An idea popped into Yuri's head, but he sure didn't like it. Looking back to the werewolf corpse beside him, he groaned as he gripped his sword with both hands. He hacked away at the corpse, splattering more blood across the tiles. Reaching down into the puddle of crimson liquid, he began to drench his hands in the warm blood and rub it along his arms, legs, and face. He even smothered some of the guts onto his shirt and pants.

If Yuri's observations were correct, then werewolves used their sense of smell to locate targets that were outside of their line of sight. They could detect the difference between werewolf and human scents and, from what he saw in the streets, the beasts did not attack their own kind.

By covering himself with werewolf blood, Yuri's masked scent would not lure any of the monsters to him. Though, if they spotted him, he would still be in trouble.

Yuri's nose twitched at the pungent miasma that came from his blood-coated body. He turned back to the streets and saw that the werewolves had finished hunting whatever civilians were on this street. Dozens of mangled corpses lay sprawled across the ground, their bodies practically shredded to pieces from the beasts' sharp claws. The monsters placed their noses to the ground like hunting dogs, sniffing for several moments. Within seconds, they had located their next targets and sprinted off on all fours, leaving the street completely devoid of life.

The boy sighed with relief, satisfied that his plan had worked. He slid his sword back into its sheath, watching as the creatures leapt onto the rooftops of buildings. His eyes widened when he realized that the beasts were heading in the direction of his home. "Damn it!" he growled in frustration, breaking into a mad dash across the rooftops.

Leaping from building to building, he raced forward. He soon saw that the werewolves had already descended upon their next group of targets, who were located on a street near his apartment. Cries of terror and agony echoed in Yuri's ears and he clenched his jaw, pressing onward as he sprinted in the direction of his home. *Mom ... Han ... please be okay!*

After several minutes of running, Yuri reached the roof across the street from his house, his heart racing. He pressed the soles of his feet against the tiled roof and leapt forward, his arms outstretched. He flew over the alleyway beside his home and used his hands to grab the top of his window, swinging his body into his family's apartment.

Landing hard on his feet, Yuri gaped at the scene before him. His eyes were wide with shock and he breathed shakily, his hands trembling. It felt like every cell in his body had just been frozen, for his body was completely numb.

His mother's body was pinned against the bloody wall, a claw lodged deep into her chest. Her head lolled forward and her arms were limp at her side. A werewolf stood in the center of the room, biting into the corpse of young Han, who was lying on the floor. The beast pulled its claw from Yuri's mother's body, causing her to crash to the floor of the apartment. Its eyes locked onto Yuri, and he tossed Han's body away like an unwanted toy. The lifeless corpse slammed against the wall on the other side of the room and slumped to the floorboards, blood pooling beneath Han's body.

Yuri's lower lip quivered as he stared at the bloody remains of his brother and mother. Shaking his head in disbelief, his quavering hands reached up to his back. He tore his sword from its sheath, his sorrow suddenly replaced by burning rage. It felt like lava now flowed through his veins. Adrenaline exploded through him and Yuri clenched his jaw so tightly that his teeth hurt. *"How ... dare you!"* he screamed, sprinting at the beast.

The werewolf ripped at the air with its claws, attempting to rend Yuri's face. The enraged man swept low, hacking his sword into the beast's stomach like a lumberjack cutting down a tree. There was a harrowing cry from the monster as it swiped downwards to attack Yuri. But the warrior quickly yanked his weapon from the beast's bloody stomach and slashed straight through the creature's arm before its claw could reach him. More blood splattered onto his face as the abomination screeched, falling onto its back.

Yuri was instantly upon the helpless werewolf, animosity blazing in his eyes. He brought the silver sword down and stabbed the beast in the chest, listening to the anguished roars of his family's killer. "That was my family that you murdered!" he roared, watching as smoke rose from the wounds of the werewolf. He rapidly swung away at the corpse of the beast, spraying more acrid ichor onto his clothes.

"You hurt them! Han and Mom ... you...," he cried out, tears beginning to fill his eyes. Soon they were rolling down his cheeks as he weakly collapsed to his knees, his sword clattering at his side. Putting his head in his hands, he began to sob. The last time he'd spoken to his mother, he'd yelled at her. "I never got the chance to apologize," he whimpered.

He cried for several minutes, the agony taking hold of his entire world. His heart was filled with abhorrence for the werewolves, but he knew that his family's fate wasn't their fault. If Beo hadn't released Faelen, then this never would've happened. It took all of his willpower to push the unbearable rage and grief from his mind.

Yuri raised his head and wiped the tears from his face. Standing up, he stared blankly at the bodies of his mother and brother, knowing that this would probably be the last time he saw them. Part of him wanted to take their bodies and bury or cremate them. But he knew that there was no time. If he wanted to live to see another day, he needed to get out of the Lower District before the werewolves completely overtook the city.

Yuri brushed some hair from his dark eyes and turned away from his family's cadavers as he moved to the window. His heart throbbed painfully and he crinkled his nose, trying to fight back the tears that wanted to flow out. Right now, he needed to compose himself. There would be plenty of time to mourn later. He needed to focus if he wanted any chance at getting to the Upper District.

The boy jumped from the window of his home and grabbed onto the edge of the roof on the opposite side of the alleyway, using his upper body strength to drag himself up. Within seconds, he was back to sprinting across the roofs of the buildings, making his way toward the Noble District, which wasn't too far away.

Yuri saw in the distance that there were barricades set up near a giant gate. At the stockades, there were dozens of knights and soldiers making a final stand, trying to defend the entrance to the Upper District. But in the end, they were only there to buy time, for it was impossible to defeat the horde of beasts that filled the streets.

The young man glanced to his side and saw that there were werewolves rushing across nearby roofs in the direction of the gateway. At least four beasts scrambled behind him, eying him hungrily. At their enhanced speed, they would catch up to Yuri in seconds.

Yuri grunted as he reached the end of the roof, diving forward. He smashed straight through a window and landed heavily on the floor of a bedroom, rolling upon impact. He scraped his arms and legs on the fragments of glass, and winced at the stinging pain. Whirling around, he saw several werewolves dive at the building after him. Some of them missed the window and slammed into the structure's walls. One did make it, and crashed hard onto the floor beside Yuri, growling.

As soon as the beast landed, Yuri took the opportunity to strike. The fighter ripped his silver sword across the monster's torso, cutting deep enough to finish the creature with a single blow. The werewolf collapsed beside Yuri, hemorrhaging blood from the fatal slash.

Yuri heard thumping noises coming from the roof. He staggered backward, startled by the abrupt sounds. But within seconds, it was quiet. He could hear the yelling of soldiers and rapid gunshots in the distance, but whatever was scampering about above him had fallen silent.

Suddenly, a werewolf crashed through the ceiling, descending upon Yuri with its fangs aimed straight for his throat. The boy grunted and stuck out his sword, slamming it straight through the beast's lower jaw. The silver blade rushed through flesh with ease, erupting from the top of the monster's muzzle.

Yuri ripped the blade from the creature's head just as another werewolf smashed through the wall on the opposite side of the room, taking the young warrior by surprise. He grunted as the beast slashed its claws across the boy's chest. A surge of excruciating pain exploded through his body and he staggered backward, gasping. He whipped his sword sideways in a clean stroke, slicing werewolf's throat.

At first, the beast seemed unfazed by the cut. But soon the creature's body began to react to Yuri's silver sword, and wisps of smoke began to drift from the monster's wound as it fell backwards, hitting the floor loudly.

Yuri panted, leaning back against the wall behind him. He lifted his shirt and examined the deep slashes that carved into his raw flesh. The bloody gashes were painful, but he was lucky that the injury wasn't worse. That werewolf could've easily torn Yuri in half.

The young man glanced around him, he knew he had to vacate the area as soon as possible. If he could just get through the gates to the Upper District, he would be a lot safer than in the Lower District. He turned as two werewolves forced their way into the room, one flying through the window while another barreled straight through a wall, sending bricks spraying.

Yuri swore under his breath and bolted across the room, diving out the window swiftly. He could hear the sounds of the scrambling werewolves behind him as he flew out of the building, dropping to the ground below. He slammed his feet on the ground, absorbing the shock through his feet, nearly twisting his ankle. Exhaling, he ignored the pain that cried through his body. *We're almost there. Come on!*

Yuri dashed out of the alleyway, back onto the main street. He could see the guards at the main gate about a hundred meters away. That was quite the distance, since he was completely surrounded by werewolves. Many of them had now marked him as their target, and he was already exhausted. His legs were numb from the fatigue of free-running all over the city, while his arms ached from cleaving his heavy sword about. Sharp pain screamed from his bleeding chest, but he knew that now was not the time to give up. One hundred meters — he could make it!

Yuri pressed his toes deep into the ground and burst forward with a surge of speed, rushing with all haste towards the soldiers at the gate. By now, they had all noticed him, since he was the only survivor that they'd seen thus far. His eyes widened when he recognized that the knight that was leading the group of dauntless warriors was Senna.

Senna stared at Yuri, surprised to find that the boy was still alive. "Focus your fire around the boy! Make sure he gets here!" he boomed, holding a blunderbuss in one hand and a sword in the other. He raised his blade as a werewolf came near the blockade and cleaved the beast's head right off its shoulders with a single stroke.

A cloud of gunpowder appeared before the group of soldiers as a barrage of projectiles soared forward, rushing in Yuri's direction. The young man continued sprinting forward, flinching as he heard the sound of bullets pounding into flesh. There was heavy thumping behind him as multiple bodies crumpled to the ground. The rooftops were filled with dozens of werewolves, raining down upon him. Some of them were knocked clean out of the air by bullets or arrows, but others landed on the street and bolted towards Yuri, saliva running down their jaws, their eyes flashing with bloodlust.

Yuri spotted a beast approaching quickly from the side and unsheathed his sword with a flourish just as the monster pounced. He grunted as he slashed the werewolf's chest open while the creature was still in the air, watching as the monstrosity struck the ground beside him. He continued onward, running as fast as he could. Closing his eyes, he bit his lower lip as he felt his aching legs screaming for him to stop. *Come on … I'm so close!*

Yuri cried out as he ran, feeling his body surpassing its limits. His bloodstained shirt was now sopping wet with fresh sweat, and every part of his body trembled, for his muscles were clearly exhausted. The physical pain that he had felt was now numbed, but he forced himself forward as adrenaline kicked in, granting him newfound energy.

Hearing claws scraping against the street behind him, Yuri glanced over his shoulder and spotted a werewolf springing at him. He quickly dodged to the side, just as the beast landed at his original position. It struck the ground with frightening force, cracking the paved street. A moment later, a lead bullet buried itself in the monster's forehead and it collapsed.

Yuri winced, realizing that he was losing his balance after shifting his weight so abruptly. He gasped when another werewolf suddenly tackled him off his feet, slamming him hard onto his back. The wind was driven from his lungs and he coughed, his grip on his sword weakened. He stared up in horror and saw that the werewolf was already leaning down to sink its fangs into his neck. His eyes widened with dread and his lips quivered, tempted to cry out for help. But there was no time for the words to even leave his lips.

An image of his bloody apartment flashed through his mind. He saw the grotesque scene and his slaughtered mother and brother. He didn't want to end up like that. *Please ... I don't want to—*

A gigantic sword skewered the werewolf straight through the side with such force that the beast was thrust off of Yuri's body. The monster collapsed beside Yuri and the boy stared at the slain creature, stupefied. He turned and saw that Senna was standing over him, offering his hand.

"Hurry up! We're going to close the gates," Senna growled.

Yuri looked past the knight and saw that the other soldiers had advanced from the gate's entrance to cover Senna. Yuri gulped and nodded thankfully as he reached up, grasping Senna's gauntlet.

Once he was on his feet, the young warrior took off towards the stockades. He ran around the wooden walls that functioned as barricades and sprinted with Senna through the gates. "Fall back!" Senna ordered to his men as the soldiers disengaged from their battle in the streets, returning to the Upper District.

There was a loud groaning sound as the gates began to close, even though there were still some soldiers that were trying to escape. Yuri watched with horror as werewolves pounced on some of the fleeing warriors. One man had his hand outstretched toward Yuri, as if the young man could somehow assist him from afar.

Yuri glanced away, wishing that he could block out the suffering knight's cries.

"P-Please! Wait for me!" a panicking soldier screamed, as he rushed towards the massive closing doors. But there was no way that he would make it. "No! Don't leave me, I—" A werewolf was already upon him and sank its fangs into his throat, squirting blood all over his neck. The man's face turned ghostly pale as he fell. That was the last thing that Yuri saw in the Lower District before the gates finally banged shut.

"There's no telling how long this gate will actually hold back those barbaric beasts," Senna said, turning away from the wall. "We need to get to the docks before all of the boats leave. Let's go."

"You've been bitten!" one of the soldiers exclaimed, pointing at one of his comrades. Immediately, all of the knights unsheathed their weapons and pointed them at the accused individual.

The frightened man raised his hands in protest, shaking his head. "N-No! Please, it's not a bite. It's just a scratch from a claw! I swear, please! Don't—"

There was a loud bang and Yuri gaped in shock as a bullet smashed straight through the accused knight's head, splattering blood on the ground. The man collapsed in an instant, and Yuri turned to find that Senna had fired his pistol.

"Why did you do that?" Yuri demanded, glaring at the knight.

Senna lifted the visor on his metal helmet so that he could meet the irate boy's gaze. "Do you honestly need to ask me that question?" he said. "We need to get out of here, *now*. Stop—" His eyes widened and he suddenly grabbed Yuri by the forearm and yanked the boy back.

Something plummeted from the sky and split the earth, creating an explosion where Yuri had been only a second before. A cacophony of anguished screams ripped through the night as a blurred figure rushed about in the cloud of dust that swallowed the area.

Yuri staggered behind Senna, squeezing the hilt of his sword with his clammy hands.

The knight stood his ground bravely, watching as the smokescreen cleared. He gaped with incredulity when he saw that all of his fellow soldiers were lying in bloody heaps on the ground before him. All of them had been slain in only a matter of seconds.

Standing in the center of the circle of corpses was an ebony werewolf that Yuri recognized. No ordinary werewolf could effortlessly climb up the side of a one-hundred-foot wall. The beast was staring up at the shining moon, exhaling through its nostrils, as if he were absorbing its energy. "Humans are so fragile and easily broken, it almost makes me feel sorry for you," the creature growled, locking its fierce gaze onto Yuri. "We meet again, boy."

"Faelen." Yuri's hands tightened around the handle of his sword. *This massacre is your fault, you damned monster. My family is dead because of you!* He bit his lower lip so hard that a small sliver of blood began to trickle from his mouth to his chin. "You'll pay for what you've done to this city."

"Is that so? Then make me pay." Faelen burst forward at triple the speed of the other werewolves. He swatted Senna out of the way before the knight was able to react, sending the man rolling helplessly across the field of grass. The creature wrapped its claws around Yuri's throat, lifting the boy off the ground with his fearsome strength.

Faelen sniffed the boy, smirking. "You're a clever one, aren't you? It took me a little extra time for me to find you since you masked your smell with werewolf blood. But I never forget a scent. That's the difference between the rest of the filthy mongrels on the other side of the wall and me. Like you, they're weak."

Yuri felt the air being choked from his lungs and grunted, jabbing outward at the werewolf with his sword. But Faelen could read his moves before they even occurred and lashed out, grabbing the blade with his free claw, halting the weapon before it reached his chest.

Suddenly the beast released Yuri, dropping the boy to the ground as he clutched his claw in agony, growling in rage. "*Silver!*" he bellowed, glaring at Yuri. "I'll have your—"

Faelen was suddenly struck in the ribs by a powerful blow from Senna's sword, causing the beast to double over in excruciating pain. Clutching the bleeding wound, the werewolf fell to its knees, gasping.

"This is our chance!" Senna exclaimed as he began to sprint away as fast as he could, waving for Yuri to follow. "Let's go!"

Yuri was on the ground, rubbing the deep scratches that sliced into his neck. He snatched his sword from the grass and dashed after the fleeing knight, his heart racing. "Senna, you go on to the docks. I'll meet you there!" Yuri said, bolting ahead of the knight in clanking armor.

The warrior's countenance contorted into a puzzled frown. "Where are you going?" he called after the agile boy.

"I need to make sure that Asmund has gotten out! Wait for me, I'll be quick!" Yuri shouted, dashing in the direction of his friend's mansion. *Please, Asmund … be alive!*

***

Faelen clutched his bleeding ribs, eying the injury. He could already feel the wound healing itself; the gash had stopped bleeding and was beginning to seal. The beast exhaled and then glanced at his claw, which was still raw, as if he'd just dipped his hand in lava. Because he'd received the wound from a silver blade, it would not regenerate as his other lesions did.

The werewolf growled in frustration, shaking his head. That boy truly was an annoyance, but he was also skilled. Yuri was coated in the blood of multiple werewolves, meaning that he had slain several of the beasts, surely using that silver sword of his. Faelen scowled, knowing that such a blade belonged to Beo.

The creature gazed off into the distance, sniffing the air. He smirked, catching the scent of a familiar target. Beo's son, the boy that had accompanied Yuri into the catacombs. Faelen recalled that he told Beo that he would slay the noble's son. The beast licked his lips. He didn't like breaking promises.

Don't Lose Your Way

"Asmund!" Yuri shouted, throwing open the door to the boy's mansion. He exhaled slowly, taking in the atrocious sight before him. The bodies of all of Asmund's maids, butlers, and fellow House members were all scattered on the marble floor of the home. Not a single person was conscious.

The boy rushed over to one of them and pressed his fingers to their neck, feeling for a pulse. The person was asleep, as were the rest of the unconscious individuals in the room. Yuri slapped several of them, trying to force them to wake up, but they did not stir. *What's going on here? Are they in a coma?*

Yuri gritted his teeth, noticing that Asmund was not amongst the sea of unmoving bodies. *There's no time. I need to find Asmund!* He dashed up the stairs, making his way to Asmund's room, where he hoped he would find his friend. Throwing open the door to the room, he was relieved to find Asmund unconscious on the floor. At least he was alive.

Yuri rushed to the noble's side, shaking him roughly. "Asmund, come on! You need to get up, we're running out of time! Otherwise—"

"My, my," an unfamiliar voice called out. Yuri glanced over his shoulder and saw a swirling black mist drifting before the door. "A gallant friend has come to his poor friend's rescue. How valiant of you." Stepping from the haze of darkness was a bald man, wearing an ebony cloak that coiled around his body. A small, diamond tattoo gleamed upon his forehead, matching the color of his violet eyes.

The man held a flower that was on fire. The stranger admired the flower's beauty, watching the flickering flames that danced upon its ruby petals. "I assume that since you've come here, you know of Beo. Did you know that he had such a prized possession?" he said, smiling.

"Who are you?" Yuri demanded, slowly rising to his feet. He unsheathed his sword and whirled it through the air, preparing to battle the mysterious man. But the stranger did not budge. Rather, he continued to gaze with awe at the beautiful flower, unfazed by Yuri's brandished silver blade.

"This is a Phoenix Heart, and it is extremely rare, only found in the northern mountains of Escalon, where the frigid temperatures turn men into statues of ice," the man spoke on, spinning the plant by its stem. "By eating this flower, a werewolf can regain their rationality. They won't be like the other slobbering beasts that are out there in the Lower District. Instead, a werewolf could become like Faelen, intelligent. Incredible, isn't it?"

Yuri's eyes widened at the mention of Faelen. *They know each other?*

"Beo must've kept this flower for himself just in case he ever did become infected. How selfish of him," the man said with a light chuckle. He turned his attention to Yuri and smiled, as if they were reunited old friends. "But you, you're altruistic, aren't you? After all, instead of running off to the docks like the rest of these fleeing pigs, you're here to save a friend."

"Tell me who you are and what you want," Yuri repeated.

"I'm Junko," the man said, bowing his head slightly. "I am a user of dark magic, and the temporary leader of an organization known as the Bounts. We intend to conquer the continent of Escalon. Satisfied?" He twirled the flower in his hand and snapped his fingers. "I don't want or need anything else for now. I'm quite satisfied with how things are going."

Yuri turned and saw that Asmund was beginning to stir, groaning as he leaned forward, his eyes squinted as if he had been sleeping for days. The man had undone whatever magical spell he had placed on the people of the mansion! He glanced back to Junko and saw that the man was now standing outside of the doorway, peering down the stairway. The cloaked stranger turned his head and gave Yuri a small smile. "But I cannot speak for the beast."

Yuri watched as the man exploded into a cloud of black smoke, vanishing. The door to the mansion slammed open and terrified screams echoed from downstairs, followed by anguished cries of dolor. *The beast?* "Faelen," he grumbled under his breath. He tapped Asmund. "Can you run?"

"Y-Yeah … what's going on?" Asmund asked, pushing himself to his feet. "Why's everyone—" His eyes suddenly bulged with fear as he stared at the doorway behind Yuri. He raised a trembling finger. "It's the werewolf!" he cried out in fear, tears gleaming in his eyes.

Yuri spun around and saw that Faelen was charging straight at him, his fur coated in blood. He grunted as he instinctively threw himself out of the way, rolling to his feet across the room. Glancing back, he was shocked.

Faelen had sunk his teeth into Asmund's neck. The boy's body was completely limp, his eyes wide with confusion as he gawked at his friend. His body trembled, his face blanching white. "Yuri … I-I feel a bit … weird. Am I—" The werewolf tore his head away from the noble, causing the boy to crumple to the floor. The beast grinned at Yuri nefariously.

"Soon you will truly understand pain. Watch powerlessly as you lose your friend," Faelen said, stepping to the side. "And then realize your insignificance in this cruel world."

Yuri's lips were quivering as he began to slowly move towards his friend. "Asmund? Are you—"

"*Get away!*" Asmund yelled suddenly, wrapping his arms around himself, gasping heavily. He glanced at Yuri, his eyes already a beastly red. Tears streaked down his cheeks as he bit his lower lip. "*Something's happening, I feel so angry. I can't … control myself. Please ... run!*' he growled, suddenly letting out an agonizing scream as excruciating pain erupted throughout his body. He roared, his head abruptly snapping backward. His spine began to lengthen, twisting and elongating until the boy had stretched to seven feet in height. Dark brown fur sprouted from his skin as his hands turned into sharpened claws. His nose lengthened into a snout while his ears morphed into those similar to a dog. Baring his dagger-like fangs, Asmund now towered over Yuri as a werewolf, an untamed monster.

Yuri staggered backward towards the doorway, his hands quavering. He hesitated, waiting to see if Asmund would recognize him.

The beast let out a bellowing roar and shot forward with a burst of speed, dragging his claws across the wall, shredding off the wallpaper. The creature's sharpened nails tore through the air at Yuri's throat but he had already thrown himself backward, scrambling away.

Asmund leapt forward and swatted Yuri with the back of his hand, sending the boy tumbling down the stairway to the lower floor. The beast let out a victorious howl as he leapt from the second floor, descending upon Yuri, about to squash his former friend.

Yuri winced in pain, his head spinning. He caught a brief glimpse of the giant werewolf crashing down upon him. Yelping, he rolled away at the last moment, bumping into the corpse of one of Asmund's slaughtered maids. His eyes widened when he realized that Faelen had already massacred everyone in the manor. The carnage was nauseating, but Yuri knew that he didn't have time to feel sick. He had to escape from Asmund before he too became a corpse.

Asmund swiped his claws at his friend just as Yuri flipped over the maid's cadaver, ripping the woman's body apart with a single slash. The beast gnarred and continued forward, drool running down his jaw.

"Asmund, it's me!" Yuri exclaimed, staggering to his feet. "Your friend—"

The werewolf did not heed Yuri's words and stabbed his claws into Yuri's stomach, sinking his sharp nails into the boy's flesh. The young man gasped in agony as he was lifted into the air and slammed heavily into the ground, the wind forced from his lungs. Unbearable pain exploded through his diaphragm and tears twinkled in his eyes as he stared up in shock at the transformed noble that now towered over him. "P-Please ... don't do this," Yuri gasped, wincing at the burning sensation that ripped through his stomach as Asmund's claws dug deeper into his diaphragm.

Asmund looked at him for a long second before snapping downward, sinking his fangs into Yuri's shoulder. The boy's eyes widened at the insufferable pain that detonated throughout his body. It felt like his entire body was on fire. He gasped, barely able to choke out any noise from his quavering lips. *I'm going to die here if I don't—*

Yuri wrapped his hands tightly around the grip of his sword, knowing what he had to do in order to survive. He closed his eyes, thrusting his silver blade into Asmund's gut. The beast looked at the injured boy with wide eyes, groaning. The lethal wound began to smolder, sending wisps of smoke into the air. Asmund choked painfully, sputtering some blood onto Yuri's chest. The beast's lips then curved into what might've been a smile before he rolled off the injured boy.

The entire house was silent except for the arduous pants of Yuri, who stared blankly at the ceiling. His shoulder and diaphragm ached, and to the boy's horror, he watched as the wounds on his body began to close until they were no more than light scars on his skin. *I've ... been bitten.* He pressed the back of his hand to his moist eyes, beginning to sob quietly to himself. *Tonight, I've lost everything ... my family, my best friend, my home, my city, and now ... my humanity.*

Faelen watched the boy from the second floor, snarling with satisfaction at Yuri's despair. He leapt to the ground floor, landing heavily beside the exhausted boy's body. "Worry not, boy. I'll put an end to your misery, so that you're not forced to become the nightmare that you fear. Consider this mercy." The beast raised his claws into the air, licking his lips as he prepared to execute Yuri.

That was when another werewolf sprung through the mansion's front door and tackled Faelen, sending the two beasts rolling across the foyer. The two monsters slashed at each other wildly with their claws, each attempting to claim the other's life.

Faelen's eyes narrowed when he recognized his opponent. "Beo."

Yuri leaned forward slowly, staring at the newcomer in surprise. The werewolf looked similar to Asmund, with the same color fur and facial features. Beo was … a werewolf?

Beo stared at Asmund's corpse, his eyes gleaming with grief. He then bared his fangs at Faelen, unleashing an enraged roar that shook the entire manor. "Yuri, run!" Beo ordered, planting his feet into the ground as he prepared to battle Faelen.

"Oh, my!" Junko's voice echoed through the foyer as a black mist surged through the upper floors. The cloaked man materialized at the top of the stairway, grinning at Beo. "You're a werewolf? Well, that's a surprise. It would seem that I've been tricked! After all, who would expect a werewolf to despise his own kind so much? Faelen, you never mentioned that he was a werewolf."

"I'm as surprised as you are," Faelen grumbled. "His scent is that of a human, not a werewolf. I thought I was the last of my kind."

Junko still held the Phoenix Heart in his hand and raised an eyebrow. "It seems that you're tame, meaning that you've already eaten a flower in the past. Then who was this for?" he asked, twirling the flower.

"My son," Beo snarled, glancing at Yuri from the corner of his eye. "What are you still doing here? I'll fend them off. You need to run!"

"But I—"

"It doesn't matter," Beo said, flashing his sharpened claws as he shot forward towards Junko and Faelen. "Live on and return one day to reclaim this city!" he boomed, sinking his teeth into Faelen's shoulder. The beast let out a ferocious howl as he tackled Beo, the two werewolves rolling on the floor as they hacked at each other with their claws.

Yuri, trembling at the ferocious battle, stole a final glance at Asmund's corpse, feeling tears welling up in his eyes. He swallowed hard and nodded to himself, scrambling towards the door. *I have to get out of here!*

Junko burst into a cloud of black smoke, surging across the foyer. The man appeared at Yuri's side, a wicked grin on his face as he reached for the boy's throat. Then his eyes widened with surprise as Beo grabbed him by the ankle. "You're that fast—" He was interrupted as the werewolf hurled the Bount straight through a wall, sending the cloaked man tumbling into the next room.

Yuri dashed off, glancing back at his best friend's father, who bravely stood against two formidable opponents. But the man-beast did not seem fazed, and didn't quiver as a terrified man would. It seemed that he had nothing left to lose.

Faelen clenched his jaw tightly, drool dripping down his chin onto the bloodstained floor as he trudged forward towards Beo, ready to tear the noble to shreds. Scrapes, gashes, and bloody wounds covered his body from his brief exchange with Beo.

Junko stepped through the hole in the broken wall, brushing some dust off his shoulder. His violet eyes gleamed and his smile was gone. Magic circled around his body, its color a combination of dark-purple infused with black, forming a misty cloud that surrounded the cloaked man. "Getting in our way is pointless. You're hopelessly outmatched," he declared.

Beo swallowed hard, his eyes flitting between his two opponents. He knew that the battle was hopeless, but he had to buy time for Yuri to escape. After all, it was the least that he could do after trying to kill the boy … his son's best friend. Exhaling, the werewolf crossed his arms before his face, as if bracing himself for an oncoming storm. "I know. But the two of you are responsible for the destruction of this city and the infection of my son. What kind of a father would I be if I simply let you mongrels walk away unpunished?" he growled, smirking at Faelen's injured body. "You'll pay for what you've done here."

***

Senna bit his lower lip, scanning the docks for any sight of Yuri. He was on the deck of the last boat in the harbor and had somehow managed to convince the captain that they were to wait for one last individual. But he knew that they couldn't stay here long.

Archers and soldiers with pistols were on the deck, ready to fire at any werewolves that appeared. But so far, there was only silence. That was … until Senna spotted Yuri in the distance, sprinting towards them. The boy was running from the castle's back entrance, clearly exhausted. Behind him were dozens of werewolves that hungrily rushed in the direction of the boat. However, their eyes weren't on Yuri; they were focused on the people on the ship.

Senna watched as his men fired at the werewolves around Yuri, but the knight observantly noticed that the beasts were purposely not attacking the boy, who was now limping towards the ship. Instead, they scurried past him, charging towards the docks. "Take off," the warrior commanded to the captain of the ship, his voice loud and full of authority.

"But the boy—" the captain began.

"Obey my orders!" Senna shouted and the captain nodded quickly as the ship prepared to take off. By the time Yuri finally stumbled onto the docks, the boat had already drifted from shore. Dozens of werewolves lay dead around him and the boy trembled.

Yuri was clutching his shoulder, gasping as he collapsed to his knees. His eyes were filled with despair. "Senna!" he yelled, panting as he felt scorching heat radiating throughout his body. It was as if all of his blood had been replaced with burning lava. "You're leaving me?"

The knight stood on the quarterdeck, watching the boy pitifully from behind the wooden railing of the ship. He pulled out his pistol and aimed it at Yuri, his expression devoid of emotion as he gazed down at the boy. The gun clicked as the knight pulled back the hammer with his thumb. "You're not human anymore, are you?"

Yuri's eyes widened. He extended one of his hands to Senna with a pleading gaze. But his irises had already started to turn red, the eyes of a werewolf. "Senna, stop! I—"

There was a final bang that shattered the night as a lead bullet smashed into Yuri's chest, spraying his blood on the wooden docks. The boy's eyes rolled to the back of his head, his body swaying back and then forward. Then he was falling off the platform and into the water, where he was swallowed by darkness.

Becoming a Beast

Yuri gasped, clutching his aching chest. He leaned forward, finding himself engulfed in blackness. Breathing heavily, he waited for a moment to allow his eyes to adjust to the dark. He recalled his last memory before he'd passed out. Senna had shot him.

The boy reached up and touched his face, which was somehow still human. Frowning, he skimmed his hand over his heart, where he had been shot, feeling the skin. The wound was gone, but such fast recovery would only be possible if he was a werewolf ... and Asmund had bitten him. How was he still in control of himself? Was he still human? No, if he were he would've bled out long ago.

As his eyes slowly adapted to the dark, he began to make out shapes in the gloomy area. There were bars to his right. To his left was a pile of hay that was supposed to be a makeshift bed of sorts. So, he was jailed then, surrounded by walls of dark stone.

Yuri's eyes narrowed when he spotted another man sitting on the ground across the cell, leaning his back against the wall, watching the boy. He licked his lips nervously. "Hello?"

"Good, you're awake."

"Archerus?"

"Yep."

Yuri let out a sigh of relief, tapping his head back against the wall behind him. "Thank the gods. Where are we?"

"The royal jail. You were lucky that I had just arrived at the docks when you fell into the water. I saved you from drowning, but then Faelen arrived and had us thrown in here. Currently, he is reluctant to kill other werewolves, since he is so unused to seeing other members of his race. But who knows how long his affinity to other werewolves will last," Archerus murmured. He smirked at Yuri's surprised look. "Yes, I'm a werewolf too. I went home to find that one of the damned beasts had already murdered my wife. Unfortunately, the monster ended up infecting me as well. I didn't have any silver on me, so my chances of escaping that situation unscathed were very slim."

Yuri lowered his head. "I'm sorry," he murmured quietly.

"Everyone lost loved ones tonight," Archerus said, slowly pushing himself to his feet. He cracked his neck and turned to look at the iron bars that trapped them in the cell. "Now we have to focus on escaping Horux before Faelen changes his mind and decides to execute us. Since we've become werewolves, we have enhanced strength, meaning that there's no way that a cell like this can hold us," he said, tapping the iron bars with his index finger. "That probably means that he's taken defensive measures to make sure that we can't escape. I expect that there are dozens of werewolves surrounding the palace. Not to mention that as soon as we alert one of them, they'll start howling like a pack of hounds. Faelen will come running in while we're off battling a horde of werewolves and wouldn't have any trouble finishing us off.

"But there's a huge difference between us and those mindless mutts out there. Sure, we have the same physical capabilities, but you and I are still intelligent. We are going to have to use that to our advantage when we decide to escape," Archerus said, turning to Yuri. He raised an eyebrow when he saw that the boy was still sitting on the ground, staring at his shaking hands with his head lowered like a sulking child. "Hey, are you listening to me? We need to escape tonight."

"I heard you," Yuri muttered. "But tell me what makes us different from the rest of those werewolves? How is it that you and I are intelligent whereas the rest of them turned into …

monsters?" He remembered how Asmund had lost his humanity in only seconds, transforming into a monster bred to kill.

Archerus watched the boy, recognizing the look of depression on his face. Surely the young man had gone through a lot tonight. He sighed, rubbing the back of his neck. "Ever since I found out about Beo's secret, I knew that I had to take precautions in case Faelen was ever let loose. So, I spent a fortune on two Phoenix Hearts. They go for a pretty hefty price since they're extremely hard to obtain. How often do you see flowers that are constantly aflame?" he said, turning back to the iron bars of the cell. "It just so happens that if a werewolf eats a Phoenix Heart, their human side reawakens. That is, they regain their lost rationality. I went home to save my wife and get the flowers, only to find that she was already dead. The Phoenix Heart that was meant for her, I granted to you." He smiled at the boy. "After all, you were the one person who was willing to help me in my time of peril."

Yuri stared at the man in surprise. He didn't know what to say. "Thank you," he said, remembering that the mysteriously cloaked man in Beo's home also had one of those flowers in his possession. "So, if we're werewolves, how are we still in our human form?"

"Werewolves that have regained their rationality are able to freely shift between their human and beast forms," Archerus explained. "You might not be able to tell that from watching one like Faelen; it would seem that he prefers to look like a monstrosity. In our human forms, we have enhanced strength and speed. However, when we shift into beasts, our physical attributes such as agility and strength are augmented, and are then triple that of when we are in our human forms. I know that you'll ask this question, so I'll answer it now," he said. "We can only infect other individuals if we sink our fangs into a person's bloodstream in our *werewolf* form. Biting someone, spitting on them, mixing blood … none of that does anything if we're in our human state. Do you understand?"

"Yeah." Yuri swallowed. "So, uh, how do we transform then?"

"The trigger to transforming is different for everyone. For me, I think of my wife. All I need to do is picture her in my mind, and I start to feel a warm sensation in my chest." Archerus's body began to suddenly shift, his body morphing into that of a beast. Grey fur sprouted from his skin and within seconds he had transformed into a werewolf. "I grasp at that feeling and then this happens."

Yuri raised his eyebrows, impressed at how easily Archerus had shifted forms. He made it seemed effortless, as if he'd been a werewolf for more than just a couple hours. Then again, he'd done extensive research on werewolves for years prior to Faelen's invasion of Horux, so it was expected that he would know a lot more than most.

Archerus nodded to Yuri. "Eventually, as we get the hang of transforming, we won't even need a trigger. We will simply be able to morph into our werewolf forms at will. But I imagine that won't be for a while. Now you try. It'll be easier to escape if you're in your beast form."

Yuri gulped and attempted to follow Archerus's advice. First, he pictured images of his slain family, which only left him vomiting in the corner of the cell. The grotesque scene was branded into his memory and was so detailed that it made him feel ill.

Archerus was extremely patient with Yuri and insisted that he try to transform again. The second time, he recalled an image of him slaying Asmund, which he was sure would be an emotional enough experience to trigger his werewolf form. But it didn't. Instead, all he felt was tormenting guilt throbbing in his chest.

The boy shook his head, pressing his forehead on the wall of the cell, cooling his skin against the stone. He was sweaty, as if he had just woken up from a terrifying nightmare. "I can't do it," he whispered shakily. "Those are two of my darkest memories."

"Sometimes it isn't a dark memory that will be your trigger. In fact, it might not be a memory at all. Maybe it is simply a *feeling* that you have locked up within," Archerus said with a sigh. He shouldn't have expected that Yuri would be able to find his trigger so quickly. There were so many memories and experiences that he would have to first sift through to find the right one. "It doesn't matter. We can't stay here. You'll have to make do in your human form. I recall that you're quite agile anyway. Perhaps we can still escape Horux in one piece," he said. "First, we'll have to retrieve your silver sword."

"Is it that important? Shouldn't we just get the hell out of here?"

"That weapon is special. It received numerous enchantments from some of the greatest mages, druids, and priests from all around Terrador. Its power is in slaying more monsters than just werewolves. It will surely be of use in the future," Archerus said, reaching out and grabbing the iron bars with his hands. The metal creaked loudly as the werewolf pried them apart, creating a gaping opening. Stepping through the hole and into the empty hallway of the royal dungeon, Archerus sniffed the air. "I have the location of your sword."

"Huh? How?"

"Werewolves use their keen sense of smell to locate everything. Even in your human form, you should have enhanced senses. Just concentrate and try to track your own scent. It should be attached to the sword, since you used it quite a lot tonight." Archerus turned to look at a pair of stone stairs that led out of the royal jail. "Looks like we have company."

Yuri could feel it, the gentle vibrations of padding footsteps in the distance, rumbling through the soles of his feet. He could hear the heavy breathing of two werewolves as they descended the stairway towards the royal jail. Their stench was acrid and reeked of raw meat, blood, and dirt. *Track your own scent.* His senses were amplified to the point where, if he concentrated hard enough, he could hear, smell, or feel things from an incredible distance.

The boy leaned down and smelled himself, familiarizing himself with his own unique scent. He then sniffed the air and immediately located something that had his scent attached to it, along with the strong odor of werewolf blood. *That has to be my sword,* he thought. Yuri met Archerus's gaze and nodded, indicating that he too had traced his weapon's position.

"All right, once we take out these two werewolves, we're in perilous territory. We're going to have to keep moving, and there will be no time to rest until we are outside of Horux's perimeter, do you understand?" Archerus said, loudly snapping two iron bars off of the cell. He looked to Yuri, who nodded. "Perfect. Let's go then."

Two werewolves burst into the hallway of the royal jail, snarling at the sound of the breaking iron bars. Archerus hardly gave them any time to snoop about. The prisoner charged towards his two opponents on all fours, pouncing from the shadows onto one of the beasts. He brought both his claws stabbing upward, sinking into the chin of the werewolf with such force that the monster's head was almost ripped off. Almost instantly, Archerus rotated his body and slammed a solid punch into the side of the second opponent's cheek, shattering the creature's jaw with a sickening crack.

Yuri sprinted through the hallway, leaping over the limp werewolf bodies as he continued up the stairs to leave the jail. Right now, they were probably underneath the royal castle. His sword was located somewhere nearby, which meant that it was probably hidden in the building. Then again, he remembered how easily he had gotten lost in the castle earlier that day. There were limitless places his weapon could be hidden within the palace. *Let's see how powerful these werewolf senses really are.*

Yuri put all of his concentration into tracking his sword. Within moments, he could see a blue misty trail before his eyes that traced a path to his weapon. *Am I insane, or am I actually seeing smells?*

Smiling, he sprinted forward with a surge of speed, moving as quickly as a horse at full gallop. His newfound speed was amazing. He skipped up the stone stairway in only seconds and was off, flitting through the castle's hallways at blinding speed. He didn't even need to check over his shoulder to see if Archerus was following him; he could hear and feel his companion's presence directly behind him.

The boy also heard the scrambling of dozens of other werewolves through the castle. All of the beasts were converging on his current position; it would be difficult to escape this citadel without a fight. Not to mention that if they spent too much time here, they would eventually end up running into Faelen. That would be trouble.

Following the visible hazy trail that floated before him, Yuri grunted as werewolves leapt at him from nearby hallways, slashing wildly at the air. While the beasts were ferocious and terrifying, Yuri noticed that they lacked grace. With his new senses and reactions, it was easy for him to weave around their attacks. He found himself reacting by instinct, avoiding and dodging the werewolves as they wildly threw themselves at him.

The boy continued onward, realizing that he was still not out of breath. Impressed by his improved physique, he bolted toward a door at the end of the hallway.

"You better be ready to close that door!" Archerus yelled at him.

Yuri slammed his feet on the floor, skidding across the remainder of the corridor, his boots giving off a sharp squeak against the marble. He could feel the bottoms of his shoes tearing off, and the smell of burning leather filled his nostrils. Grabbing the doorknob, the boy swung the door open and scuttled inside. He waited for the opportune moment as Archerus dove through the entrance and slammed the door abruptly, pressing himself against the wood.

There was a heavy thump as the door jolted against Yuri's weight, causing the boy to wince as he held back the dozens of werewolves in the hallway. Grunting, he turned around and saw that Archerus was stumbling about, desperately searching for Yuri's sword. The room looked like a messy armory filled with dozens of piles of armor and weapons. Ordinarily, Yuri knew that he could never have found his sword. But with his enhanced senses, he saw a blue cloud circling around a particular pile on the left side of the room. "There!" he exclaimed, pointing to a heap of armor and weapons.

Archerus rushed to the pile and tore through it for a moment before pulling out the silver sword. Relief showed on his face. "Got it," he said and turned to the door, watching as the werewolves suddenly barreled through the entrance, sending Yuri flying across the room.

Yuri landed hard on a mound of armor, wincing slightly as he slammed into the metal. But he was grateful that he had landed on an iron breastplate instead of the blade of a sharpened sword. He spotted a window on the far side of the room that led outside. That was their way out of this castle.

It was odd, seeing Archerus wielding a sword in his werewolf form, but the warrior was slashing through beasts left and right with fluent strokes, eradicating each enemy with powerful slashes. Glancing over his shoulder for a brief moment, he met Yuri's gaze as the boy rushed in the direction of the window. Nodding, Archerus swung his sword outward in a sweeping cut, rending three werewolves with a single blow. He then whirled around and quickly followed Yuri.

Yuri jumped forward, bringing his legs upward so that he smashed through the window with his boots. He winced as shards of glass scraped the soles of his feet through what was left of his shoes. The boy grunted when he realized that he was falling at least thirty feet towards the castle's lawn with nothing to cushion his fall. Expecting to shatter the bones in his legs, or at least twist an ankle, he closed his eyes, bracing himself for a world of pain.

The earth quickly came up to meet him. Yuri slammed heavily into the ground, sending dirt spraying everywhere. But surprisingly, he didn't break any bones. In fact, it felt as if he'd only fallen three feet as opposed to thirty. He'd nearly forgotten that he was a werewolf. Surviving thirty-foot drops was nothing to him now.

Archerus had landed beside Yuri and was already sprinting away. He tossed the sword over his shoulder to Yuri and the boy caught it by the hilt, careful not to touch the silver blade.

Squeezing the handle of his weapon, Yuri glanced up to see that the pursuing werewolves were pouring through the window, raining down around him. He yelped and quickly bolted after Archerus, dashing across the royal lawn towards a giant wall in the distance. He recalled that this was the wall that surrounded the castle grounds and was where Senna had met him to escort the boy to the dinner earlier that night.

Yuri gulped, not particularly sure how he was going to be able to scale the wall. He watched as Archerus jumped upwards, digging his claws deep into the stone before propelling himself upward and vaulting over the top. Yuri knew that he would not be able to climb like that since he was still stuck in his human form. Perhaps his strength had been enhanced enough that he could simply jump over the wall. *That's a big gamble. I don't really know my own strength yet. This could completely fail!*

The boy bit his lower lip as he approached the wall. There was no room for error here; the other werewolves were catching up to him. If he jumped and slammed into the wall, then those beasts would be upon him in a second.

Yuri brought his arms forward and then down, shifting his weight to his legs as he smashed his feet deep into the earth and propelled himself as high as he could. Dirt sprayed from underneath him and he blinked with surprise when he saw that he cleared the wall by a reasonable margin, soaring through the air with his arms flailing, like a baby bird flying for the first time.

While in the air, he got a clear view of the gloomy Lower District. Werewolves were everywhere, feasting upon the corpses of slain humans. Carnage filled the streets and the walls of buildings were painted in blood. The bloodbath was horrific and gruesome. Yuri had no idea how he and Archerus were going to force their way through the rest of Horux with that many beasts populating the Lower District.

Descending to the earth, Yuri rolled on a patch of grass as he struck the ground. Scrambling to his feet, the boy saw that Archerus was waving for him to come quickly. He took off dashing towards his companion, listening to the howling creatures that were landing behind him. "The division between the Lower and Upper Districts will be the next hurdle that we will have to climb," Archerus shouted, pointing to the gigantic wall in the distance. "It'll be difficult for you to leap over that one."

"Faelen did it," Yuri said, remembering when Faelen had jumped over the Upper District's wall and slaughtered all of Senna's men. He clenched his jaw as he eyed the wall and winced, realizing that this one was at least double the height of the previous obstruction. Archerus was probably right; the chances of him scaling the wall in his human form were slim.

"You either have to transform into a werewolf right now and climb that wall," Archerus said, "or you can jump onto my back and I'll do the climbing. It'll slow us down by a reasonable amount, though. The werewolves are bound to catch up to us with me carrying you."

"I'll try to transform," Yuri said, shutting his eyes.

"Don't close your eyes, we're running!"

"I have to concentrate!"

"Now's definitely not the time," Archerus grumbled. "Just jump on my back, the wall's coming up!"

Yuri threw himself onto Archerus's back, mounting the werewolf like a horse. But soon he was grabbing fistfuls of Archerus's fur as the beast accelerated to his maximum speed, charging straight for the wall. The boy's legs dangled loosely in the air as the blistering wind rushed into him, blowing back his hair. His body was practically horizontal as he clung onto Archerus for dear life.

Yuri glanced over his shoulder and noticed that the gap between them and the werewolves was closing. Soon, the beasts would be upon them. "Faster!" he cried out, panicking.

"I'm working on it!" Archerus growled, partially out of breath. He pounced through the air and sank his claws into the stone wall, and began to clamber up the side of the barrier. Archerus brought his hands over the top of the wall and was about to haul himself up when suddenly he felt a sharp pain bite into his ankle. He let out a bellowing howl, clenching his teeth tightly.

Yuri glanced down to find that one of the werewolves was clinging to Archerus's ankle, stabbing the warrior's flesh with its sharp nails. Drawing his sword, Yuri dismembered the pursuer with a swift slash. Archerus then managed to climb onto the wall's walkway.

Clutching his bleeding ankle, Archerus groaned, watching as other werewolves dragged themselves onto the wall. His eyes narrowed and he panted as the horde of beasts swarmed around the two escaped prisoners. "Damn my luck," he grumbled, wincing at the excruciating pain in his ankle, blood oozing from the fresh wound. Running at full speed was certainly going to be difficult with this injury.

"Go on ahead," Yuri said, whirling his sword as he stepped towards the snarling werewolves. Despite being outnumbered, he wasn't that afraid. He had already killed plenty of them as a human. Now that he was a werewolf, he knew that he would have little trouble fighting these beasts. "I'll hold them off for a bit, then I'll catch up with you."

"But—"

"Trust me," Yuri said, grinning confidently. "I can handle them."

***

Faelen watched Beo through the iron bars of a cell that had been custom designed by the king for the royal family's greatest enemy. The noble had shackles around his wrists that were chained to the ceiling, holding his limp body up. The man was in his human form and had his head lowered, his face smeared with blood that dripped off his nose and lips into a crimson pool at his dirt-caked feet. "How does it feel? To be chained up like an animal, your freedom deprived," Faelen snarled. "I can't wait to see the light fade from your eyes as I pry you apart, piece by piece, for what you've done to me."

The werewolf reached out and grabbed one of the iron bars, squeezing it, grinning wickedly. The metal creaked as it was crushed by his powerful grip. "I know that these silly chains won't be able to hold you. But I am not a cruel overseer, as you were. I will not keep you surrounded in a cell of silver. Instead, I will return here every night at midnight, and I will break you as I have done tonight. Don't worry, though; as long as I don't strike your flesh with silver, you'll heal quickly." He heard footsteps approaching from the dark corridor behind him.

Glancing over his shoulder, he glared at Junko, who emerged from the shadows. "What do you want?"

"It would seem that your two prisoners have escaped," Junko said, folding his arms. "This is what happens when you do not follow my advice. You should've killed them while you had the chance."

"What?" Faelen barked, wincing at the news. "They are surrounded by at least a thousand werewolves in the citadel! Where are they now?"

"Battling off your horde of beasts in the Lower District," Junko said.

"How is that possible?"

"The boy is rather skilled with that sword of his. He's probably killed a hundred of your werewolves in the past hour. The werewolf with him must've given him a Phoenix Heart. He is in complete control over himself," Junko said, his arms folded over his chest, nodding at Beo. "I would stop them, but I exhausted all of my magic battling Beo. You head after them, and I'll stay here and keep watch."

"Damn it all!" Faelen roared in frustration, sprinting down the corridor. *Yuri has slain a hundred werewolves?* He recalled the boy's agile movements when he had been dodging Asmund's attacks earlier that night. *He's taking advantage of his enhanced werewolf strength. I spared him because I thought he would become like the rest of these mindless creatures. Archerus had another Phoenix Heart to spare?* The beast swore under his breath. *I was going to wait a day before I executed those mongrels. It looks like their heads will be mounted on my wall a little earlier than expected.*

Druid of the North

Yuri grunted, spinning around as he cleaved a werewolf in half with a clean swing of his sword, the blade whipping around like an untamed whirlwind, cutting down multiple beasts around him. The boy was on the rooftops on the Lower District, drawing the majority of the werewolves' attention away from Archerus, who was sprinting through the streets on his injured leg. Luckily for him, the werewolves followed their instincts and were focusing their attention on Yuri, since he was currently the bigger threat, having slain well over a hundred werewolves.

Free running on the rooftops had never felt so smooth and easy as with Yuri's newly obtained werewolf powers. The boy hopped from building to building with ease, skipping gaps effortlessly. In fact, he could completely leap over the entire street with his current strength if he wanted. Not that it really made any difference if he did. These werewolves were actually faster than he was, despite his augmented attributes. However, their attacks were so predictable that battling them was not difficult. The only real issue was their numbers.

Having gained the attention of a majority of the Lower District, a myriad of werewolves now chased the two fleeing prisoners. Countless beasts dashed on the rooftops after Yuri while several of them were in the streets chasing Archerus. The two escapees had pushed their way through most of the city already, but the number of werewolves kept increasing. It was already a miracle that the duo had not been overwhelmed and killed yet.

Archerus lashed out with his claw, opening the throat of a werewolf that scampered from a nearby alleyway. He charged forth, his breathing heavy. His eyes were trained on the gigantic walls that surrounded Horux. That was their final obstacle. "Once we get past the walls, we'll be safe!" Archerus yelled, ducking as a werewolf pounced towards his head.

"That so?" Yuri yelled back, thrusting his blade into the chest of a beast that was in his path. Tearing his sword out of the corpse, he continued sprinting forward. "I'm pretty sure these guys will follow us outside of the city," he called as he rolled onto another rooftop.

"Trust me, we'll be fine!"

Yuri located an enormous scaffold that was near Horux's main gate. He could use that to get to the top of the wall, instead of having to cling to Archerus's back again. "We're almost there!" he said, suddenly stepping onto a weakened part of a roof. His eyes widened as the tiles beneath him gave in and the entire roof collapsed inward, causing him to lose his foothold and fall into an abandoned warehouse. He grunted, landing hard on a wooden box that was crushed underneath his weight.

The boy gasped as a werewolf dropped upon him from above, and quickly rolled away before it could stab its claws into his flesh. *Crap, they're all going to catch up to me now!*

Yuri scanned the gigantic warehouse in an attempt to find an exit, but he couldn't see past the crowds of werewolves that were now falling around him. He swallowed hard, holding up his sword as he retreated into a corner, his back pressed up against a wall. *There's no way that I can fight my way out of this one.*

The wall behind Yuri suddenly exploded. A werewolf tore its way through the wood, grabbing Yuri by the arm and sinking its fangs deep into the boy's shoulder. Blood soaked into his shirt as he screamed in agony, instantly causing the rest of the beasts to rush forward towards him. Yuri gritted his teeth, biting back his pain, and swept his sword outward, the blade causing the werewolves to halt their advance. None of them wanted to be struck by silver.

Yuri swung his elbow backward, smashing it into the werewolf behind him with superhuman strength, sending the beast rocketing back through the hole in the wall. The warrior winced at the raw wound in his shoulder and watched in horror as the werewolves all suddenly blitzed him at the sight of watching one of their comrades being hurt. One of the werewolves tackled Yuri, pinning the boy to the ground. It dug its dagger-like teeth into Yuri's forearm while other beasts began to bite at his legs.

Unbearable pain erupted all over Yuri and tears welled up in his eyes as he cried out in anguish, wishing that someone would come to his rescue. He didn't want to die like this ... being eaten alive by countless werewolves. That was when an image flashed into his mind. It was a memory of him watching Asmund transform. *Watch powerlessly as you lose your friend.*

Faelen was right. Humans were feeble, weak ... *powerless.*

Yuri's eyes suddenly turned from their turquoise color to a shining violet, and his teeth began to sharpen. The werewolves suddenly lifted their heads from the bleeding boy, watching with surprise as Yuri's body began to morph into that of a monstrosity. Black fur, the color of night, sprouted from his skin, and his nails lengthened into claws that were sharper than swords. His spine cracked as it arced and elongated, causing his shoulders to snap forward. Within moments, he went from an ordinary teenage boy to a ferocious werewolf, his bloody linen shirt tearing apart.

Rage coursed through his veins and instinct conquered his mind. Before he knew what was happening, he had lacerated the werewolves that were upon him with swift movements. He grabbed the beast that had pounced on him by the throat and quickly smashed the creature into the ground. Raising his foot, he squashed the monster's skull under his heel.

His brutish eyes gleamed with malice. All feelings of pain, fear, or guilt had been vaporized. Yuri felt nothing. It was odd;

even though he was still conscious and had not fully succumbed to whatever bestial instinct called to him, he could still feel a separate presence telling him what to do. It was as if a malevolent entity had taken the reins of his mind when he had transformed.

Yuri reached down and snatched his sword off the ground as werewolves rushed towards him. He tore his weapon through the air, mangling and rending his enemies with a barrage of fierce attacks. Yuri's speed and strength were even better than before. He felt invincible. Covering himself in the blood of his opponents, Yuri was soon alone in the warehouse, surrounded by piles of corpses.

Beasts that were standing on the rooftops watched Yuri, noting his superiority, and were skeptical about descending into the warehouse to challenge the powerful beast. Yuri let out a ferocious roar in their direction and then turned away, dashing through the hole in the wall and back out into the streets of Horux. His violet irises suddenly turned back to their original turquoise color, though he remained in his werewolf form.

Yuri blinked as he regained control of his body. He glanced back at the warehouse, bewildered by what had just happened. He was certainly glad that he was alive and had somehow escaped that precarious situation, but he'd felt very … different when he had first transformed. Certainly not different enough to make him wonder if he was losing control like the rest of these barbaric werewolves. But it was enough to make him question his own actions and whether or not they were truly his own. *I'll think about that later. Right now, I need to find Archerus and we need to get the hell out of here.*

Yuri spotted Archerus, already climbing the side of Horux's outer wall, digging his claws into the stone as he ascended. Scrambling to keep up with him were dozens of other werewolves that were having trouble climbing such a height. Most of them had fallen, while a very few managed to keep up with Archerus, who was actually clambering up the wall at a fast pace despite his injured ankle.

Yuri glanced down at the blood splotches that matted his fur, his arms and legs covered in bite wounds from the werewolves. It was odd; he didn't feel the pain from the injuries as he expected he would. Instead, most of his body was just numb. *That's probably not a good thing.*

The werewolf dashed forward, taking off into Horux's streets on all fours. Even though his senses had been heightened when he was in his human form, being a beast was completely different. All of his natural faculties were enhanced to the point where he could hear a person as far away as the royal castle if he concentrated hard enough. In this case, he could *feel* a particular murderous aura that filled the air. It was difficult to explain, but there was a certain atmosphere that surrounded a rapidly approaching individual.

Yuri stole a glance over his shoulder, and his heart nearly stopped when he spotted Faelen springing from building to building, his malicious gaze searing into Yuri. He was the one with the malevolent aura. Swearing under his breath, Yuri increased his speed, sprinting as quickly as he could, clutching his silver sword in his teeth. *Damn, damn, damn! I'm almost there! Faelen, what bad timing!*

"Hurry up!" Archerus boomed from the top of the wall, battling several werewolves as he waited for Yuri to join him. He swiped a beast across the jaw, knowing that he wouldn't be able to hold this position for much longer. But he had no intention of leaving Yuri behind. "He's going to catch up to you!"

"I know that!" Yuri barked, a tingling sense tickling the back of his mind. He turned his head slightly and spotted Faelen descending upon him. He grunted, slamming his hind legs into the ground, cracking the floor beneath him. Pouncing like a frog, he leaped from the street onto the rooftop of a nearby building just before Faelen made impact.

Faelen smashed into the street, shattering the ground with his god-like strength, creating a crater beneath himself with the force of his fall. He growled in frustration, glaring at Yuri as the transformed beast sprinted off. "You won't get away from me!" Faelen roared, taking off after Yuri.

At the sight of their pack leader, the other werewolves were spurred into action, once again pursuing Yuri. The horde of dark beasts glided over the rooftops agilely, surging towards the fleeing lone werewolf.

Yuri saw that Faelen was swiping his right claw through the air in his direction. Even though Faelen was a reasonable distance away, Yuri felt a chilling shiver trembling through his body. But there was no way that Faelen would be able to strike Yuri from that range. Right?

Jump. A word forged itself in his mind, dominating the countless threads of panicky thoughts that jumbled through Yuri's head. The word echoed in his ears, almost sounding as if someone were ordering him to take action. Instinct took over, and he followed his mind's command and sprung as high as he could.

To his surprise, black energy surged off of Faelen's claws and smashed into the building beneath Yuri. The structure groaned loudly before toppling entirely, crumbling to pieces. Faelen slowed to a stop, staring in bewilderment at Yuri's action. The only way the boy could have avoided that magical attack was if he'd predicted the strike beforehand. Clenching his jaw with frustration, Faelen let out an irritated howl.

Yuri had reached the scaffold along Horux's outer wall and pounced on it, landing upon the wooden platforms with such force that the beams supporting the wooden structure cracked. Soon the entire scaffolding began to collapse, crushing pursuing werewolves that were climbing up after Yuri.

The warrior grunted and leapt off the final platform of the scaffolding just as it was about to give way. He lashed out with his claws as he slammed into the side the massive wall. Digging his sharp nails into the stone, Yuri gritted his teeth as he began to climb vertically, with some difficulty. His clambering was neither as elegant nor as efficient as Archerus's, but after several moments he had made it to the top. He stood still and panted, eager to catch his breath.

Archerus shoved another werewolf off the wall and nodded to Yuri, jumping off the walkway, down onto the dirt outside of Horux. "We need to keep moving; we aren't safe until we get to the forest!"

Yuri nodded and was about to jump after Archerus when suddenly something tackled him straight off the wall and sent him tumbling through the air. The world spun around him, and he gasped as he slammed heavily to the ground, a sharp pain biting through his arm. His eyes widened and he tried to cry out, but it only came out as a hoarse wheeze. His vision was becoming blurry, and he could feel himself losing consciousness. The corners of his perception were blacked out.

Visceral fear burned in his chest when he saw Faelen towering over him, the beast baring his blood-stained fangs as he glared down at the defenseless boy. Yuri grunted, attempting to move his body, but he was physically drained. His body didn't listen and he lay still, watching Faelen as the werewolf reached down, ready to tear his arm off.

"Damn it, Yuri!" Archerus's muffled voice cried out. The werewolf dashed into Yuri's line of vision and tackled Faelen, sending the two beasts sprawling in the dirt fighting for dominance. Hundreds of werewolves on city wall's walkway watched their master slam Archerus to the ground effortlessly.

"You should've run when you had the chance," Faelen snarled. He was raising one of his claws to slash open Archerus's throat when he glanced upward and grunted. A bright bolt of energy, which looked like a shooting star, sliced through the air and buried itself in Faelen's chest. The projectile detonated, sending the monster flying backwards and crashing into Horux's outer wall, sending clouds of dust sweeping out in all directions.

Yuri groaned as he was engulfed by a wave of dust. He closed his eyes, feeling his consciousness slipping away. And then a word screamed out in his mind. *Awaken.*

***

Yuri's eyes snapped open and he grunted in surprise, finding himself in the room of his family's apartment. The room was spotless, without even a single drop of blood on the wooden floorboards, despite the massacre that had ensued not a day before. However, the apartment was not empty. There was a small candle positioned in the center of the room, illuminating the darkness.

Yuri turned to look behind him at the window, to see what time of day it was. Outside the window was a black sheet of nothingness. It was as if the room existed in a void of darkness. He reached one hand out through the open window, and felt a current of freezing air that did not belong to Horux. His hand felt as if it had just been dipped in the coldest arctic waters of the north.

Withdrawing his hand in confusion, Yuri staggered back, his heart racing. Outside of this room it was terribly cold, but the temperature inside this isolated apartment was relatively average for a spring night. *What's going on here?*

Swallowing hard, he glanced around the room and saw a door on the other wall. Skipping over the flickering candle, he tried the door, only to find that it was locked. Wincing in frustration, the boy gave the wooden door a swift kick to see if it would budge. It didn't.

A gust of cold air suddenly swept through the room and blew out the candle, immediately blanketing the apartment in darkness. Yuri's back tensed as he felt the presence of something behind him. "Who's there?" he said, unable to see the gray mist slowly creeping from the end of the candlewick. This small wisp soon transformed into a gigantic cloud that swept about the room with eyes that glowed red as a devil's, watching Yuri as a starving beast would its prey.

As soon as Yuri turned around, the mysterious smoke retreated, seeping into the cracks in the wall. The boy gulped, knowing that he felt the presence of something. He looked at the floor and saw that a circle was smeared on the floor in some type of purple liquid, a small star in its center. "What's this?"

"*A portal,*" a voice spoke from all around Yuri, causing him to jump with surprise.

Yuri spun around, trying to pinpoint where the voice was coming from. "Why are you hiding from me? Show yourself!" he declared. He watched with disbelief as the smoke emerged from the walls, coming together to create a floating, demonic entity that towered over the young man. Yuri gaped at the being, pressing his back against a wall, as he met the monster's glowing gaze. "By the gods, what are you?"

"*I am Malyios,*" the being said. "*I was once a great Titan that dominated over the realm of Terrador. That scripture on the floor is a portal, one to Oblivion.*"

"Oblivion? I don't understand what that—"

"*You will understand soon, boy.*"

***

Yuri lurched forward suddenly, his eyes wide with terror. He slammed his forehead on the low wooden ceiling and fell back, clutching his throbbing head in pain. "Ow!" he groaned, rolling off his bed. "Eh?" he yelped as he hit the hard, stone floor.

"You seem lively this morning, hm?" an unfamiliar voice said. Yuri turned to find an unusually tall man in the next room, standing over a black cauldron. He was using a gigantic stick to stir the mysterious contents in the large pot. The stranger had long silver hair that streaked down to his lower back, and strangely large ears that pricked up. His eyes were white and lacked irises, which was even more disconcerting. But the part of this man that startled Yuri the most were the gigantic antlers protruding from the top of his skull.

"W-Where am I? Who are you? Is this another dream?" Yuri said, sitting up.

"Another dream? That, my friend, it is not," the man said, setting down his wooden stick as he sauntered into Yuri's room. He was dressed in a long blue robe with elegant designs of violet and green streaking throughout. On his shoulders were giant pauldrons that glowed a brilliant turquoise color every couple of seconds. The stranger reached up and stroked the wispy beard on his chin. "You are in my home. I am Moriaki, the Druid of the North. Archerus is an old friend of mine. I was on my way to pay Horux a visit when I stumbled across the two of you, unconscious and at the mercy of Faelen." He sighed, scratching the back of his neck. "I never would've imagined that werewolves would overrun the city. I haven't seen one in centuries. To think someone like Faelen is still alive after all this time."

"You know Faelen?"

"We met centuries ago. I doubt he remembers," Moriaki said, pointing to his ears. "I assume that you've never left Horux before; that would explain your expression when you first saw me. I am an elf, and thus I am immune to aging."

Yuri raised an eyebrow, impressed. "That must be nice."

"It is, to an extent," Moriaki said with a gentle smile. "Throughout my centuries of living on Terrador, I've come to meet many people, see plenty of places, and experience countless adventures. But you also are forced to watch as the world deteriorates around you. I was there at Horux's inception and it is sad to see the city crumble so soon. That was actually when I first met Faelen, back when he was a human."

"Faelen was human at one point?" Yuri said, stunned.

"Yes, as all werewolves are," Moriaki said. "He—"

"Yuri?" Archerus's voice called from another room. "Ugh, where are we?" Moriaki met Yuri's gaze and winked at the boy. "We'll finish this conversation later," he said, turning to walk to Archerus's room.

Yuri followed the elf, noticing that none of the rooms in Moriaki's cottage had any doors. Every room was open and connected. He peeked into Archerus's room and saw his friend was lying in a bed of white sheets that were stained with blood. Despite the tainted cloths, Archerus's wounds seemed to have already healed. "Moriaki, my old friend!" Archerus said with a broad grin as he embraced the druid. "It's been too long!"

"Really? It feels like I last saw you just yesterday," Moriaki said.

"That's probably because ten years feels like nothing to you, you ageless bastard," Archerus quipped, giving the elf a friendly slap on the back. "How long were we asleep?"

"About two days."

"What?" Yuri exclaimed, his jaw dropping open with surprise. "T-Two days?"

"You'd better get used to long naps," Moriaki said with a chuckle. "After sustaining damage, werewolves tend to sleep so that they can heal their wounds. While sleeping, you regenerate three times faster than when you're awake."

Yuri crinkled his brow. "Really?" He looked to Archerus. "So how did my wounds heal so quickly after only being asleep for a couple hours when I woke up in the royal jail with you?"

"Call that a special case," Archerus said. "You had just become a werewolf, so all of your cells were being altered. You were regenerating at probably ten times the ordinary rate. If you sustained that type of damage now, you'd probably still bleed out. You were in pretty bad shape when I pulled you from the water. It would take a miracle for you to survive with wounds like that now." The man looked to Moriaki. "We're lucky that you came to save us. Faelen would've slaughtered us both."

"He's strong. I'm surprised that the three of us managed to get away in one piece, especially with the myriad of mindless werewolves that now follow him," Moriaki said with a groan. He shook his head at the situation. "I'm sure that the two of you are hungry, yes? I've made some stew that should nourish you. We shall talk about the next plan of action over lunch."

The stew that Moriaki made was absolutely delicious. Then again, if Moriaki's culinary skills were lacking after living for several centuries, then Yuri would've been surprised.

The boy sat on the floor of the kitchen, holding a stone bowl filled with brown soup. There were vegetables poking out of the broth while bits of red seasoning floated on its surface. The stew was extremely hot and it radiated its heat throughout the bowl, stinging Yuri's hands slightly. But his growling stomach cared not for the burning sensation in his fingers. He found himself gulping down the stew and asking for seconds.

Archerus had explained Horux's dire situation to Moriaki, who seemed unsurprised by the events, as if he'd dealt with similar issues before.

"As the Druid of the North, it is my duty to help maintain balance in the continent of Escalon," Moriaki said, using a ladle to pour some more soup into Yuri's bowl. "Surely you understand the gravity of this situation, Archerus. The werewolf virus has been released. If it manages to travel to the mainland, the human race on Escalon will be endangered. The disease must be contained within Horux's peninsula."

Archerus nodded in agreement, taking a sip from his hot bowl. Scrunching up his face at his burned tongue, he gently blew on the soup. "But the three of us cannot contain it alone. We'll need help."

"I believe that calling upon the Iradian Empire would be our best choice of action," Moriaki suggested.

Yuri licked his lower lip. He'd heard that Escalon was home to multiple races, including the undead and vampires. Iradia was the human empire in Escalon. Within it was every human-based settlement on the continent, with plenty of resources and a powerful army. Receiving assistance from such a dominant force would surely be beneficial.

"The only issue is that the Iradians are all human," Archerus grumbled. "If one of the werewolves manages to bite one of their soldiers, then the virus could take hold. Yuri and I have seen how quickly the disease spreads. Within hours, most of Horux had been infected. Aren't the elves immune to the infection? Wouldn't it be—"

"The elves have refused to set foot on the unholy lands of Escalon. The continent is one of the most dangerous places in the world. They are not interested in creating a settlement here. They live on another continent to the east," Moriaki said with a light shrug. "Iradia is the only possible ally that we could reach out to. Unless you'd rather go off and ask the vampires and undead if they want to help."

Archerus set his emptied bowl on the floor and raised his hands into the air, defeated. "Point taken. Fine, we'll reach out to Iradia for their assistance. I'll be counting on you to get the king's approval then. I expect that he already favors you," he said.

Moriaki scoffed. "Favors me? Hardly. The Iradians dislike anything non-human," he said, looking at both Archerus and Yuri. "You two might want to work on controlling your physical forms. There would be complications if you … transform. It would be easier if you two maintained the façade of being human."

"We'll work on it on our journey to Iradia," Archerus said, refilling his bowl with Moriaki's delicious stew. "My concern is how we'll keep the werewolves at bay in the meantime."

"I may have an idea," Moriaki said, standing up and walking out of the kitchen. "Come outside when you two are ready to depart," he called over his shoulder, strolling out of the cottage.

Yuri and Archerus exchanged confused glances before quickly finishing their servings of stew. The two men then walked outside after the druid. As soon as Yuri stepped outside of Moriaki's cottage, his eyes twinkled, fascinated with the towering trees that surrounded him. The cottage was located in the middle of a gigantic forest. The mountainous trees around him had trunks that stretched so high that they made Yuri feel tiny. A sea of green leaves covered most of the sky. Somehow the sunlight managed to trickle through cracks in the layer of leaves, shining ribbons of light onto the forest floor.

Yuri whistled and walked over to one of the trees. He rapped his knuckles against its tough trunk in awe. "These trees make Moriaki's cottage look like a mere pebble in comparison. I've never seen anything so tall before. They're double the size of Horux's outer wall! Are you sure that we're only a day's journey from Horux?" he said to Archerus.

Archerus folded his arms and smirked. "The whole world isn't like Horux, Yuri. If anything, I would say forests like these are more common than the ominous one outside of our city. Wouldn't you say so, Moriaki?"

Moriaki was trudging from the woods, shrugging at Archerus's comment. "What was that? I didn't catch what you said."

"It doesn't matter. Where'd you go off to?"

"I was setting up some magical wards around the area," Moriaki said, squinting slightly as he turned to look back the way he had come. "Faelen and his werewolves will have to pass through this forest in order to leave the peninsula. Hopefully these nature wards will create enough barriers to stall their advance." He nodded to Archerus. "It will take a couple days to get to Reidan, even with your werewolf speed. Are you ready to depart?"

"Yeah," Archerus said, his body shifting into his werewolf form. He glanced at Yuri. "Can you transform?"

Yuri tried to remember what had triggered his transformation in the warehouse in Horux. It was all just a haze, a misty memory that he hardly remembered. All that he could recall was the savage rage that had pulsed throughout his body. He sighed and shook his head, disappointed that he still didn't have control over his ability to transform.

Archerus knew that he had been lucky to find his own trigger so quickly, and understood that it would take Yuri time to master his. The man glanced at Moriaki. "You should go on ahead and inform the king of the situation. Our journey will be prolonged if Yuri is not in his werewolf form and I am forced to carry him. You'll save a lot of time if you go ahead."

Moriaki set his hand gently on Archerus's shoulder, nodding to his friend. He shot Yuri a warm smile and morphed into a raven, winnowing into the air with several flaps of his wings. "I will see you two at the city then. May the gods keep you safe," the druid called out, soaring up towards the sea of leaves above.

Yuri gaped in awe at the elf's swift transformation. "Wow, was that magic?"

"If you want to call his connection to nature 'magic,' sure. He's a powerful druid, able to shift to the form of any animal that he has once eaten. That isn't even including the countless other abilities that old fool has," Archerus said, getting down on all fours. He nodded to his back, indicating to Yuri that he was waiting for the boy to mount him. "We'd better get out of here. I want to put as much distance between us and Faelen's legion of werewolves as possible."

***

The refugees from Horux had landed in Teolan, a port city of Iradia in southern Escalon. Princess Violet watched as waves of survivors poured out of their boats and onto the docks of Teolan. A line of Iradian soldiers, armed with rifles and swords, were standing at the end of the docks, preventing any people from entering the city.

Violet followed her parents off their ship, stepping onto the wooden docks in her torn dress. She swallowed hard, shaking her head at the situation. *Yuri was right after all. Beo was hiding a werewolf underneath Horux. But how was the beast released? Look at what's happened to our city.* Her gaze drifted over the crowds of hungry and exhausted refugees. *We can't recover from this.*

"Milady," Senna said, sliding his way through a line of people. He halted before the princess and bowed respectfully. The knight turned his head, looking at the line of Iradian soldiers positioned at the end of the docks. "As expected, they won't allow us into their city without proper explanation for why we have brought dozens of unauthorized ships into their harbor." He raised an eyebrow and pointed to a man in long robes that emerged from the row of warriors. "Look."

Violet's gaze followed the direction of Senna's finger, seeing a bald man wearing a long robe that draped down to his wooden sandals. The stranger's attire was white, with a single stream of gold running from his collar to the base of his dress. At first, Violet thought that this man was a priest of some sort. But as soon as she saw the necklace of black beads dangling from the figure's neck, she knew that he was an elder of this city.

While elders were not necessarily associated with politics, they still had a major impact on the decisions made within a settlement. "He must be here to speak to my father," Violet said, watching as the crowd of civilians separated to create a pathway for the royal family. The king and queen walked through the passage with their heads held high, despite their lost city. "We should head up there too."

Violet, accompanied by Senna and several other knights, walked through the open pathway. The civilians had quieted, their eyes on the royal family as they strode past. Suddenly, a young man shoved his way through the crowd and stepped before the princess, causing her to halt in surprise. She blinked, recognizing the person as the thief she'd seen in Horux's marketplace several days ago.

The knights all drew their weapons in unison, pointing them at the panting man. But the stranger did not flinch, nor did his resolute gaze waver. He stared at Violet, his hands balled into clenched fists at his side. "Where's Yuri?" he demanded, his eyebrows knit together into a scowl. "He was at dinner with you when the attack happened, right? Why isn't he with you?"

"Learn your place," Senna snarled, about to take a step forward. He raised his eyebrows with surprise when Violet held up her hand, halting the warrior. All it took was a swift nod of the knight's head to cause the rest of the soldiers to lower their weapons.

"I don't know about Yuri's whereabouts," Violet said. "He left our dinner early to see if there truly was a werewolf underneath the city. It would seem that he was correct." The crowd gasped in unison and Senna glanced away, scrunching up his nose as if he smelled a disgusting odor.

"He must've released the werewolf then!" one civilian cried out.

"Yeah, he was the only person who knew where the werewolf was!" another person exclaimed.

The survivors exchanged glances as they all began to speak up, voicing their opinions. But Violet simply shook her head and the people all hushed into silence once more. "No, several people knew about the werewolf's existence," she said to the townsfolk. "As for Yuri—"

"He's dead," Senna said quietly.

Violet turned and looked at the warrior with surprise. "What?"

The young man in front of Violet was now shaking, his eyes wide with rage. "How did he die?"

"I shot him." Senna's face was expressionless, but his words struck like daggers.

A look of shock registered on the man's face. The crowd quieted as they watched the trembling stranger. The thief suddenly sprinted forward, about to throw a punch right at Senna. He grunted when several knights stepped forth and subdued him, slamming him hard to the wooden docks. "You killed him?" he barked through his clenched teeth. The man glared at Senna from the floor as one of the knights pinned his arms behind his back. "Why the hell would you do that?"

"Yuri had been infected and was beginning to transform. I did him a favor by putting him out of his misery while he was still human," Senna said apathetically, looking down at the man as if he were nothing but a bug. "Take this fool away," he ordered the soldiers.

"I have a name," the man growled as he was hauled to his feet and carried away. "Terias! You'd best remember it."

Senna watched as the man was dragged through the crowds of spectators and towards the brig of one of the ships. He looked at Violet and saw the sorrowful look on her face. "Milady, killing him is not what I wanted. He was dangerous and poised a direct threat to—" He bit his lower lip when he remembered the moment he had pulled the trigger. Yuri had been on his knees, pleading for mercy. *A direct threat, huh?*

Violet shook her head and continued down the walkway. She had not known Yuri for long, but her heart still felt as if it had been penetrated by the sharpest of blades. Wiping tears from her eyes, she made her way to the end of the docks, where she found her father and mother talking to the elder.

"Werewolves? Why, I was under the impression that such beasts were extinct," the elder said, rubbing the top of his head. He pursed his lips and narrowed his eyes. "If your city has truly been overrun by such beasts, the infection is likely to spread if it is not contained within the Horuxian peninsula. Come, we must get you to the capital at once. We must inform the king of this precarious situation." The elder turned around and the Iradian soldiers immediately stepped to the side to open a path for the royal family. "I am not sure what we will do with so many refugees. It is not possible for us to feed and shelter your people for longer than a week. We will do our best to help, but they'll have to be put to work if they want to live here."

"I'm sure my people will have no problem with that," the king said, following the elder.

"As long as they work, I'm sure that Teolan will be able to take your people in for the time being, until we can figure out future accommodations. We'll just have to see what the king says when you arrive at Reidan," the elder said, glancing over his shoulder and spotting Violet. "Is that your daughter, Lord Emon?"

The king of Horux smiled and nodded. "Indeed, she is."

"How youthful," the elder said, meeting Violet's gaze. "Horux's queen and princess have the eyes of angels. I've never seen irises of that color before. Are there any other members of your family with eyes like that?"

"My brother," Violet said. "He used to have violet eyes as well, but he passed away a long time ago."

"I'm sorry to hear that," the elder said, dipping his head.

As the royal family was escorted deeper into the streets of Teolan, Violet found herself fascinated with the wooden structures around her. The buildings were much larger than the ones in Horux, with colorful, tiled rooftops that gleamed in the sunny afternoon. There were hundreds of civilians in the streets, wearing cloth garments of a variety of colors. All of them stood by and watched as Violet's party strolled through the streets.

Violet couldn't push Yuri's demise from her mind. She bit her lower lip, remembering how the boy had promised that he would return to the castle. Yuri had seemed genuinely worried about the wellbeing of Horux's civilians. Violet didn't believe that he was the one that released the werewolf.

The princess tapped Senna on the shoulder and the knight immediately turned to her. "Can you do me a favor before we leave for Reidan?"

"Anything, milady."

"Release that young man that was just arrested, Terias," Violet said. "He was just worried about his friend. He doesn't deserve to be condemned to the brig."

Senna nodded and struck his fist to his chest, saluting his princess. "I'll retrieve him now."

***

The salty smell of brine filled the dark cell where Terias was confined. The brig was completely empty. Any prisoners that had filled these cells during the invasion of Horux had been thrown overboard to make room for civilian refugees. The young man sat in silence, his head lowered, as he recalled his last encounter with Yuri in the alleyway, where he'd ambushed Yuri countless times in the past.

Guilt seized him, and Terias bit his quivering lip. The boy stared blankly at a tiny spot of light that gleamed on the wooden floor of the brig, shining from an open window in his cell. Terias exhaled through his nose, and glanced up suddenly when he heard a heavy bang echo through the brig.

Clanking towards him from the shadows was Senna in his metallic armor. The knight halted in front of Terias's cell, dangling a pair of bronze keys before the man. He tossed the keys through the metal bars. They landed right in front of Terias. "You can go," Senna said, expecting the young man to quickly free himself. But he didn't. Instead, he simply sat on the floor, staring at the knight. "What are you waiting for?"

"What did you see in his eyes just before you shot him?" Terias asked. "Was he thankful that you killed him before he transformed?"

There was silence as Senna watched Terias. He averted his gaze and turned around, about to exit the brig. "Tell me the truth," Terias demanded, his words freezing the knight.

"It was sorrow." Senna exhaled heavily, his back to the young man. "He was distraught that he'd been left behind. There was a hint of disbelief; he was in shock that he'd been infected and that he was losing sight of himself. Of course he wasn't thankful that I murdered him. Everyone fears death, but I thought that putting an end to him was certainly better than letting him become an uncontrollable abomination. In my eyes, Yuri died the moment that virus entered his bloodstream." The warrior glanced at Terias over his shoulder. "What would you have done? Let him live on as ... a mindless creature? I'm sure that's not what your free-spirited friend would've wanted."

Terias gritted his teeth and reached up, rubbing his palms against his moist eyes. "The rest of my family is gone. All of my friends in the Lower District have perished. Out of all the people in Horux ... I expected that Yuri would've been the most likely to survive an invasion like this," he said quietly, tears trickling down his cheeks. "He's strong ... stronger than anyone I've ever met. Every time I've ever seen him get knocked down, he always recovered and grew stronger than before."

Senna said nothing.

"I just wish that I had the chance to apologize to him for all the wrong that I've done to him in the past ... and to thank him for the good that he's done for me recently," Terias said, dropping his arms to his side. "Damn it! I'm tired of depending on others to fight my battles for me. Why am I so weak?"

"Come with me, then," Senna said. "I'll soon be departing for Reidan, the capital of Iradia, to accompany the royal family in their negotiations with the Iradian king. If you don't want to depend on others, then start depending on yourself. I'll help you obtain the strength that you desire by training you to become one of my knights. You have potential. Will you use it?" He turned to fully face Terias, who was looking up at the warrior in surprise. "You have a choice. You can either stay here in Teolan and work to survive or you can join me on my journey to Reidan, where I will train you to become a true soldier. What is your decision?"

Terias glanced at the keys on the floor and reached down, feeling the cold metal in his hands. He swallowed hard, remembering the countless times where others had fought his battles. His parents had always taken the burden of feeding the family, while he was off screwing around in streets of the Lower District. His friends would assault whoever he ordered them to and, like a tyrant, he would simply sit there and watch others suffer. And then, finally, Yuri had been there for him when he needed help the most. Continuing as he was would bring no rewards, he knew that. Perhaps training under Senna was the best path for him.

"Why are you offering me such an opportunity?" Terias asked, squeezing the keys tightly in his hand.

"Most of my knights were killed during the massacre. Many soldiers lost their lives several nights ago. Right now, our forces are low in numbers. In order to survive in Escalon, we'll need a lot more manpower than what we currently have," Senna said, folding his arms over his chest. He hesitated for a moment. "To tell the truth, I also see a little bit of my past self in you. Weak and spineless, with nothing to cling to except a fading hope that things will get better. I was given the rare opportunity to rise from the slums of Horux and become a powerful knight. Now I will pass that chance on to you. So, what will you do?"

Terias pressed his hand to his knee, slowly rising to his feet. Hope ... that was something that he had lost sight of when his parents had passed. Now it had returned, in the form of a knight in gleaming armor. There the symbol of Terias's newfound hope stood, on the other side of the cell's iron bars. This was his door out of poverty, out of desperation, out of powerlessness. He met Senna's gaze with a look of resolution. "I'll come with you."

The Accord

"**M**oriaki!" Faelen roared, storming into Beo's cell with rage coursing through him. He lashed out and rocketed his fist into the wall behind the noble, striking the stone several inches from the man's face. The wall cracked under Faelen's tremendous force, but Beo hardly even flinched. "That bastard druid will pay for meddling in my affairs. Archerus and Yuri should be in pieces, damn it! I should've killed them when I had the chance."

Beo stifled a chuckle, his lips curving into a smile.

Faelen glared at him with murderous eyes. "Is something amusing?"

"You need not worry, Faelen. You'll see Yuri again. There is no doubt in my mind that he will return for your head." The noble spoke with a bold smirk.

Faelen raised his eyebrows. "My head? You think that he'll return to try and kill me? Are you a moron? I could tear that youngling limb from limb if I wanted. If that insolent fool has the audacity to return to my city, then I'll rip off his head and eviscerate his damned corpse! DO YOU HEAR ME?" he boomed, his snout inches away from Beo's ear.

The noble closed his eyes, trying to hide his fear behind his dauntless façade. But Faelen could see that the man was trembling. "I have returned to ask you the same question that I've asked at the beginning of each day. Now, you will either give me a proper answer or you will feel my wrath. I have no more patience," Faelen snarled, grabbing Beo's thigh and stabbing his claws deep into the noble's flesh. He listened to the man's agonizing cries that echoed through the cell. "*Where is the portal to Oblivion?*"

"Piss ... off!" Beo snarled through clenched teeth, tears of pain gleaming in his eyes.

Faelen's eyes flashed with fury, and he jammed his nails into Beo's chest, sinking his claws into the man's heart. Shock registered on the noble's pale face as he stared at the werewolf. Blood dribbled down his chin. Beo slumped forward when Faelen pulled his claw from the corpse. "You kept me imprisoned for decades, and you think that you can afford to defy me? Pitiful," he growled, storming away from Beo's unmoving body. He grabbed the iron bars of the cell and pried them apart, not even bothering to use the door.

"Where are you going?" Junko asked, emerging from the shadows behind Beo. He glanced at Beo's cell, spotting the noble's corpse, hanging from the ceiling. Raising his eyebrow, he turned his attention back to the irate werewolf. "I'm not sure how you plan to find the portal to Oblivion since you've murdered the one man in Escalon who knew of its location."

"I'll find it. It's miracle that I didn't tear his head off his shoulders days ago, after what he's done to me," Faelen grumbled, turning to look at Junko. His gaze then went to the shadows, where he saw another mysterious figure. "Who is your companion?"

"This is Tanya," Junko said. Emerging from the shadows was a young woman with straight, dark, shoulder-length hair. She was wearing a black cloak that was similar to Junko's, except it was sleeveless, revealing her toned muscles. The woman certainly did not seem native to Escalon. Her skin was far too tan for her to be from this continent, where people commonly had paler skin tones. The Bount met Faelen's gaze with her dark eyes and smiled slightly, as if she found something humorous. "She is from the continent of Dastia. I'm sure that you've heard of it."

"Yes," Faelen muttered. "I've heard of the oceans of sand that stretch across its desolate land. I've never seen a desert for myself, but it certainly sounds impressive. Why have you brought her?"

"As the leader of your pack of werewolves, you will have to stick with the beasts in order to maintain their allegiance. If you are not with them, they will have no one to follow, and will wander about like the mindless creatures that they are. That means that it will be difficult for you to search for the portal to Oblivion, since it is somewhere in Lichholme, in northern Escalon. With a pack of werewolves this large, you can focus on dominating the continent," Junko said, nodding to Tanya. "Tanya can take a small group of werewolves to northern Escalon. They will be able to search for your portal. It may take longer, since you impatiently murdered the one man who knew its exact location, but she will certainly find it."

"I don't need help," Faelen insisted.

"I don't care that you think you don't need help," Junko snapped, causing Faelen to raise his eyebrows with surprise. The Bount took a step towards the werewolf, bringing his face so close to the beast's that Faelen could've easily bitten the man's head clean off. Junko's voice dropped to a whisper. "Understand that my decisions are final. Without me, you'd still be trapped underground behind silver bars." He reached into his cloak and pulled out a Phoenix Heart, which blazed in his hand. "Your next order is to infect Tanya."

"What?" Faelen blurted out.

"You heard me. Bite her and turn her into a werewolf," Junko said, walking back to Tanya. He handed her the flower and smiled. "Once the virus has entered Tanya's bloodstream, eating the Phoenix Heart will allow her to tame the beast that she'll become." He reached up and stroked the woman's cheek gently, gazing into her dark eyes. "She will allow you to focus on your task at hand — the total eradication of Escalon's humans."

"You expect me to entrust the quest of finding the Oblivion portal to her?" Faelen snarled, edging towards the Bounts. "The journey alone is treacherous. Surviving in Lichholme is difficult for anyone who lacks experience, even if she becomes a werewolf."

"The Bount organization is known for recruiting some of the strongest beings in the world," Junko said, his hands dropping to his side. He darted a glare at Faelen over his shoulder, freezing the werewolf in his tracks. A sly smile crept over his lips, and he let out a gentle chuckle as he stepped to the side, beginning to walk back into the shadows. "Your quest for omnipotence can wait, Faelen. For now, you must focus on fulfilling your end of our bargain. Be grateful that I've found someone to search for the Oblivion portal in your stead. Would you rather not have Tanya here? If that's the case, your hunt for the Oblivion portal will have to wait until Escalon is conquered."

Faelen gnarred through his clenched fangs. "Fine, I'll take her."

Junko smirked as he faded into the darkness. "I'm glad that you can be accommodating. Best of luck to you two."

Faelen watched as the cloaked man vanished, using his magic to teleport away. Silence swept over the two Bounts as they gawked awkwardly at each other, unsure of what to do next. The werewolf stomped over to Tanya, towering over the young woman. "Are you not afraid?"

Tanya simply looked up at him and gave the monster a broad smile, like a child on her birthday. "In order to gain power, one must make sacrifices. To become stronger, I'll gladly cast away my humanity," she said, tilting her head to the side, exposing the smooth skin on her neck. She averted her gaze from the werewolf and bit her lower lip. "Just be gentle. I'm not a fan of pain."

Faelen snorted with amusement and leaned down, baring his sharp fangs. He hovered his mouth over Tanya's neck to see if she would flinch, but to his surprise, she stayed intrepid before him. *To think people exist in this world that would gladly become a monster.*

The beast sank his teeth into the flesh of Tanya's neck, feeling her warm blood trickle onto his tongue. He could feel his natural instinct tickling the back of his mind, ordering him to bite deeper and devour her flesh. But he knew better, and his control was unmatched.

Faelen pulled his head back, licking his lips slightly, watching as Tanya collapsed to her knees. He stuck out his large index finger and pointed to the Phoenix Heart in her hand. "*Eat it.*"

Tanya had one hand clutching the bleeding wound in the side of her neck. She was leaning forward, panting as if she were out of breath. Heat coursed through her veins, making it feel as if there were a burning sun within her chest. Energy surged through her, causing her to shudder uncontrollably. Her widened eyes turned bright red, and she began to giggle to herself. "I've … never felt power like this before." She leaned down and consumed the flaming flower, munching it. Swallowing hard, the humanity returned to her eyes and her lips quivered slightly.

Faelen raised an eyebrow at her and then turned away, beginning to walk down the corridor to leave the dungeon. "Perhaps right now you feel powerful, as if you can control the newfound power that comes with becoming a werewolf. That's because you just ate the Phoenix Heart. But trust me, within a couple of days your enhanced senses will torment you to no end, unless you learn to adapt. I will teach you." He glanced over his shoulder at the Bount. "Are you coming?"

Tanya blinked and then scrambled to her feet, jogging after the werewolf. "Y-Yes sir!"

***

"How is it possible that you haven't found your trigger? You already transformed once before!" Archerus snapped impatiently while they were sitting on the bank of a river. "The way that you felt when you morphed into a werewolf should be engraved into your mind by now. I'm tired of lugging you around!"

Yuri groaned and fell back, sprawling out on the moist dirt. "I just don't really remember transforming that well! It's like I became someone else for a second. I wasn't myself," he murmured. "I don't even remember shifting back into my human form. That must've happened while I was asleep. So even if I managed to turn into a werewolf, it would be a new matter entirely to change back."

Archerus was in his werewolf form, wading into the shallow waters. He shrugged, feeling the cool water rushing against his hairy legs. The beast's eyes scanned the clear river, his legs spreading out as he prepared to catch them some dinner. It had been a long day of travel. The two adventurers were extremely hungry and were in need of rest. "Yuri, you can always be productive. If you're tired of trying to transform, then work on controlling your senses. As werewolves, it is essential that we learn how to tune out the world around us and focus all our senses on one task," he said, stabbing his claw through the water and snatching a fish. He tossed the catch to Yuri, where it landed in his hands and flopped about. "Go on, give it a try."

Yuri raised an eyebrow as he stood up, the convulsing fish rolling off his lap and onto the dirt. He sauntered towards the river and reached down, rolling up his torn pants. Moving into the water, he winced at the chilling sensation that nipped at his skin. But within moments, he had adjusted to the river's cold temperature and waded out until the water reached his waist. He glanced over his shoulder, watching as Archerus walked back onto shore with one massive fish in each hand. The werewolf went off to go fetch firewood.

Yuri narrowed his eyes, irritated. *By the time he gets back I'll have a whole pile of fish caught, he'll see! I could catch fish with my hands easily when I was human. Now that I'm a werewolf I can ... huh?* As he glanced down, he noticed that his vision was all over the place.

He could see every fish that rushed through the river. His eyes caught any movement within his line of sight, from the gentle sway of pondweed and the drifting of crabs across the sandy bottom of the river to even the tiniest of ripples on the water's surface.

Seeing all of this was not anything new to Yuri; he'd seen a river before. But he found that it was extremely difficult for him to focus on one fish to target. He could see the tributary before him in more detail than ever before, but was unable to narrow his vision to focus on one particular thing.

Biting his lower lip in frustration, he jabbed at the water at the area where he predicted the fish was going to go. The animal darted inches to the right of his hand. His prey was certainly not faster than him; Yuri had simply missed. Blinking several times, he tried to clear his vision so that he could focus on one fish. But the vast detail of the river was still tampering with his mind. He attacked the water ferociously, his hands stabbing at the water, but to no avail. He'd completely missed the fish.

After several tries, Yuri brushed back his hair and frowned. "How is it that I had the coordination to kill dozens of werewolves earlier and now I can't even catch a damned fish?" he grumbled to himself, irritated.

"All werewolves react differently when they ingest the Phoenix Heart," Archerus called, already returning with his fish under one arm and wood kindling in the other. "You and I were lucky. When we ate the flower, we maintained our coordination as if we were still human, even though our attributes had been enhanced tenfold. We could still perform physical tasks normally. But that effect wears off quickly. It was gone when we woke up in Moriaki's cottage. Every werewolf eventually faces the reality of adjusting to master their new abilities."

"So you're saying that because my vision has been strengthened … I have to *train* to be able to focus my vision on individual objects?" Yuri said with narrowed eyes. He kicked at the water in annoyance. "Then how the hell did you manage to adjust your eyes to your new werewolf vision, huh? I didn't see you do any training."

"I've been lugging you around all day," Archerus said, setting the wood on some dry dirt so that he could begin making a fire. "My training was when I was running through the forest. After traveling for a full day, I've gotten used to my new vision."

"Oh, so that's why you were running into bushes at the beginning of our journey," Yuri said, stifling a laugh. "You nearly rammed straight into a tree!"

"Hilarious." Archerus rolled his eyes. "The reason you haven't synchronized your coordination yet is because you've spent the entire day clinging to my damned back instead of moving on your own. We're done traveling for the day, so you might as well spend some time getting used to your new werewolf senses. The effects of the Phoenix Heart aren't here to help you stay coordinated anymore, so unless you want to continue looking like a fool, I'd get started."

Yuri rubbed his hands together and licked his lower lip. "All right, let's do this."

"As an incentive for you to succeed in catching a fish, you'll need to catch your own dinner tonight," Archerus said with a gentle smile, striking two stones together with tremendous force. Sparks ignited between the rocks and fell onto the kindling, the wood smoldering as it began to glow orange. Soon the sparks became tiny flames that flickered on Archerus's pile of wood. "These two are mine."

"Huh, catching this fish will be easy!" Yuri said, tackling the water as he attempted to grab a fish. Once again, he missed by a slight margin. Rising from the river, drenched, he groaned. "I expect that it'll take a couple tries, though."

After several hours, Yuri had only managed to catch one lousy fish. Darkness settled in the sky and the glistening moon shined down on Yuri and Archerus's camp. The two men were sitting around a reasonably sized fire, using it to cook their fish, which were skewered on sticks.

Yuri devoured his fish in a single gulp and sighed, leaning back. He was exasperated from trying to catch prey all afternoon. He had stopped because he was becoming far too frustrated to continue with such tedious training. He grabbed his stomach, which moaned in complaint. *Damn, I wish I'd gotten a bigger catch.*

Archerus chuckled and tossed him half of his second cooked fish. The food landed on Yuri's stomach and the boy looked at his friend, raising an eyebrow. "Go on and eat it. I'm not going to let you go hungry just because you haven't gotten used to your vision," he said.

There was silence between the two men as Yuri munched on his food.

"It's bothering you too, huh?" Archerus said.

"Yeah, I never knew the world was this loud," Yuri grumbled, swallowing the last piece of his meal. He lay back in the dirt, folding his arms behind his head to cushion him. Gazing at the sea of stars that glistened in the night sky, he let out a long sigh. To any ordinary person, it would've seemed like a tranquil night underneath the stars. However, to Yuri and Archerus, the night was noisy. Nature's sounds were constantly harassing the two werewolves.

They could hear everything from the howling of the slightest of breezes to the droning noises of insects in the night. The sounds were not exactly loud, but they all bombarded the eardrums of the both of the werewolves in unison, creating a dissonance of agonizing noise that made relaxation impossible. The world hadn't been this loud when Yuri had first left Moriaki's cottage. He imagined that the effects of consuming the Phoenix Heart had worn off for him sometime while he and Archerus were traveling.

It wasn't just his hearing; his sense of smell was even stronger than it had been when he first became a werewolf. He could catch the scent of anything within a mile's radius of his position. Twitching his nose, Yuri tried to block out everything, all of the smells, all of the sounds. Right now he just wanted to rest. It was certainly not easy, but as he closed his eyes and relaxed, he felt his senses toning down, as if they had been switched off.

"Do you think we'll ever be able to return to Horux?" Yuri asked quietly.

"Who knows?" Archerus said, finishing his meal with a final gulp. He turned his head, gazing across the stretching plains of grass around them. "The city is infested with monstrosities that are each capable of massacring a small village. We shouldn't be bothered too much with the idea of retaking our city. Rather, we should focus on preventing the virus from spreading to the rest of Escalon. Otherwise, it will just be a repeat of Lichholme."

"Lichholme? What's that?"

"That's what many inhabitants of Escalon call the northern section of the continent," Archerus said. "At one point in time, it was home to multiple thriving empires. But then a powerful necromancer spread a plague that annihilated every human in the area. That was what gave rise to the undead. Constructed abominations, skeletal creatures, and zombified monstrosities swept across the land, slaughtering and conquering all living things in the name of the necromancer. Eventually, the human race was eradicated completely from Lichholme. Their corpses became the undead warriors that now roam the land, but it is said that they are bound to Lichholme. Otherwise, they would've conquered the rest of Escalon by now."

Yuri whistled. "That sounds like the worst-case scenario for our situation."

"It does, yes. But it certainly is within the realm of possibility if we do not contain that virus," Archerus said, leaning back onto the grass. "We need to get to Reidan as soon as possible, so get some rest. We've got a lot of ground to cover tomorrow. "

***

Yuri found himself standing at the edge of a frozen cliff, overlooking a blackened abyss. The skies were filled with dark clouds that blanketed the land in an ominous shadow, but they were rushing overhead with incredible speed, as if time were passing at an accelerated rate. The boy was wearing boots that crunched the icy ground beneath him. He gazed across the ridge and found that there was a figure on the other side, staring at him.

The figure was completely black, as if it was a mere shadow, and had no definite form. While it was shaped somewhat like a man, there were black wisps of darkness that drifted off its body. Horns protruded from the top of its head, and its eyes … they glowed like two flaming coals dipped in lava, burning Yuri with their fiery gaze.

Yuri could feel a knot in his stomach, his fear seizing control of his mind. He retreated several steps, feeling the stranger's unrelenting gaze tearing him apart. Turning around, the boy was about to flee, and he found himself face to face with the ominous being. His heart jumped, and he gasped in surprise when he suddenly felt a hand pressing against his chest. Looking down, he saw that the stranger had pushed him.

Losing his balance, Yuri's eyes widened as he fell from the edge of the cliff and into the dark abyss below. He screamed in terror, watching as the cloudy skies got farther and farther away. The icy walls of the ridge became darker, until they were nothing but blackness. The sky eventually faded into nothingness. Within moments, Yuri had descended into the void, surrounded by sheets of black.

Yuri suddenly felt something grab his back, and he sank downward into something hard. He glanced over his shoulder and, to his horror, saw that he had fallen into a pit of hideous undead monstrosities. They had no eyes, only blackened sockets.

Bloody boils had sprouted over their decaying flesh, and their rotted teeth chattered, chilling the terrified boy to the bone. Resounding screeches, sounding like banshee cries, left their mouths as they grabbed at Yuri, proceeding to rip the boy limb from limb.

Powerlessness. Remember that feeling.

Yuri blinked, finding himself transported to a valley of lush grass surrounded by snow-covered mountains. His heart was still racing and sweat rolled down his face as he stared at the clear skies. He had heard a voice, the same voice that belonged to that mysterious being that had spoken to him in a previous dream. Was this all still a nightmare?

The boy leaned forward and exhaled shakily when he saw that the black figure from the ridge was standing several meters in front of him. The mysterious being watched him for several moments before turning his head and pointing to something. Yuri reluctantly followed the stranger's gaze and spotted an entire field of Phoenix Hearts, blazing brilliantly.

Yuri pushed himself to his feet, staring at the field. *That's enough Phoenix Hearts to cure the werewolves of Horux!* He glanced at the ebony stranger, who was now staring at him once more. "Are you Malyios?" he asked, recalling the name of the mist of darkness from his previous dream.

"*Indeed.*" The voice was the same.

"Where is this?"

"*You are in Lichholme.*"

"But how did you bring me here?" Yuri asked, looking around him. "All of this feels so real, as if it isn't a dream. But it has to be … I remember that Archerus and I are still in southern Escalon."

"*Well, young Yuri, this is not an ordinary dream,*" the being said. "*I've come before you to offer you a deal, one that might interest you. I've been watching you. You do not understand yet the full extent of your power. But I know what you are capable of. Your boundless strength allowed you* to overcome that horde of werewolves in the warehouse in Horux's Lower District. Do you remember?"

Yuri remembered vaguely that he had somehow lost control of himself and slaughtered every werewolf within that vicinity. He narrowed his eyes, watching the being. At the time, it had felt as if … someone else had taken control of him. "Was that you?" he demanded. "Did you take control over me at that time?"

"I did, in order to show you what you are capable of." Malyios pointed to the field of Phoenix Hearts. "Finding that field would be a miracle for you, wouldn't it? You could save your people and reclaim Horux without having to massacre the transformed citizens of the city. There could be a solution with minimal bloodshed. I could tell you where this supply of Phoenix Hearts is — and how you can control your werewolf powers."

"I don't need your help to control my powers," Yuri mumbled, though deep within his mind he doubted whether he would ever discover the triggers to his transformations.

"Do you think Archerus will have the answer to all of your questions? His knowledge of werewolves comes from words in books, not real experience. He can't even tell you how to transform from a human to a werewolf and then back. Are you going to entrust everything to him? Especially when time is so limited," Malyios said with a gentle chuckle. "I can sense that you have questions. Go on, ask."

"How were you able to control me when I first transformed?"

"My real body is far away, beyond the physical grip of Terrador. I used my magic not to control you, but to save you from your demise," Malyios said. "I can also use my magic to communicate with you when you are asleep. Do not be deceived by my actions, Yuri. I do want to see you succeed and I am prepared to offer you the information that you seek, should you agree to my accord."

"What do you want me to do?"

"I want you to find the Oblivion Portal and enter it."

Yuri remembered that there had been markings on the floor of his home, in his past nightmare. Malyios had said that was the portal to Oblivion. "What is on the other side of this ... portal?"

"*It is a gateway to the realm of the dead. There, you will be able to speak to those who have passed. In fact, you could even exchange a few words with your deceased family. You could apologize to your mother. You two were on poor terms the last I checked,*" Malyios said, holding out his hand. "*Worry not. All you have to do is step through the portal. Then you will be free to leave whenever you would like. Your life will not be in danger. Just shake my hand and the accord will be sealed. Once you do so, I'll tell you the secret to controlling your werewolf powers and the location of this field.*"

Yuri stared at the being's hand, contemplating the deal. There certainly was more to this accord than what he was hearing. Why would he be asked to simply step through a portal and not complete another task? Perhaps Malyios was lying about the exit and was condemning him to his ultimate doom, trapped in the alternate world.

He bit his lower lip. Malyios's offer was quite tempting, though. Yuri was caught at a particularly desperate time. Getting to Reidan right now was their top priority; they would need to get reinforcements to trap the werewolf virus as soon as possible. He needed to get control over his werewolf transformation so that they could get to the city quicker. Right now, he was slowing Archerus down. In addition, if he could find out where the field of Phoenix Hearts was, they could retake Horux without having to massacre the werewolves. If all he had to do was go through a portal — maybe this wasn't such a bad idea after all.

Yuri reached out and grasped Malyios's hand, suddenly feeling a surge of heat rushing into his hand. His eyes widened when images of Lichholme began to race through his mind, burning into his memory like hot iron. Within moments, he had memorized how to get from Reidan to the field of Phoenix Hearts — and from there, to the portal of Oblivion.

***

Archerus stirred slightly, his eyes cracking open against the sun's dazzling rays. He groaned as he rolled over in the grass, hearing a boisterous splash in the river next to him. Raising an eyebrow, he turned to find that Yuri was already awake with a pile of fish flopping on the riverbank, and a bonfire blazing beside it. Even more surprising was that Yuri was in his werewolf form, grasping two large fish with one hand and holding them up in the air, as if he'd just won a contest.

After taking several minutes to fully wake up, Archerus stood up and sauntered over to the riverbank where Yuri was beginning to cook their breakfast. The man raised his eyebrow at the werewolf, one hand on his waist. "You've been busy. I'm impressed. You've managed to transform and regain your coordination. How long have you been awake?"

"Three hours," Yuri said, pulling a fish from the fire that was burned to a blackened crisp. He raised an eyebrow and sighed, eating it anyway. "Unfortunately, I'm still a poor cook."

Archerus guffawed, sitting down beside his companion. "What was the secret trigger to your transformation? A specific memory that you had locked away?"

"No," Yuri said, shaking his head. "It was a feeling, a relatively specific one. It was the feeling of being powerless, watching someone that I've loved perish. For the past couple of days, I had been sifting through my most tragic memories, like the death of my family and Asmund. But all of this time, my trigger to becoming a werewolf was the empty feeling of weakness that I'd endured when I watched my best friend transform into a werewolf — and when I walked into my home and saw that I was too late to save my family."

Archerus watched his friend for a moment and nodded. "Have you managed to figure out what trigger can turn you back into a human?"

"Yeah," Yuri said with a gentle smile. "It's a memory. One with my father, long ago."

Archerus bit his lower lip, feeling a gloomy ambiance in the air. He reached out and touched the Yuri on the shoulder. "Well, that's quite the surprise that you managed to grasp control over your transformations so quickly," he said, smirking. "That's outstanding."

Yuri cracked a half-smile but said nothing.

"Now that I won't have to lug you around anymore, we could reach Reidan before the end of the day," Archerus said, grabbing a fish from the pile. "So be sure to eat up. We've got a grueling day ahead of us."

The Quest of Peril

Moriaki soared over Reidan in his raven form, looking down on the grand city. He descended from the clouds, sweeping down to the capital and morphing back into his elven form. There were several startled outcries of surprise from the civilians, but he paid them no attention as he walked through Reidan's packed streets.

Structures of all sizes surrounded him, mostly made of either stone or wood. The architecture in Reidan was just as Moriaki remembered it. The buildings were slightly ostentatious in their vibrant colors, and had steeply slanted tiled rooftops. They were gigantic, making the citizens seem like mere insects that strolled in the buildings' shadows.

The civilians in the city also wore very colorful attire, and were well prepared for the arctic weather that haunted Escalon. Citizens typically wore multiple layers of clothing and scarves to protect them from the bitter cold. Squadrons of soldiers and knights patrolled the city streets, clanking about in their heavy, metallic armor. Most of them had blue tabards draped over their armor, bearing the golden insignia of Iradia.

"I could've sworn that I sensed a familiar aura," a voice said from behind Moriaki. The elf turned around, recognizing an old friend from several centuries ago. "It's nice to see you, Moriaki."

"Likewise, Zylon," Moriaki said with a broad smile. Zylon had spiky red hair, the color of fire, which pointed towards the sky like sharp blades of grass. The man wore a dark cloak over his white attire. It was rare to see someone lacking a weapon, as Zylon was, but Moriaki knew that the man had no need for a blade in order to defend himself. After all, he was renowned for being one of Terrador's greatest heroes. "It's been centuries, and

GHOST WOLF

you haven't aged a day. You still look like you're in your twenties."

Zylon walked forward and embraced the druid with a hearty chuckle. "Is that so? Well, they don't call me an immortal for nothing. It's been, what, two hundred years since we've last seen each other? You're just as I remember you. Maybe your ears got a little longer."

"I highly doubt that," Moriaki said, laughing. He smiled at the quiet boy standing by the immortal. "Who is the youngling beside you?"

"Ah, this is my son," Zylon said, nodding to the boy. He looked to be around the age of twenty and was wearing a pair of glasses. His dark hair brushed down just above his shy eyes and his lips were pursed in a pout. He wore a perfectly fitted black suit, which had clearly been tailored by a professional. Underneath one arm, he held a large book that was thicker than his entire arm. "Noah, this is Moriaki. He is the Druid of the North and has maintained the balance of Escalon for centuries."

"To an extent, Lichholme is a realm beyond the reach of my power," Moriaki said, rubbing the back of his neck. "So, what are you two doing on Escalon? I thought that you'd settled on the human continent of Etherica."

"I've come to recruit young mages to assist me in combating an organization known as the Bounts," Zylon said. "Surely you've heard of them; they're an infamous terrorist group. And you? What business do you have in Reidan?"

"I'm here to try and save Escalon from falling out of balance, as usual," Moriaki said, looking at both of the men before him. "Actually, I could use your help. The continent is in quite a dangerous predicament at the moment. The city of Horux has been overrun by werewolves."

"Werewolves?"

"Indeed. One was imprisoned underneath Horux for centuries, but was recently released. He's infected the people of

155

Horux, and now the virus will become a threat to all of the humans of Escalon if it leaves that peninsula," Moriaki said, folding his arms.

Zylon whistled, not as fazed by the situation as one would think. He tapped his chin, deep in thought. "That does seem like a problem. Then you've come here to request assistance from Iradia to try and contain the virus while you search for a solution to this ... werewolf issue," he said, smiling when the druid nodded. "Interesting. How exactly do you plan to get an audience with the king? He's a busy man, you know. He won't see even the Druid of the North immediately, even if you claim that it is an emergency."

Moriaki narrowed his eyes and groaned. He knew the immortal was right. "Yeah, I'd planned to just turn into a mouse and sneak into the throne room to force his attention."

Zylon chortled, holding his belly as he gave the elf's shoulder a friendly slap. "Oh gods, that is a dangerous decision to make, my friend. Here, I'll get you an audience with the king. We're old friends."

"As you are with most people that I stumble across," Moriaki said, rolling his eyes. Nevertheless, he grinned. "Go on then, lead the way. I'll fill you in on what I know."

***

The three of them strolled through Reidan's busy streets, making their way to the grand castle gates that led to the royal family's land. All of the guards recognized Zylon, and he was clearly a celebrity of sorts amongst the people of Iradia. Citizens constantly greeted him in the streets and the charming man would respond with a friendly wave.

Noah was silent, reading his book as Moriaki explained Horux's current situation to Zylon in detail. The boy suddenly closed his manuscript and looked at the druid. "So, do you have a particular plan for after those werewolves are contained on their peninsula? In fact, what is preventing them from leaving Horux and journeying out into Escalon as we speak? Is trapping them even an option anymore?"

Moriaki raised an eyebrow at the boy's barrage of questions, but soon found himself smiling. These were good questions to ask, as he expected of the son of one of Terrador's immortal heroes. "I've set up several wards forged from nature magic throughout the forest outside of Horux. In addition, I've laid out a second defensive layer of magical barriers in another forest near the edge of the peninsula. The soonest Faelen could've departed was yesterday. It would take his forces four days to defeat my wards and get through them."

"In order to meet that deadline, you'll need to have the king's soldiers riding with all haste towards Escalon's southern peninsula by tomorrow morning," Zylon said with a raised eyebrow. "That is assuming the worst — that the werewolves left Horux yesterday."

The immortal led his son and the druid across a long, grassy yard towards a gigantic, towering iron fortress. This castle was very different from various other citadels Moriaki had visited in Terrador. Unlike the other structures in Reidan, this stronghold was built to withstand raids and invasions. Its roofs had jagged spikes protruding from its iron top, and a fortified door made of the hardest steel covered the entrance to the building. Soldiers surrounded the perimeter of the building, and dozens of squadrons of guards patrolled through the castle grounds, marching past them.

Moriaki played with the hem of his robe, shrugging as they approached the giant door of the fortress. "I didn't say that I had much time to plan things," he said, watching as one of the soldiers raised his gauntlet, halting the group just outside of the steel door. The door groaned open, and one of the guards went into the citadel while the other stayed with Moriaki's party.

Noah looked to his father. "What's going on?"

Zylon smiled at the soldier, who saluted the well-known hero. "They need to inform the king that I am here with the Druid of the North. Surely, Lord Reimos will understand that our visit is important if both of us are here together," he said, raising his arms into the air as the soldier began to search the party for weapons.

Moriaki's face contorted into a frown when the soldier relieved him of his staff, but he understood that it was merely protocol. The guard that had entered the castle minutes before returned promptly and nodded. "King Reimos has postponed his meeting with his military advisors to see you now," he said with a slight nod of his head. "Please, follow me."

Walking through the iron halls of the stronghold, Moriaki noticed that the inside of the castle lacked any sign of extravagance. The walls did not have ostentatious paintings, as many other royal palaces did, nor were there any other pieces of artwork throughout the halls of the citadel. Instead, lit torches were secured to the walls on sconces, illuminating the corridors. The doors were all made of solid steel, and there were triple the amount of guards of any ordinary citadel. The building seemed to be packed with warriors were ready for any surprise assault. Moriaki understood that such defenses were necessary, especially within Escalon. Many enemies wanted the king of the human empire dead.

Walking into a massive, circular room, the elf found himself facing the king of Reidan, who sat upon a golden throne on the far side of the space. Knights armed with pikes surrounded the perimeter of the throne room, watching the newcomers as they were escorted before the king. Moriaki, Zylon, and Noah all halted in the center of the throne room and knelt in homage to the lord.

Lord Reimos looked more like a viking warrior than an ordinary king. He was dressed in a suit of heavy armor, and wore the pelt of a white bear over his head instead of his crown. At the side of his throne was a gigantic mace; it was the size of a man, and enchanted so that it barely weighed thirty pounds. Scratching his grizzly beard, Reimos chuckled as he gazed upon his visitors. "The Immortal Zylon and the Druid of the North — it's wonderful to see both of you after so long. I believe I was a child when I last saw you, Zylon."

"Yes, milord," Zylon said, raising his head. He slowly rose up and struck his chest, saluting the king. "I am glad to see that you are well."

"It's interesting to see a human who doesn't age," Lord Reimos said, looking at Noah. "Who is the young man beside you?"

"That would be my son."

"Ah, and I'm sure that he's equally as talented," the king said, thrumming his fingers against the arm of his throne. "If you're together, I'm assuming that you've both come here for an important reason." He leaned his chin against his knuckle, ready to listen. "Tell me."

***

Yuri fell onto his hands and knees, morphing back into his human form. He could finally see Reidan in the distance. Exhausted after a long day of running, he exhaled with great relief. Sweat poured down his face, soaking his torn shirt, and he closed his eyes, bathing himself in sunlight. They had moved across Escalon at double the speed that they had anticipated, arriving at the capital of Iradia several hours after noon.

Archerus gave Yuri a slap on the back, walking past the boy. "You moved swiftly today. Now that you can transform freely between your forms, covering ground will be a lot easier," he said, gazing at the massive walls of Reidan in the distance. "We'd better continue the rest of our journey on foot. We wouldn't want to startle the guards with two werewolves charging towards the city."

Yuri groaned, pushing himself back to his feet as he stumbled forward after Archerus. "Gods, please spare me of this agony."

"What happened to all of that energy you had earlier, eh?" Archerus jested, smirking at the wearied boy.

"Oh, shut up."

***

Lord Reimos listened to Moriaki's tale and raised his eyebrows as the druid finished, closing his eyes. "Horux's collapse is certainly a tragedy. Earlier today, its king arrived in Reidan, requesting that we aid the refugees that are now flooding into Teolan from the fallen city. The story that the royal family told me aligns with yours, Moriaki. But they did not mention this Faelen individual that you've described. He leads this pack of transformed beasts? Why is it that the werewolves turned to him for leadership?"

Moriaki looked at the king with an expression of surprise, not having expected the royal family of Horux to arrive in Reidan so quickly. Yes, he had anticipated that they would eventually come to the capital to request aid of Iradia's king. However, they truly must've traveled with all haste to arrive here before the druid. "Werewolves, like many beasts, look to their strongest for leadership. Faelen is by far the most powerful werewolf in history, because he has dark magic at his disposal."

"Dark magic? So, he is an intelligent beast," King Reimos murmured. "At the request of the king of Horux, I have already agreed to send a small force to the southern peninsula of Escalon in order to contain these werewolves. However, after speaking with you, I am beginning to think that we may require a larger army if we are to push back the monsters. Not to mention, there is always the risk that the infection could spread if any of my soldiers are bitten."

"Might I suggest a tactic, Lord Reimos?" Noah spoke suddenly, catching everyone in the room by surprise. The boy had been silent since their arrival. "I've read that werewolves are vulnerable to silver. If we can buy time to build barricades of silver, and perhaps eventually a wall, we will be able to contain the werewolves indefinitely."

"A wall across the southern peninsula," Lord Reimos said with a laugh. "That would surely take a lot of resources, boy."

"Then perhaps not a wall, but barricades … some form of fortifications will surely be needed in order to prevent the werewolves from leaving the peninsula. I believe that is a good plan," Zylon said, smiling proudly at his son. His attention went back to the king. "I am willing to travel to the front along with a small force to buy time for the transfer of supplies."

Lord Reimos narrowed his eyes and groaned, reaching up and rubbing his temples. He was clearly stressed out by this entire situation, knowing that he needed to find a solution to this urgent problem immediately. Understanding the importance of trapping the werewolves, the king nodded reluctantly. "All right, immortal. You'll leave with a force of five hundred soldiers tonight. I expect that you'll be able to protect them from the werewolves until reinforcements and supplies arrive the following week." The king lowered his hands to his side, his expression relaxing. "What is your plan for the long-term handling of these werewolves? We cannot just keep them permanently caged on the peninsula. Something must be done about them."

Moriaki was about to open his mouth when suddenly there was a loud bang behind him. He glanced over his shoulder and saw that Yuri and Archerus were standing in the doorway to the throne room, drenched in sweat. They looked absolutely exhausted. Behind them were three guards with weapons pointed at their backs. The druid blinked as he looked at his two friends and stifled a laugh. "You two arrived a lot quicker than I thought you would."

"We rushed here as quickly as possible," Archerus said, pouting at the iron pikes that were prodding at his back. "Oh, come on. You can lower your weapons. We pose no threat."

"Milord, these two claim to be companions of the Druid of the North and have come here regarding news of the—" one soldier said but was silenced by a gentle wave of the king's hand. The warrior bowed his head and left the room with his colleagues, closing the door to the throne room behind them.

Lord Reimos indicated the two newcomers with a calm gesture. "Who are your friends, Moriaki?"

"This is Yuri," the druid said, pointing to the boy. He then nodded to the man. "That's Archerus. The two of them are survivors of the Horuxian massacre. They were the ones that gave me the information that I've relayed to you."

The king smiled at the two visitors. "You two must be tired. You're free to stay here for the time being. I'll have my servants set up rooms for you." Watching as both Yuri and Archerus bowed in appreciation, Lord Reimos then turned his attention back to Moriaki. "Let us return to the task at hand. We'll begin by containing the werewolves. What's the next step after that to ensure the safety of Escalon? The complete eradication of their species?"

"No," Yuri said, arousing confusion and surprise amongst the other individuals in the room. "There is another way. The werewolves can be cured of their beastly rage and regain their human rationality if they ingest a rare plant known as the Phoenix Heart."

The king looked at Zylon and Moriaki. "Is this true?"

Moriaki nodded, and the king raised his eyebrows in amusement.

"But Phoenix Hearts are extremely rare, milord," Archerus said, stepping forward. "I understand that Yuri wishes to grant the werewolves mercy because they were once human, but such a plan is impractical. It is impossible for us to find enough Phoenix Hearts for that many werewolves. Even if we were to plant and cultivate the rare flower, it takes at least a year before they grow and fully bloom. In that amount of time, Faelen and his pack of beasts likely could break out of the peninsula and spread the virus to the rest of Escalon. I support your idea; the monstrosities must be annihilated."

"I know of a place!" Yuri exclaimed, claiming the king's attention. "There is a field in Lichholme that is full of Phoenix Hearts. There are thousands of them, enough to cure Horux's beasts of their fiery rage."

The king stared at the boy, unconvinced. "Lichholme? How could you possibly know of such a field? Entering such an unholy area and returning alive is nearly impossible. Not to mention that you live on the other side of Escalon. I don't believe that you have been there before."

"I haven't," Yuri said confidently. "But if you give me a map, I can show you its location."

"But how are we supposed to know it exists?" Zylon said, with his arms folded. "You could mark any place on a map, but it could be a barren wasteland of naught but ice."

"He's right," Archerus said.

Yuri winced. He didn't want to have to tell them about Malyios and the deal that he had secretly made with the Titan to gain this information. But at this rate, he would have no choice. He gritted his teeth, wishing that someone would believe him.

"I could check using my clairvoyance," Moriaki said suddenly and everyone's eyes went to the druid. "If my staff is returned to me, I could use my magic to see a particular area for a small amount of time. If Yuri marks the location on a map, then I could confirm whether or not this field of Phoenix Hearts truly exists."

Zylon clapped his hands together with a hearty laugh. "It's settled then. Let's get the boy a map of Escalon!"

The king had one of the guards race out of the room to retrieve a map of Escalon and Moriaki's staff. The location was burned into Yuri's mind; it only took him moments to mark its exact spot on the piece of parchment. Archerus curiously looked over the boy's shoulder, skeptical that Yuri had somehow discovered a field of Phoenix Hearts.

Moriaki squeezed his wooden staff and closed his eyes, activating his clairvoyance. Everyone in the throne room watched the elf as he began to tremble. When the druid reopened his eyes, they were glowing bright blue. His vision had extended to the very corners of Terrador and narrowed in on the site that Yuri had marked. His mouth gaped in disbelief, but it soon twisted into an elated grin. "The youngling is correct. There is a field of Phoenix Hearts there." His eyes stopped glowing and he shook his head, eying Yuri. "I do not know how you managed to find such a miraculous place, but perhaps you've found a peaceful solution to the werewolf threat on Escalon."

"How did you know?" Archerus asked Yuri.

"I saw the field within a dream that I had last night," Yuri said with a shrug. "The location … it was somehow just engraved in my mind. It's hard to explain." He received an unconvinced stare from Archerus.

"Is that all?" he pressed.

"Yeah, that's all."

Moriaki raised an eyebrow at Yuri's response, but said nothing.

"Perhaps the gods are on our side, then, and have given you a vision. We should not waste the information that they've granted us," Zylon said, turning to the king. "But there are two issues that lie before us regarding this plan. A journey to

Lichholme will be an extremely dangerous quest. I will not be there, since I must travel to southern Escalon to fight back Faelen's forces. The other problem is how to get the Phoenix Heart's antidote into the bloodstream of the werewolves."

Yuri winced. Those were certainly large problems to deal with.

"If we send an elite force to travel to Lichholme, perhaps they could make it to the field and back unharmed," the king said. "The party would have to be small enough to travel unnoticed. The horde of undead abominations that plague the land would be attracted to a large army. Whether or not the group survives is entirely up to their skill ... and a lot of luck."

Everyone in the room nodded in agreement.

"As for the second issue, Iradia does have an alliance with a small settlement of gnomes that live in Lichholme," Lord Reimos said, getting off his throne. The king strode forward and knelt down by the map on the floor, pointing at a particular spot near the eastern mountains of Lichholme. The location that he indicated was conveniently on the way to the field of Phoenix Hearts. "If you take this path here, you'll come across a gnomish fortress known as Etaon. There are Iradian engineers there, talented ones trained by the gnomes themselves. They're the only engineers on Escalon capable of fixing up an invention that could inject the Phoenix Heart substance into the werewolves. We are merely assuming that they're still alive, though. We haven't been in contact with Etaon for a couple of months."

"That's better than nothing," Moriaki said with a smile. "I believe that we're onto something here. Who do you think should embark on this perilous quest? I wou—"

"Pardon me, Moriaki," Zylon said. "But I would feel a bit safer if you were to come with me to the southern front to combat Faelen's army. I don't believe I can handle such formidable opponents alone, even with a force of Iradian soldiers as support."

The druid nodded. "Perhaps that is for the best. If they break through the defenses, this whole quest is pointless," he said, turning to Archerus, Noah, and Yuri. "I'm assuming that you three would like to volunteer to go to Lichholme?"

"What? I—" Noah began but sighed when he spotted a disapproving glare from his father. He shrugged sluggishly. "Yeah, I'd love to go," he murmured.

"We have another issue. How are we going to carry thousands of Phoenix Hearts with us from Lichholme?" Archerus asked.

Noah held out his hand, his face expressionless. Clearly, he wasn't too happy about having to journey to one of the most dangerous places in the world. A bright red light began to glow in his palm, growing until there was an evanescent flash. His hand now held a small bag made of an arcane ruby-colored substance. "My father and I have the magical ability of creation. I can make any physical object that my mind pictures, and I can give it a function," he said, reaching into the small bag. To Archerus's surprise, the boy pulled a sword, made of the same magical material, from the tiny bag. "This is essentially a bottomless bag that I can use to store whatever I want. I'll be able to keep all of the Phoenix Hearts in here."

Yuri whistled. "That's handy."

"Well, I'm pretty sure that going on this trek with only three people is going to end poorly," Archerus said, folding his arms. "Who else can we bring?"

"I believe there are several skilled champions that arrived with Horux's royal family. Perhaps we should ask if they would like to volunteer for this quest," Lord Reimos said, waving for Yuri, Noah, and Archerus to follow him out of the throne room. "Moriaki and Zylon, I will have your soldiers meet you at Reidan's gates tomorrow morning at sunrise. If you ride with haste, you'll arrive at the southern peninsula before Faelen can break through Moriaki's wards."

Moriaki and Zylon both gave the king a bow of reverence. "Thank you, Lord Reimos," Moriaki said. "Your assistance in this affaire will surely help maintain balance in Escalon."

"I hope it does, druid. Best of luck to you two."

Witness the Secret

Yuri followed King Reimos through the twisting maze-like corridors of the castle. Archerus and Noah walked beside him, with three burly knights tailing closely behind. The young man blankly watched the lord's clanking armor, his mind wandering.

The memory of Senna shooting him on the docks of Horux flashed through his mind. There was no doubt that Senna knew that he was a werewolf. If the knight revealed his identity, things would only become complicated, and Senna was certainly here with the royal family.

Yuri exchanged glances with Archerus, who gave him a nod. *Keep it a secret for now. They'll find out when we reach Lichholme.*

The boy blinked back to reality when the king opened a door, entering a large room that was expensively designed. The bed was massive, and there were extravagant pieces of furniture scattered throughout the huge chamber. Yuri followed the king into the room, his eyes widening when he spotted Terias. "T-Terias? What are you doing here?"

Terias stared at Yuri as if he were looking at a ghost. "Yuri! You're alive?" The young man was dressed in clanking iron armor and had a giant broadsword sheathed at his side. Standing next to him was Princess Violet, and on his other side was Senna, who was already reaching for his weapon.

Yuri narrowed his eyes; his werewolf senses could spot the knight's intentions before he'd even touched the handle of his sword. It was as if everything were moving in slow motion, as his natural instincts caused adrenaline to kick in. He saw that the soldiers behind him were beginning to react to Senna's abrupt movements, for they also reached for their own weapons. A blur of movement flashed before Yuri and the boy watched as

Archerus flitted across the room, grabbing Senna's wrist before he was able to unsheathe his sword.

"Calm down," Archerus commanded.

"Don't give me orders, you insane—" Senna began, but swallowed back his words. He had no right to call Archerus crazy, not after he'd been right about the werewolf underneath Horux. The warrior bit his lower lip in frustration and darted an irate glare at Yuri. Senna squeezed the hilt of his sword so tightly that his weapon rattled, but Archerus's superior strength prevented him from brandishing his blade. "You've gotten stronger since I last saw you, Archerus. Have you also become a monstrosity?"

"I don't know what you're talking about," Archerus said with a cold gaze.

"You know exactly what I'm talking about!" Senna barked angrily.

"Senna, what's going on?" Princess Violet demanded, puzzled by what was happening. She looked at Yuri. "I thought you said that Yuri was—"

"I *shot* him," Senna insisted, releasing the handle on his sword. "Yuri was infected by a werewolf. I saw the beasts run past him. They considered him one of their own and disregarded him as a threat!"

"I wasn't infected," Yuri said.

"If you weren't infected, then show me your damned chest! There's no way that any ordinary human could take a bullet to the heart and escape a horde of werewolves!" Senna shouted, scowling when he saw Lord Reimos's soldiers stepping forward to restrain him. He held his hands up. "I'm not lying."

"A lot of things happened that night, Senna," Archerus said, putting his hand on the man's shoulder. "I understand you're shocked that he's still alive, but you need to calm down. We're on your side. In fact, we've come to you requesting your help to try and retake Horux."

"Retake Horux?" Princess Violet said. "How would you do that?"

Senna listened as Lord Reimos explained the plan to find a field of flowers. Everyone seemed diverted from Senna's accusations, now that their attention was focused on the king and his words.

However, Senna could not tear his gaze from Yuri. Rage channeled through every part of his body, and he ground his teeth, infuriated that no one believed him. He knew what he had seen. There was no doubt in his mind that Yuri had been on the brink of transformation at the time. He'd fired a lead bullet right into Yuri's chest. Yet ... here the boy stood. Rational. Calm. Human. How was this possible?

When the king was finished explaining the plan, Senna simply nodded. "I'll go," he said. "I would go through Oblivion itself to reclaim Horux."

Yuri's eyes fluttered at the warrior's mention of Oblivion, but he said nothing. He was surprised that Senna suddenly seemed relaxed. Only moments ago, he had been enraged. Perhaps he'd convinced himself that he had been hallucinating. He watched as the knight left the room, his eyes on the carpeted floor as he stormed away. Yuri looked at Archerus, but the man simply shrugged. He too was unsure of Senna's mental state.

"As Senna's apprentice, I'll also journey to Lichholme," Terias stated, reaching up and striking his chest. This was the salute of a dauntless soldier, not of a young man from Horux's Lower District.

Yuri was surprised that Terias even knew Senna, and that the former thief was now dressed like a knight. What had happened in the past couple of days?

Lord Reimos nodded with approval. Senna was the most renowned knight from Horux, infamous for his expertise in swordsmanship. It was said that he could cleave three men in half with a single swing. Any man apprenticed to such a grand knight must show some promise.

Yuri had his eyebrows raised with surprise, about to protest Terias's embarking upon such a perilous journey. But the words were locked in his throat, and he merely gaped at the soldier. There was no way that Terias had somehow managed to learn to fight in only a couple of days. How had he even managed to get an apprenticeship underneath one as renowned as Senna?

Yuri sighed. Allowing an inexperienced knight to take up a quest like this was foolish, but the king seemed willing to take up any volunteers that would attempt this near-impossible task of infiltrating Lichholme.

"I'll go as well," Princess Violet said.

"That, I'm afraid, is out of the question," King Reimos said with a shake of his head. "Only those with combat experience will be allowed to go to Lichholme. Milady, I'm afraid that your chances of surviving such a journey are extremely low. No offense to you, but I believe it best if you stay here."

"But—"

"I understand that you want to help in this time of dire need, but you can do so in other ways," Lord Reimos said. "Raising the morale of your people is what you should focus on. In this period of desperation, Horuxian survivors will be looking for leadership. They'll look to the king, the queen, and you. You must fulfill your role as one of their leaders and give them hope." He watched as the princess lowered her head in understanding. Nevertheless, he could still see the distraught expression on her face.

The princess rushed past Yuri without another word and quickly fled the room, clearly upset by the king's decision.

Yuri bit his lower lip, knowing that it was best if Violet stayed away from Lichholme. Nevertheless, Yuri felt that he should go after her. He turned to walk after Violet but was halted by a gentle hand from Archerus.

"Give her some time," Archerus said with a pitiful visage. "The princess feels helpless. But as King Reimos said, there are other ways she can assist our people."

She feels powerless, just as I have. Yuri relaxed his shoulders, exhaling. "What's our plan?"

"I'll gather a small party of my greatest warriors to travel with you to Lichholme," Lord Reimos said. "The situation is indeed disastrous and calls for immediate attention. I think it best if you all depart tomorrow morning, if you can manage it. I understand that you're all tired so if you must—"

"We'll go tomorrow," Yuri said.

The king smiled. "Good, then get some rest. I'll have my servants lead you to your rooms, where you may bathe and get some sleep. Hopefully by morning, you'll feel refreshed and will be ready for your trek."

***

Faelen trudged through the forest outside of Horux, after spending several days training Tanya to adjust to her newly obtained werewolf senses. She'd been a quick learner, and Faelen was impressed with her progress.

As Junko had promised, Tanya was naturally skilled in combat. She could wield nearly every weapon that Faelen could name, but she chose to use a chain-whip, a unique weapon native to her home continent of Dastia.

Faelen had seen Tanya use the weapon one night. Her form was graceful and fluid, flowing elegantly as her chain whip sliced through the air. One false move and she could lop off her own head with the sharp blades. On one end of the chain whip was a scythe, made of abyssalite, Terrador's hardest metal. It was also incredibly light, which allowed it to tear at her opponents with frightening speed. On the other side of the metallic chain was an ordinary blade that glowed bright red, as if it had just been dipped into a hot forge. The werewolf could see that this blade had been enchanted by several magicians, for many arcane spells twisted around the steel, making it as deadly as the abyssalite scythe. Maybe even more so, for these enhancements enabled the blade to cut through the skin of most living beings.

As Faelen watched Tanya perform her dance, slashing her chain whip in the night, he'd realized that he'd taken quite a liking to her. He enjoyed her company; it was nice to have a rational person to talk to as opposed to him barking pointlessly at the other werewolves. He only hoped that she could meet his expectations and find the Oblivion Portal.

"Do you not use a weapon yourself, Lord Faelen?" Tanya asked, walking beside him in her human form. She'd taken it upon herself to start calling him *lord*, for some unexplained reason. Nevertheless, Faelen did not complain. He'd thought they were partners, as Junko had said, but if she insisted on declaring him as superior, then he was fine with that.

"I have no use for a weapon," Faelen said, holding up one of his hands to his face. He knew that his claws were probably stronger than a majority of the world's blades, able to shred most metals apart with ease. His claw began to glow ominously as wisps of dark magic streamed from his fingertips. "But I've dedicated my life to search for a particular item. Have you ever heard of Sacred Treasures?"

Tanya nodded. "They're items that are crafted by the gods. They're extremely rare, aren't they?"

Faelen smiled, impressed with Tanya's knowledge. "Yes, they certainly are. Sacred Treasures have magical properties that can accomplish wonders. That is why I seek the Oblivion Portal, for within Oblivion lies a Sacred Treasure that I've dreamed of obtaining. With it, I'll never have to fear being locked away again."

"Now that you're part of the Bounts, I imagine that you don't have to worry about being caged," Tanya said, flicking some dark hair from her eyes with a slight toss of her head. "Our organization has many powerful members, some of whom have already acquired a few Sacred Treasures."

Faelen smirked, shaking his head. "I know better than to put my faith solely in others," he said, glancing over his shoulder. He gazed at the legion of werewolves that scampered through Horux's forest behind him. He sniffed the air. The atmosphere was filled with powerful magic that was so intense that it was almost palpable. *Something is wrong.*

The werewolf's face twisted into an angrily scowl as he saw glimmering magic shining on the trees around him. He held up a hand, halting Tanya and the werewolves behind him. The beast watched as a pair of glowing viridian eyes cracked open on the trunk of one of the trees in front of him. The branches snapped and crackled as the tree groaned to life, practically tearing itself from the earth, exposing massive tentacle-like roots that functioned as legs.

The moan of the tree echoed throughout the forest. Faelen soon realized that a number of other trees had also been brought to life, but they did not move. They merely stood there, blocking the path, waiting for the werewolves to come and attack.

Faelen gnarred, dropping to his hands, digging his claws into the dirt. "It would seem that the Druid of the North has set up some obstacles to keep us at bay while he goes to find help. Tanya, let's eradicate them."

"Yes, Lord Faelen," Tanya said, beginning to morph into her werewolf form. She gripped her chain whip tightly, squeezing the metal links in her claws as she eyed the dozens of lumbering trees before her.

Faelen let out a boisterous howl that split the night as he dashed forward, his eyes on the prey before him. His subordinate werewolves mirrored his yowl and followed his example, striking at the trees ferociously. The beasts were much faster than the slow plants, but their slashes and bites were hardly enough to penetrate the creatures' tough bark. Within moments, however, the werewolves had discovered that tearing off the trees' branches caused the plants significant pain. Dozens of werewolves pounced upon each living tree, bringing the magical beings crashing to the ground underneath their weight.

Several of the silent oaks swung their thick branches downward, driving werewolves into the earth. Faelen watched as one of his companions was lifted into the air by one of the grand trees and slammed into the ground with tremendous force, shattering every bone in the creature's body.

Faelen snarled and charged, dark energy gathering on the tips of his claws. He swiped outwards and shredded the tree's trunk apart from a distance, using demonic magic to strike the oak with ferocity. The plant let out a shrill screech that sounded like it came from a witch, a piercing noise that greatly contrasted the grumbling groans the trees had made only moments ago.

The werewolf turned and saw that Tanya was slicing the trees apart with ease, her chain whip ripping through the creatures' trunks. Faelen growled, baring his fangs as he rushed back into the battle. *A minor setback, that's all this is. It'll take a lot more than a couple lumbering trees to halt my advance, druid.*

***

Yuri rubbed down his soaked hair with a towel, having taken a hot bath. It'd been so long since he'd last bathed, and he felt refreshed after spending an hour scrubbing the dirt, grime, and dried blood off himself.

He'd changed into new clothes that the king had granted him, eager to try them on. His attire included a black cloak that wrapped tightly around his body, one that was enchanted to shield him from Lichholme's bitter weather. He wore a white shirt, the color of snow, and heavy pants that were woven to keep him warm. He slid into leather boots that rode up past his ankles, matting warm fur against his skin. On the table beside his bed was a pair of gloves and an extra long-sleeved shirt that he could wear in case the cold of Lichholme truly was unforgiving. Everything seemed to fit comfily.

Across the room from Yuri, Terias was sitting on his own bed. He whetted a dagger while he waited for Yuri to finish using the bathroom. The soldier was dressed in comfortable nightwear, a blue robe with slippers. "I still can't believe that you're alive," Terias said. "Senna scared the crap out of me when he told me that you got turned into a werewolf. I went to his room to check on him an hour ago. He still seems convinced that you're one of those beasts."

Yuri felt a knot twisting in his stomach, but he hid his nervousness behind his smiling facade. "Well, I don't look like a werewolf."

"That's what I told him." Terias shrugged. "He'll come around in time. I wouldn't worry about him." The soldier got off his bed and walked towards the bathroom. "Are you nervous? About this journey, I mean."

"Nervous?" Yuri rubbed the base of his neck. "I am, but I'll try not to let it get to my head."

"Yeah," Terias said, opening the door to the bathroom. He let out a startled yelp and staggered backward. The young man lost his balance and fell onto his back, cringing and holding out his arms as if bracing for an attack. "H-How the hell did you get into our bathroom?" he yelped, flustered.

Yuri turned to find a woman standing in their bathroom, clad in tightly-fitted ebony armor of leather that made her look like an assassin. She had her dark hair tied back into a ponytail, and a black cloth masked her mouth and nose. An array of knives and shuriken were strapped to her belt, and a short-sword was sheathed across her back. Her apathetic gaze sent shivers through the two young men. Yuri saw a long scar cutting across her left eye, carving into her skin.

"I snuck in. It wasn't too hard," the intruder said simply.

"There are no windows or alternate doors into our bathroom, and you weren't in there a moment ago," Yuri said with a raised eyebrow. Even with his enhanced senses, she'd snuck by undetected. How was that possible? "Who are you?"

"My name is Kura. I'm a warrior of Iradia, one of the best," the stranger boasted. "Lord Reimos has summoned me to escort you through the precarious land of Lichholme. But I'm unimpressed with what I see thus far." The assassin looked down at Terias, who was still on the floor. She smirked. "Nevertheless, I merely wanted to introduce myself before we leave tomorrow. After all, we'll be spending a lot of time together."

"That doesn't mean you can just sneak into our bathroom," Terias growled, climbing to his feet. "Haven't you heard of privacy?"

"Are you going to force me out? Then do it." Kura said, staring at the soldier with her cold gaze. When Terias averted his eyes, the female warrior smiled, victory gleaming in her eyes. "Well, I'll see you boys tomorrow morning. Get some rest. Tomorrow will be an arduous day."

Yuri and Terias watched as the woman left their bedroom. Terias folded his arms over his chest, pouting. "I hate her already," he murmured, storming back into the bathroom, scanning the area to see if there were any more intruders. "This certainly will be a laborious adventure if we have to deal with the likes of her the whole way." He closed the door behind him as he prepared his bath.

Yuri laughed. He walked to his bed and sat down, embracing the tranquility of solitude.

But the serenity did not last long. Soon he was swamped by thoughts of Violet. The boy shook his head, knowing that it was best if he just stayed away from the princess. The longer the silence dragged out, the more Yuri itched to check on her.

The boy suddenly stood and ambled out of the room, realizing that if he left the next morning without seeing the princess, he would forever regret that decision. After all, there was always the possibility that he wouldn't return. The chilling thought of death made him shiver.

It took about an hour of asking around to locate the princess's room, but eventually he found it. He was surprised to find that there were no guards at her doorway. He rapped his knuckles against her door gently and blinked when the door cracked ajar on its own, giving him a narrow view of the princess's room. He gulped, knowing that he probably shouldn't peek, but found himself doing so regardless.

Princess Violet was standing at her balcony, looking over the city; she had an excellent view. She was wearing a white nightgown, and her hair was down, flowing to her lower back. The beautiful woman glanced over her shoulder at the sound of creaking door and saw Yuri standing there in the doorway. "What are you doing here?" she said softly. It was clear that she had been crying. Dried tears lingered on her face.

"I came to see if you were okay," Yuri said, closing the door behind him. "I haven't really had a chance to talk to you since our dinner in Horux. I was worried that you hadn't made it." He walked a few steps into the room and paused. "I just wish that I had been able to prevent Faelen's escape. Then none of this would've happened."

"Who was it?" Violet whispered. "Who released him?"

"I don't know. I think it was a man named Junko. He's an ally of Faelen's."

The princess's eyes widened with surprise as she spun around, turning to fully face Yuri. Her eyes were watery now, and Yuri wondered if he had accidently said something wrong. Violet's lips parted slightly, trembling. "Wait, Junko is … alive?"

"You know of him?"

"He's my brother!"

Now Yuri was baffled and he gawked, unsure if he had heard Violet correctly. He did see some resemblance, the primary feature being their uniquely colored irises. But if Junko really was Violet's brother, then he was the prince of Horux and heir to the throne. There had been stories surrounding Violet's older brother, who had been kidnapped at a very young age by a group of raiders, just after the princess had been born. It was said that those brutes had killed the prince, but they never did find the body.

Yuri ran a hand through his hair in disbelief, closing his eyes. That mysterious man ... he was powerful, perhaps even more so than Faelen. Their encounter had been brief, but it was enough for Yuri to understand Junko's formidable strength.

"I need to go on this journey to Lichholme," Violet blurted out, shattering Yuri's train of thought.

"Huh? Wait, no—"

"I can't just stay here in my chambers, doing nothing! If it's leadership that my people need, my parents will be there to fill that role," Violet exclaimed. "But if my brother truly is out there and helping Faelen, then I need to help stop him."

"Violet, it's too dangerous. Even for ordinary warriors—"

"I don't care! I can handle myself," Violet said, growing annoyed. She took a moment and exhaled her frustration, trying to calm down. "Look, I don't intend to stay in Reidan, regardless. I'll take a horse and follow your party tomorrow. By the time you reach Northern Escalon, the group will be forced to take me in. All I need is for someone to leave a trail that I can follow. Please, I need your help, Yuri. I'm sure you understand how I feel. Everyone thinks that I'm too feeble to do anything except sit here and be an idol for the people, while others are out there, risking their lives to fight the real battle. I want to do more than just make speeches and tell the citizens of Horux that it'll be all right. Because the truth is, unless your party succeeds and the Iradian forces are able to contain the werewolves, it won't be all right. No one in Escalon will be safe. Knowing that so much depends on what happens over the next few weeks … I can't stay here. I just can't."

Yuri stared at Violet, biting his lower lip. He walked to the balcony, leaning against the marble railing as he gazed at the full moon in the sky. "I know what you're going through. Feeling powerless — it's a sensation that I've been accustomed to my whole life. I was always beat down by guys like Terias or giant soldiers like Senna, who made me think that I would never have a chance to escape poverty. I trained myself to fight so that I wouldn't have to feel weak, so that I could have power. But in the end, none of that mattered. When I went home after Faelen was released, I found my family slain. That realization, that there was nothing I could've done to prevent their deaths … it's haunting," he said, his lips quivering. Lowering his head, he closed his eyes, feeling them beginning to moisten. "And when Asmund was bitten, I had to watch as he transformed into a monster before my eyes. What could I do? Even if I could go back in time to that moment, I know that I couldn't do anything to prevent the inevitable."

Violet watched with shock as Yuri's body began to morph and he grew in size, stretching his clothes slightly. The boy morphed from an ordinary human into a ferocious beast that looked at her with glowing eyes. But it did not lash out and attack her. Instead, it spoke. "But if I were given the chance to make a difference … I would grasp it in a heartbeat," Yuri said, causing the princess's eyes to widen. "You deserve that chance. When we depart for Lichholme, I'll leave a trail behind us for you to follow." Following Violet's gaze to his dark fur, he snorted. "I'm surprised that you aren't screaming with fear right now, to be perfectly honest."

"Senna was right … you were infected. But you ate a Phoenix Heart, didn't you? Otherwise, you wouldn't be able to maintain such control," Violet said softly, fighting the urge to step backward in the presence of such a terrifying creature. "Why don't you just tell everyone? I'm sure they would understand that you aren't a threat."

"Archerus says that people fear that which they don't understand," Yuri said, his body already shifting back into its human form. He stretched his back, cracking it. "It's better if it stays a secret until we leave Reidan. We wouldn't want any complications before our departure."

"Is Archerus a werewolf too?"

"Yes."

Violet pursed her lips and smiled. "Well, I'm honored that you decided to show me your secret, Yuri."

Yuri blushed slightly and scratched the back of his neck, feeling heat burning his cheeks. "Y-Yeah, well I just feel like I can trust you, for some reason. You're easy to talk to."

"Thank you."

"For what?"

"For letting me come on this quest with you," Violet said. "I know that everyone else would disapprove. They don't think much of me. But for some reason, I knew that if I asked you to help me, you would. You see me as more than just a helpless princess, don't you?"

"Helpless? Hardly," Yuri said, grinning. "You're undoubtedly brave, volunteering for a precarious journey to Lichholme. Most people I know would piss themselves at the very thought of going to such a forsaken land." He walked forward and got down on a knee, taking one of the princess's hands and planting a kiss upon her soft skin. "I suppose we should both call it a night. After all, we'll have to wake up early for tomorrow's expedition."

Violet smiled. "Indeed."

The Creator's Wall

In the morning, Yuri and his companions met at Reidan's front entrance. A party of mounted knights was already prepared to depart when Yuri arrived. Leading them was Zylon, an inspiring smile on his lips. He gave Yuri a slight nod of acknowledgement as he approached the young man. The immortal watched Noah, who was stuffing supplies into his magical bag. "Keep an eye on my son, will you? I only have one," Zylon said, winking.

Yuri nodded. "He seems strong," he said, glancing in Noah's direction. "I haven't seen much magic myself. We don't have many magic users in Horux. But with the power of creation, I'm sure that he'll be fine. At least, I think that he has a better chance at survival than the rest of us."

Zylon chuckled. "All that he knows is from training. He has yet to experience real battle."

"Yet you're sending him on a journey this dangerous?" Yuri said incredulously, mentally questioning Zylon's parenting.

"One grows the most in situations of great risk," Zylon said, pulling on the reins to turn his horse around. "I'm sure that on this adventure you'll find that you will change as well, hopefully for the better." He raised his hand into the air and waved to the young warrior. "I wish your group all the best on your end. Don't take too long. I don't plan on spending the rest of my days fighting werewolves."

Yuri smirked, folding his arms as he watched the immortal gallop away. While the adventurer had the body of a middle-aged man, everything else about him seemed to reflect his experience. The way he spoke, how he rode his horse, even his walk seemed heroic. The immortal, they called him. But how old was he really?

"You don't have to worry much about the front lines," Moriaki said, clamping his hand on Yuri's shoulder as he stepped beside the boy. The druid beamed proudly as he watched his friend gallop off with his squadron of knights into the distance. "Zylon is one of the strongest magicians in the world. Buying time against a couple of beasts won't be too much of a challenge, I imagine."

Yuri chortled. "To be honest, I wasn't worried so much about your task as mine," he said, thinking about the pact that he had made with Malyios. But he didn't dare speak of it. "I've heard tales of Lichholme's danger. The monstrosities that exist there are frightening. I fear for the wellbeing of those traveling with me."

Moriaki nodded, his hands dropping to his side. "You'll have to proceed into the territory with caution," he said, his expression suddenly hardening. He looked around him to see if anyone was listening and then leaned in close to Yuri's ear. "You've been having dreams, haven't you? About Malyios."

Yuri's eyes widened with surprise, his heart pounding at the very mention of the name. A chilling sensation crept under his skin. He shivered. "How do you know?"

"I can sense his unholy energies clinging to you like a leech. I would recognize the mark of Malyios anywhere. You've made a pact with him, haven't you? How else would you know the location of a field of Phoenix Hearts?" Moriaki said, his countenance reflecting worry. "I don't know how you came into contact with such a nefarious being ... but I would be careful when dealing with a God of Demons."

"He's *the* God of Demons?"

"He's one of them, and is by far the most dangerous. Malyios has created some of Terrador's most horrific creatures, including the werewolf," Moriaki said, biting his lower lip. "At the cottage, I never finished telling you about how Faelen became such a powerful werewolf, did I? Malyios is the one who granted him his demonic power and transformed him into the beast that he is, making him Terrador's first werewolf." The druid gazed into the distance and sighed, realizing that he needed to catch up with Zylon. "I wish I knew more about Faelen's past, but even Archerus's vast knowledge of werewolves contains little understanding of the first werewolf's life. It would seem that Faelen's tale has been lost in the fabric of time."

"Would Archerus know anything about Malyios?" Yuri asked as Moriaki walked towards Reidan's massive gate.

"There is not a lot of recorded information on the deity. He's been sealed in Oblivion for eons," Moriaki said over his shoulder, tossing something to Yuri. The boy caught the item and examined it, recognizing a small seed. "I have a feeling you'll need that where you're going, Yuri. I have to go. Best of luck to you on your quest, and be careful."

Yuri was about to ask what the seed was, but the elf had already transformed into an eagle and taken off into the sky, soaring after his comrades. Puzzled, the boy tucked the seed into his pocket, unsure of its purpose. Perhaps its function would be revealed with time.

He bit his lower lip, thinking about what Moriaki had said. *Malyios is locked away in Oblivion? Then our pact ... he must want me to free him.* He frowned. *But he never specified in the accord that I am to release him from Oblivion, or even that I was required to meet him there. All I have to do is go through the portal, so then what are his plans?* Turning around, he saw that the rest of his group had gathered and were preparing to depart. *If Malyios created werewolves, that would mean that Faelen has been to Oblivion before, since there's no way that they met before the god's imprisonment. Could it be that Faelen's power originated in Oblivion?*

"Hey," Archerus called, snapping the boy back to reality. The man raised an eyebrow at Yuri's startled expression, pointing to Kura and a few of her fellow warriors that would be accompanying them on their quest to Lichholme. "Kura is giving a talk before we depart. Better listen up."

Kura introduced a dozen men and women, whose names Yuri instantly forgot. She went on to explain their vigorous travel pace and what route they would take to reach the entrance of Lichholme. A giant glacier separated Lichholme from the rest of Escalon, but there was a supposed fissure in the ice that cut a straight path to the forsaken land. Every hour had been planned out, and Kura emphasized that they had to stick to their strict schedule. Time was a precious commodity and every second counted.

Yuri pursed his lips as he listened to Kura talk. The warrior certainly seemed to know what she was doing. This was going to be an exhausting journey indeed if she was in charge. Yuri wondered if Violet would be able to keep up on horseback. Last night, just before they'd gone to bed, they had set up a system of markings that would help Violet track Yuri's party from a distance, since Archerus would be able to sniff her out if she came within a mile of their party.

Yuri felt a tap on his shoulder and found that Princess Violet was behind him. With her was the royal family of Horux and King Reimos. The boy smiled politely at the lords and bowed respectfully. "I've come bearing you a gift," Violet said, biting her lower lip. She held out her hands, presenting a beautifully woven scarf, the color of rubies. "I expect that Lichholme will be cold. This will help protect you from the bitter weather."

Yuri stared at the gift in awe, the corners of lips curving into a broad grin. He accepted the scarf and put it on immediately, unsurprised by its warmth and softness. It was well knit, surely an expensive piece of attire. He turned his head slightly and caught a glimpse of Senna, who glared at him with noticeable animosity. But the knight said nothing and stomped off to speak to Terias.

Turning his attention back to the princess, Yuri nodded. "How kind. Thank you," he said, noticing that the other members of his party were already beginning to mount their steeds. Archerus led two horses over, handing the reins of one over to Yuri. The boy gripped the leather reins in his hands and looked back at Violet. "I'd better get going. Like Kura said, every second counts."

"Best of luck on your quest, Yuri," the king of Horux said with a gentle nod. "Help us retake our kingdom."

"You need not worry, milord," Yuri said, striking his chest with a courageous soldier's salute, a respectful gesture that Asmund had taught him. "We shall not fail." He dug his heels into the side of his horse, starting the mare off at a slow trot as he moved through the gigantic gates of Reidan with his fellow adventurers.

"The princess has taken a liking to you then?" Terias said with a sly smirk, riding up beside Yuri, acknowledging the boy's new scarf. He gestured to Senna, who was conversing with Kura near the front of the group. "Senna seems a little jealous."

"He's always fancied her," Archerus said, mounted on Yuri's other side. "It's why he worked so hard to become her closest protector, I imagine. It's almost disheartening to see that Yuri has won her favor in only days when Senna's been trying for years." He snickered, accelerating to a gallop.

Terias whistled. "That's tough," he said, watching as the other warriors started to increase their speed as well. "Come on, let's go." He increased his speed to a canter and within moments was sprinting with the rest of the unit, moving as one.

Yuri cantered behind the squad, stealing a glance back through the gates of Reidan and locking his gaze with Violet's in the distance. Perhaps she couldn't see him, but he could certainly see her. Yuri touched the soft scarf around his neck, caressing the warm cloth gently. He sighed and dug his heels into the side of his steed, taking off after his friends.

***

Faelen stomped on the corpse of one of Moriaki's tree spirits, shattering the animated bark underneath his hairy feet. The triumphant beast snarled as he stormed over a sea of lacerated trunks and snapped branches. This was the seventh skirmish that he'd had with Moriaki's damned creatures. The druid had summoned rock golems and tree spirits to defend the forest outside of Horux, and they were becoming more than just a nuisance. Faelen had counted three dozen of his own werewolves killed by these weaklings.

He ground his teeth in annoyance, his eyes gleaming with rage. "How many of these accursed trees has Moriaki enchanted?" he barked, his claws quavering at his side. At this rate, the Iradian soldiers would arrive before the werewolves could enter Escalon's mainland. He would be trapped again, isolated and sealed away like a—

Faelen felt a gentle hand on his shoulder. He turned to find that Tanya was standing at his side, giving him a worried look. He felt his shoulders relaxing beneath her soft touch and his furor drifted away with the breeze. Why was it that she could calm him like this? His wrathful nature was a relentless tempest; it could be not tamed. Yet, just a gentle touch from her was enough to erase his frenzy and return his sanity. "Thank you," he grumbled.

"What's wrong?" Tanya asked. "You've been extremely angry about, well, nothing. We've defeated all the enemies that we've come across and we're well on our way to spreading the infection across Escalon."

"At the rate that we're pushing through Moriaki's magical barriers, we won't be able to leave the peninsula without running into an army of Iradian soldiers. The Druid of the North will go to the humans for help," Faelen said. "I'm just worried that I'll be locked away again. The very thought terrifies me, to have my freedom stripped away and be forced into a cage like … an animal." *But that's what I am, isn't it? An animal. An abomination feared by all.* He remembered what it was like to be stuck inside of Beo's catacombs, remembered the claustrophobic feeling of his throat tightening every time he looked at the solid walls around him. Sometimes he thought the room was closing on him and that one day he would be crushed. Most days, he wished that it would so that he wouldn't have to live such a purposeless existence behind silver bars. The moment his freedom was torn away, centuries ago, was also the moment that he'd lost his reasons for living.

"Then we will overcome them, as we will the rest of our enemies," Tanya said confidently.

"That is easier said than done," Faelen said. "The renowned druid, Moriaki, will stand with them. He'll be a formidable opponent and it will take time to defeat him, time that we may not have. If we do not defeat Moriaki quickly enough, Iradia will send reinforcements that will ensure that we never escape this peninsula. Then it's only a matter of deciding how they'll destroy us." He closed his eyes, exhaling from his nose. "They don't understand what it's like … to be caged away for centuries. My rage increased with every second that I spent in that confined hell and they will know my wrath. Perhaps alone, smashing through Iradia's ranks would be difficult. But with you by my side, Tanya, things may be different."

Tanya smiled at him. "Lord Faelen, things *will* be different."

"I can only hope so."

***

It took Zylon and his soldiers several days to reach the southern peninsula of Escalon. It would take a lot of manpower to cover the entrance to the mainland, manpower that they didn't have. Currently, Zylon had five hundred knights with him.

Against the thousands of werewolves that Faelen was probably commanding, they were vastly outnumbered. Not to mention that the beasts were already physically stronger. Zylon understood that he would have to make up for their disadvantages with his creation magic.

The knights had set up camp on the strip of land that connected the peninsula to the mainland of Escalon. Surrounding the land bridge was the endless ocean, extending as far as the eye could see. The encampment faced a forest of giant trees where the werewolves supposedly were, still battling through Moriaki's magical fortifications. Though the druid claimed that most of them had already been torn down.

Zylon crossed his arms over his chest, watching the peninsula. The werewolves could emerge from various parts of the forest, but eventually they would all have to converge on the land bridge where Zylon's forces were located. At least that meant that all of the beasts would be coming from one direction. As long as Zylon's army did not enter the forest, there was no threat of ambushes. All of the confrontations would be direct.

Zylon's main concern was how they would deal with all of the werewolves. The monsters would slam into the Iradian knights with tremendous force. Their numbers could overwhelm Zylon's soldiers within moments, and individual battles with the werewolves would surely end in the soldiers' demise.

"The last of my barriers were just torn down," Moriaki said tensely, stepping beside Zylon. The druid kept his eyes trained on the forest before him, stealing a glance back at the dauntless ranks of knights that were in formation behind him. None of them had ever seen a werewolf before; they had no idea what the vicious creatures were like. "What's our plan?"

"You and I are going to have to do the majority of the work here," Zylon said, scratching his nose. "If the werewolves manage to overwhelm our knights, we'll crumble within moments. I imagine that you won't have to be as careful as the rest of us, with your healing magic and immunity to the werewolf disease."

"Right," Moriaki said, understanding. "The knights will handle any stray beasts that aren't caught by our magic." He exhaled, feeling the ground rumbling underneath his feet. The werewolves were approaching. The druid gripped his staff tightly and held it out in front of him, pointing its tip towards the forest. "Reinforcements arrive in a week. Do you think we'll be able to hold out for so long? We can't just keep casting spells forever. We'll tire before help arrives."

"We have to hold out; we have no choice," Zylon said, watching as the dark monstrosities pounced from the trees. Countless beasts piled out of the forest, the frenzied creatures scampering towards Zylon's force with mindless rage burning in their eyes. The immortal had never seen a werewolf for himself, despite his centuries of existence, but they were just as he had imagined them. Whatever humanity they once had was now gone, replaced with pure bestial instinct. "Don't get bitten!" Zylon roared to the knights behind him, who courageously held their ground before the legion of monsters.

Glimmering energy surged into Zylon's palm as he forged a pistol made of the immortal's creation magic. The weapon was the color of fire, initially looking more like a toy than a gun. However, when he pointed and fired a bullet into the breast of an approaching werewolf, the knights all watched as the creature crumpled behind its fellow beasts, howling in pain.

Zylon swept his arms upward, materializing multiple walls that formed barriers between his force and the werewolves. He knew, however, that the werewolves could scale the walls with ease. Watching as the beasts clambered up the magical hurdles that Zylon set out, the experienced magician simply snapped his fingers and the walls came crashing down, squashing dozens of werewolves beneath their weight.

Moriaki's irises faded, and his eyes glowed as he summoned an enormous amount of power to animate the trees of the forest. The giant oaks groaned to life, lashing out with their massive branches, and snatching werewolves off the ground and hurling them into the earth. The bewildered beasts stared at the familiar enemy, now engaging in a battle with the forest as well.

The druid felt slightly sapped of energy after casting such a taxing spell, but he knew that there was no time to rest. Even with Zylon casting his creation magic, the werewolves were only being slowed. At this rate, they would still descend upon the small force of knights.

Moriaki sprinted forward, his body morphing into a massive rhino with three horns, one that was the size of an elephant. The charging beast surged forward with incredible speed, barreling into the front lines of the werewolves, sending the monsters scattering in all directions. The druid felt bones crunch underneath his feet as he trampled everything in his path, forcing his way into the heart of the werewolf army. He'd gotten the attention of most of the creatures and knew that now he would have to stand his ground.

The rhino then transformed into a polar bear of equal size, with fur the color of snow and sharp claws that could shred flesh from bone with ease. The ferocious bear roared as he brought his claws swiping about, mangling the werewolves around him.

The knights watched with shock as Moriaki bravely charged into battle. But soon they saw that there were hundreds of werewolves now advancing towards their position, avoiding Zylon's creation magic. "Shields up!" one of the commanders shouted. The first two lines of soldiers stacked their silver shields together, one atop another, to create an insurmountable wall.

The werewolves slammed into the shields, some of them roaring in agony as their skin was scorched by the silver. The knights jabbed their swords and pikes through the tiny gaps in the shield-wall, stabbing the wounded beasts.

Some of the creatures leapt over the shield wall and descended upon the force of prepared knights, who brought their weapons upward to fend off the monsters. Things were going according to plan, at least until *he* arrived.

***

Faelen sauntered onto the battlefield, his overwhelming presence stealing the attention of every living being in the area. His eyes flashed with malice as he trundled towards Moriaki, who was tearing apart his brethren. His eyes widened when he saw a flash of bright light break into his peripheral vision. As he tilted his head, a spear made of golden magic grazed his cheek.

"Zylon, the immortal," Faelen breathed, scowling as he spotted the man that had thrown the spear. He'd heard stories of the renowned hero. "You're here as well?" He turned his attention to the hundreds of knights guarding the land bridge that led to Escalon's mainland. Reinforcements were indeed here. Grinding his teeth in frustration, memories of confinement flashed through his worried mind. *Damn it, they're already here?*

Tanya smashed an animated tree into the ground, slamming her claws through the bark. The oak choked out a moan, its leaves withering and branches deteriorating as it died. The Bount stood up and rushed to Faelen's side, recognizing the distraught look on the werewolf's face. "It would seem that our opposition is stronger than expected. Their numbers are low, but the druid and magician are formidable opponents."

Faelen nodded, swallowing hard. "There is only one way to break through their defenses, and that is if you go ahead without me," he said, seeing the look of surprise on her face. "If I charge them, both Zylon and Moriaki will temporarily focus their attention on me. That is when you must rush through the land bridge. I imagine that you can bypass some lowly knights with

192

ease." He sighed. "It is only the druid and the immortal that we have to worry about."

"But then you'll be trapped here. You can't defeat the two of them alone—" Tanya began.

"They cannot defeat me either," Faelen said with a weary smile. "But if you go ahead and begin infecting the humans of Escalon, they'll have to turn their attention back to the mainland. I will be trapped on this peninsula, but only for a short time. Once you infect one village of humans, that will be enough to scare Iradia into withdrawing their troops from this peninsula. Then you'll travel north to Lichholme to search for the Oblivion Portal."

"Only one village? Are you sur—"

"I'm positive," Faelen said, stretching his body forward so that he dropped on all fours. "Do as I say. Now go!" the werewolf shot forward with inhuman speed, accelerating to a mere blur to the ordinary eye.

Just as Faelen had predicted, Zylon and Moriaki both turned their full attention to him. The druid morphed into a rhino as he rushed after the sprinting beast while Zylon materialized a wall right in front of Faelen in an attempt to slow him down.

"You aren't going anywhere, Faelen!" Zylon shouted, holding out his hand. Dozens of needles, made from green magic, sliced through the air straight towards the werewolf. "Escalon is under our protection!"

Faelen grunted as he slammed his feet into the dirt, sliding to an abrupt stop before the magical wall that Zylon had created. He brought his forearms upward, the sharp needles slamming into his flesh, stinging him slightly. Smirking, he knew that Moriaki was just about to impale him from behind in his rhino form. He spun around and grabbed the druid by his horns, the werewolf's muscles bulging as he swung the mighty beast straight into Zylon's wall, shattering it an instant.

Moriaki hit the ground, rolling to his feet, immediately transforming into an ebony panther. He gnarred, baring his sharp teeth.

"I know," Faelen said with a wild grin. "But she is."

Zylon saw something flicker across his peripheral vision. His eyes widened as he spun around, watching as a female werewolf sprinted with abnormal speed towards his battling knights. There was something about this creature that was different from the rest. It wasn't dashing forth wildly like the rest of the crazed beasts. It was clear that every movement was chosen as she avoided Zylon's obstacles. *No way....* "Stop her!" Zylon boomed, holding out his hand to materialize a cage around Tanya.

But Faelen was not going to let that happen. The Bount was already upon Zylon, slashing his claw through the air with a murderous look in his eyes. The immortal grunted, instinctively creating a shield to block the sudden attack. Faelen's blow struck Zylon's magical shield with unstoppable force, sending the man flipping backwards.

Zylon slammed onto his back, the wind driven from his lungs. He panted, relieved that his shield had absorbed a majority of Faelen's strike. Wincing at the aching pain that pounded in his arm, he saw that Moriaki was sprinting after the female werewolf as a cheetah. Behind him was Faelen, who was somehow moving even faster than the druid was. "No, you don't!" Zylon extended his hand, fabricating a purple chain that shot from his sleeve, constricting the werewolf's ankle.

Faelen's eyes widened as he was yanked to the ground, his pursuit of Moriaki abruptly halted. There was a powerful tug on his leg and the beast grunted, digging his claws into the dirt, realizing that Zylon was trying to yank him back.

Werewolves dashed at the immortal from various directions but Zylon moved with perfect reaction. He ducked, leapt, and dodged the various beasts that threw themselves at him. The ground was marked with footprints from the magician's boots, proof of his amazing footwork.

Zylon stomped into the ground, conjuring red spikes that scattered on the ground around him. The startled werewolves all halted their assault, surprised by the man's arcane magic. The immortal extended his arm, unleashing another chain that curled around one of Faelen's forearms.

The Bount winced, feeling the magical chain tighten around his bicep. The veins in his strained muscles bulged as he fought back against Zylon's jerking force. He clenched his jaw tightly, saliva pooling in his mouth. *He can't beat me in a contest of strength; he's just a human!*

Zylon pulled both of his arms backward, the glistening chains clanking from his sleeves. A smirk cracked across his lips as he snapped his fingers. Two gigantic mammoths materialized behind the mage, forged from his magic. Zylon's chains mystically slipped from his sleeves and floated to the colossal beasts, wrapping around their thick legs.

Faelen's eyes widened at the size of Zylon's summoned creatures. *So that is the power of creation.* The mammoths groaned as they trampled over dozens of werewolves, yanking Faelen behind them. The Bount grunted as he slid helplessly through the dirt, dragged by the gargantuan beasts that now dominated the battlefield. He slid past Zylon, who smiled.

Suddenly a sapphire-colored anchor materialized above Faelen and smashed down into the werewolf, creating an explosion that trembled the earth. The chains that were latched onto Faelen snapped and dust wildly swept through the area like a hurricane.

Conjuring an orange bow with a quiver of blue arrows, Zylon began to unleash volleys of projectiles on the waves of werewolves that still sprinted towards his force of fighting knights on the land bridge. His heart skipped a beat when he saw a silhouette rise from the smokescreen of dust beside him.

Before Zylon could even react, a heavy punch caught him in the jaw. The man's head snapped back and he tumbled back across the ground, his bow flying from his hands. He landed heavily on his back. There was hardly a moment for him to breathe before a werewolf pounced on him, prepared to take a bite out of the immortal.

Magic flowed from his chest, channeling through his forearm into his palm. A black dagger appeared in his hand and he gripped the handle tightly, thrusting the knife's blade into the side of the creature's neck. Knowing that wasn't enough to halt the inexorable monster, Zylon also created a blunderbuss in his other hand. He pressed the gun's barrel to the werewolf's gut and fired, spewing blood onto his cloak.

The immortal shoved the dead beast to the side and turned to find that Faelen was limping towards group of struggling Iradian knights. Zylon gritted his teeth and rose to his feet, extending his hand outward as he drafted an enormous amount of power. He summoned a gigantic spiked wall that slammed down before Faelen, sealing the werewolves away from the land bridge.

Faelen's eyes widened with rage as he froze, shocked at how tall and wide the wall was … it covered the entire land bridge. How was it possible for one to create such a massive structure? He turned and saw that Zylon was trembling, barely standing. Surely using so much magic in such a short time was taxing. Faelen was surprised that the man could still stand.

Zylon panted, sweat dripping down his face. He smirked victoriously, satisfied that he had stopped Faelen's advance. Though he wasn't sure how he would escape this situation alive. Now surrounded by countless hairy enemies, the lone magician faced impossible odds.

"No barrier can trap me forever, human," Faelen barked.

"Well, there's a first for everything." Zylon's hands balled into tight fists, and suddenly gigantic white gauntlets materialized on his hands. Pieces of magical metal began to form on the immortal's body, until he was completely encased in mystical armor. Two red swords appeared in his hands, the razor-sharp tips scraping the dirt.

Faelen scowled, his eyes narrowing as he watched his subordinate beasts charge the lone warrior. He was surprised by Zylon's prowess. He'd never seen such a talented human before. The man's expertise with various weapons seemed to exceed that of a majority of skilled warriors. Zylon's knowledge and experience in combat was certainly unmatched by any living being, as could be expected of a man that has lived through centuries of chaotic war.

The magician was clearly growing tired, after using so much magic. His movements were becoming sluggish, and his attacks weakened with each beast he struck down. While he could still hold his own against the myriad of werewolves that encased him, Faelen knew that he could easily smash through the immortal's defenses. "You're impressive." The Bount launched himself forward, his body a mere blur as he raced towards the unprepared mage. He rotated his body and swung his fist straight into the side of Zylon's helmet. The man's head snapped to the side and his body twisted as he spun through the air, smashing into the dirt like a lifeless doll. "But you're still only human."

The armor dissipated, and all that was left on the ground was the broken body of Zylon.

Faelen stood before the unmoving immortal, his jaws clenched in frustration. It truly was a remarkable feat to bring down the infamous Zylon, but he didn't intend to kill the defenseless man. He had other plans. The werewolf reached down and grabbed his unconscious opponent, slinging the limp body over his shoulder. Shrugging, he began to trudge back towards the woods. Remaining confined to the peninsula was the last thing that he wanted, but he knew that letting Tanya go ahead was the best course of action. Glancing over his shoulder at the massive wall that Zylon had created, he let out a deep sigh. Bypassing such an obstacle would be difficult unless the immortal deactivated the magic himself. Luckily for Faelen, he was good at forcing a man's hand.

***

Tanya rushed towards the army of knights that lay between her and freedom. The warriors were all preoccupied with dealing with the werewolves that had broken through their ranks. But soon their attention would turn to her, the true threat.

The Bount leapt gracefully over the wall of silver shields that the knights had formed to halt her. The soldiers stared incredulously as she landed on the other side of the wall, wielding her chain whip. They didn't know that werewolves were capable of wielding weapons.

Tanya swung her whip back, the blade slicing through the armor of every knight in the front lines. Their agonizing screams created a cacophony of wails as the warriors collapsed, dismembered and hemorrhaging blood from fatal wounds. The shield wall collapsed along with them, the protective pieces clattering to the ground.

Surging forward elegantly, Tanya weaved her way around the soldiers. Her chain whip carved a perfect path for her, for it was powerful enough to shred the armor of the warriors. Zylon's men were incapable of dodging Tanya's attacks, for her blades cut through the air with blinding speed. Even if they could see her weapon, it wasn't physically possible for them to avoid its path.

Tanya heard a loud boom behind her that sounded like an explosion. Stealing a glance over her shoulder, her eyes widened when she saw that a massive black wall, fabricated from Zylon's magic, had sealed off the entire land bridge. It was so tall that even werewolves would have trouble climbing it. Her heart thumped, realizing that Faelen truly would be confined to Horux's peninsula. Biting her lower lip, she knew that Faelen was depending on her to get to Escalon's mainland. She would not let him down, not after he'd granted her this incredible power.

Tearing her way through the army of Iradian knights, Tanya finally smashed through the final ranks and dashed freely onto the mainland. Her heart raced; she'd done it!

Looking once more over her shoulder, Tanya saw that the druid was no longer pursuing her. Most likely, he had to help the wounded knights eradicate the rest of the werewolves. It was probably best if Tanya put as much distance between her and the elf as possible. Tucking her chain whip into her cloak, she sprinted onto a field of grass, her unwavering gaze trained forward.

The Awakening Dead

Days of vigorous traveling made Yuri feel like his body was falling apart. Every bone in his body ached. He didn't understand how the horses were still able to move, since even he felt fatigued, just from riding them. They would travel for about fifteen hours a day, and spend the rest of the time setting up camp, eating, or sleeping. Kura's travel plan was grueling, exhausting even her experienced comrades. Nevertheless, no one opened their mouths to complain, so Yuri kept his shut.

The landscape consisted mostly of hills and fields until they reached Northern Escalon, approaching Lichholme. The weather became chillier as they moved north, and the grasslands were now covered in a thin layer of snow. There were not many trees around. The terrain became mountainous, with boulders scattered throughout the land. The party had gradually traveled into high elevation when they finally reached the giant glacier that marked the entrance to Lichholme.

Yuri rubbed his aching back as he dismounted, his boots sinking into the snow as he looked up in awe at the towering cliffs of ice looming over the small party of warriors. Scaling the massive glacier was impossible, but it seemed that they wouldn't need to. As Kura had said, there was indeed a gaping rip in the glacier that cut a clear path into Lichholme.

The boy watched as his comrades began to trudge through the snow, making their way towards the giant passageway. He swallowed hard, suddenly recognizing the glacier. He had been here before in his second dream with Malyios; this was where he had fallen into an abyss of darkness. Yuri looked to the top of the icy cliffs, licking his lower lip nervously. That was where the Titan had pushed him into an army of undead.

It didn't look like there were any undead abominations in the passageway ahead, but Yuri couldn't be too sure from this distance. He returned to reality when Terias tapped his shoulder. The knight had a swollen eye since he spent each night training with Senna, using every free opportunity to try and better himself in the art of fighting. Terias always emerged from his sparring lessons with more than a couple of bruises, but he never complained. He seemed euphoric ever since he'd become a knight-in-training. "Archerus saw someone pursuing us. Looks like it's the princess," Terias said.

Yuri turned and spotted Princess Violet behind them on horseback, clearly exhausted from the long journey. Nevertheless, she was galloping at a rapid pace, swiftly moving across the snowy lands. He let out a sigh of relief, glad that Violet had managed to follow them all this way. He'd had his doubts about whether or not she'd be able to keep up with their ridiculous pace, but it seemed that she was tougher than he gave her credit for.

"What the hell is the damned princess doing here? This is not a quest for fragile damsels!" Kura growled, her irritated scowl showing her clear disrespect for the princess. "Tassan, Oma, the two of you will escort her ba—"

"I don't think that will be necessary," Yuri said, feeling a wave of unease tremble through his body as Kura darted him an irate glare. But he gulped back his perturbment and continued. "We're going to need every member of our group for this journey. Lichholme is dangerous. We can't afford to sacrifice two of us just to escort Princess Violet back."

Kura raised her eyebrows, putting her hands on her hips. "I don't give a crap! She'll hold us back and get us all killed. Weak links in the group should be severed," she said, stealing a glance in Terias's direction. The trainee slunk behind Senna, clearly understanding that he still had a lot of room for improvement.

"I can't help but agree with Yuri on this one," Noah said, watching as Princess Violet slowed to a canter, approaching the group. "We have the resources to include another person, and we are already low on manpower as it is. Taking the princess in may be the better option."

Kura's right-hand man, Tassan, raised his hand. "What if we just leave her behind?" he suggested.

"Who knows whether or not she would be able to make it all the way back to Reidan. It's a miracle that she managed to follow us all this way without running into any danger," Noah said. "Not to mention, she may not have the supplies for the return trip. Turning her away would be the same as condemning the princess to her demise. I don't think King Reimos would approve of such a decision."

Kura narrowed her eyes and groaned, rubbing her palm against her forehead. Turning away, she spat into the snow as she tramped towards the passageway into the glacier. "Fine, she can stay. But she won't get any special treatment just because of her title. In the wilderness, royalty means nothing."

"Understood." Noah nodded, adjusting his glasses with a gentle poke to his lenses.

Yuri exhaled. *Nice save, Noah.* He turned and saw that some of the warriors were helping Violet off her horse.

She had heavy bags under her eyes, and her arms drooped weakly as she stumbled off her mount, wearily smiling at Yuri. "Made it," she breathed out, her voice barely more than a whisper.

"Don't worry, you just have to push a little further." Yuri nodded to the glacier. "Once we get into Lichholme, I think we'll set up camp. You can rest then."

Violet noticed that the rest of the group had started moving towards the glacier's giant fissure. She shivered slightly, not from the cold weather but because of the ominous feeling emanating from the passageway. "That's the entrance to Lichholme?" she murmured to Yuri, a wisp of mist drifting from her lips as she spoke. "There's something eerie about it."

"It would seem it's the only way," Yuri said, seeing the look of disconcertion on her face. He wanted to say something to comfort her, to affirm that there was no danger ahead. But he couldn't. He could sense something menacing about the atmosphere and the air stank of the familiar scent of fresh corpses. He saw that Archerus also felt uneasy, but the two werewolves kept their feelings to themselves as they moved forward.

Finally out of the snow, the group now walked into the ice canyon. Yuri saw that Kura's warriors were all concerned about the possibility of an ambush. They were all looking up, scanning the cliffs for any signs of an enemy. But all they saw was the dark cloudy skies, blotting out the sun's rays.

It was as painfully silent as Horux's forest. He recalled when he and Asmund had journeyed outside of the city to search for the entrance to the underground catacombs. Yuri felt just as he did then, like someone was watching them. Except this time, there was a tingling sensation in his body. He could tell that there was *something* in this gorge, but he didn't know what.

"Weapons out," Archerus commanded and everyone in the party brandished their swords in unison, looking around for their enemy in confusion. "There's something here."

"I don't see anything," Senna said.

"Neither do I," Kura murmured, whirling her short-sword.

Yuri heard it now, the sound of a piece of ice crunching underneath the boot of someone's foot. *Above.* He glanced upward and saw a blurred figure rushing down at Kura with blinding speed. The boy sprinted forward, putting himself between Kura and the attacker, ripping his sword upwards. There was a hard clang that echoed through the canyon as Yuri parried a powerful blow from the assailant's rapier.

The cloaked attacker was a middle-aged woman with skin as white as snow. Her eyes, orange as blazing flames, flashed with surprise when she saw that Yuri had managed to block her strike. Amusement crossed her face as the assassin disengaged, flipping backwards. Landing several meters away, she licked her blood-red lips, revealing pointed fangs. "My, my, it's been far too long since I've seen one of your kind," she said, gazing at Yuri lustfully. She smirked at Archerus. "Two werewolves and a dozen humans, what a pleasant surprise. What are you lot doing so far from home?"

"Werewolves?" Senna said, staring at Yuri in shock. He scowled angrily. "You lied—"

"Can we save this for later?" Archerus grumbled, darting the knight an irritated glare. "Yuri and I are not a threat to you. If we were, you would all be infected by now, wouldn't you? So shut up and focus on the real enemy." He pointed the tip of his sword at the cloaked assailant. "The vampire."

"Vampire?" Kura's grip on the hilt of her sword tightened.

The vampire shrugged, lowering her steel rapier. "I can't defeat two werewolves on my own, so I'll be on my way," she said with a chuckle, nodding to Yuri. "You, what is your name?"

"Yuri."

"And I am Malyssa," the pale lady said with a respectful bow to the werewolf. A broad grin crept across her lips and she snapped her fingers. "If you do survive here, Yuri, I look forward to crossing paths with you again. Few have ever blocked a strike from me. I'm impressed. You're very quick." She tilted her head to the side, acknowledging the rest of Yuri's companions. "As for the rest of you, I doubt that you have what it takes to survive in the harsh wasteland of Lichholme. That is, if you even make it through this gorge. Enjoy yourselves."

Yuri could feel the ice underneath his feet beginning to rumble, with minor tremors that soon turned into a thundering earthquake. The pungent scent of decaying flesh suddenly filled his nostrils, making his stomach heave. He gasped, feeling sick as he collapsed onto his knees.

"Yuri, what's wrong?" Terias exclaimed, as he and Violet quickly rushed to the boy's side.

"We're in trouble," Archerus grumbled, scrunching up his nose.

Malyssa let out a wicked cackle as she slammed her feet into the ground, propelling herself hundreds of feet into air, leaping out of the canyon and landing on one of the cliffs. She glanced down at Yuri and licked her lower lip slowly, thinking about how delicious the werewolf's blood would taste. "Until next time." She vanished from view.

Yuri grunted, forcing himself onto his feet. Wincing at the powerful miasma, he pointed forward. "We need to run, now!" he growled, just as the ground began to crack. Monstrosities began to tear their way through the icy floor, dragging themselves into the glacier's gorge. The creatures had putrefied flesh attached to bone, with green pus spewing from the bloody boils on their faces. They had no eyes — only empty sockets that stared blankly at Yuri's party. Letting out horrific screeches, the undead hobbled forward. What started as an irregular limp soon turned into a frantic sprint as the horde of zombies surged towards the shocked group of warriors.

Archerus did not hesitate to transform into a werewolf, his body shifting in an instant. Kura's companions yelped in surprise at his physical alteration, but were relieved when they saw the beast pounce onto a group of undead instead of them. "Get moving!" he barked.

Everyone stood frozen with fear as the swarm of monstrosities rushed at them. Violet could sense the panic that now took hold in the warriors' minds as they stared at the ghastly creatures. Even Kura's feet were rooted to the ground as she stood there gaping at their army of opponents. Never before had she seen such atrocious beings.

Violet reached out and grabbed Kura by her wrist, squeezing the assassin until her skin stung. The female warrior blinked, her sense returning to her eyes. "We can't stay here!" Violet shouted, the words registering in the warrior's mind. "You're the leader, right? Stop panicking and take control of the situation!"

Kura licked her lower lip nervously and exhaled shakily, her hands quivering at her side. Resolution suddenly swept over her visage and she struck her chest, the group's brave warrior returning to command. "Archerus can only buy us so much time. We're retreating, follow me!"

The adventurers rushed behind Kura, their brandished weapons smashing into whatever undead creatures lay in their path. The monsters were not particularly hard to slay; it was their numbers that made them dangerous. The zombies continued to crawl out of the gaping holes in the canyon's floor, soon filling the gorge with a myriad of abominations.

Yuri ripped his sword sideways, catching one of the creatures in the throat. His blade cut through the foul monster's putrid flesh with ease, decapitating it with a swift motion. The boy's heart raced, his weapon hacking wildly into the swarm of undead. He thought about the moment when he had lost control in Horux's warehouse and had brutally slaughtered dozens of werewolves. Glancing over his shoulder, he watched as one of the monstrosities pounced on Kura's friend, Oma. The woman was pinned to the ground, screaming in agony as the undead creature tore open her breast with its claws. *I need to do something.* His clammy hands squeezed the hilt of his silver sword. *The power to save everyone is within my grasp. I can't be afraid of it ... more importantly, I can't be afraid of what I've become.*

"Noah, clear a path!" Yuri shouted to the magician.

Noah nodded and extended his hand outward, creating a herd of elephants, fabricated from blue magical essence. The triumphant beasts stampeded forward, trampling all of the undead creatures in their wake. The magician nearly fell over, exhausted after casting such a massive spell, but was caught and supported by Violet. Letting out an exasperated sigh of relief, Noah smiled at the princess. "Thanks."

"Go while it's clear!" Kura shouted, swiping her short sword across the breast of a monster. She swung her other arm outward, hurling three shuriken that buried into the forehead of another abomination.

The battling warriors hacked their way through the remainder of the undead ranks, sprinting through the open area that Noah had cleared. Nevertheless, the living corpses kept prying themselves out of the ground, crawling and sprinting after the group.

Yuri sheathed his sword and closed his eyes, recalling his memory with Asmund. Watching powerlessly as his friend perished before his eyes, untamed rage built within him. His turquoise eyes changed into those of a beastly monster and his body contorted into that of a ferocious werewolf. Letting out a bellowing roar, he burst forward and rent bodies apart with his sharp claws. Dismembered limbs flew through the air as Yuri entered a state of bloodlust, swiping and slashing the undead creatures relentlessly. It was an elating sensation ... to butcher these abominations, to feel so powerful.

Terias stared at Yuri, watching as the beast slaughtered the creatures with ease. He gulped, continuing on with the group, leaving the werewolf to his massacre. The undead were all being drawn towards Yuri and Archerus, allowing the contingent to escape.

"We're almost there!" Senna yelled, cleaving his broadsword across the torso of a creature. The knight rushed to Noah's other side, wrapping the boy's arm around his shoulder to help Violet support the magician. "I can see the other side!"

Gunshots sounded as bullets whizzed around Yuri, slamming into the undead. The werewolf grabbed one zombie by the face and squashed its skull into the icy cliffs. Fetid liquids oozed from its crushed head as the werewolf let the cadaver crumple to the ground.

Adrenaline surged through his veins and he felt as if he could fight these unholy abominations forever. Part of him wanted to stay and continue mutilating the undead until all that remained were mounds of body parts. But he knew where he had to be, and that was with his friends.

Yuri scampered after the group of fleeing warriors, knocking away any monsters in his way. To him, they were nothing but crushable bugs. There were just so many of them. Why were there so many corpses inside of this glacier? He clenched his fangs irately, remembering the vampire. How had Malyssa been able to summon so many undead?

Yuri leapt out of the gorge, landing hard on a layer of solid ice. He slipped slightly, nearly losing his balance, and turned to find that he was standing on a massive wasteland of flat ice. It was as if an entire ocean had just been frozen over. His throat tightened when he saw that beneath the frigid layers of ice were pale corpses, entrapped. *More bodies?*

"Yuri's out, that's all of us," Archerus said, looking to Noah. "Can you seal the gorge?"

"Yeah. It'll take the rest of my energy, though."

"Do it."

"What do you mean? We're missing three people, at least!" Kura exclaimed, storming up to the werewolf. Fearlessly, she jabbed her finger into the beast's chest. "I'm not leaving without my warriors. They'll come."

Archerus met the assassin's gaze with his own unsympathetic visage. "Seal it," he commanded Noah, his eyes still on Kura. "Unless you want to battle that horde of undead storming onto this unstable ice."

"Don't do it!" Kura barked to the conflicted magician. "My men are still—"

"They're dead!" Archerus roared, his voice even more ferocious in his werewolf form. Towering over Kura, the female leader slunk back in the shadow of the monster. "And we will be too if we don't seal that canyon now!" Already dozens of undead monstrosities had begun to pile out of the glacier's entrance, sprinting wildly towards the group of survivors.

Yuri watched as some of the ice started to crack underneath the feet of the oncoming horde of zombies. The fracture then started to split throughout the ice-covered surface, spreading uncontrollably until it seemed like the entire frozen lake would shatter. "You have to seal it!" Yuri exclaimed to the magician.

Noah nodded in understanding, realizing the direness of the situation. He brought his hands upward, forging an image of a gigantic wall in his mind. Then he made it a reality. The magician conjured a magical blue wall that sealed the entire entrance to the gorge. Groaning, he fell onto his knees, his skin blanching white. He looked sick, as if he were about to vomit. "Ugh ... maybe I pushed myself a bit too far today."

Bullets and arrows sliced through the air as the remainder of Kura's force unleashed hell on the small force of undead that had squeezed through the canyon's entrance prior to Noah's conjuring of the wall. The volley of projectiles pounded into the front lines of the frantically sprinting zombies, causing them to fall over and smash heavily into the ice. Some of them lost their footing and ended up sliding across the slippery surface while others simply fell through the cracks of the unstable ice, dropping into the freezing waters.

Within minutes, Yuri's party had eradicated the remainder of the undead force and stood in silence, staring blankly at the monstrosities that they had just battled. Yuri breathed shakily. He'd thought that such abominations existed only within his darkest nightmares. Yet he'd just battled a legion of them. "This place really is hell," he murmured aloud.

The boy turned and saw Kura advancing towards Noah, who was barely conscious. The assassin's gaze was fiery. From her expression, one might assume that she was about to murder the exhausted magician. "How dare you disobey *my orders?* I am leading this expedition!" she snarled angrily, her hand moving towards her sheathed short-sword.

Senna was suddenly behind her and quickly grabbed her wrist, halting the woman before she could brandish her weapon. "There is no need for violence. The boy is not your enemy."

"What about these werewolves?" Kura growled, shooting a glance towards Yuri and Archerus. "The two of you might've wanted to mention that you were infectious beasts when you decided to come on this quest! That might've been good information to know."

"It only would've complicated things," Archerus said, his face stern.

"You lied to us because you thought it would *complicate* things?" Senna spat, taking a step towards the werewolf. He winced when his metallic boots cracked the ice beneath him.

"We are not a threat to you," Yuri said, morphing back into his human form. He held out his hands, showing that he was not the same as the uncontrollable beasts that Senna remembered in Horux. "The two of us have already ingested the Phoenix Heart, giving us control over our werewolf bodies. Haven't we already demonstrated to you that we are your allies? Without Archerus and I, none of you would've survived in the gorge." He knew that he sounded like a jerk, insisting that the werewolves had been the ones to save the day. But it was true, and the rest of the group knew it.

"I trust them," Violet said and suddenly all eyes were on her. "If they had ill intentions, they could've just infected everyone in Reidan while they were there. But they didn't. Archerus and Yuri have had plenty of chances to spread their infection or kill all of us, but they haven't." She looked to Yuri and gave the boy a friendly smile. "The werewolves we saw in Horux were just as mindless and brutal as the undead we just battled. But Yuri and Archerus are completely different. They're as human as we are."

"I trust them too," Terias murmured, his arms folded over his chest. When Senna glared at him, he shrugged. "It's clear that without them, we would've died in the gorge. Noah cleared a path for us, but we never would've been able to escape without the werewolves' help." He raised an eyebrow at his mentor. "We have other enemies to worry about. Lichholme is a dangerous place."

Senna stared at his apprentice for a long moment and then nodded hesitantly. Even Kura had to agree, though she was grumbling swears to herself. "But there are no more lies," Kura growled to everyone. "I don't have time to think about whether or not my companions are trustworthy."

"That's right. You'll encounter countless formidable opponents along your adventure," a familiar voice hollered.

Yuri turned and saw that Malyssa was standing at the top of the glacier, looking down at the adventurers. The vampire had a sadistic grin on her face, as if she'd enjoyed watching them battle for their lives within that ice canyon. "But your journey has only just begun, hasn't it?" she said, folding her arms. Then her eyes flashed a slightly brighter shade of red. Yuri had noticed it before when they were in gorge, just before she'd summoned the horde of undead. Did that mean—

"Vampires have an innate ability that allows them to control certain individuals with weak minds," Archerus murmured, staring at the massive glacier that towered over them. His eyes narrowed and began to slowly take steps backward. "Things are not looking good for us."

Yuri understood why Archerus was beginning to panic. The ground was quaking, just as it had when the zombies had awakened. However, this time it felt like a real earthquake, as if the ground itself were alive. Fear shot through him as he saw the cracks in the ice deepening. He watched with horror as a massive hand tore itself from the icy floor, shattering the frozen lake like glass.

The hand grabbed onto Kura's right-hand man, Tassan, and squeezed him tightly. The warrior shrieked with surprise, fear and shock on his face as he was pulled downwards into the depths of the frigid lake. Freezing water splashed onto the cracking ice, which was now beginning to give way.

Yuri heard Kura's anguished cry of sorrow at the sight of her friend's demise. The rest of his comrades broke into a mad dash across the frozen lake, fearful of the creature underneath the surface. But Yuri stood frozen in his tracks, the image of the enormous hand still burned freshly into his mind. The size of that hand had been colossal … as if it belonged to a Titan.

The werewolf's eyes widened when he heard the icy ground explode behind him, feeling sprinkles of freezing water bite at his neck. He gulped back his fear and spun around to find a frost giant, the size of the glacier itself, towering over him.

The creature looked like a monster from mythology, with a long beard made of sharp icicles that dangled down to its large belly. Its skin was pale as snow, and its eyes were large gems that glowed an icy blue. Black antlers that looked like they belonged to a deer protruded from the top of the giant's head. In its left hand, the frost giant held the frozen body of Tassan. In its right hand was a massive spiked club made entirely of crystallized ice.

Oh gods. Yuri swore under his breath as the monster raised the weapon over its head. He quickly transformed into a werewolf and spun around, dashing away. Lichholme was truly one of the most dangerous places in Terrador.

Native

Yuri was thrown high into the air, his arms flailing wildly, as the frost giant brought its club smashing down onto the frozen lake. The icy surface exploded, sending ice, snow, and water spraying in all directions. The werewolf screamed as some of the freezing water burned his skin as if it were acid. Every droplet that touched him felt like molten lava.

His landing was less than graceful as he landed painfully on his arm, rolling and sliding uncontrollably across the fractured ice. Terrified that the floor would give way beneath him, he quickly scrambled to his feet and continued fleeing.

It was easy for Yuri to predict the giant's attacks since its movements were so sluggish. But each time that the creature struck the ice, it dealt devastating damage to the lake's surface. If all of the ice was annihilated, Yuri would fall into the sub-zero water and perish within seconds. Remembering the floating corpses trapped in those waters caused him to shiver. He increased his speed, sprinting as fast as he could in a poor attempt to escape the giant's enormous reach.

Several of the knights had fallen through the ice and into the water. Yuri saw one man was flailing about for a moment, but his clanking armor weighed him down and he quickly sank to his doom. The man probably froze to death before he could drown.

Yuri saw that Archerus was carrying Noah on his back. The magician was unconscious, completely taxed after having used up so much of his energy to conjure magic. The boy winced, realizing that the frost giant was wading through the water towards the group of fleeing adventures. They weren't moving away fast enough — at this rate, the creature would surely catch up and kill them all.

Skidding to a stop, the werewolf turned to face the frost giant. *I have to buy the group time.* Licking his lower lip, he exhaled a wisp of chilly mist as he scanned the creature for its weak points. Everything about the giant seemed impenetrable; did this thing even have a weakness?

The goliath swung its spiked club downward once more and Yuri dodged to the side, grunting as he slid away from the crumbling ice. He was certainly running out of places to land, and avoiding the monstrosity's brutal attacks was a lot harder with less available space.

Yuri suddenly caught sight of the gleaming crystal eyes of the giant. Maybe those could be shattered, but reaching them was nearly impossible. Then the werewolf looked at the club, feeling his heart beginning to race at the idiotic idea that flashed into his mind. Unfortunately, it was the only plan that he had. "Desperation at its finest," he said, taunting the creature by waving his hands in front of him. "Hey, fat-ass! How is it that you keep missing me? Come on, finish the job!" *Can this thing even understand me?*

Malyssa, sitting on top of the glacier, raised her eyebrows in surprise at the boy's bold actions. Intrigued, she leaned forward, gazing at Yuri with profound interest. "How exciting," she said, licking her lower lip. For anyone to bravely confront the giant directly was an unexpected turn of events.

Yuri yelped as the club smashed into the ice several feet from his position. The ice beneath the werewolf collapsed but he'd already lashed outward and grabbed onto two of the spikes on the giant's weapon. Luckily for him, the creature pulled his club from the water before it sank too deep. Yuri's legs, however, had been temporarily dipped in the freezing water and were now trembling. He couldn't feel or move his legs anymore after only a brief moment of being in the water. Gritting his teeth, he watched as the giant pulled the club up near his head, as if to examine his weapon. With its other hand, it dropped Tassan's corpse into the lake and reached for Yuri.

A smile of victory split across Yuri's lips. *Good thing you're an idiot.* Using the remainder of the strength in his arms, he launched himself upward through the gaps between the giant's massive fingers and landed on the monster's face. His claws lashed out, grabbing the glowing crystal eyes of the giant. A howl of agony escaped the creature, but Yuri wasn't done yet. Heaving back, the werewolf yanked the icy spheres straight out of the goliath's sockets, gripping one in each hand. *I did it! I—*

Yuri saw a shadow suddenly looming over him, and grunted when he saw that the giant's palm was coming to squash him. Yelping in panic, he released his grip on the creature's face and fell. His eyes widened when he saw that there was no ice underneath him ... only the bitter-cold waters of the lake. His mouth opened slightly to scream in terror in the face of death. But he stopped himself and instead closed his eyes, bracing himself for what was to come.

Smashing through the chilly waters, the werewolf immediately felt every joint in his body freezing entirely. Within a second, he couldn't move. It felt as if he had been dropped into a scorching furnace, for every inch of his skin was burning. The pain was immeasurable, worse than any agony Yuri had ever endured. Then came numbness, sweeping over his mind and overcoming all his senses. He stared blankly at the sea of corpses that drifted underneath the water. Blackness coated the perimeter of Yuri's vision, but he could swear that all of the bodies trapped underwater ... they were alive.

And then came darkness.

***

Violet watched with horror as Yuri plummeted into the lake, disappearing beneath the surface. She knew that he'd frozen to death. The frost giant was still alive after Yuri's courageous act, but was clearly drastically injured. The massive creature groped at his face in a futile attempt to find his crystallized eyeballs, roaring in dismay.

"Who are they?" Terias called out, turning and pointing to a group of pale humanoids that were skating across the ice on sleds pulled by reindeer.

The newcomers had dark-blue hair and glowing eyes that were similar in nature to the frost giant. Their cerulean attire was fabricated from cloth, most of them wearing skimpy outfits despite the unforgiving weather. Leather pauldrons layered with white wolf fur covered their shoulders. There were dozens of these native warriors, wielding bows and axes that looked like they were made from ice, just like the frost giant's club.

The animals that pulled their sleds weren't ordinary beasts either. Their eyes also glowed like glistening crystals. Their coats were the color of the snow, with stripes of icy blue streaking down their fur. Massive antlers protruded from the creatures' heads as they snorted, galloping across the ice with ease. Somehow, despite their hooves, they did not slip, nor did the ice crack beneath them.

"Are they on our side?" Kura said curiously, halting to watch the warriors as they engaged the blinded frost giant. The rest of the group also stopped, turning to witness the combat.

The natives unleashed volley after volley of ice arrows upon the giant, assaulting the monstrosity with waves of needle-like projectiles that somehow pierced its tough skin. One of the natives reached down into the sled and pulled out a massive harpoon gun and fired it straight into the knee of the frost giant. The creature bellowed in excruciating pain.

Other ice warriors also revealed harpoon guns and fired more projectiles, which stayed lodged in the creature's legs.

Attached to the ends of the harpoons were glistening wires that were so slim that they were barely visible. The natives attached their wires to their sleds and steered their white reindeer towards Violet and her group, riding at full speed. The combined force of all the sleds yanked the frost giant's legs out from underneath him, causing the colossal monster to fall backwards. The creature let out a boisterous cry as it smashed into the lake, sinking beneath the surface.

The victorious hunters detached the wires from their sleds with swift slashes of their axes. Dismounting their sleds, several natives with thick ropes wrapped around their shoulders walked casually towards the freezing water. One person tied the rope around their waist and handed the other end to their partner, who planted their feet firmly on the ice. They seemed rather confident that the floor wouldn't collapse beneath them.

"Are they going into the water?" Terias said, puzzled.

"Maybe they're immune to the cold. That frost giant sure is, since it was sleeping in there when it attacked us," Archerus murmured. "Even if they are immune, it isn't safe to go into the water. That giant is still alive, the water won't do anything to him."

"The Lake of Eternity freezes all, even that giant," a female warrior called as she walked toward them. Unlike the rest of her comrades, she was wearing a dress that looked like it was fabricated from ice. Nevertheless, Violet knew that the attire was made from the same material as the frost giant's club. The clothing was far from delicate.

The woman had her hair tied back into a bun. Her lips were as blue as the lake's chilling waters, and they curved into a polite smile as she approached Violet's party, bowing respectfully before them. "I am Lady Amara. They call me the Frost Mistress," she said, tapping her thumbs together. "I haven't seen a live human in Lichholme in quite a while."

Archerus stared sorrowfully at the glistening waters of the Lake of Eternity, biting his lower lip softly. "Why are your people diving into the water?"

"We are saving your companions."

Violet's eyes widened, newfound hope surging through her. "Y-You mean, there's a possibility that everyone that fell in is still...."

"Alive? Yes," Lady Amara said. "The Lake of Eternity does not kill its victims. It is enchanted so that anyone who falls in will freeze, but they will not die. Instead, they are eternally frozen beneath the icy surface of the lake, forever condemned to suffer in the frigid waters."

"So all of those people in the lake...."

"They're alive. Though they could be undead, which is why you have to be careful about who you decide to save," the Frost Mistress said, turning to see that two of the natives had collectively pulled a young man out of the water. She smiled wearily. "That werewolf, he is brave. Especially if he committed such a bold act without knowing of the Lake of Eternity's true nature."

Something caused Violet to sprint forward, even though she knew that the ice was unstable. Before she knew what was happening, she had rushed to Yuri's side as the boy lay on the ground, his face pale as snow. The princess reached out and touched his neck for his pulse, shivering at how cold his skin was. But by some miracle, he was still alive.

Warm tears glistened in her eyes and Violet fell forward, pressing her cheek to his chest, overwhelmed with joy. For the second time in only weeks, she'd thought he died. "Stop scaring me like that," she whispered.

Archerus sighed with relief when Violet waved excitedly to the group. "Thank the gods."

"Yes!" Terias exclaimed, pumping his fist.

Senna simply closed his eyes and smiled. But he said nothing.

Kura watched as Lady Amara's men dragged her frozen knights from the lake's waters. "What of the giant? Surely the creature was not felled."

"That giant was sealed underneath the lake by a legendary necromancer named Alice," Lady Amara explained. "As I said, any being that falls into the Lake of Eternity will freeze forever. The only way that one could escape is if they are physically pulled out … or if powerful magic is involved." The Frost Mistress glanced over her shoulder at the glacier, but there was nothing there. She scowled. "The presence of the vampire, Malyssa, lingers around this area. I expect this is her doing."

"It was her," Kura growled angrily. "That accursed wench is the reason half of my men are dead."

"Perhaps you can explain your situation at my fortress," Lady Amara said with a friendly smile. "You all look like you could do with some rest." She nodded towards Noah, who was still unconscious on Archerus's back. "Especially that one; his magical pool is nearly empty."

Kura looked between all of her companions and saw their elated gazes, ecstatic about the idea of resting. Even Senna looked joyful for once. The leader rolled her eyes and nodded. "We appreciate your kindness and assistance, Lady Amara. Please, lead the way."

***

Zylon groaned, his head hanging limply. His body was marked with bruises from Faelen's relentless beating. He had been knocked unconscious every other day for an entire week, but he knew that the werewolf was still holding back. The Bount could've torn off his limbs if he wanted, but he never did. Every day, Faelen marched into the chambers demanding that Zylon bring down the magical wall that blocked off the peninsula from the rest of Escalon. But the immortal never complied, and so he was punished.

Blood dribbled from his lips into a pool at his feet. Zylon's arms were chained to the ceiling, his hands hanging limply in the air. Both of the immortal's eyes were so swollen that he could barely see past his inflamed flesh. But he could see the mutilated corpse at his feet. The body belonged to a man named Beo, according to Faelen. Beo had supposedly been Faelen's previous jailor, and death was his punishment. Now that Zylon was the warden, having entrapped most of the werewolf population within Escalon's southern peninsula, he wondered what his penalty would be. After all, what was worse than death?

There was a loud creak on the far side of the prison corridor, and Zylon could see Faelen approaching. However, today the werewolf did not seem as wrathful or furious as he had in previous days. He was not storming about and slamming doors like an irate child. Today, he seemed composed.

He was dressed in the black cloak of the Bounts, recognizable attire that made the immortal tremble. Zylon hadn't known that the Bount organization was involved in this werewolf affair, but now that he thought about it, it made sense that they would be. With Faelen on their side, the Bounts could obtain influence and control over the entirety of Escalon, if the werewolves managed to get to the mainland to spread their infection.

Faelen's eyes reflected an emotionless gaze as he watched Zylon's broken body through the iron bars of the cell. But the werewolf did not enter the chamber. He stood outside the cell, his arms folded over his chest. "How long do you think you can keep this up, old man?" he said. "Do you enjoy pain?"

"It's like you said," Zylon wheezed with a raspy chuckle. Gods, it hurt to talk. "I'm an old man. I'm used to pain."

Faelen was not amused by the prisoner's response, but his countenance did not change. Ordinarily, he would've thrown an angry fit. "I don't feel like knocking you around until you pass out today," he said. "I understand now that your pride, selflessness, and resolve are strong enough to withstand any physical abuse that one may inflict upon you. Ripping off your limbs would do nothing, would it?" He nodded in the direction of Beo's corpse. "Like me, you've lived for a very long time. You don't fear death."

Zylon said nothing, his chains clanking as he lowered his head to look at the stone floor.

"I've thought about infecting you," Faelen said. "But then there would always be the slim chance that you would acquire a Phoenix Heart, and then you'd become unstoppable."

"Then what are you going to do?"

"I'm going to offer you a chance at your freedom," Faelen said with a sly smile. "I know that you are one of the Bounts' greatest enemies, Zylon. You've been hunting down this organization for years, haven't you?"

Zylon gritted his teeth, glaring up at the werewolf.

"But I've been forced into this band of terrorists," Faelen said with a shrug. "The only thing that binds me to them is my accord with Junko, who freed me from Horux's catacombs. I care nothing for the absolute domination of Escalon or Terrador. My vengeance upon the inhabitants of Horux has already been achieved." A broad grin split across his lips. "Junko might want you dead, but I don't care whether you live or die, as long as you don't get in my way and you grant me my final wish."

"What is it you want?" Zylon murmured.

"It is said that within the dark realm of Oblivion lies a vault of Sacred Treasures, forged by the gods themselves," Faelen said. "In the past century or so, the gods placed a seal on the legendary Oblivion Vault. Now, in order to enter, one must know a certain incantation. Rumors circulate that you know what it is." The werewolf held up his right hand. Flexing his claw, the Bount gave Zylon a sadistic smile. "You'll tell me the incantation and you'll have Moriaki relay a message to Tanya."

Zylon winced. Tanya must've been the female werewolf that escaped to the mainland. "The items within that vault—"

"Do not worry. I don't care for any more objects of power. I've had enough experience with corruptive Sacred Treasures," Faelen said with an annoyed scowl. "I am searching for a potion that will turn me into a human again."

Zylon's eyes widened, disbelieving what he was hearing. Human?

"Did you know why I was jailed for centuries underneath Horux?" Faelen asked the immortal. He reached out with his claw, crushing one of the iron bars of the cell with his hand. "The founders of Horux saw me as a ferocious beast and nothing else. They attacked me and locked me away because of what they saw. Their fear of the unknown was what left me behind bars of silver for hundreds of years." He held out his claw before his face, anger flashing in his eyes. "I didn't choose to become this. This power was forced upon me, and I would see it vanquished."

Zylon gulped and said nothing.

"If you do as I say, I will release you. You will be free to go back to your comrades and leave the wall up, keeping us trapped on this peninsula. Currently, Tanya has orders to infect a village, which will undoubtedly spread the werewolf disease throughout Escalon, given time," Faelen said. "If you help me, I will give her orders to bring the infected with her to Lichholme, where she will search for the Oblivion Portal."

"You plan to have her fetch this rare potion for you?" Zylon murmured. "How do I know you will keep your word?"

"My honor prevents me from breaking any accord. Otherwise, I would've detached myself from the Bounts the moment I had eradicated the people of Horux," Faelen said, prying the iron bars of the cell apart as he walked into the chamber. He lashed out with his claws and slashed the chains that bound Zylon, letting the immortal drop to the puddle of blood on the floor. "If you refuse my offer, I will dismember you slowly until you drown in your own blood, and Tanya will fulfill my orders and allow the werewolves of Escalon to scatter freely throughout the continent, spreading the infection. Eventually, I will find that incantation and you will have died for nothing." He looked at the defeated immortal with pity. "You can still do a lot of good for this world, Zylon. There is no need for you to be a martyr."

Zylon worked his jaw, chuckling lightly to himself. "Looks like you're not leaving me much of a choice here," he muttered. "Fine, you have my word. I'll help you become human again."

***

Malyssa was completely invisible to the naked eye, standing at the top of a massive glacier as she watched Lady Amara escort Yuri's party away. The vampire had the ability to temporarily make her physical appearance imperceptible to most living beings. She reached up and gently dragged her fingernails down her cheeks, feeling that her hands were quavering. Oh, how she wanted to leap down there and rend those pathetic humans to pieces. She wanted to take the unconscious werewolf, Yuri, to become her blood-bag.

Licking her lips, Malyssa imagined the taste of the werewolf. People who were more courageous and heroic tended to have tastier blood. She'd noticed that. But she knew that facing Lady Amara and her band of warriors alone was suicide, even if she was more skilled.

Malyssa sat at the edge of the icy cliff, kicking her dangling feet outward as she pouted in frustration. "Why did that lousy hag have to get involved? I was having so much fun, too," she murmured. Her ears twitched and she sighed, recognizing the presence of someone behind her. Their nefarious aura was too noticeable to miss. "The infamous Junko is paying me a visit? How blessed I must be. What is it that you want? If you're coming to ask me to join your band of terrorists, I've already told you that I'm not interested."

The cloaked Bount was indeed standing on the glacier's peak behind the vampire. A small smile crept across Junko's lips and he chuckled, moving towards the sitting woman. "I've actually come for a different reason today," Junko said, gazing at Yuri's unmoving body in the distance. He raised an eyebrow. "It's about that boy."

Malyssa smirked, recognizing Junko's reaction to seeing Yuri. "You know him? Yuri's extraordinary. I want him to become my blood-bag." She salivated at the very thought of being able to suck the blood from him every night.

Junko raised an eyebrow at the vampire. "He is a survivor of the Horuxian massacre," he said, watching Yuri as Lady Amara's associates carried him away. His eyebrows furled together as he scowled. "Malyios has chosen him. I can smell the powerful magic of the Titan's mark from here."

"Malyios?" Malyssa said, suddenly leaping to attention. She narrowed her eyes and leaned forward, staring at the unconscious werewolf. The Bount was right — dark magic swirled around the boy. Such a powerful aura could only be emitted by the mark of a deity. "What could the Titan possibly want with Yuri?" she asked.

"An accord, I imagine. The Titan will attempt to lure the boy through the Oblivion Portal," Junko said, folding his arms. He shook his head. "But forget that. Right now, I've come to you for a favor. I want to slow down Yuri's party. Are you interested?"

"I owe you a favor, don't I?" Malyssa said with a yawn. "Just tell me what to do."

Junko knew that the only reason Yuri's party would be in Lichholme is for the field of Phoenix Hearts that were in the far north. They wanted to cure the werewolves of Horux. But even if they did manage to obtain the Phoenix Hearts, what was Yuri's plan to administer the antidote? Etaon was a gnomish fortress in northern Lichholme that was widely renowned for housing various infamous engineers. Junko smirked. *I am always one step ahead.* "I want you to infiltrate Etaon and eradicate their engineers."

"Eh? How will that slow down Yuri's party?"

"Just do as I say. I will be monitoring your progress," Junko said, turning away to walk away from the vampire. "And if you encounter Yuri and his party again, it would be great if you could exterminate them. I hate having weaklings foiling my plans."

Malyssa pouted, watching as the Bount's body burst into black mist. Then she was alone again. "Always the bossy one. Why can't you complete these damned tasks on your own?" she grumbled, standing up. "Well, I suppose I ought to get my vampires ready for an invasion. How annoying. Gnomish blood is so unsatisfying."

***

Yuri found himself standing in a mysterious graveyard, engulfed by an ominous mist. He'd somehow witnessed Faelen's conversation with Zylon and Junko's meeting with Malyssa. It was as if he'd been there in person, witnessing the events unfold firsthand. "Where am I now?" he muttered to himself, his voice echoing as if he were in a cave. *Could this be another dream?*

The boy sensed something slithering in the thick fog around him; a creature was watching him. Disconcerted, Yuri started through the mist, stepping around the dozens of stone gravestones that covered the dirt ground.

His stomach twisted when he felt the stare of his stalker intensifying. Glancing over his shoulder, he turned and saw a blurred silhouette of darkness in the fog. The creature's red eyes glowed through the haze, making it look like a demonic being.

Fear seized the boy and his body froze. "Is that you, Malyios?" Yuri croaked, staring at the mysterious entity. "Why ... why did you show me all of that?"

"*I am helping you realize who your true enemies are to help you stay alive, so that you will not be killed before you reach the Oblivion Portal,*" Malyios's familiar voice grumbled. "*Understanding your enemies is important.*"

"When I enter the Oblivion Portal ... what will happen?"

"*Nothing. It will be the same as if you entered a portal to anywhere else. You'll be whisked to a far-off land. You will arrive at Oblivion and then our accord will be complete. Once you walk through, you are immediately free to turn around and leave, should you decide to do so,*" the Titan said. "*But you are also free to walk amongst the realm of those who are lost in Oblivion. You may recognize a few souls that are wandering there.*"

Yuri suddenly saw that another shadow had appeared to his right. The figure was walking towards him, the silhouette's figure unfamiliar at first. But within moments, the stranger came into view. It was Beo.

The deceased noble calmly strode through the gloomy mist, his eyes darting about as he scanned the fog for any signs of life. His gaze went straight through Yuri, as if the boy was transparent, and he continued forward.

Yuri watched as the sojourner disappeared as quickly as he had come. The next figure that walked forward was someone that the werewolf recognized immediately. The shape of the man's body had been burned into Yuri's mind since he'd last seen the person years ago. "It can't be—" Yuri said, his eyes going wide with disbelief. It was his father, a parent that had perished a decade ago. But … he looked the same, as if he hadn't aged a day.

"Dad?" he said, taking hesitant steps towards his father. But the man did not acknowledge him. He was looking about frantically, his body trembling with terror. He looked exhausted. There were heavy bags underneath his dark eyes, and his skin was covered in bloody lacerations.

"Please, look! It's me, I—" Yuri exclaimed, reaching out to his father. Then the man phased straight *through* Yuri's body, stepping out on the other side of the shocked boy. The distraught werewolf spun around, staring at his dad. His eyes glistened with tears and his quavering hands clenched into fists at his side. Biting his quivering lip, he glanced at Malyios. "Why can't he hear me?"

"Because he is in Oblivion, while you are still in the material world. You can see and meet him again in Oblivion," Malyios said. *"I believe there have even been occasions when souls have escaped Oblivion."*

"Escaped Oblivion?" Yuri echoed. In other words, Malyios was saying that it was possible to bring people back to life. Could he do that too? Images of his deceased family jolted through his mind and he clenched his jaw, knowing that he would do anything to bring them back. Even if it was just one of them … he would pay any price to resurrect them. "Why are souls put in Oblivion?"

"When a person dies, their soul is judged. They are either placed in Heaven or condemned to Oblivion for eternity. However, your father is special. He was not judged," Malyios said with a chuckle. *"Certain individuals are chosen by the gods of death. These souls are given the option to participate in a test known as the Oblivion Trials. Survivors of these trials, regardless of their morality while they were alive, can have any wish granted. They can even be revived into the world of living, if that is their wish. However, those that fail the trials are condemned to Oblivion, even if they were meant for Heaven."*

Yuri looked at his father, who had just vanished into the fog. "My father participated in those trials?"

"*He did.*"

Yuri sighed. Could this be some kind of trick? Was Malyios merely trying to lure him deeper into Oblivion? He shook his head. It didn't matter. Even if there was the slightest chance that he could bring his father back to life, he needed to pursue that path. After all, Yuri knew that he wouldn't be the person he was today without his dad. "The accord hasn't changed," he said. "After I complete my task and retrieve the Phoenix Hearts ... I will enter the Oblivion Portal."

"*I understand.*" Yuri couldn't quite tell through the thick fog, but he could've sworn that the god was smiling. "*I will be waiting.*"

***

Yuri suddenly jolted awake, his eyes snapping open fully. He was breathing heavily, his shirt completely soaked in sweat. There was a wet towel on his forehead and he gulped, understanding that he was back in reality. Scanning his surroundings, the boy saw that he was in a room entirely made of sculpted ice. He was on the ground, lying on a warm mat made from the hide of some hairy animal. Sleeping soundlessly beside him was ... Violet?

The boy covered his mouth with both of his hands, nearly crying out with surprise. His face turned as red as a beet. He heard a light chuckle and turned to find Archerus, sitting in a chair on the far side of the room. The man was studying a map of Lichholme, attempting to memorize it.

"Another dream?" Archerus said, prying his eyes from the map to look at the boy. He lowered the piece of parchment and nodded in Violet's direction. "The princess cares a great deal for you. She's been by your side from the moment they pulled you from the Lake of Eternity."

Yuri blinked. He wanted to ask how he had survived the freezing temperatures of the lake, but there were too many mystified thoughts rushing through his mind. "Where are we?"

"Lady Amara's fortress. She's a Frozarian, a humanoid descendant of the frost giants. The Frost Mistress has been kind enough to let us take refuge here from the bitter cold while you recover. How are you faring?" Archerus said, standing up as he walked over to Yuri.

"I'm fine, but we need to get going immediately!" Yuri said, attempting to lean forward. There was a surge of sharp pain that jolted through his joints and he winced, finding it difficult to even move. Most of his bones were tremendously sore and the majority of his body ached. Gasping, he collapsed back to the floor.

"You won't be able to move for a while," Archerus said. "Look, I understand that we're in a rush to get these Phoenix Hearts, but pushing yourself too hard isn't going to help anyone."

"You don't understand," Yuri growled, shaking his head. "Etaon is in trouble! Malyssa is going to attack it and have all of the engineers there murdered. We need to ride to the gnomish fortress with all haste so we can warn them of the oncoming danger!"

"And how is it possible that you can foresee such an assault?" Archerus said curiously, raising an eyebrow. "You just know, is that it? Just as you *knew* of the Phoenix Heart field and its exact location, despite never having set foot on the mainland. I am tired of the act, Yuri."

Yuri averted his gaze. "It's difficult to explain."

"We have time," Violet said, her voice gentle. She rubbed her tired eyes with the back of her hand as she leaned forward. "Especially since you're temporarily paralyzed."

Yuri stared at the princess and let out a defeated groan. Perhaps it was time that he was completely honest. He didn't like leaving his friends in the dark about what was happening; he just thought that it would be bizarre to tell them about an ancient deity that was contacting him through his dreams. The very idea of it all seemed insane. Nevertheless, he started talking. He told them everything that he knew, from the existence of the Bount organization to Malyios's accord, and all of the nightmares that he'd had.

When he finished his explanation, Yuri was surprised to see that neither Violet nor Archerus disbelieved him. Then again, he supposed that they'd been through enough unusual experiences that perhaps a Titan contacting him through dreams wasn't the most preposterous idea around.

"So, this Malyios wants us to succeed in our quest," Violet said, clapping her hands. "I mean, that can't mean that he's malicious, right? He's forewarned us of the future attack on Etaon."

"You don't know what force you're dealing with, Yuri," Archerus murmured, his expression grim. "Malyios doesn't want *us* to succeed. He wants Yuri to succeed; that's the only reason he's granted Yuri precious information regarding Faelen and Malyssa. For all he cares, the rest of us could perish. Not much is known about the ancient Titan. We only know that he's a god of darkness, and at one point, he was the most dangerous deity on Terrador and Heaven alike."

"Look, I can't do anything about the accord that I've made with him. It's already been done," Yuri said. "I know to be careful when dealing with him."

"It was foolish of you to make such a deal with him in the first place," Archerus said harshly, causing the boy to lower his head. "I knew it was suspicious that you'd gained absolute control over your werewolf powers in one night. You shouldn't have made such a bold decision without consulting me first."

"I'm sorry," Yuri said, closing his eyes. "But—"

"Apologizing won't help when you walk through that Oblivion Portal and end up condemned there for eternity," Archerus snapped, exhaling his frustration through his nostrils.

"A-Anyway," Violet said suddenly, trying to change the topic. "We should focus on the information that Yuri got from Malyios's projected visions. If there is going to be an attack on Etaon soon, we should send some messengers to tell them to bolster their security so they can defend themselves against Malyssa and any possible incursion."

Archerus and Yuri nodded in agreement.

"Now we also know that there is a werewolf approaching Lichholme that will be searching for the Oblivion Portal and the vault full of Sacred Treasures," Violet said, tapping her chin with her index finger. "That's certainly an issue."

"Right," Yuri murmured, running a hand through his hair. "Now we also have to worry about stopping this Bount, Tanya. We have to assume that she has the incantation needed to get into the Oblivion Vault."

"But doesn't Tanya work for Faelen? I thought that she would only be retrieving a potion for him, so that he can return to being a human," Violet exclaimed. "S-So maybe we don't have to regard her as a threat?"

"Wrong," Archerus said. "She will certainly take the potion for Faelen, but I believe that she is subordinate to the Bounts before Faelen. There is no doubt that she'll attempt to take other Sacred Treasures from the vault, items that will pose a great danger to the world. We'll need to stop her." He turned and started to walk towards the doorway. "But for now, she's still searching for the Oblivion Portal, and it'll take her some time to find it. We'll use that time to complete our quest. Hopefully Yuri can fulfill his end of his accord with Malyios without dying."

"That would be nice, wouldn't it?" Yuri said with a weary chuckle. "Where are you off to?"

Archerus waved to Yuri and Violet over his shoulder. "I'm going to get a small party ready to ride at full speed for Etaon. Get some rest, Yuri."

Yuri watched as his friend left the room and sighed, leaning back into the soft, furry mat. He gazed blankly at the flat icy ceiling above him. There was a moment of awkward silence between him and Violet, but he finally mustered the courage to speak his mind. "Given the opportunity to revive someone that you love, you would grasp it, wouldn't you?"

"I would do whatever it took to bring that person back," Violet said, initially thinking of Yuri. But she quickly realized what he was talking about. "But what if that opportunity wasn't real? Yuri, you don't know if Malyios is telling you the truth or not. You can't be sure that your father can be brought back, or if he's even in Oblivion at all! Malyios might be just trying to lure you into some trap. Why else would he just ask you to enter the Oblivion Portal? That seems too easy, doesn't it?"

"I would be free to leave Oblivion whenever I like," Yuri said, wetting his lips. "I know that it's risky and that this whole situation is dangerous, but there is a slim chance that he could be telling the truth. I would forever live with regret if I simply left Oblivion without knowing if I really could bring back my dad."

Violet lay down, folding her hands over her stomach and looking up at the blank ceiling. The boy's mind was made up and she knew that there was no way that she could change that. She liked that Yuri's decisions weren't swayed by the opinions of others, but she truly thought that this time his choice was too dangerous. "What was your dad like?" Violet asked.

Yuri looked at the princess. It'd been a decade since he'd openly talked about his father. But maybe it was finally time that he told someone what Dad was like. He smiled. "My father was a kind man. More than anything, he cared about our family. Our household was poor, and scraping by was sometimes hard. But

Dad would often do whatever it took to get the money that we needed to survive." He closed his eyes as he spoke, his mind whisked away by the fresh memories of his father that flashed through his mind. "He worked during the day, but his wage was only enough to support him, not a family of four. On some days, I was surprised that he stayed with us instead of running off to live on his own. For most of my early years, I felt like a burden to him. He'd sacrifice so much for us ... he always put himself last, even though he was the reason we had food to eat in the first place.

"My father would give his portion of meals to Han and me. He always said that growing boys needed to eat, and insisted that we didn't worry about him. But as the years went by, I saw him growing weaker and weaker. Eventually, he was fired from his job at Horux's warehouse. Without income, my father became desperate. He felt that he needed to do whatever it took to survive," Yuri said, his expression hardening. "The economy was in a recession and no one was hiring. My father assured us that he would find a way to make money. And so he became a thief, stealing from whoever he could in the streets."

Violet bit her lower lip and said nothing, allowing Yuri to continue his tale.

"At first, he stole small things and sold them, making enough money to feed the family. But when the rent was due, he still couldn't pay it," Yuri choked out, his voice dropping to nearly a whisper. "We lived in a very dangerous area of Horux at the time. It was the fourth month that we couldn't pay the rent, and my father refused to leave. So the landlord had one of Dad's fingers cut off. He claimed that for every month that he didn't pay the rent, he would slice off another."

"That's horrible! Why didn't you tell the guards? I'm sure they would've—"

"The guards didn't care about lowlifes like us," Yuri murmured, shaking his head. "No one did. In their eyes, we were just dirty scumbags destined to perish in the streets, bathed in our own filth. After my father lost his finger, he realized that he needed to steal bigger things to get enough money to pay the rent. So, he did. He started sneaking into the Noble District and stealing from the rich. For several months, we lived better than we ever had. Then he got caught. As the princess, I assume that you know the names of all the nobles in Horux. My father broke into one of the mansions in the Wolf House ... the home of Asmund and Beo."

"The manor of your best friend?" Violet said with surprise.

"Yes, but we weren't friends at the time. I didn't even know he existed," Yuri said. "Asmund discovered my father, who was trying to steal a valuable flower that they had sealed away in a safe. In desperation, my father tried to silence Asmund. But Beo appeared and defended Asmund, killing my Dad. For a decade, I wondered why it was that my father had to die for a mere flower. I didn't even realize its value until I became a werewolf. It was a Phoenix Heart. If he'd sold that, my family would've never had problems with money again. In my father's eyes ... that would have been his last theft."

Yuri pressed his forearm to his moist eyes. "With his dying breath, he apologized to the nobles and asked them for a favor — to watch over my family after he passed. Beo arrived at my home several days later, explaining my father's demise. I think that he felt somewhat guilty that he had taken my dad away, which is why he treated me like one of his own for the next couple years. Beo did as my father asked. He made sure that my family was financially stable through me. He understood that Dad was stealing out of desperation as opposed to malicious intent.

"There is one memory of my father that I'll always recall, and it's the one that helps me revert from my werewolf form back to a human," Yuri said, smiling slightly. "On my seventh birthday, he brought me an entire baguette. He told me that I could have it all to myself, and that it was my day. I knew that he didn't eat that day, and that he'd spent his earnings on that baguette and small portions of food for my mom and brother."

Violet reached out and interlocked her fingers with his. She gave the boy's hand a tight squeeze. "Your father sounds like a great man."

"He was. It was his selflessness and determination to preserve the wellbeing of his loved ones that influenced me to become the person that I am today," Yuri said, tears trickling slowly down his cheeks. "He would do anything for his family, I know that. That's why I have to go to Oblivion. If there's any chance that I can bring him back, I have to grasp it. He would do the same for me."

"I understand," Violet said. "I think you should go then. Just be careful. You've been close to death so many times that I'm surprised I haven't had a heart attack yet."

Yuri laughed. "Thank you."

"For what?"

He grinned. "Everything."

Fire and Ice

Moriaki had been watching over the peninsula's entrance for several days, his heart full of worry for Zylon's safety. The magical wall that the immortal had created was still in place, but the druid expected it to come crashing down at any moment. Faelen would torture Zylon to force him to release his magic. Moriaki had to be prepared to battle an army of werewolves when the wall finally faltered.

King Reimos upheld his promise, having sent a reasonable force to assist in holding the ground. That day a force of five thousand soldiers had flooded onto the land bridge, fully armed. With them came caravans with much-needed supplies of weapons, ammunition, and rations. Upon their arrival, the Iradian warriors began to set up silver barricades and fortifications to hold back the werewolves. Once they were established, most of the beasts would be trapped. Although Moriaki was a bit skeptical about whether the barriers would be able to hold back Faelen.

Moriaki scanned the sea of soldiers for their commander. He had to inform the man that a female werewolf had escaped several days ago and that he needed to chase after her. With her speed, she could've already infected multiple villages over the last few days. The druid gritted his teeth, recalling the cloak that she had been wearing. It belonged to the Bount organization. There was no doubt that she had ingested a Phoenix Heart. Her swift actions and ability to wield her chain whip was proof that she wasn't any ordinary werewolf. Even if Moriaki caught up to her, he wondered whether or not he was strong enough to defeat such a fearsome opponent. *It doesn't matter. I need to stop her and anyone she's infected thus far.*

There was a loud groaning sound, and gasps suddenly spread throughout the surprised Iradian force. Moriaki turned around and saw that a small door had suddenly appeared in Zylon's magical wall. The druid watched as the door creaked open.

Standing in the entrance was Zylon himself. The immortal was covered in bruises, but was still in one piece.

Zylon smiled at the hundreds of rifles that were pointed at him. "I'm back," he said jadedly. Directly behind the man was a myriad of werewolves, led by Faelen himself.

"Moriaki! Come forth," Zylon hollered, standing in the doorway. The immortal didn't walk forward; he stayed exactly where he was. There was no look of fear on his face. Instead, there was simply exhaustion. He looked as if he were about to collapse.

Moriaki slipped through the confused ranks of the Iradian soldiers, moving towards the magical wall. The druid met Zylon's gaze and continued forward, greeting the immortal with a tight embrace. "What's going on?" he said, indicating the werewolves behind Zylon.

"I've made an accord with Faelen so that I may be freed," Zylon said with a weary shrug. He glanced over his shoulder to the Bount, who simply nodded. The man stared at the legions of tamed werewolves that stood behind their alpha leader. "I am about to ask you to do something, Moriaki, that you may find odd at first. But I will explain to you why it is necessary afterward. I will only be freed once the task is complete. Do you trust me?"

Moriaki looked at Faelen and saw that the werewolf was at least twenty feet behind the immortal. Regardless of the distance, even if the druid pulled Zylon through the doorway, he knew that Faelen would be able to strike one of them down in that time. The beast was not one to be challenged. The elf let out a sigh. "Looks like we're in a predicament, huh? Okay, tell me what to do so we can free you."

***

Tanya had invaded two populated villages with ease, infecting most of the population. The elderly and children were all slaughtered, since she had no need for weaklings in her army of ferocious beasts. She hadn't yet sent the werewolves off to spread the infection throughout Escalon. The beasts still instinctively followed her. They recognized her as the strongest and therefore considered her their leader.

The Bount had traveled deep into Northern Escalon, having gathered a force of almost a thousand werewolves behind her. There was no doubt that Iradia had already noticed the pack of rowdy beasts, but she didn't care. No human army would be strong enough to face a force this big, not with her at its head.

Tanya intended to disperse the werewolves once she reached the border between Escalon's mainland and Lichholme. She would take a few companions into the dangerous territory with her, but the rest of the beasts could be scattered throughout the continent to spread the infection.

The Bount had just reached the top of a hill and could see the massive glacier that marked Lichholme's border. She glanced over her shoulder and saw her army of hairy creatures scampering about behind her, waiting to see what she would do. They would mindlessly follow.

A pounding headache suddenly assaulted Tanya, feeling as if a mace has just struck her skull. Wincing, she collapsed onto one knee and gasped. This was no ordinary migraine; she could sense that arcane magic was involved. She could feel her mind being infiltrated by the presence of a stranger. "Get out," she growled, grabbing her head in agony. The fortifications of her mind crumbled before the mental incursion, the layers of her cerebral defense peeled back until her mind opened up to the stranger. Every thought, every secret was free for her intruder to browse, like an open book. Whoever had magically entered her mind was powerful, Tanya acknowledged that. But she noticed that they did not rummage through her mind. Instead, they only left a message.

A voice spoke, sounding like Faelen. *Tanya, I have made an accord with Zylon. You will not let those werewolves loose on Escalon, at least not yet. For now, you will take whatever infected beasts you've accumulated and lead them through Lichholme to the Oblivion Portal. I will not be able to leave Horux's territory as planned. Instead, I want you to go to Oblivion in my stead and retrieve a particular Sacred Treasure for me.*

Tanya listened to the rest of Faelen's message, frowning at what he was asking for. Faelen wanted to put off Junko's plan to uphold this accord that he'd made with the damned elf and the magician? How preposterous! Then again, in exchange for delaying the domination of Escalon, Faelen had received priceless information — an incantation that would allow for one to enter the Oblivion Vault.

She'd heard of the renowned vault, a sealed place where countless Sacred Treasures, forged by the gods of death, were stored. In there were items that could easily lay waste to an entire continent. And yet, Faelen specified that he only wanted Tanya to take one item from the vault. A potion, one with mysterious properties that he hadn't specified. What were the effects of consuming the liquid? Would it grant omnipotence?

Tanya sighed, turning to look at the army of werewolves staring at her, awaiting her command. Originally, she'd only intended to find the portal. Entering such a perilous place as Oblivion had never been on her agenda, but this was indeed the opportunity of a lifetime. Power was something she'd always sought. When Faelen had turned her into a werewolf, she regarded the transformation as one of the greatest gifts one could've granted her. But within that vault ... she could obtain limitless strength. "Faelen, I'll fetch your potion," she said gently to the wind. A sly smile cracked across her lips. "But I cannot promise that it'll be the only thing I take from that vault."

***

The next day, Yuri still felt extremely fatigued and weak. He could barely walk, but he managed to lumber his way over to an ice balcony that had a grand view overlooking Lady Amara's territory. In all directions, snow coated the ground and the pine trees that were sprinkled across the land. Mountains loomed in the distance, and the sun beamed its morning light on the snow, making the whiteness shine brighter than diamonds.

For a wasteland known for being home to the undead, Yuri found that the landscape itself was quite beautiful. He'd never seen this much snow before. Looking down, he saw that several Frozarian warriors were leading half a dozen reindeer to the front of the fortress. He watched as Senna, Kura, Terias, and several Iradian warriors were given mounts. *So that's the group that'll be heading to Etaon.*

Terias glanced up and caught Yuri's gaze. He smiled broadly at his friend. "Hey, what are you doing up? Go back and get some rest! We'll be waiting for you at Etaon."

"Make it in one piece," Yuri called down.

"Could say the same for you when you come," Terias shouted back with a sly smirk. He mounted one of the reindeer with a Frozarian manning the reins. None of the humans knew how to ride the reindeer efficiently, so Lady Amara was kind enough to send several guides that would lead the party of messengers to Etaon. It looked like a dozen people were embarking on the journey, six humans and six Frozarians.

Yuri watched as the group rode off on the reindeer, sprinting across the snowy lands. He squeezed the icy railings of the balcony until his knuckles turned white. The cold air bit at

240

his reddened cheeks and he let out an exasperated sigh, staring helplessly at the snow.

Many troops had to stay in Lady Amara's Fortress to tend to the wounded. Most of Kura's warriors that had fallen through the ice into the Lake of Eternity had been saved. Everyone was still recovering from the magical waters, and the traumatic experience of losing many companions.

Kura had already been distraught over the loss of several comrades when they had fought the undead in the glacier. She was particularly upset over the death of her close friend, Oma. When she saw that the Frozarians were pulling survivors from the Lake of Eternity, she'd hoped to see that her right-hand man, Tassan, had survived. But the knight had been crushed in the hands of the frost giant. There was no coming back from that.

The previous night, the Frozarians had held a ceremony in reverence to those who had passed over during the last couple of days. The robust Iradians and Horuxians had attended, but victims of the Lake of Eternity's chilling waters couldn't be present, since most of them were still paralyzed.

Violet had returned later that night to tell Yuri of the ancient ritual. She described how Lady Amara had used some type of magic to create hundreds of tiny blue lights that floated into the night. The small orbs were meant to represent the spirits of the deceased that were moving on to the afterlife.

Yuri now watched Lady Amara, who was standing at the entrance to the fortress. She waved to the departing messengers as they rode away. For a complete stranger, she was very kind. She'd offered the hospitality of her home, saved the lives of dozens of knights from the Lake of Eternity, and brought down the frost giant, thus saving the lives of everyone in Yuri's group. But there must've been some alternative motive, Yuri had a feeling that the Frost Mistress wanted something in return for her benevolence.

"Up and moving already?" Violet asked, walking from the room to the balcony. Since they'd reached the fortress, she'd been spending a lot of time with him. Nearly every hour, actually. Sometimes she would go to talk to Senna, but for the most part she stayed with Yuri. They would talk for hours, eat meals together, and last night they even slept beside each other. Not that anything else happened, though Yuri wouldn't have minded if something had.

The boy grinned at the princess, scratching the back of his neck. "Yeah, after lying around all of yesterday, I was excited to move around again. It's still a little difficult to walk, though," he said, glancing over his shoulder for a brief moment. In his peripheral vision, he caught sight of a forest in the distance. A foolish idea sparked into his mind. "Hey, do you want to go on an adventure? Just the two of us."

Violet blinked, astonished that Yuri would even suggest leaving the fortress. "What? Shouldn't you be resting? I doubt that it's healthy for you to move around too much … and this is Lichholme! It would be imprudent for us to leave the Frozarian fortress without escorts!"

"If there's any danger, I'll sense it coming," Yuri said, pointing to himself with his thumb confidently. "I'm a werewolf, remember? I'm sure that I'll be able to protect us if something happens. Come on, who knows when we'll get a chance like this? Would you rather sit around inside this fortress, waiting until everyone else has recovered?"

"But you haven't even recovered yet," Violet murmured.

"Werewolves heal a lot faster than ordinary humans, I'm fine!" Yuri insisted, knowing that it was partially the truth. He could move a lot better than the rest of Kura's knights, who were still paralyzed. But it would still take him another day or so to return to his normal self. His body still ached. He extended his hand to the princess, who gave him a questioning look. "We won't go far, I promise."

A tiny smile creased Violet's lips as she reached out and took Yuri's hand. The boy pulled her close to him, taking her up in his arms. "Hold on," he said, leaping off the side of the balcony. The werewolf slammed heavily into the snow below, surprised that Violet hadn't screamed. Glancing over his shoulder, he saw that Lady Amara was watching him from the fortress's entrance. Two Frozarian warriors stepped forward, about to halt Yuri, but the Frost Mistress held out her hand. The guards stopped, looking to their superior.

Yuri put Violet down and shot Lady Amara a broad smile before pulling the princess away. The two rushed towards the distant forest on foot.

One of the guards gave Lady Amara a perplexed look. "How is the werewolf even moving? He's only had a day of recovery from the Lake of Eternity's waters," the soldier said. "Lady Amara, are you sure that you should let the two of them go off on their own?"

"We are not their guardians," Lady Amara said. "This fortress is not a prison to keep them locked up. They are free to leave when they choose." The Frost Mistress turned around, walking back into the building. "Let Archerus know that the pair left. They are of his concern."

***

Yuri and Violet walked for an hour through a nearby forest of snow-covered pine trees, talking as they went. The two learned a lot about each other, and Yuri found his interest in the princess burgeoning as they conversed. Violet was an intelligent woman of many skills, some of which were unexpected, such as cooking and sword fighting. Not many princesses needed such talents, since they had loyal chefs and warriors that were subordinate to them.

Violet was also one of the smartest people that Yuri had ever met; her extensive knowledge of Terrador exceeded that of most scholars. She'd spent countless hours in Horux's royal library, studying. Even in her free time, she loved to learn. The princess told Yuri of faraway lands that were in Horux's records. There were continents with vast deserts that covered thousands of miles, while others were filled with exotic beasts that did not exist in Escalon.

Hours went by as the pair wandered the forest, walking wherever their feet took them. They were too lost in each other's words to care for their destination. Violet's incredible tales of floating islands and frightening dragons captured Yuri's mind. His whole life, he'd been limited to the city of Horux, without wondering what else was out there in the world. After talking to Violet, Yuri came to realize that he had only adventured through a speck of Terrador. There was so much more that he hadn't seen yet.

Yuri brushed aside some bushes as he led Violet out to a frozen pond where he saw a pair of penguins sliding across the ice on their stomachs, skating around playfully. Instead of black coats, these penguins had silver hides, making their bodies camouflaged by the snow. However, their beaks were still bright orange. "Wow," he drawled in awe. "I've never seen a penguin before."

"These penguins are native to Lichholme, so you won't see them anywhere else in Escalon," Violet said, tucking some hair behind her ear. She giggled when two of the penguins bumped into each other, spinning on the ice. "Gods, they're adorable."

Yuri wanted to go out onto the ice and join the animals, but he had no intention of walking over frozen water after what had happened at the Lake of Eternity. The boy pointed to a massive bear that sauntered from the forest on the far side of the pond, stepping onto the ice. The penguins looked at the beast, but clearly did not deem him a threat, because they continued to skid around instead of fleeing. "I've never seen a bear with white fur like that!"

"Some in Escalon call it a polar bear," Violet said. "Others call it a ghost bear."

"Ghost bear? That sounds intimidating."

"Well, it's just a name," Violet said, watching as the beast began to roll around on the ice with the penguins. The princess smiled. "After all, it doesn't look like a threat to anyone."

Yuri grinned, temporarily mesmerized by Violet's beauty. Suddenly, his eyes caught an ominous glow that flashed from a cave behind the princess. His eyebrows went up and he walked past her, moving towards the mysterious grotto. A blue light was intermittently shining from the inside of the cave, giving off a bright glow every couple of seconds. "What could that be?" he said curiously.

"Don't you want to find out?" Violet said, grasping Yuri's hand as she pulled him along. "Let's go!"

Yuri's eyebrows went up, realizing that now she had taken the reins of the adventure. He laughed heartily as he followed her to the mouth of the cave. The shimmering light reflected off the grotto's stone walls, but its source came from deep within the cavern. To his surprise, the princess boldly ambled into the cave. She admired the glistening lights that flashed across the stone.

Yuri followed her carefully, his senses on full alert. But there did not seem to be any danger lingering about this cave. The two adventurers journeyed deeper into the grotto, until they finally came across the source of the flashing lights. A pool of water filled a dome-like crater in the floor, the liquid glowing. Beneath its surface was a mystical rock that glowed with arcane energy, releasing bright flashes of blue that radiated throughout the cavern.

"It's … beautiful," Violet said in awe, taking in the view. The color of the water was almost turquoise from the stone's light. Whenever the rock stopped glowing, the cave would temporarily be swallowed in darkness.

Yuri looked at the smiling princess. "It is," he said, releasing her hand. He rolled his pants up to his knees, tugged off his boots, and stripped off his shirt. He walked towards the pool. "Stay right here."

"W-What are you doing?" Violet exclaimed, blushing slightly. Her gaze wandered over his skin, across his muscular build, and finally fixated on his grinning face.

Yuri waded into the pool, the chilling water biting at his skin. The very thought of entering water after his terrifying experience in the Lake of Eternity made him feel uneasy. But he disregarded his hesitancy and continued onward, feeling the chilly water engulf him as he dove beneath the surface. This cold was nothing compared to the freezing Lake of Eternity.

The boy emerged from the pool several seconds later, brushing some of his dark hair from his glistening eyes. In his hand, he held the glowing stone. Stepping out of the water, Yuri went to Violet. He gently took her hand and placed the tiny rock in her palm. Despite its small size, it radiated like a miniature sun, beaming its light all over the two adventurers. "This is a memento," Yuri said, closing her fingers around the rock, "so that you will forever remember this moment."

Darkness reigned over the cave as the stone's glow was sealed by Violet's hand, tiny trickles of light streaming through the gaps between her fingers. Yuri felt something in his chest, an unfamiliar warmth that comforted his shivering body. He felt himself drawn forward to Violet like a magnet and he gently pressed his lips against hers in a passionate kiss.

The princess was surprised at first, but she did not resist. She dropped the stone on the ground, where it radiated its light throughout the grotto once more. She was completely enthralled by the kiss, her arms wrapped around Yuri's neck.

Yuri curled his arms around the princess's waist, pulling her close. Violet pulled away for a moment, her lips inches away from his. "I don't need a memento to remember this," she whispered.

Yuri grinned. "Neither do I."

The Trickster

It took Senna's party several days to reach Etaon. The Frozarian guides managed to steer the party clear of most dangers, but they still encountered a group of undead as well as a frost troll. Luckily for them, the native warriors knew exactly how to deal with most of Lichholme's creatures. They'd defeated all their enemies with no casualties.

One of the guides told Senna of an infection that had once swept across Lichholme, eradicating the entire human population and transforming many of them into the undead. The disease was created by a powerful necromancer, who used the plague to kill humans and extract their souls so that he could gain power. The pestilence had traveled to all corners of Lichholme within months, wiping out millions.

Senna saw plenty of uninhabited villages on his journey to Etaon. It was clear that, at one point in time, Lichholme had hosted various human civilizations. It was shocking to think that a disease could kill and warp countless people, turning them into zombies. He realized that Escalon's mainland was now in a similar situation, threatened by the werewolf infection. If Faelen did succeed it wouldn't take long before Escalon became just like Lichholme, infested with monstrosities.

"There it is!" Terias exclaimed, pointing into the distance.

Senna followed Terias's gaze and indeed saw Etaon, a fortress of massive proportion. A wall of steel surrounded the stronghold, equipped with spikes that were sprinkled over the top. Gnome sentries patrolled the walls, already spotting the group of approaching strangers. The metal bastion was shaped like a pyramid, with various entrances and windows.

The knight raised an eyebrow when he saw that cannons were mounted on top of Etaon's walls. He'd heard that the gnomes were the best inventors and engineers in all of Terrador, and that cannons were their most recent creations, able to unleash hell on distant enemies with explosive power.

"Do we even have to warn these gnomes?" Kura grumbled as they rode towards the fortress. "They seem like they're ready for a war. This place looks impenetrable."

"To humans," a Frozarian said. "But vampires have their ways of accomplishing the impossible, and they could easily infiltrate Etaon as it is now. The gnomes must bolster their defenses if they are to stand a chance against Malyssa's bloodsucking creatures."

The group of messengers reached the gates of Etaon within the hour, relieved when the doors swung open. A tiny gnome strolled into the opening, standing in the path of the reindeer. He was only three feet tall, and wore orange-tinted goggles that shielded his eyes from view. His face was smeared with soot, as if he'd just cleaned a chimney, and he wielded a rifle that seemed far too large for him.

"What is a group of humans and Frozarians doing at Etaon?" the gnome asked in a high-pitched, squeaky voice.

Senna saw that there were at least a dozen other gnomes behind the leader, all armed with rifles. The gnomes wore unsympathetic expressions; they were fully prepared to open fire on the strangers. The knight glanced at his apprentice, Terias, who was trembling. *You still haven't learned to control your fear, have you?*

"We hail from the Empire of Iradia, under the command of King Reimos. We've come to Etaon requesting aid. I believe that you are housing several engineers from our kingdom," Kura said, dismounting her reindeer. She indicated the Frozarian warriors around her. "These kind Frozarians serve Lady Amara. They escorted us here."

"Is that so?" the gnome said, lowering his rifle as he eyed the Iradian badge that glistened on Kura's cloak. He held up his hand, and the other gnomes behind him also put away their weapons. "It is a relief to see another living being, anyone other than undead, vampires, and damned frost trolls for once. As for your Iradian engineers, most of them have perished. We only have one left, the only human left in Etaon." He glanced over his shoulder, acknowledging a young woman that was carrying several rifles out of the fortress. She seemed to be having great difficulty and tripped, dropping all of the weapons. Flustered, the woman quickly scrambled to pick up the guns. "Her name is Lena. She's my apprentice." The gnome sighed, slightly embarrassed by the girl's clumsy display.

"And your name?" Senna said, looking down at the gnome leader.

"Twinklehart."

"Twinkle … hart," Terias echoed, receiving a glare from his mentor. He raised his hands into the air, indicating that he meant no offense.

"Well, come in," Twinklehart said, walking towards the entrance to Etaon's fortress. "I feel uneasy whenever the gates are open. We will have to search you, though. It's precaution; I'm sure you understand."

Senna and his group were frisked and relieved of their weapons, and were then led into Etaon's stronghold, where they gathered in a grand hall. They were served hot tea to warm their bones, a welcome treat after being in Lichholme's unrelenting weather for several days. Twinklehart sat down in a tiny wooden chair while the humans and Frozarians stood. Beside him was Lena, who awkwardly stared at the group of strangers before her.

"Uh, why am I here?" Lena asked aloud.

"These humans are from Iradia," Twinklehart explained. "They've come requesting the aid of the Iradian engineers that were here and since you're the only one left—"

"Right," Lena muttered, not wanting to hear anymore.

The young apprentice was in her late teens and had brown hair that was tied back into a ponytail. She reached up and rubbed her hazel eyes, clearly distraught over the mention of her deceased classmates. The engineer wore brown clothing that was caked in dirt, as were most of the other gnomish engineers. A utility belt was wrapped around her waist, equipped with a variety of knives, tools, and even a holstered pistol.

"We've also come with a warning. The rest of our group is still at Lady Amara's fortress and will be arriving later. But we came earlier to inform you that it is essential that you bolster the defenses of Etaon immediately," Kura said, dipping her head respectfully. "A vampire by the name of Malyssa intends to assault this fortress. She will target all of the inventors and engineers in Etaon."

Twinklehart wrinkled his nose, frowning at the news. "And where did you hear this?"

Kura winced, not really sure how to explain where the source of the information came from. Even she wasn't sure how Archerus had found out about Malyssa's malicious plan. "We just know," she said simply. "It wouldn't hurt for you to maximize your defenses, would it?"

"Our defenses are always maximized," Twinklehart said. "This is Lichholme. We try to be as prepared as possible. But we are merely a band of gnomes with only our gadgets and rifles to defend ourselves. Malyssa leads a settlement of vampires to the west of Etaon. The best we could do is gather materials that would help us combat vampires."

"What do you need?"

"Lichholme doesn't have any wolfsbane; the plant would be outstandingly useful. The hard part about killing vampires is that they tend to regenerate extremely quickly. Even if we manage to pump them full of lead, they could still survive. Sunlight would make the vampires weak and vulnerable to attack, but Malyssa would only strike at dark. When exposed to fire or silver, their healing abilities are vanquished and they can be killed. You can also decapitate a vampire to kill it, even if it hasn't been weakened," Twinklehart explained, folding his arms over his chest. "You're positive that Malyssa plans to attack us?"

Kura was reluctant to say anything. She wasn't positive; she was merely taking Archerus's word that Yuri's prediction was correct. "We're positive," Senna said suddenly, taking the Iradian warrior by surprise.

"Then we'll have to gather all of the silver that we've got and use it to forge bullets. In addition, we'll want to set up torches all over fortress … not just these tiny candles," Twinklehart murmured, indicating to the dozens of candles and lanterns that illuminated the room. "Defeating vampires will be a difficult task indeed."

"We have expertise in murdering the vampires," one of the Frozarians said, bowing. His colleagues followed his example. "The Frozarians have been at war with them for decades, ever since they started kidnapping our youths to turn them into blood-bags."

"What are blood-bags?" Terias asked Senna.

"Live beings that are enslaved by the vampires. They exist merely to have their blood harvested daily," Senna whispered to his apprentice. It was horrible, what the vampires did to blood-bags. They abused, tortured, and worked the slaves until they wished that they were dead. But the vampires constantly supervised them, making sure that whenever their blood was spilt, it was into a goblet to be drunk.

Twinklehart nodded to Kura. "I will strike a deal with you then. If you're certain your prediction is correct, and Malyssa's forces will attack, then you will stay here and help us combat the vampires. If you do so, we will help you with your current quest to the best of our ability."

Kura opened her mouth to protest, knowing that they were short on time. They couldn't just stay here in Etaon since there was no telling when Malyssa would strike. It could be days, weeks, or months from now! But Senna spoke up once again, silencing the assassin. "That sounds perfect. Thank you," the knight said with a bold smile. He ignored the hostile glare from Kura. "We'll get started on helping to prepare Etaon for the vampire attack immediately."

***

Ever since their exclusive adventure, Yuri and Violet had been quite open about their relationship. Archerus, who had scolded the two for hours for leaving the ice citadel, seemed to be the only one who wasn't surprised about their sudden bond. Yuri and Violet spent most hours of each day together, exploring the area around Lady Amara's fortress. The more time they spent with each other, the stronger Yuri's feelings for Violet became. He'd never felt this way about someone before. Initially, he'd merely had a crush on the princess because of her beauty. He'd never gotten the chance to really meet her until he was invited to have dinner with the royal family. But with every minute that he spent with Violet, Yuri felt that he was learning more about the type of person that she was, and he knew that he was falling deeply in love.

A week had passed since Yuri had kissed the princess. He knew that soon it would be time for them to depart for Etaon. Most of the Iradian knights had recovered from the Lake of Eternity's freezing waters. They were mostly waiting for Noah to regenerate the rest of his magical energy. But it seemed that he was also ready to leave the stronghold, eager to get out of his bed.

Yuri and Violet stood at the foot of the magician's bed. They had visited him daily. "Archerus said that we should leave today at noon," Yuri said to Noah. "Are you going to be okay with that?"

Noah nodded quickly. "Oh, please. I need to get out of this accursed bed. I've already finished a hundred books since the beginning of my recovery," he said, indicating the stacks of massive tomes that were piled beside his bed.

Yuri winced. *Is it even possible to read that fast?*

"At least you're feeling better," Violet said with a smile. "You used a lot of magic. I imagine that most magicians wouldn't be able to cast half the number of spells that you did against those undead."

"Oh, my father would be furious with me if he knew what I did." Noah laughed. "He always tells me to conserve my energy and not to use massive amounts of magic at once. You see, if I cast small spells, my body has time to regenerate the energy that I've just burned. But using magic all at once, like creating massive walls or stampedes of fabricated animals ... then I'd just drain myself and pass out — which I did."

"Well, you saved the day." Violet grinned.

"I suppose."

Yuri frowned, feeling an odd sensation quivering throughout his body. It was the same feeling that he'd had when he'd walked through the glacier's canyon or when he'd first stepped foot in Horux's forest. No, it was more comparable to the dream that he'd had when he'd encountered Malyios in the foggy graveyard. It was that feeling that he was being watched ... except this time, he could sense murderous intent. *Outside.*

Yuri bolted to the window and his eyes widened. Standing in the snow was a cloaked figure ... Junko. The Bount stood there, staring right at Yuri, as if he'd been waiting for the boy to go to the window. A dozen Frozarian guards lay on the ground, their bodies buried in the bloodstained snow.

Enraged, Yuri gritted his teeth, his turquoise eyes changing red as animus surged through him. He leapt outward and smashed through the ice window. Slamming into the ground before the calm Bount, Yuri rose to his full height, now in his werewolf form. *"Junko!"* he boomed.

"It is nice to see you again," Junko sneered, his tone mocking. He gave a sarcastic curtsy with the corners of his cloak. "I am surprised to find that you are still alive."

"I don't plan to die anytime soon," Yuri said, flexing his claws before his face. "Back in Horux, it was you who released Faelen, wasn't it?"

"Yes, it was me," Junko admitted, raising his hands into the air. "The mystery has been solved! Looks like I—" He swiftly ducked as Yuri ferociously rent the air, trying to rip the Bount to shreds. The cloaked man staggered backward, raising his eyebrows with amusement at werewolf's enraged countenance. "Oh my, now that's quite the look."

Yuri was beyond angry, every part of his body wanted to lunge at Junko and eviscerate the bastard. Pouncing outward, he swiped his claws rapidly at the agile Bount, but his efforts were futile. "You caused the deaths of thousands!" he roared, snapping his jaws where Junko's head was, hoping to clamp his fangs into his opponent's throat.

But Junko was highly experienced. He read Yuri's moves with ease, maintaining a calm expression as he dodged Yuri's attacks. Grinning, he stepped forward and slammed his palm into Yuri's shoulder. Dark energy pulsated through his forearm to his palm and detonated against the werewolf's body.

Yuri was launched backwards, his body rolling through the snow. He grasped his stinging shoulder, smoldering smoke rising from his body. Surprisingly enough, Junko's attack didn't hurt much.

The Bount shrugged. "Sorry, I'm not exactly meant for direct combat! But don't worry. I'll have a match for you soon enough," he said, smiling wickedly. "Anyway, I'm not here for you." He glanced up at the window, meeting the shocked gaze of Violet — his little sister. "I'm here for her."

"Violet, get away from the window!" Yuri yelled, sprinting at Junko.

But the Bount had already vanished in a wisp of black smoke. The mist appeared at the windowsill before Violet and the princess staggered backward, her eyes wide. She clenched her jaw, watching as her brother's body began to emerge from the darkness, stepping towards her.

Junko ... he was one of the main reasons Violet had come on this journey. Now that she was facing him in reality, she couldn't just quiver in fear uselessly. She needed to do something.

"Noah!" Violet shouted, her expression hardening as she glared at her brother.

Noah grunted as he extended his hand to the princess, conjuring a golden rapier in the air just above her head. During one of her visits, she'd mentioned that she had trained for several years using a rapier. But that was training. Noah could only hope that she was ready for a real fight.

Gripping the handle of the weapon, Violet jabbed the sword towards Junko with ferocious speed. The Bount, having just appeared at the window, had not expected such an abrupt attack. He'd expected her to be unarmed; suddenly seeing a weapon driving for his face was a surprise. Using his inhuman reactions, he tilted his head to the side as the blade sliced his cheek slightly. Blood oozed from the cut and Junko stumbled to the side, his purple eyes flashing with malice. "My, my. It looks like you've learned a few tricks. You're better than mother and father," he said, reaching into his cloak. He pulled out two golden necklaces that belonged to the king and queen of Horux and dropped them at Violet's feet. "They fell without a fight."

Violet stared at the bloodstained jewelry with disbelief, her lips trembling. "You ... killed them?" she choked out. Her attention snapped upwards and she saw that Junko's hand was lashing out for her throat.

"I *assassinated* them. That's what I'm good at!" Junko cackled, his gaze reflecting his madness. "And you're next!" His eyes flickered to the side as he spotted a mystical hammer swinging at his chest. The Bount quickly skipped to the side to avoid to blow, spotting Noah. The magician had rolled out of bed and had forged himself a weapon. "Creation magic? So, you're the son of the legendary immortal, Zylon. I heard rumors that he had a brat."

"I'd back off if I were you," Noah snapped. "Soon, you'll be hopelessly outnumbered."

"I don't mind a challenge," Junko said, sensing the presence of Yuri pouncing at him from behind. The werewolf had climbed up the side of the ice fortress to attack him? "Interesting tactic." The Bount spun around and grabbed Yuri by one of his legs, swinging him down with tremendous force, cracking the icy floor. "I told you that I'm not here for you." Junko drove a heavy kick into Yuri's side, sending the werewolf smashing through one of the walls. He glanced back to Violet. "Our reunion is long overdue, little sister."

"Why are you doing this?" Violet screamed, tears streaming down her cheeks. She thought of the last time that she'd seen her parents. She thought they would be safe in the Iradian Empire. How had this happened?

"Hope," Junko said with a malicious grin. "My duty in the Bount organization is to cause despair. Our parents were a beacon of hope to the survivors of Horux. Now that they're dead, the people will have no one to look to for guidance. When that happens, they'll fall into a state of disorder. That'll make it easier for the werewolf infection to spread." He pointed his index finger at Violet, purple energy gathering at the tip of his finger until a small ball of arcane magic floated there. "Don't look so distraught, Violet. You'll see our parents soon."

Violet planted her feet on the icy floor and rotated her body as she jabbed her blade at Junko's throat with blinding speed. The Bount grunted, narrowly avoiding her attack by stepping to the side. But Violet was not finished; she unleashed a flurry of fast blows that stabbed at Junko's body.

Junko raised his eyebrows, impressed with Violet's expertise with the rapier. He could sense the burning rage and animosity behind every one of the princess's brutal strokes. Her blade flashed with frightening speed, able to drill a hole through a human body. But her inexperience in combat would prove to be her downfall.

Violet's sword ripped through the air inches from Junko's face. The man grinned wickedly, his hand catching Violet's wrist. A slight application of pressure would snap the princess's bones like fragile twigs. From there, striking her down would take only a fraction of a second. Not even Noah would be able to react fast enough to forestall Junko's swift movements.

An arrow of ice pierced the air, whistling straight for Junko's face. The Bount released Violet and caught the projectile by the shaft, blood trickling onto the floor from the chaffed skin on his palm. He glanced at the hole in the wall and saw Lady Amara stepping through the opening with Archerus and Yuri at her side. "You are infiltrating my fortress, Bount," the Frost Mistress said with a wry tone. "Do not expect mercy."

Junko whistled, smashing the arrow into tiny bits of ice that crumbled to his feet. "I wondered who owned this fortress. Malyssa told me to steer clear of you, Lady Amara," the Bount said, his mouth pinched into a thin line. The smile on his face had faded. "You pathetic annoyances just love to get in my way, don't you?" He took a step back and sighed. "Oh, well. I've accomplished what I came to do."

Yuri gritted his teeth, unsure of what Junko meant. He watched powerlessly as the cackling man turned into a poof of smoke, vanishing in an instant. He saw Violet on the floor, gripping the bloody necklaces of her now-deceased parents. The princess was sobbing, clutching the jewelry to her chest.

Yuri watched her sympathetically, knowing what it was like to lose family. Had Junko come merely to cause her sorrow?

"Everyone, we have a problem," Noah said, pointing out the window. The stables that housed the reindeer had been completely destroyed. All of the animals had been crushed beneath the collapsed debris. "How are we going to get to Etaon?"

Archerus gritted his teeth, shaking his head. "He's trying to slow us down."

Yuri gritted his teeth, realizing what Junko had planned. Malyssa would strike Etaon while Yuri's contingent was stuck at Lady Amara's fortress. Without those mounts, they wouldn't be able to get to the gnome stronghold in time to provide reinforcement before the vampire assault. It seemed that most of the members in the room also realized what was going on.

"I have my private carriage stationed away from our stables," Lady Amara said through clenched teeth, clearly trying to stay calm despite her rage. She nodded to Archerus and Yuri. "You werewolves should be able to move on foot. I'll lead you to Etaon using the safest and quickest route I know."

"We appreciate your help," Archerus said thankfully.

"The vampires are the greatest enemy of my people," Lady Amara said. "I am simply aiding the enemy of my enemy." The Frost Mistress stormed out of the room, fuming. "We cannot waste any more time. We must leave immediately. It'll take us several days to reach Etaon."

Yuri ran his hand through his hair, closing his eyes. He wanted to punch something, but out of respect for Lady Amara, he didn't take his anger out on any of her icy furniture. Junko had already eradicated the reindeer before Yuri spotted him. All the Bount had done was kill precious time. "Violet, we need to go," Yuri said, walking to the distraught princess.

"I … can't," Violet whispered shakily.

"We don't have much time," Yuri said, suddenly feeling impatient. The images of scattered corpses in Etaon flashed through his mind. If his group didn't get there in time, there was no telling whether or not there would be a massacre. "Look, I understand that you're distressed and that you need time alone, but we can't just—"

"Can't just what?"

"Waste any more time…," Yuri finished, immediately regretting his words.

"Is my mourning just a waste of time to you?" Violet snapped, making Yuri feel as if a sharp dirk had penetrated his heart. Her frustrated stare made him feel naked before her gaze, his courage stripped away. "My brother, who I thought was dead for most of my life, murdered my parents!"

Anger seized his mind and he wanted to yell, to tell Violet that she was being selfish and that there were other lives at stake. But Archerus stopped him, grabbing his shoulder before he lost control and said words that he'd regret. "She's not herself, and neither are you," Archerus said softly, pulling the boy away. "We'll leave some Iradian soldiers here to stay with you, Violet. We'll come and fetch you on our way back. Take as much time as you need. We understand."

Yuri was silent as Archerus led him out of the fortress and to where Lady Amara tended to her personal sled. It was pulled by four reindeer that had been put in her private stables. Luckily, Junko hadn't found Lady Amara's personal mounts. Dozens of Frozarians were outside, tending to the wounded victims of the Bount's assault.

"You need to calm down," Archerus said, clamping his hand on Yuri's shoulder. "Both of us know what it's like to lose family. Think of the position that she's in. You can't expect her to race to Etaon, having just found out her parents were assassinated."

Yuri shook his head. "I know. It's just that we don't have time to sit around and grieve. So many things are happening and we've already wasted enough time resting here!" he growled, his body morphing into a werewolf. He turned to Lady Amara, who had gotten into her sled with Noah and another Frozarian. "Are we ready?"

The Frost Mistress nodded. "Follow me," she said, swinging down her reins as the reindeer sprinted forward across the snowy lands, dragging the sled closely behind.

Archerus watched as Yuri took off after Lady Amara's sled in his werewolf forms, moving at a hurried pace. He sighed and quickly morphed into a beast, rushing after his companions.

Yuri could feel it, the enormous weight of failure hovering over his shoulders. He didn't want to be too late, like he had with his mother and brother's demises. He didn't want to be powerless either, like he had when Asmund had transformed into an uncontrollable monster. The lives of so many depended on the success of this mission. If Malyssa really did manage to execute all of the engineers in Etaon, then there would be no way for them to invent a method to deliver the Phoenix Heart's antidote into the werewolves' bloodstream without forcefully feeding the beasts. All of this strife would've been for nothing. *Everyone's counting on us. Please, we need to make it in time!*

The Fall

It had been several days since they'd arrived at Etaon. Terias hadn't trained with Senna since they'd been in Etaon, but that was because the two of them were always being tasked with something to do to help prepare the fortress for the predicted invasion. Torches had been placed all over the bastion, and the doors of every entrance in the stronghold had been layered with silver so that the vampires would have trouble entering. Tons of silver ore were smelted and then turned into bullets or swords that the gnomes would wield when the vampires came.

However, as the days dragged on, Terias began to wonder whether or not Yuri's prophecy was just a hoax. No one really knew if they should trust what Archerus had told them, except Senna. Oddly enough, the knight seemed confident that Malyssa would attack and had the most enthusiasm of all the warriors in the building.

Terias had noticed that Senna gained newfound respect for Yuri after he'd risked his life at the Lake of Eternity. He no longer worried about Yuri being a potential threat after his selfless actions. Kura's troops also saw the boy as a courageous hero, having risked his life against a horde of undead and a frost giant for the sake of the group.

Terias wiped his brow as he secured yet another lit torch on a sconce in an empty corridor. It was nighttime, so he had to make sure that all of the torches were aflame. He turned to the sound of echoing footsteps as someone descended the stone stairway nearby. He watched as Lena staggered into the hallway with a box full of silver weapons in her arms. The apprenticed knight crinkled his brow at the engineer, surprised that she was able to carry around such a heavy load.

"Here, let me help," Terias offered, walking to her.

"Thanks," Lena said, with a sigh of relief, as the young man gripped the other side of the box, sharing the weight. "We're taking this to the armory, if that's all right."

"No problem," Terias assured her. The two walked in silence for several minutes. He hadn't noticed it before, but it was frighteningly quiet tonight. Usually the gnomes would be arguing about something outside or there would be an explosion or two from some failed experiments. But tonight, there was nothing. A disconcerting feeling swept over him, and it was affirmed when he saw a gnome frantically sprinting down the hall, his shirt covered in something other than just soot, dirt, and oil. There was blood, and it was everywhere.

"H-Help!" the gnome screeched, his eyes bulging with terror. In one hand he was holding an iron wrench, and in the other was a silver dagger. This was one of Etaon's engineers!

Terias and Lena nearly dropped the box in unison when suddenly a black shape slithered from the shadows behind the gnome. The apprenticed knight stared in shock as a cloaked creature grabbed the engineer and sank its fangs into the side of the poor gnome's neck. It was a vampire, its skin pale as snow and eyes the orange of boiling lava.

The humanoid monstrosity pulled away from the corpse, which was now drained of blood. The body crumpled to the ground, the gnome's skin as blanched as the vampire's.

Terias stared at the cadaver for a moment, his expression hardening. He reached to his side and gripped his silver sword, tearing it from its scabbard. Brandishing the blade with a flourish, the warrior felt adrenaline channeling through him. The need to slay the unholy beast drove him towards the vampire, his weapon tearing in a sideways cut.

The vampire was agile, elegantly ducking beneath Terias's attack. Licking the gnome's blood from his lips, the creature's hand shot out and grabbed the knight by his throat. The monster lifted Terias off the ground as easily as a grown man could pick up a puppy. The apprentice could feel the vampire's nails digging into his flesh, drawing small slivers of blood that trickled from the cuts in his neck.

The vampire was enraptured by Terias's pain, his crazed eyes flashing with elation at the sight of fresh human blood. A loud bang sounded, and the creature suddenly was forced backward as something heavy thumped into his shoulder, penetrating his pale flesh. Ichor splattered onto the floor of the corridor, and the vampire released Terias to grab his hemorrhaging wound.

The monstrosity glared at Lena, who was wielding a rifle. "Silver!" he screeched as he charged towards the engineer. He bared his fangs, prepared to leap upon the young woman, but grunted when a metallic gauntlet grabbed his ankle. The vampire screeched as Terias brought him slamming to the ground. The knight snatched one of the torches off the wall and pressed the blazing flame against the skin of the ghostly creature.

The undead monster let out a shrill scream of agony as his flesh began to deteriorate, the layers of his skin peeling away beneath the fire. The vampire suddenly burst into flames as if he had been covered in oil, screaming and writhing about. In only moments, the scathing monster lay still.

Lena was panting as she reloaded her rifle. "It looks like Malyssa's forces have already infiltrated Etaon. We need to find the others; it'll be a lot easier to handle the vampires if we're together."

Terias touched the bleeding cuts on his neck, gulping nervously. He nodded in agreement and hastily sprinted down the corridor, leading the way. The two apprentices dashed through the lifeless halls of Etaon, where the corpses of numerous gnomes were slumped against the walls. All of their blood had been drained. Sorrowful whimpers escaped Lena each time she saw a familiar face.

Terias and Lena pushed deeper into the stronghold, eventually making their way to one of the doors that led to a large foyer. They found Kura, Senna, and Twinklehart fighting off a swarm of vampires, beside numerous Iradian soldiers, gnomes, and Frozarians.

The undead creatures outnumbered Kura's small force, but the assassin did not falter. She was enraged, after what Malyssa had done to her companions at the entrance to Lichholme. Rushing forward, the female warrior's speed matched those of the vampires. Her blades bit into the flesh of several enemies as she flipped about, her image a mere blur to Terias's eyes. He could barely follow her movements, but she left behind a trail of dead vampires.

"We should go and hel—"

"Wait," Terias said, clamping his hand over Lena's mouth as he pulled the apprentice away from the entrance, hoping that no one had seen them. He peeked his head into the room, his heart pounding heavily. It was *her*.

Malyssa marched through the main entrance to the room, stepping around the silver door that lay broken on the floor. "If we go out there now, we won't accomplish anything. Not with her out there," Terias whispered.

"What are you talking about?" Lena said through gritted teeth, pulling Terias's gauntlet from her face. "My people are in that room, fighting with their lives on the line. I'm not going to sit here and hide!"

"Malyssa's objective is to kill all of the engineers," Terias snapped. "You can't just throw yourself at her. She'll—"

"I don't care. I'm not going to sit here and do nothing!" Lena snapped, prying herself from Terias and stumbling to the arched doorway to the foyer. She gripped her rifle bravely, aiming down the sights. It only took her a second to fire a silver bullet that sped towards Malyssa.

The vampire turned her head, astounded by the riflewoman's quick accuracy. She'd hardly even noticed the apprentice's presence. However, the projectile never reached her. One of Malyssa's subordinates shielded the vampiric leader with her body, the bullet biting into the monster's back. The creature crumpled to the ground, convulsing for a moment as the body smoldered in its reaction to the silver projectile.

Malyssa glanced at the corpse with pity, and then turned her attention to Lena, raising an eyebrow at the engineer. She waved her hand and a horde of vampires flooded through the doorway behind her, racing for Senna and his comrades. But her murderous gaze stayed on Lena. "This one is mine."

Terias's eyes widened as the tide of battle abruptly turned. The vampires outnumbered Kura's forces five to one. Within seconds, the gnomes and humans fell victim to the nimble creatures. Even the Frozarians were slaughtered, though they put up a fierce fight.

Senna grunted, realizing that he, Kura, and Lena were the only ones still standing, watching as the respected Twinklehart joined the victims of the vampires. He let out a fierce battle cry, cleaving two enemies in half with a single strike of his sword. But he was not fast enough to counter the speed of all of his opponents. Every time he slashed, the vampires would strike him with puncturing strikes of their fists, hammering his armor with a barrage of attacks. The dauntless warrior squeezed the hilt of his sword tightly, his hands quivering from the sharp pains that exploded from his numerous wounds.

Rotating his body, the knight spun, slicing every vampire around him in a powerful stroke. Dismembered bodies rained down around him and Senna panted, spitting some blood onto the floor as he glared at Malyssa. "Keep coming, I'll kill you all!" he barked, wincing at the grievous injuries that he had sustained. Deep slashes carved through his armor and into his bloody flesh, and he had the several broken ribs.

Malyssa smirked at the injured knight, impressed. "To think that feeble humans would prove to be such formidable warriors," she said, catching sight of Kura.

The assassin was sprinting along the wall of the foyer, decapitating three vampires with brutal strokes of her sword. Kura kicked off the wall, flipping through the air, and hurled ten silver knives in Malyssa's direction. The projectiles smashed into four of Malyssa's comrades that stood around her. The vampire leader watched as they collapsed at her feet, not even flinching.

"I'll deal with them," Malyssa assured her subordinates, licking her lips as she eyed her three opponents hungrily. "Search the rest of Etaon for any survivors and kill them all. Cleanse this forsaken fortress of all life." Her executive command sent her minions scattering as they left their leader to battle Senna, Kura, and Lena.

Malyssa reached for the rapier at her side, gripping its hilt tightly. She whipped the weapon out into the air, grinning sadistically, and dragged her tongue across the glistening blade, remembering its metallic taste. Soon, it would taste of delicious blood. "Who's first?"

Terias listened the sounds of clanging blades, pressing his head back to the wall. His heart raced and he could feel tears coming. They didn't stand a chance here — they were all going to die, weren't they? Even if they did manage to defeat Malyssa, the other vampires would return and slaughter them. He reached up and grasped at his breastplate where his heart was, feeling its rapid palpitations.

Fear dominated him and prevented him from going to his comrades' aid. *I'll just end up like the rest of the corpses on the ground.* He bit his lower lip, remembering how Lena had dauntlessly charged into the foyer. *How can she be so brave in the face of definite death?*

The knight brought his gauntlet upward and slammed it into his cheek, sending a twinge of pain into his face.

Terias shook his head and forced himself to his feet, grasping the handle of his sword. It was certainly okay to be afraid, but it was not okay to be a coward. Not if he was to be a knight. "Wake up, Terias!" he mumbled as he pulled his silver weapon from its sheath with a scraping hiss. "If we're all going to meet Death anyway, then we might as well be fighting when it happens."

Kura ripped her short swords at Malyssa, scowling as the vampire parried the blows with graceful ease. "You damned abomination," Kura snarled, her eyes flashing with rage. "You'll pay for the atrocities that you've committed!" She stamped the sole of her foot on the ground, and a small blade protruded from the tip of her boot.

Malyssa blinked as the assassin kicked upwards, slamming the blade into the vampire's forearm. She winced at the explosion of agony that sliced into her flesh. It was soon replaced with a burning sensation that felt as if her entire arm had been lit aflame. "Silver," she seethed, staggering back.

Adjusting her grip on her rapier, Malyssa quickly jabbed outward in three quick successive blows. The blade flashed forward with unimaginable speed, the air shimmering around its fluent movement.

Kura's eyes widened as three holes appeared in her chest and stomach. The vampire's attacks had been so fast that she hadn't been able to react. An agonizing gasp escaped Kura's lips before she fell backwards, slumping against the wall of the foyer, blood pouring from the fatal wounds. Her lips quivered as her body was embraced by bitter cold.

"Damn you!" Senna yelled, rending the air with his massive sword. But his blow was far too slow to strike someone as agile as Malyssa. The woman easily ducked underneath the attack and was about to strike the knight's chest plate, sure that her rapier could puncture the metal.

But Malyssa had not forgotten Lena, knowing that the riflewoman was still taking aim. The bullet exploded from the barrel of the engineer's gun, spiraling as it bolted towards the vampire. Malyssa smirked, grabbing Senna and thrusting the unsuspecting warrior in the path of the projectile. There was a heavy thud as the bullet smashed into Senna's back, causing him to lurch forward in pain.

Malyssa leaned forward and licked some of the blood that trickled from Senna's lips. "Delicious. Let me try some more." She tilted her head to the side and sank her teeth into the knight's neck, sucking the warrior's body dry in an instant.

"Gah…!" Senna gasped, his eyes widening. His face paled as he felt himself weakening. It was as if his very soul was being sucked out along with his blood. He shivered, the hairs on his body straightening as a deadly cold took hold in his body. At first, he could hear his heart pounding rapidly, for he was terrified of the unknown fate that was to come. But as his vision began to blacken, his heartbeat calmed … slowing until he could count individual beats. Then the darkness swallowed him with his final breath.

Malyssa grinned, wiping some blood from her lips. The stout knight collapsed at her feet, unmoving. She tapped the metal armor of the corpse, smirking. "To think you had the audacity to—" Suddenly a silver sword ripped upward, dismembering her left arm completely. Her eyes bulged as she stared at the hemorrhaging stub where her arm had been a moment ago. Trembling, she turned to see Terias, standing over his fallen mentor, sword in hand.

The shocked vampire stared at Terias with disbelief, her body quavering with rage. She knew that such an injury would not heal; he'd used a silver weapon to mutilate her. "You … filthy human!" she gasped, her rapier clattering to the ground as she stumbled back, holding her bleeding wound. "You'll regret that!" She was screaming now.

Lena had reloaded her rifle, tears glistening in her eyes as she looked at Senna's corpse. Biting her lower lip, she brought the gun up and aimed at Malyssa. His death would not be in vain. This shot would put an end to this monster!

Terias expected to hear a gunshot go off behind him, but instead heard a thud. He glanced over his shoulder and saw a vampire standing over Lena's unconscious body. *Wait, no!* His heart skipped a beat, realizing that he'd turned his attention away from Malyssa for a brief moment. But the woman was already upon him, striking him across the face with a powerful blow from her knee. The warrior flew across the room with frightening speed, his body crunching as he struck the wall on the far side of the foyer. His eyes rolled back as he fell forward, slamming to the floor.

With that, the room fell silent. The entire fortress was quiet, with only the sounds of scampering vampires echoing through the area. Malyssa winced at the excruciating pain exploding from her hemorrhaging wound. She needed to return to her camp immediately to get her injury treated. "Take these two as bloodbags," she growled, nodding to Lena and Terias.

"Milady, your arm—" the vampire started.

"I know about my goddamned arm, you pathetic sycophant!" Malyssa barked angrily, storming out of the room. "Just get them and don't bother me. I'm already in a terrible mood as it is."

***

As soon as Malyssa returned to her camp, her wound was bandaged and tended to. The bleeding had stopped, but her surge of rancor hadn't. She'd been clumsy and hadn't seen that boy approaching from behind the large knight's body after she'd sucked out his blood. Her ineptness was the cause of her lost arm.

The vampire sat on a surgical table, her head lowered. This injury was not worth the favor that she'd promised Junko. Irritated, she glanced up and found that the Bount had mystically appeared before her. "What do you want?" she grumbled, glaring at the cloaked man.

Junko looked at her dismembered arm. "It seems that your opponents were quite fearsome," he said, little expression in his tone. "Did you accomplish your task?"

"Yes, I did," Malyssa growled.

"You're in a terrible mood."

"One of the brats lopped off my damned arm."

"I noticed," Junko said, frowning. "I delayed Yuri and his friends so that they wouldn't interfere with your incursion."

"Yeah? Well, it turns out that some of them were already there," Malyssa spat, her words catching Junko by surprise. "I took home two blood-bags—"

"You took hostages?" Junko shook his head. "I highly advise that you just execute them. You don't know if Yuri's group will come looking for them."

"Do you think I'm afraid of a couple of fragile weaklings?" Malyssa snarled at Junko, clearly still grieving over her lost arm. She reached up and pressed her palm to one of her eyes, clenching her teeth. "The very fact that a *human* was the one to take off my arm disgusts me. Now if you'll excuse me, I need to rest. Please, just get out of my sight."

Junko nodded in understanding. "I came to warn you that Yuri might try to assault your encampment of vampires in order to avenge those that he's lost. When he sees Etaon destroyed, he'll blame himself. Who knows what irrational behavior he'll indulge in?"

"Your warning is acknowledged. Now leave."

Junko snapped his fingers and a mist of black magic swirled around his ankles, curling up his body as he began to disappear. His eyes stayed on Malyssa's stump of an arm. Only a silver blade

271

could've caused such damage. The inhabitants of Etaon must've been prepared for Malyssa's assault. When he'd entered the encampment, Junko noticed that the vampires had suffered crippling casualties during the assault on the gnomish fortress.

That meant that the attack had been foreseen and Yuri's party had sent forth messengers to warn the gnomes of Etaon. But how was it possible that Yuri's group knew of Malyssa's plans?

***

Violet knew that she should've left with Yuri, to rush to Etaon to make sure that everyone else was okay. After an hour of crying her eyes out, she'd returned to her senses somewhat. Her sorrow no longer blinded her, and she realized the mistake that she'd made. Yuri was the reason that she had been able to embark on this quest in the first place, and just like that she'd quit on him. There was nothing she could do about her parents' demise. Sitting around and crying would solve nothing.

The princess sat on the ledge of a windowsill, gazing out over the snowy land outside of Lady Amara's fortress. She squeezed her parents' bloody necklaces in her hand, brushing her cheeks where dried tears stained her skin. *Knowing that the fate of so many depends on what happens over the next few weeks … I can't stay here. I just can't.* The pleading words that she'd said to Yuri on that night in Reidan echoed in her mind. Time was precious and every second counted, even the ones that she spent sitting here at this windowsill staring at nothing.

Violet bit her lower lip and dropped the necklaces into the snow, where they struck the ground. To her surprise, the jewelry burst into black mist as soon as it touched the snow, vanishing instantly. The princess gawked at the dark magic that drifted into the air, her mouth gaping. *They weren't real?*

Junko had fabricated those necklaces, using his magic to hurt her, to waste time. That was his plan all along.

Grinding her teeth, her sorrow was now replaced by anger. Violet stepped back into the room where Noah had rested, standing in silence. She needed to get to Etaon.

Violet immediately took off into a sprint, racing throughout the fortress. She spent the next couple of hours asking Frozarians if they could lead her to Etaon. But none of them were willing, especially without any mounts. Lady Amara had taken the last of the reindeer. None of the Iradian warriors wanted to leave the fortress, either. They seemed content with the idea of leaving Lichholme when Archerus returned to fetch them.

Wearing a thick cloak of warm fur, Violet stormed out of the fortress. She stared in the direction that she'd seen Yuri leave. The tracks that the werewolves and reindeer had left were covered up by the snow falling from the darkened skies. Violet swallowed nervously. Sheathed at her side was a short sword that one of the Iradian soldiers had given her. She knew the general direction of Etaon, though it would still take a miracle for her to get there.

Nevertheless, she knew that she had to go. The distraught princess was about to take a step forward when she heard a familiar voice behind her.

"Milady, what do you think you're doing?" a voice said.

Violet whirled around, surprised to find the druid, Moriaki, standing there. "The Druid of the North? W-What are you doing in Lichholme? I thought that—" She stopped speaking. She knew of the accord that Zylon had created with Faelen from the details that Yuri had told her.

"Zylon and the Iradian forces can hold off Faelen and his werewolves without me," Moriaki said, folding his arms. "I was flying around when I sensed some of Junko's magic coming from this area. I didn't know that you were part of Yuri's party," he said with a raised eyebrow. For a moment, Violet thought the druid would scold her for leaving Reidan without permission. But he smiled instead. "I am glad to see that you are still well, princess. Where are the others?"

"They've gone onward to Etaon."

Moriaki glanced at Lady Amara's fortress, watching the Frozarian warriors that were eying him curiously from the stronghold's entrance. "You've made allies with the Frozarians? Interesting choice. You'll have to fill me in," he said, his body morphing into that of a massive bird, the size of a fully-grown tiger. Layers of red and orange feathers blazed upon the exotic creature, making it look as if the falcon were aflame. The druid indicated his back with a gentle nod. "Get on. We'll fly to Etaon."

***

Yuri could smell the thick miasma of blood from a mile away, so he wasn't surprised when he walked into Etaon and found that all of the gnomes had been massacred. There was a twisting knot in his stomach as he walked into the gnomish fortress, stepping over many corpses. He feared the moment where he would recognize one.

Archerus patted Noah's back as the boy vomited, nauseous at the sight of the vampires' victims. The bloodless cadavers of the gnomes were covered in bite marks, their bodies mangled and mutilated, and some were eviscerated.

Lady Amara and her Frozarian comrade also seemed repulsed with the bloodbath as they moved through the bloodstained hallways of Etaon's fortress. "The soldiers of Etaon were wielding silver weapons, and there are torches everywhere," the Frost Mistress said observantly. "It seems they were prepared for the vampires."

"Yet this still happened?" Archerus murmured, shaking his head. He watched as Yuri stormed deeper into the stronghold. "Yuri, wait. Let's slow down—"

Yuri blocked out Archerus's words as he continued forward; he'd recognized a familiar scent. The boy halted at an open entrance that led into a large foyer, where dozens of vampire bodies lay sprawled on the ground. Stepping over their corpses, he saw a massive silver door on the ground that had been ripped cleanly off its hinges. He froze, his eyes widening as he stared at the sight before him. The entire foyer was filled with dead humans, gnomes, Frozarians, and vampires.

Senna was lying with his face pressed against the floor, the blood sapped from his body. There were dozens of heavy dents and rips in his plated metal, and a gigantic cavity in the back of his armor.

Yuri trembled as he hovered over the knight's unmoving body. He remembered when he'd first met Senna in the tavern in the Lower District, and the dozens of disagreements that they'd had. But even though they had their differences, it was impossible for Yuri to say that Senna wasn't a great and honorable soldier.

Senna had always seemed like such a triumphant warrior, able to aptly handle stressful situations with ease. He was like one of the heroes that Yuri had read about as a child. Everyone in Horux knew of the great knight. But to think that he would be felled like this.

This ... can't be happening. Yuri dropped to his knees, feeling for Senna's nonexistent pulse. He closed his eyes, grief overtaking him. Grotesque memories of his mother and brother's bodies in their apartment flashed through his mind. *Again, I'm too late.*

"Yuri...," a gentle voice croaked.

Yuri turned and saw Kura, slumped back against the wall of the foyer. There were three punctures in her flesh, but it looked like the bleeding had stopped. The assassin's skin was blanched of color, and she was clearly weak. Nevertheless, she extended a quivering hand to Yuri.

The boy rushed to Kura's side, holding onto her cold hand. "We have a survivor!" he shouted, a hint of hope in his voice. "Someone, please—"

"We couldn't … hold them off," Kura whispered, chuckling softly to herself. "To think... that we ever thought we stood a chance against monsters like them. Malyssa, she's truly a formidable adversary."

Yuri gritted his teeth at the mention of the vampire. *I'll make Malyssa pay for this!*

Kura coughed, sputtering some blood onto her lap. "They're still … alive. You can still save them." Her eyes were barely open, it was clear that she was fighting to stay conscious. "Malyssa … she took Terias and—"

"Stop," Yuri whispered, his eyes twinkling with moistness. "Conserve your energy."

"Save them," Kura said, as a tear made its way down her cheek. "In the end, I couldn't protect anyone. But maybe you can." She squeezed Yuri's hand with her last bit of energy. "Promise … me." The life faded from her eyes before she could receive a response and the fallen warrior's head slumped forward.

Yuri bit his lower lip. He released Kura's limp hand and stood up, exhaling shakily. *I promise.* He turned away from the assassin's body, only to find himself gazing upon the sea of bodies that blanketed the foyer's floor.

Archerus stood at the entrance of the room, watching his pain-stricken friend. He reached up and squeezed his chest, breathing heavily. The sight of Senna's body was an excruciating blow; the two knights had known each other for decades.

Noah left the room to retch once more, unable to stand the sight of so much carnage.

Lady Amara also looked away, distraught at the sight of her slain kin. "This is brutal."

"What did Kura tell you before she…." Archerus trailed off.

"She told me that Malyssa took Terias. She said *them*, so there might be other survivors that were also taken captive. I'm going after them."

"Yuri—" Archerus began.

"Look, we need to save him before—"

"Yuri!" Archerus raised his voice to a shout, breaking the silence. "It's over. Without the gnomish engineers, there's no way that we can fashion an antidote to cure the werewolves. We need to turn back and return to Reidan, and we'll make another plan to deal with Faelen's beasts."

"We haven't failed yet!" Yuri insisted.

"We have. Look around you, everyone is dead!" Archerus barked harshly, storming towards his friend. "Without the engineers of Etaon, there is no quest. I understand that you want to try to save Terias, but there's no way to successfully do that! Malyssa will kill us all."

"What the hell are you talking about? We can beat those vampires!" Yuri shouted, his eyes flashing with frustration. "We can't just leave Terias to die or become a blood-bag for the rest of his life. Think about what you're saying. Isn't that cruel?"

"What's even more cruel is if we mindlessly throw ourselves at Malyssa's forces, only to become blood-bags ourselves," Archerus retorted. "If Kura and her warriors couldn't handle a small force of vampires, do you think we could defeat an entire encampment of them? We are few in number, and just because you and I are werewolves doesn't mean that we're invincible. Malyssa would slaughter us if we even came close to her vampire city."

"I can't stand this," Yuri gritted his teeth, closing his eyes. "Always feeling like I'm too weak to do anything!" His clammy hands crunched into tight fists at his side. "I thought that when

I became a werewolf that things would change, that I would never fail again, like I did with my family and Asmund."

"Yuri, this isn't your fault."

"You're wrong, it all is!" Yuri yelled, tears now streaming freely down his cheeks. "If I was stronger, I could've stopped Faelen back in Horux. If I had power ... I could've saved everyone in the glacier's pass, I could've defeated the frost giant at the Lake of Eternity without wasting so much damned time!" He lowered his head, sobbing as he collapsed to his knees. "And I could've made it here ... I don't want to see anyone else die. I don't want to feel like this anymore."

Archerus opened his mouth slightly, watching his distressed friend sympathetically. He didn't want to feel this way either; it was excruciating. To lose so many people that he'd shared memories with in such a short period of time was an agonizing pain that no one deserved. Memories of his wife crept into his mind and he could feel his eyes beginning to water. He couldn't blame Yuri for feeling like this. The boy was only nineteen, and he'd lost his family, his city, and most of his friends to the cruelty of the world.

Yuri didn't know who else to blame but himself. If he was strong enough, every conflict could've been avoidable. If he was perfect, he could've prevented everyone's demise. But even when he trained relentlessly to become powerful, even when he cast away his own humanity and became a werewolf, his strength was still not enough to face the world. Powerlessness was his reality.

Archerus bowed his head to Yuri, tears dripping from his eyes onto the bloody floor of the foyer. "I'm sorry." That was all he could say.

The Shadow Realm

*W*ake up.

Yuri opened his eyes, lying in the small bed of one of the deceased gnomes. It was the middle of the night. Everyone was asleep after grieving over Etaon's massacre. After crying away his pain, Yuri had agreed to return to Reidan with Archerus, where they would create a new plan to deal with Faelen. He knew that he was too weak to do anything on his own. In the face of real opponents like Faelen, Junko, and Malyssa, he didn't stand a chance.

The boy looked across his empty room and watched as a shadow slithered across the room, morphing into a physical entity that floated before the shocked werewolf. This certainly wasn't a dream, yet Yuri knew that it was Malyios, somehow manifesting before him. He swallowed, slowly rising from his bed, standing before the mist of darkness.

Malyios took the same foggy form that he had in Yuri's graveyard dream. The Titan's glowing red eyes stared at the boy, who hid his fear behind an expressionless façade. "*You cannot leave Lichholme without first completing the accord. However, you will be pleased to hear that, within Oblivion, you can make all your dreams become reality.*"

Now Yuri was listening. "What do you mean?"

"*Your quest does not end here, should you choose to journey into Oblivion and seek out its vault. Within there, you can acquire the power that you need to fell any opponent. Malyssa, Faelen, Junko ... all of them would be forced to grovel at your feet. Never again would you have to feel powerless. Never again would you have to feel as you do now. Empty, so accustomed to the bitter taste of defeat that it has become a numbing sensation. Frustrated that every action you perform has little to no effect on the world around you. The fate of your loved ones always remains the same. I can see the despair in your eyes. You only know failure."*

Yuri grinded his teeth but said nothing.

"You wonder if it is simply destiny that has forced you to suffer for the remainder of your days. Perhaps you blame the gods for your misfortune." Malyios's ominously rumbling voice echoed in Yuri's head. *"But if you claim the Sacred Treasures within the Oblivion Vault, you can change this haunting destiny."*

Yuri kept quiet.

"Your friend, Terias, is still alive within Malyssa's camp. Will you let another friend perish?" Malyios said. *"Trapped with him is an engineer, a survivor from Etaon."*

Yuri's gaze went up and met Malyios's, staring at the Titan with disbelief. One of the engineers was still alive? *That must be the other survivor that Kura referred to.* If he somehow infiltrated the Oblivion Vault, he could use the Sacred Treasures to free Terias and the engineer. Hopefully, the engineer could then invent something that would efficiently deliver the Phoenix Heart agent. Malyios was right. The quest wasn't over yet.

"There's an incantation, isn't there?" Yuri said, remembering the conversation between Faelen and Zylon that Malyios had shown him. Unfortunately, he hadn't heard the actual incantation. "One that must be spoken in order to open the Oblivion Vault."

"You're right, and that's why I've used an enormous amount of my magic to become a physical entity to get your attention tonight. There is a female werewolf that has found the Oblivion Portal. She will be entering it tonight, and you can follow her if you leave now. She knows the incantation for the Oblivion Vault."

Tanya.

Yuri's eyes widened at the information that Malyios was giving him, his hands quivering at his side. This was his only chance to make things right. He could still finish the quest that they'd all started. If he could acquire the power he needed to save

Terias and the Etaon engineer, then everyone that perished on this perilous journey wouldn't have died for nothing.

"Perhaps you'll get the chance to bring back your father as well."

Yuri rushed past Malyios and out of the room. He didn't know if the Titan was just tossing bait at him, but he knew that he needed to go into the Oblivion Portal. The chance that Malyios could be telling the truth was enough to push Yuri to sneak out of Etaon. He moved as stealthily as possible, for even the slightest of abrupt sounds would awaken Archerus.

The location of the Oblivion Portal was freshly burned into his mind; he knew exactly where it was. Once he was out of range of Archerus's senses, he broke into a mad sprint in his werewolf form. The frigid cold nipped at his cheeks and chilled his claws as he dashed across the snowy plains of Lichholme with all haste. He ignored all forms of discomfort, his mind focused on only one task — reaching the Oblivion Portal.

An hour passed, and Yuri knew that he was getting close. The snowstorm had worsened, becoming a roaring blizzard. Ice sliced at his fur and Yuri squinted, wading through the thick snow against the blistering wind. It became extremely difficult to see through the layer of whipping precipitation, but soon he could spot a lone, towering rock that lay in the center of the blustering tempest. The Oblivion Portal would be there.

The werewolf grunted as he fought against the relentless winds, his black fur coated in snow. He shivered as he reached the giant rock, noticing fresh footprints leading to a cavern in the mountainous boulder. Heading through the opening, Yuri reverted to his human form. He shook some of the snow from his boots, hearing echoing footsteps coming from deep within the cavern.

Yuri crept into the grotto, making sure to minimize the amount of noise he made. Those footsteps must've belonged to Tanya. He'd made it just in time. Now, he just needed to follow her into the Oblivion Vault without being noticed. A loud whirring sound suddenly filled the cavern, and a brilliant flash of purple light temporarily blinded Yuri. And just like that, every trace of Tanya vanished completely.

Yuri sniffed the air, trying to catch her scent, but his eyebrows furled when he realized that she was no longer in the cave. He broke into a sprint, rushing deeper into the stone cave. The ceiling was lower than most caverns, and rocky stalagmites towered around him. As the werewolf progressed deeper into the grotto, the setting became more disturbing.

Hanging from the ceiling were bloody slabs of meat that were so mutilated and disfigured that Yuri couldn't even tell what race these corpses had been. They were fresh, meaning that someone had hung them up here within the past week.

Dozens of wooden cages, clearly built to hold hounds, were placed against the walls of the cave. Within these prisons were the skeletons of human children, their ancient bones completely bare, as if all their flesh had been stripped off.

Yuri's heart pounded as he forced himself to journey further into this madhouse, no longer able to contain his fear. Sweat formed on his brow and he felt his stomach twisting and contorting as he encountered more atrocities. He felt sick, but his determination pushed him onward.

He finally reached a ring of dead men and women sprawled on the ground. In the center of them was a glowing circle that had been carved into the stone floor of the cave by some arcane substance. Within that circle was a star, forged by the same purple smearing. It was the same marking that he'd seen in his first dream with Malyios, burned into the floorboards of his home. *This is the Oblivion Portal.*

Yuri stepped into the center of the ring and the markings responded to his touch. They flashed a violet glow that reflected off the cavern walls, filling the area with vibrant light. A mechanical whirring sound started, the same one that he'd heard

moments before Tanya vanished. Several seconds later, he felt
something grasp his ankle. It was hard and had a tight grip.

Yuri glanced down to find that the circle beneath him had
now become a swirling maelstrom of darkness. A skeletal hand
had reached through the void and grabbed him, pulling him
down with profound force.

The terrified boy felt his body sinking like quicksand
through the darkness, sending a chilling sensation rushing
through his body. His skin felt like needles were pricking every
inch of his flesh as he descended through the portal. Panic
gripped him as he lost feeling in every body part that was
swallowed by the mysterious void. He gasped as the darkness
crept up his neck, preparing to engulf his head, and within
moments he lost consciousness.

Opening his eyes, Yuri found himself lying on hard volcanic
rock. He stared up at the night sky, which twinkled with red stars.
A purple moon shone through the sea of darkness, casting its
ominous light across the forsaken world. A searing pain erupted
in his head, and suddenly the exact location of the Oblivion
Vault engraved itself into his mind. He leaned back, gasping.
Welcome to my realm. Malyios's voice echoed through his mind.

Yuri sluggishly pushed himself to his feet, shaking the pain
out of his head. He knew that he could turn around and leave;
his accord with Malyios had technically been fulfilled. But he
needed the power of the Sacred Treasures. He heard a heavy
bang, and turned to find that he was at the top of a hill of
volcanic rock. In the near distance, he saw a female werewolf
battling a monster of massive proportion. The werewolf was
certainly Tanya. Yuri recognized her Bount cloak, flapping in the
air as she danced about, smashing her chain whip's blades against
her opponent.

The monstrosity that Tanya battled was a colossal golem,
made from ebony volcanic rock that clumped together to create
this creature. Lava burned in the elemental's glowing eyes and

churned within its toothless mouth. Its fingerless hands were gigantic boulders of molten rock, which coruscated with heat.

Tanya's blades glanced off the golem's impenetrable skin. Nevertheless, the warrior continued to battle the monster fiercely. The elemental was certainly slow, and it seemed easy for Tanya to avoid its strikes. But if it managed to hit Tanya, she would die instantly. Yuri found himself charging forth, knowing that he couldn't let her die. After all, Tanya was his key to the Oblivion Vault.

Morphing into his werewolf form, he scampered onto the scorched earth. Ashes drifted in the hot air, and Yuri grunted as he tackled the golem's foot with his full force. Sharp pain jolted through his shoulder, but he managed to take out of one the creature's legs, causing it to lose its footing. The elemental groaned as it lost its balance and fell backward, a wave of dust sweeping out and swallowing Yuri and Tanya in a giant cloud.

Within seconds, Yuri had grabbed Tanya by her forearm and was dragging her away. "We need to run!" he insisted, meeting the Bount's bewildered gaze. "Look, we can save our introductions for later. We can't fight a monster like that, not with weapons like these."

"I've never come across a creature that I couldn't defeat," Tanya insisted, eager to turn around and continue dueling the molten abomination.

"In Terrador," Yuri said. "But this is Oblivion, and things are not the same. Now let's go." He tugged on Tanya's arm again, leading her away from the elemental. This time she didn't resist.

The two werewolves dashed across a plain of desolate earth, charred by flames. The dirt was black and the trees were all dead, the majority of them having burned to the ground. Around them were live volcanoes that spewed lava which drooled down the mountains towards the obliterated valley that Yuri and Tanya ventured through.

"We've gone far enough!" Tanya called out. "We don't even know where we're going. The land extends endlessly."

"We're heading to the Oblivion Vault, no?" Yuri said, glancing over his shoulder. Now the Bount was even more confused. She tilted her head to the side, demanding an explanation. "Like you, I'm from Terrador."

"I figured as much. What is your name and business in Oblivion?"

"I'm Yuri—"

"Never heard of you."

Yuri narrowed his eyes, already slightly annoyed with Tanya's attitude. But he cast away his irritation and smiled wearily. "That's fine. Like you, I'm here to enter the Oblivion Vault. I heard that you know the incantation to get inside."

Tanya's eyebrows went up with surprise. "How do you—"

"Let's save the explanations," Yuri said, holding up his hand. A wave of satisfaction swept over him as Tanya's face contorted into an aggravated scowl. She was not used to being interrupted. "Someone told me where the Oblivion Vault is, just as someone told you the incantation to get in. Do the details really matter? The point is that we can help each other. There are more than enough Sacred Treasures in there to arm a myriad of warriors. I'm sure you can share some of the loot with me."

Tanya pursed her lips, hesitating in deep thought. Then she nodded in understanding. She had no intention of wandering this forsaken land for eternity. She wanted to reach the vault as soon as possible. The realm of Oblivion was supposedly massive, even larger than the entirety of Terrador. "My main interest is a particular potion."

"Fine, it's yours. I'll lead you there so long as you can get us in," Yuri said, gazing off into the distance. The location that Malyios had inscribed into his mind was pointing him in this direction. Far away, there was a gigantic volcano ... was that

where the Oblivion Vault was? He supposed that he would find
out once he reached it.

"My name is Tanya, by the way," the Bount said.

Yuri pretended it was the first time he'd heard her name. He
smiled at her politely. "Stay close. We don't know much about
this forsaken land. We need to tread carefully."

The two werewolves sprinted across the wasteland for
several hours, eventually stumbling across a desolate field. The
few trees there had rotted trunks with limp branches. Decayed
leaves were scattered amongst the ocean of lifeless grass.
Countless gravestones were embedded in the earth, with the
names of the deceased inscribed in the moss-covered rocks.

Yuri froze at the sight of this dismal field. It was like the
graveyard that he'd seen in his dream with Malyios. This was
where he'd seen his father and Beo. In the distance, he saw a
small child holding a lantern, its tiny light shining through the
world of darkness. The little boy was shirtless and wore torn
shorts. He stood motionless, with his back facing Tanya and
Yuri.

Tanya slung out her chain whip, gripping the weapon in her
hands. She trudged towards the mysterious stranger, unfazed by
the menacing ambiance that lingered in the air. "Turn around
and show yourself," she demanded of the child.

The stranger glanced over his shoulder, meeting Tanya's
gaze. Yuri's eyes went wide, his body tensing up. "H-Han?" he
choked out.

Han's expression was apathetic. He gazed at his brother as
if unsurprised by Yuri's appearance in Oblivion. "Why would
you willingly come to the realm of the dead, Yuri?" The boy's
eyes were black, like two voids of darkness. "The two of you are
still alive."

"What's happened to you?" Yuri whispered, staring at his
brother's inhuman eyes. While this stranger before him certainly
looked and sounded like Han, he did not act like him. There was

something more mature about this boy, as if he were a hopeless old man trapped within the body of a child.

Han turned to fully face his brother, dangling the lantern at his side. "Millennia within this forsaken realm has molded my mind to this hardened form," he said. "Forced to heal every wound, no matter how terrible. Forced to exist eternally without aging. Forced to purposelessly suffer at the hands of the cruel, demonic overlords that dominate this hideous land. I am cursed, brother.

"Every minute in Terrador is a year in Oblivion. While merely a month may have passed for you, I've been trapped in this dark world for over forty thousand years. What has happened to me? I've been eternally cursed to confinement within Oblivion."

"Forty thousand ... years?" Tanya echoed incredulously.

Yuri clenched his jaw tightly, lowering his head. "How is it that you ended up here, Han?"

"I made a gamble with Death, a game of his called the Oblivion Trials." Han closed his eyes as he reached deep within his mind to retrieve his old memories from millennia ago.

Yuri remembered that Malyios had told him about the Oblivion Trials. If the participant failed the trials then they would be placed in Oblivion even if their soul was originally judged to be in Heaven. "Why would you agree to such a game? Those who participate are unsure of whether or not they will make it to Heaven. But you were only a boy when you died, Han. You certainly would've been placed in Heaven."

"Yes," Han said. "But I was unsure about mother."

The hairs on Yuri's arms pricked up and he bit his lower lip.

"Death offered me a proposition. He said that if I participated in the Oblivion Trials, then Mom, regardless of her judgment, would be sent to Heaven. And I would also have a chance to get into Heaven, if I completed Death's trials," Han said, shaking his head. "But it was impossible. It would take a miracle for a person to survive such an impossible test. Obviously, being an inexperienced child, I failed the Oblivion Trials. Since then, I have been trapped in this hell."

I believe there have even been occasions when souls have escaped Oblivion.

"Is there … a way that I can free you from this horrible fate?" Yuri asked.

"There is," Han said. "Every prisoner of Oblivion has their soul locked away in a soul gem. Shattering a person's soul gem will free the person's soul from Oblivion." The boy's expression hardened. "However, all soul gems are heavily guarded by monsters with strength beyond your realm of power. If they defeat you, understand that you will also be imprisoned here for eternity.

"You've come to Oblivion seeking something else though, haven't you? So long as you have something to live for, don't bother trying to free me. You bear the risk of never returning to Terrador." Han lifted the lantern higher and its light began to beam brighter than before, emitting a dazzling light that blinded Yuri. "The overseers are approaching. Leave, now."

"What?" Yuri saw that Tanya was looking behind them. He turned and saw an army of figures in the distance, marching across the desolate plains of Oblivion. Most of the strangers had tattered rags for clothing and stumbled about as if inebriated. They looked emaciated and frail, similar to the zombified abominations that Yuri had seen in Lichholme.

Behind the pack of moping slaves was a group of mysterious reapers, shrouded in misty cloaks of darkness. The inhuman creatures glided across the scorched earth, levitating several inches above the ground. They wielded flaming whips that they relentlessly cracked down on the poor humans, who cried out in agony.

Yuri recognized Beo amongst the suffering humans and bit his lower lip, tempted to call out to him. The man's face was weary and expressionless, evidence of his hopelessness.

Yuri felt a tight squeeze on his wrist and saw that Tanya was urging him to leave. A part of him wanted to stand their ground instead of running away. He would battle these "overseers" and free Beo and Han from this dreadful fate. But he could sense the overwhelming power radiating from the mystifying reapers. *As you are now, you don't stand a chance.*

Clenching his jaw in frustration, Yuri turned to his brother. "I'll come back for you, I promise."

Han smiled. "When you acquire the strength to free us from these chains of eternal suffering, return to Oblivion. I look forward to seeing you again, brother. I'm glad that you are well." He bowed his head respectfully and watched as Yuri and Tanya took off across the gloomy graveyard, sprinting into the distance.

A tear found its way down Han's cheek and the boy reached up to touch the moistness, surprised that he was crying. It was the first tear that he'd shed in thousands of years. He'd thought, having enduring this agony for millennia, that he'd become numb to pain. But seeing his brother, after so long, he couldn't help but feel a twinge of anguish in his heart. Han's forgotten memories, lost to the endless stream of time, had reawakened upon seeing Yuri.

A gentle smile spread across his lips and the boy, once emotionless, dipped his head as he heard the anguished screams of the human slaves drawing closer. *I'll come back, I promise.* Yuri's words echoed in Han's head. For the first time since his arrival in Oblivion, the boy felt a tiny spark of hope igniting within his chest. Perhaps one day he could escape this hell. Even if it were eons from now, Han was willing to wait.

I look forward to seeing you again, Yuri.

***

As Yuri continued through Oblivion, he tried his best to push his thoughts of his brother out of his mind. Right now, he had to concentrate on finding the Oblivion Vault. He needed to succeed in saving Escalon first; more than his families' lives were at stake. If he managed to preserve Escalon, he would return to free Han from this vile place.

"So, what will you do with the Oblivion Vault's treasures?" Yuri asked Tanya, trying to make conversation after walking for hours through the desolate wasteland in silence.

"Is that any of your business?"

"No," Yuri murmured, shrugging. "I was only curious. Most treasure hunters that are crazy enough to journey to Oblivion must have a powerful resolve behind their madness."

"I am here to retrieve an item for a friend," Tanya said.

"A potion?"

The Bount nodded.

Yuri pursed his lips. "You must really value this person if you're willing to venture through this forsaken hell for him."

"I do," Tanya said, biting her lower lip. Her expression had softened and Yuri could see that her mind was wandering as she spoke. "My friend granted me a gift unlike any I've ever received before. But more than anything, he's the only person that I've known that's like me. He's gone through hell and survived."

"What about your parents?"

"I never knew them. They were killed before I could walk."

Yuri exhaled. "I'm sorry to hear that."

Tanya shrugged, clearly unfazed by the grim topic of her deceased parents. "Don't be. I never knew them." She rubbed the back of her neck. "The world is a cruel place. I've been thrust into the heat of battle since I was only a child. Enslaved by my parents' murderers, I was abused and forced to do horrible things. Living like an animal, with not even the freedom to choose where you piss, truly makes you hate the world."

Yuri bit his lower lip. Slavery was not practiced in Escalon, but he'd heard that there were faraway lands in Terrador that barbarically stripped people of their freedom and dehumanized them, considering them to be beasts and property. He couldn't imagine living such a lifestyle. Confined, restricted, and tortured … it would be horrible. *It's no wonder you're angry at the world, Tanya. But you don't seem like you belong with the Bounts.* "I'm sorry."

"Stop apologizing."

Yuri and Tanya traveled in silence for several hours, eventually coming near the massive volcano that towered in the distance. Carved in the molten rock was a gigantic open doorway, large enough to fit a frost giant. Through that entrance was the Oblivion Vault. Yuri could feel it. There he would find the power to save Escalon from its doom.

Yuri felt a rumbling sensation underneath his claws as he dashed forward. *We're almost there.* Worry soon swept over him as the tremors intensified. He and Tanya exchanged puzzled glances when suddenly the ground beneath them erupted like a geyser, sending blackened earth spewing into the sky. A colossal being made of a shadowy substance tore itself from the rock. Misty darkness coated its body, and its eyes gleamed like two coals freshly dipped in the scorching lava of a volcano. The earth behind Yuri and Tanya split as the gargantuan beast crawled out of the thick fissure.

The monster rose to its full height, slamming its huge feet into the ground. Each foot was large enough to squash a small village, and the creature itself was as tall as the volcano. Never before had Yuri seen such a terrifying being. He could sense tremendous power emanating from its dark body. The giant groaned, its eyes coruscating as it lifted one of its feet and brought it down near the two fleeing werewolves.

Yuri shivered as he was cast in the shadow of the frightening creature. He clenched his jaw, accelerating to his maximum speed. His arms and legs ached as he pounded them against the ground, his eyes locked on the entrance to the volcano. He could see Tanya sprinting beside him, her expression fearless despite the danger that threatened them. *Come on!*

The creature crashed its foot to the ground, missing the two werewolves by a slim margin. A shockwave pulsated outwards as the earth exploded, sweeping Yuri and Tanya clean off their feet as they were engulfed by a rushing cloud of dust. A blistering wind sent Yuri rolling across the rocky ground, buffeting his flesh. The windstorm tossed him around like a flailing doll.

Digging his claws into the rocky ground, Yuri grunted as he dragged himself to his feet. Squinting through the cloud of whipping ash and dust, he spotted Tanya's silhouette as she bolted off into the distance. Yuri grunted, scampering after her, realizing that the Bount no longer needed him now that she knew the location of the Oblivion Vault. *Is she going to leave me behind?*

The smokescreen suddenly dispersed as a powerful gust of wind blasted across the ground, blowing back Yuri's dark hair. His eyes widened, realizing that another giant shadow had been cast over him. He glanced over his shoulder, horrified to find that the gargantuan monster was about to flatten him with its fist.

A metal chain curled around Yuri's waist, and he yelped as he was yanked out of the way of the giant's strike, which shattered the ground like glass. The werewolf was hauled near the entrance of the volcano, where he landed at Tanya's feet. The Bount was in her human form now and had a hand on her hip, raising an eyebrow at Yuri. "Don't stop moving," she said simply as she ambled through the dark entrance.

Yuri gulped and scrambled to his feet, quickly following her. He transformed back into his human form and glanced back at the shadow giant. There was surely no way that the creature would be able to follow them into this volcano, unless it decided to tear the entire mountain apart. Fortunately, it seemed content to wait for its prey to return, for it did not pursue them into the volcano.

The two partners strolled into a room of absolute darkness. They couldn't see a thing. Then there was a click, and torches, fastened tightly on iron sconces, burst into flames, illuminating the area. They now stood in the center of a massive hollow room made of deteriorating stone. Carved statues of various gods were secured throughout the area, and upon the walls were inscribed markings of an ancient language that Yuri didn't recognize. Everything about this area seemed venerable.

On the far side of the room was an enormous phosphorescent vault made of unalloyed gold. The ominous ambiance that radiated from the mysterious vault was almost palpable, freezing Yuri's body as if a spell had been cast over him. He looked at Tanya, who was enraptured now that she finally arrived at the Oblivion Vault. All of the dangers that she'd had to overcome since she'd arrived in Lichholme ultimately led to this moment.

Tanya closed her eyes and whispered an incantation, foreign words that Yuri didn't recognize. But the vault reacted, groaning as it shimmered for a moment and then vaporized, as if the gold had never existed to begin with. Now a circular opening led into a room filled with glistening treasures of all types. There was an assortment of weapons, from daggers to swords to bows. Treasures, like special armor, and enchanted objects, such as flutes, were also piled upon each other.

Yuri followed his partner into the room, his eyes glistening in awe as he gazed across the sea of loot before him. He wished that Noah were with him to haul all of these Sacred Treasures home in that magical bag of his. He watched as Tanya skipped off to search for the potion that would turn Faelen into a human again. Meanwhile, he needed to find something that could grant him the strength to eradicate Malyssa and her forces.

He spent several minutes examining an array of weapons that caught his interest. Suddenly, the boy caught movement out of the corner of his eye and jerked his head to see what it was. He stared at the figure that had somehow appeared beside him. "It can't be—"

It was Yuri's father. The man smiled at his son, tears twinkling in his eyes. "Dad?" Yuri let out, his hands twitching at his side. "W-What are you doing here?"

"My soul has been trapped in the Oblivion Vault for many eons, my son," the man said, reaching out to embrace Yuri. But his ghostly hands phased straight through the boy and he quickly retreated, staring at his hands sorrowfully. "But you ... you can free me."

"How?" Yuri said, recalling that Han had said he needed to break something called a soul gem to free an individual from Oblivion.

"All you need to do is take those claws over there," his father said, pointing to a pair of ebony gloves that were lying on a pile of treasures. "They're known as the Oblivion Claws, one of the strongest Sacred Treasures in existence. With its power, you'll be able to shatter that urn." His father pointed to a golden urn that was sealed within a cage made of a black metal known as Abyssalite, the strongest alloy in Terrador. "My soul is trapped within there. If you break the urn, I'll be free."

"Father, I have many things to ask you," Yuri began.

"That may wait until I am freed," his father said with a gentle smile. "Please, I have been sealed away for too long, my son. I cannot bear it any longer. Once you release me, we'll have all the time in the world to talk."

Yuri nodded and walked over to the gloves that his father had called the Oblivion Claws. These gloves were one of the strongest Sacred Treasures? His lips curved into a relieved smile.

With this power, he could free his father and bring him back to life. He could save Terias and Etaon's last engineer. He could restore peace to Escalon.

The boy's hands hovered over the glistening gloves, feeling a powerful aura pulsating from the Oblivion Claws. Touching the fine cloth of the treasure, he felt an electrifying jolt crackling against his fingers. He ignored it and bit his lip, hesitating. *Why am I afraid?* He squeezed the gloves tightly, and then pulled them onto his hands, his heart racing. *This is the moment that I've been waiting for. This is when everything changes.*

"*Indeed.*" Malyios's wicked voice cackled.

Yuri glanced over his shoulder and found that his father was no longer there. His ghost had been replaced with the misty darkness of Malyios. Yuri's heart skipped a beat and he stared down at his hands in shock. The cloth had fused to his flesh, turning his skin as black as charcoal. His breathing grew heavy as ebony claws of darkness tore from his fingertips, potent with magical power. He crumpled to his knees, his eyes widening at the unfathomable amount of raw energy that rippled through him.

A vortex of dark magic spiraled around the boy, vaporizing his cloak and shirt. Ancient black tattoos appeared on his back, like scarred brandings had been seared into his flesh. Yuri's irises turned violet as his body trembled with the invincible power that he now wielded. He let out an agonizing scream as a shockwave erupted from his position, sending piles of Sacred Treasures scattering across the vault.

Yuri lowered his head, his bangs falling across his closed eyes. His hair was no longer black; it was now the color of snow. Swiping his white hair from his face, he flexed the Oblivion Claws before his eyes. With a weapon like this, he could bring down entire kingdoms. No one could stand against him, now that he wielded the power of Oblivion.

Malyios watched the young man, grinning nefariously. "*This is what you wanted, isn't it? You claimed that you would do anything for power. Today, you sacrificed your mind in order to gain the immeasurable strength that you have sought for so long. Now rise, my champion. Free me from my bindings so that I may exact my revenge on the gods that bound me here.*"

Yuri pressed his palm to the floor, slowly rising to his feet. His mind was cloudy and his body moved automatically, as if a puppeteer controlled him. He was expressionless as he sauntered towards the golden urn that kept Malyios captive. He raised one claw, knowing that a single slash would shatter the Abyssalite cage and the vase.

A shimmer of movement bolted behind him and he spun around, grabbing a chain out of the air. A blade halted inches from Yuri's apathetic face and he raised an eyebrow when he saw that it was Tanya that had assaulted him. "Is this how you repay me for leading you here?" he said, squeezing the metal chain tightly. A malicious smirk crept across his lips. "You've got guts, attacking me. Do you want to die so badly, Tanya?"

Tanya's lips pinched into a thin line. "I sense corrupt energy radiating from you," she growled, tugging hard at her chain whip, to no avail. Her strength was nothing compared to Yuri's now. "I know a murderer when I see one. You don't plan to let me leave this vault alive."

Yuri smiled, releasing the chain, allowing it to slither back to its owner. "You're awfully observant, aren't you?" He brushed his hair back from his forehead, his violet eyes gleaming like shining gems. "I see that you've gotten what you've came for." Tanya held a tiny vial of pink liquid in her left hand. "It's a shame that you won't be returning to Faelen."

Tanya's facial features twitched with surprise at the mention of her partner, but she said nothing. She swung her chain whip to the side, the scythe blade tearing at Yuri's shoulder. The knife end of her chain sliced from the other side so that Yuri was forced to deal with attacks from both the left and right. An ordinary man would not have the reflexes or speed to avoid both blades. Even a werewolf should have trouble. But Tanya's eyebrows furled at the sight of Yuri's calm and composed expression. His eyes were on her until the moment before her weapons would cut into his flesh.

Yuri held up both hands and effortlessly deflected Tanya's blades with the Oblivion Claws, knocking them to the floor. He charged forward with blinding speed, nearly teleporting across the vault room. Lashing out, he grabbed Tanya by the throat and lifted her off of the ground. The shocked woman thrashed about, transforming into her werewolf form. But she still wasn't strong enough to escape Yuri's iron grip. The boy looked up at Tanya, gazing into the struggling beast's dying eyes. "Is this what it's like?" he whispered to himself, squeezing Tanya's throat tighter. "To have the power to do *whatever I want*."

Yuri closed his hand, crushing the Bount's windpipe remorselessly. The vial that Tanya clutched in her left hand slipped from her limp fingers and shattered on the ground, its rare contents pooling at Yuri's feet. The boy released Tanya, tossing her corpse to the ground like an unwanted toy. He watched emotionlessly as a tear trickled from one of Tanya's eyes, rolling down her cheek.

Stop this madness. A voice called to him from the back of his mind, but Yuri ignored it. Turning around, he faced Malyios's shimmering figure as it levitated beside the urn that served as his cell. A headache suddenly ravaged Yuri's mind and he winced, reaching up and grabbing his head. *Give me back my body!* The boy tightened his jaw; the pain that detonated in his head had intensified tenfold.

"Free me!" Malyios's commanding voice boomed.

Yuri could feel the layers of his mind denying his former self, which was buried deep within his consciousness. Within moments, the demanding voice that echoed in his head faded.

The old Yuri had been weak. He did not deserve the Oblivion Claw's power. The throbbing pain in the werewolf's head also subsided and he slowly rose to his feet, feeling Malyios's steady gaze watching his every movement.

He hovered over Tanya's corpse and picked up her cloak, sweeping it around his body. Most of his clothing had been incinerated. Yuri glanced over his shoulder at Malyios, staring at the Titan from the corner of his eye. "My father ... where is he?"

"*That has nothing to—*"

"*Tell me,*" Yuri growled, his bitter aura filling the area. "You once showed me a dream of my father wandering through the graveyard of Oblivion. Where is he now?"

Malyios was silent.

"Is he still here in Oblivion?"

"*No. Your father participated in the Oblivion Trials and passed. He is currently in Heaven with your mother. Now, please, free me from these chains of confine—*"

Yuri's face was hard as he stared at Malyios. "Our accord was fulfilled the moment that I stepped through the Oblivion Portal. I owe you nothing," he said, a hint of anger glinting in his piercing gaze.

"*I am the one that granted you that power, you ungrateful bastard!*" Malyios screamed. "*How dare you defy me?*"

"You pretended to be my father to trick me into freeing you. You deceived *me*," Yuri replied, turning his back to the enraged Titan. He clutched his hand into a tight fist before his face, feeling powerful magic flowing through his fingertips. "You can spend eternity within that urn, Malyios." He walked out of the Oblivion Vault, blocking out Malyios's enraged curses. If he willed it, no voice would reach him.

Yuri inhaled deeply through his nose as he stepped out of the volcano, a dark mist swirling around the Oblivion Claws at his side. Before him towered the colossal monstrosity that had ambushed him and Tanya only an hour ago. The enormous creature let out a boisterous roar that quaked the earth, terrifying enough to shatter the courage of a thousand warriors. But Yuri did not falter, nor did his indifferent expression change.

With every second that Yuri wielded this unholy power, he could feel a part of himself being sapped away. Soon, he understood, there would be nothing left except an empty shell. The Oblivion Claws, in exchange for limitless power, would consume his soul if he didn't learn to control it.

The monstrous being brought it fists crashing towards Yuri, eager to smash him to pieces. The boy brought both of his claws slashing downwards, dark magic rippling in the air. Raw power left his fingertips and a massive explosion detonated the creature's chest, filling the air and sky with black energy that blazed with heat. Pieces of the colossal monster crashed to the molten earth around Yuri.

The power that Yuri had just emitted was strong enough to level a mountain with ease. It was frightening, this degree of strength. *What will you do with this limitless power?* He could hear his old frightened self, still cowardly whispering in the back of his mind.

Yuri smiled, finally willing to answer. "I'll eradicate anyone in my path."

Any Price for Power

The power that flowed through Yuri felt limitless. The Oblivion Claws granted him strength comparable to the gods. He'd torn the molten giant, which had been wandering near the entrance of the Oblivion Portal, to pieces. His ebony claws had shredded the elemental's rocky hide apart as if it were paper. With his Sacred Treasure, he no longer feared anything, even in the ethereal realm of Oblivion.

The white-haired boy ambled to the area where he had first landed in Oblivion, spotting the same purple markings engraved in the volcanic ground that he'd seen at Lichholme's portal. Stepping into the center of the mysterious symbol, he felt himself being drawn upwards, as if he were being sucked into a void. A cold sensation flowed over him as he was whisked away from Oblivion, returning to the freezing temperatures of Lichholme.

Yuri opened his eyes, absorbing his surroundings. He recognized the cave and the cloaked corpses that lay at his feet. Ordinarily, he would've felt elated after surviving a trip to Oblivion, even though his journey had been brief. But he currently felt no emotion. Even if he tried to appear euphoric, he knew that it wouldn't be genuine. He felt indifferent about everything except the mission he'd set for himself: go to Malyssa's encampment and exterminate the vampires that had slaughtered his friends. Saving Terias and the engineer had been pushed to the back of his mind. Right now, he thirsted for the taste of vengeance.

The boy strode out of the cave and found an army of at least a thousand werewolves loitering in the snowy cold. They raised their heads at the sound of approaching footsteps, and seemed disappointed when Yuri emerged from the grotto. The beasts had come to await their master's return. *They must be Tanya's werewolves, monstrosities that would be set upon Escalon's innocents.* Yuri licked his lips, his violet eyes flashing sadistically. *I'll destroy them.*

The werewolves sensed a murderous aura radiating from Yuri, all of them dropping to their battle positions as they bared their fangs at the lone boy. To their surprise, the human's body began to change. Yuri transformed into a werewolf that was larger than ordinary, matching the size of Faelen. He had white fur that blew in the thrashing winds of Lichholme, and his eyes retained their violet color. "A thousand enemies," Yuri boomed, looming over his opponents. "A perfect warm-up."

One of the beasts pounced at him, indicating to the rest of his comrades that it was time to attack. The werewolf army charged at Yuri, but the lone monster was not worried. He raced forward with triple the speed of an ordinary werewolf, his claws slicing across his enemies. Bellies and throats were ripped open, each blow powerful enough to tear a body apart.

Tanya's werewolves didn't stand a chance. They rushed straight into a massacre. But they fought Yuri anyway, their frenzy triggered by the potent scent of their leader's blood on the boy's clothes.

Yuri could feel the werewolves' untamed rage as they slashed at him, but that didn't make them any more formidable. His movements were too quick for them, with his senses augmented tenfold by the Oblivion Claws. His every physical attribute had improved, especially his strength.

The Ghost Wolf pounced over one of his enemies, grabbing the creature by the jaw and snapping its head back with a forceful crack. Landing behind the collapsing beast, Yuri lashed out and sank his magical claws into the chest of another monster. He ripped his arm to the side, tearing out a bloody chunk of the werewolf's body, causing the opponent to spiral to the snowy ground.

It only took Yuri thirty minutes to massacre a thousand werewolves, their corpses scattered in the ichor-soaked snow. He panted, watching their unmoving bodies, hoping that one of them would get up so that he could continue fighting. His blood boiled from the heat of battle and he could feel his claws twitching, eager for more carnage. The Oblivion Claws hungered for more souls, and he would feed his beloved Sacred Treasure.

Looking off into the distance, Yuri sniffed the air and caught the scent of a gathering of vampires, located forty miles away. Shaking with anticipation, the werewolf's lips curved into a nefarious grin. "A perfect place to test my new power."

***

Terias felt sapped of energy and hope as he lay on the cold floor of his cell. He had been thrust into a tiny chamber with dozens of other blood-bags. They were well clothed for Lichholme's frigid weather and the vampires fed them fairly. But at night, the blood-bags endured a terrible burden. Over two pints of blood were extracted from the prisoners every night.

But Malyssa had given Terias special treatment; she personally came into the cell every night and took his blood. She made sure to leave enough to keep him alive, but Terias was always left unconscious. He constantly felt dizzy, as if the world were spinning around him. Even now, his stomach knotted as he lay on the cold floor of the cell. He shivered and softly licked his lips, which tasted of bile.

The weakened knight had his head in Lena's lap. She stroked his head gently. Every day, she tried to reassure him that things would be okay, that one day someone would come to rescue them, that this hell wasn't permanent. But Terias didn't know how much more torture he could endure. He had only been a blood-bag for several days, but already he looked pale as a ghost and was so feeble that he could barely even move on his own.

Most of his days were spent in darkness, resting in a desperate attempt to recover, only to have his blood sapped once again each night.

Lena could see the despair in Terias's dark eyes. The young man didn't even have the energy to mourn his deceased mentor. She hadn't heard him talk since the second day they'd been in this prison. Biting her lower lip, she wondered if help would ever come. There were no more human settlements in Lichholme, and the only civilization that might have the strength to stand against the vampires was the Frozarians. The chances of them shattering Malyssa's forces were slim. Lena had seen that there were thousands of vampires here. Malyssa called this place an encampment, but Lena thought it was more of a city than anything else. Infiltrating such a place would require a legion of skilled warriors.

Lena lowered her gaze, tears welling in her eyes. No one would be coming after them. After all, the only comrades that she'd had in Lichholme had all perished by Malyssa's hand. On their first day as blood-bags, Terias had promised her that his other friends would come to save them. But that was a pointless hope that he'd fabricated in his deluded mind in an attempt to cope with this horrific reality.

The other people in the cell had already accepted their inescapable fate. Several of them had committed suicide since Lena and Terias had arrived, using their fingernails to tear out chunks of stone from the floor. They would then use the shards as weapons to inflict wounds upon themselves until they died. Lena had originally tried to stop them, but the more time that she spent within these chambers, the more she realized that perhaps hope truly was out of reach. Perhaps death was the only way to escape this hellish prison.

Lena closed her eyes, remembering Twinklehart's face as clearly as if she'd seen it yesterday. She missed her mentor, and all the gnomes of Etaon. But like the other Iradians that she'd accompanied to Lichholme, they had perished in this perilous land. Would her time to join them come soon, or was she destined to suffer the rest of her days in these chambers?

The distraught woman glanced up at the sound of a metal bar sliding. Malyssa stood outside of the cell, her eyes on Terias's unconscious body. Her emotionless gaze swept across the room, and the prisoners all cringed as they felt the vampire's terrifying stare boring into them. She finally stopped at Lena, a crooked smile flickering across her face. "Do you find me cruel?" she asked, her hand on the bandaged stump of her dismembered arm.

Lena said nothing.

"This is simply our nature," Malyssa said. "Just as you humans breed cows and harvest their meat, we breed you so that we can extract your blood. It's intriguing to see how shocked you are when you realize that you are being treated no better than a farm animal. Because that is what you are now, an animal, with no purpose but to feed my people." The vampire grinned as Lena dipped her head, on the brink of tears. "Don't be upset. This isn't your fault. Nature put you below us on the food chain." As she reached to her belt for the jingling keys to the cell, she heard a heavy bang.

"There has been a breach in our southern wing!" a voice shouted. "H-He smashed through the wall and has killed over a hundred of our troops already!"

"What?" Malyssa exclaimed, her eyes wide with disbelief as she stared at an exhausted vampire that had rushed into the blood-bag prison. The creature was covered in blood ... vampire blood. "He? Is it only one person?"

"Yes! It's a Ghost Wolf, one from the legends," the vampire cried out.

"A Ghost Wolf?" Malyssa echoed. She knew the tale. It was said that a werewolf, fused with the darkest magic of Oblivion, would become a Ghost Wolf, achieving levels of power that exceeded all other supernatural beings. In all of history, only one Ghost Wolf had been recorded, and it was one of Terrador's deities. Never before had a mortal obtained such strength.

At first, Malyssa contemplated denouncing the messenger as a liar. The chances of encountering a Ghost Wolf were nearly impossible. But then she felt a heinous aura that was so filled with hate that her body started to quiver on its own. Sweat formed on her brow and she clenched her teeth, frustration on her face. She also recognized the scent of the intruder, but could hardly believe that it was *him*. "Gather everyone. We'll need our full force to bring down the Ghost Wolf."

***

Yuri dashed towards Malyssa's settlement with all haste, his confident gaze trained on the high walls of the encampment. He swiped his Oblivion Claws to launch forth a magical projectile of darkness that shattered through the barriers of the city. Debris rained down on defenseless vampires, squashing them beneath boulders of stone. The white werewolf charged forth, his claws sinking into the snow as he sprinted towards the city.

Vampire soldiers, clad in shining armor, flooded through the gaping hole in the city's barriers. They raised their steel swords as they prepared to engage the sole attacker. The creatures flashed across the snowy plains, moving even faster than Tanya's werewolves had. But their speed meant nothing to the Ghost Wolf.

Yuri jammed his ebony claws into a vampire's chest plate with such speed that the monster didn't have time to react. Before the enemy knew what was happening, Yuri's dark nails had pierced straight through metal and entered flesh. Skewering the vampire with his cursed claws, a burst of magic channeled through his forearm into his fingertips. A beam of black energy discharged from the tips of his nails, exploding out of the vampire's back and engulfing a dozen of his comrades, incinerating them instantly.

The other warriors stared at Yuri's tremendous power with disbelief, unable to fathom how quickly the werewolf had eradicated a dozen vampires. But the Ghost Wolf wasn't going to give them a moment to marvel at his strength. He bolted forward, his body stretching into a blur as he shot across the battlefield, felling enemy after enemy with fierce blows that struck his opponents down.

The snow became coated with blood as lifeless bodies crumpled to the ground, collapsing beneath Yuri's frenzy. A vampire swiped at Yuri's face in a desperate attempt to strike the werewolf, but he ducked and brought his nails scraping up the creature's chest and finally across his face. Watching as his final opponent dropped to the snow, Yuri saw that the remainder of the vampire force had retreated behind the walls of their city, hoping to regroup.

Yuri's heart was pounding, satisfied by the agility and talent of his enemies. His mouth twitched at the sea of bodies that lay sprawled at his feet, but he said nothing. Trudging through the bloodstained snow, he continued towards the city. He would continue his onslaught until this entire encampment was razed to the ground. He felt that he was being somewhat merciful to the vampire race. Rather than condemning them all to extinction for the atrocity that they'd committed at Etaon, he would only annihilate Malyssa's city.

The Ghost Wolf stormed through the city's streets, a single slash of the Oblivion Claws able to crumble an entire street of buildings. The dark magic that surged from his claws ignited several wooden structures, causing them to burst into flames. Soon a conflagration swallowed the southern district of Malyssa's city, lighting up the area like a blazing torch in Lichholme's dark night.

Yuri moved through the scorched city, slaughtering every vampire in his path. Whether they were children, elderly, or soldiers didn't matter. They were all monsters, and he was relentless as he dealt doom to his enemies. He could feel a twinge of pain in his head, knowing that his past self was desperately struggling to regain control of Yuri's body. *This body isn't yours anymore, Yuri. It belongs to Oblivion.*

"Aren't you satisfied that you've finally obtained the power you've always dreamed of?" Yuri's corrupted voice cackled as he stepped over the bloody cadaver of a slain vampiric child. "Never again will you feel powerless! Never again will you be too feeble, too late, too incapable to save those that you hold dear to you."

Please, stop this! This is not what I wanted! The true Yuri's voice was filled with dismay, his pleading cries echoing in the Ghost Wolf's mind.

But the werewolf did not respond as it continued deeper into the city. Bloodlust usurped his mind as he attacked every living thing in his path. Piles of mutilated corpses towered around the malicious monster. The boy in Yuri's mind continued to scream for the beast to stop this carnage, but it did not heed the pleading cries.

"Yuri!" a voice called out.

Yuri stood in the middle of a burning plaza, surrounded by hundreds of charred corpses. He glanced over his shoulder, his eyes flashing violet as he gazed at Malyssa and an army of her vampires. Licking his lips, he turned to face the woman responsible for Etaon's destruction. "Finally, you show yourself," Yuri growled and cackled wickedly, holding his hands outward as if he expected an embrace. "Do you like what I've done to your home, to the people that you cared about?"

"What's happened to you?" Malyssa said, her eyes wide as she stared at the sinister being before her. Such corrupted magic swirled around this creature. The Ghost Wolf showed little resemblance to the old Yuri other than physical appearance and scent. The aura that he emitted was stronger than anything she'd ever seen before; it was comparable to that of a god. His personality, his strength, and everything else about him had been altered since the last time Malyssa saw him. It was as if he were a different person. "To sacrifice your soul to gain power," she murmured, gripping the hilt of her rapier. She squeezed the weapon's hilt and tore it from its sheath, whirling the weapon as she pointed its tip towards Yuri. "I was wrong about you. You're pathetic."

"Pathetic?" Yuri shouted, slashing his claws downward. Massive currents of black energy left his hands, smashing into the crowds of vampires on both sides of Malyssa. The vampire gaped in shock as dozens of her comrades were vaporized by the foul magic, their ashes drifting around her. Yuri grinned sadistically. "My power is far from pathetic."

Malyssa retreated a step as dust swirled around her body. She could smell the potent scent of fear from her subordinates. None of them wanted to face the Ghost Wolf. She looked down at her hand and saw that it was trembling uncontrollably, her sword rattling. Was she afraid as well?

Yuri kicked off the ground, obliterating the earth beneath his feet, soaring towards the myriad of vampires. Both his claws slashed at Malyssa's face, but the vampire quickly ducked, maneuvering beneath the Ghost Wolf's attack. Yuri frowned. This was the first time that he'd missed a strike since he'd acquired the Oblivion Claws.

Malyssa thrust her rapier forward, jamming it into the werewolf's stomach. A pulse of force erupted from the tip of her blade, sending Yuri rocketing backwards into a flaming building. Cheers erupted from her fellow vampires as Malyssa rose to her full height, swiping some of the werewolf's blood across the ground. "Power is one thing, but skill is another," she said, watching as Yuri rose from the wreckage. "Your ineptitude will be your downfall."

Pieces of rubble rolled off Yuri's shoulders and he snorted, glaring at Malyssa. He touched the bloody splotch of fur on his stomach, as if disbelieving that he'd been harmed. His irises coruscated like two purple suns about to detonate into supernovae, the magical aura around him intensifying until the air became thick and heavy. The perimeter of his body glowed with black energy and he gnarred, baring his sharp fangs angrily. "Now you've done it."

Malyssa grunted as she rolled to the side out of pure instinct, barely dodging the Ghost Wolf's pounce. The beast landed on a group of vampires, mauling the poor creatures. The vampiric leader stared with shock as her soldiers valiantly charged forth to strike the werewolf, but were swatted aside like flies. Yuri crushed them with powerful swings of his hands, shredding all of his nearby opponents to pieces. He'd completely forgotten about Malyssa, his mind focused on annihilating the vampires around him.

Fear gripped Malyssa for the first time in centuries, and her throat tightened as she watched as the monster effortlessly slaughtered her warriors. She gripped her bandaged arm and fled. There was only one way to stop this rampaging beast. She would need to take a hostage. *Terias, the two of them were together at the glacier!*

The vampire ran to the prison where the blood-bags were kept. The guards had already abandoned the area, tearful for their lives. Malyssa slammed the jail door open, staggering into a hallway filled with the pleading cries of the frightened captives. She stumbled past dozens of arms that stretched toward her, ignoring the inmates that begged for their freedom.

Malyssa halted before Terias's cell and saw that he was now awake. The distressed knight whimpered when he saw her, fearful of the torture to come.

Malyssa turned and saw a guard at the far end of the hallway. He had broken into one of the cells and killed the blood-bags inside, having drunk their blood. "You!" she commanded, reaching out and prying the bars of Terias's cell open. "Take these two and hold them hostage; otherwise I'll personally have you punished for feasting upon our blood-bags."

The guard vampire quickly wiped his bloody mouth and scrambled over to the cell, bowing his head in apology, not wanting to enrage Malyssa. He quickly lashed out and grabbed Terias in one arm and Lena in the other. The knight was too pale and weak to resist but the engineer thrashed about, screaming for the vampire to release her. "Stop squirming or I'll rip off one of your limbs," the soldier snarled, tightening his grip on Lena. His threat struck the woman like a hammer and she froze, weeping silently. "Will these hostages really stop the Ghost Wolf?" the vampire asked Malyssa.

"I don't know," Malyssa murmured. "Hopefully the sight of his friends will stop his onslaught. For now, just—" The wall of the prison exploded as a blurred creature smashed through the building, tackling Malyssa off her feet and sending her tumbling through the wall behind her. Rolling in the snow, she staggered back to her feet, snapping to attention.

Yuri moved towards her with such frightening speed that she could hardly see him, like a hazy fog gliding through the air. The werewolf appeared in front of Malyssa, tearing his claws at her throat, but she retreated just out of range of his attack. The beast roared in frustration, slashing once more at the woman with his other hand. Malyssa foresaw the movement, jamming her rapier into the werewolf's wrist. Blood spurted from Yuri's flesh and the Ghost Wolf clenched his jaw, pulling back his wounded arm.

Malyssa squeezed the hilt of her sword, stabbing outwards in quick succession at the beast's massive body. Her blows were quick, striking like a needle, poking holes in the werewolf's body with a barrage of jabs. Blood soaked into Yuri's white fur and splattered onto the snow.

The monster let out a bellowing snarl that detonated in Malyssa's eardrums, and the vampire stared in shock as the Ghost Wolf struck out, catching her with a hard strike to the chin.

Sharp pain exploded through her head as she flipped through the air, crashing into the top of a nearby building. Malyssa smashed through stone, rolling onto a flat roof. A stream of blood trickled down from a gash on her forehead and she leaned forward, her body aching. She gasped when she looked up and saw Yuri in the air above the building, descending upon her position.

Pressing the tips of her toes against the roof, Malyssa propelled herself forward, diving off the building. The vampire grunted as she struck the snow, rolling on impact. There was a deafening boom behind her as Yuri brought the entire structure crashing to the ground. "Bring them out!" Malyssa yelled to the guard, who hesitantly dragged Lena and Terias out of the destroyed prison.

Debris erupted upwards like a geyser as Yuri burst from the collapsed structure, glaring at the wounded vampire. About to spring at Malyssa, he suddenly turned, catching sight of Terias and Lena. His violet eyes reverted back to their original turquoise for a brief moment. "Terias," he whispered, sounding like his old self.

"Y-Yuri?" Terias choked out weakly, staring at the Ghost Wolf. "What ... what's happened to you?"

Yuri was about to speak when an explosion of pain suddenly erupted in his chest. Malyssa had thrust her rapier straight through the werewolf's body, the bloody blade protruding from his back. An arduous gasp escaped his lips as the warm, metallic taste of ichor seeped into his mouth. His vision became blurry and he felt himself descending into madness. *Fight it ... don't lose control!* He let out a barbaric yell as he slashed a claw across Malyssa's chest.

Malyssa's eyes went wide as blood sprayed across her neck, her cloak torn to shreds by Yuri's strike. Even the Abyssalite armor that she wore under her cloak had been penetrated by his powerful Sacred Treasure. The vampire groaned, releasing her rapier as she clutched at her hemorrhaging wound. "Kill the hostages!" she cried out, as she collapsed to the snow.

Yuri's gaze flickered to the other vampire and he launched himself at the guard. The soldier had turned his head, opening his mouth to sink his teeth into the Terias's neck. *No!* Yuri tackled the vampire, sending the two of them rolling through the gaping hole in the prison wall.

Lena screamed as she was tossed aside with Terias, the two apprentices falling to the ground.

Yuri grunted, ignoring the stinging pain that cried out from all over his body. He was on the ground and staring at the bloody blade that was stuck in his body, his stomach churning. He grabbed the hilt of Malyssa's rapier and began to pry the weapon from his chest. Blood splattered everywhere. He felt as if he were going to be sick, his head whirling at the gruesome sight of so much gore. When the blade finally came out, he exhaled painfully. Turning, he saw that the injured guard was crawling away, one of his legs twisted in an unnatural position.

Boiling rage forced Yuri to slowly stagger to his feet and limp over to the terrified vampire. He squeezed the hilt of the rapier until his hands trembled. The boy decapitated the defenseless guard with one fluent strike, watching as the lifeless creature's skull rolled on the ground.

Reverting back to his human form, Yuri looked at his blackened hands, staring at the bloodstained Oblivion Claws. Images of the countless lives he'd taken flashed before him and he bent over, retching beside the vampire's headless corpse. He gasped, willing the Sacred Treasure to remove itself. As if obeying his command, the claws reverted to their original form of ebony gloves.

The boy tore the cursed gloves off his hands, throwing them to the ground at his feet. His breath was shaky, and sweat poured down his face as if he'd just awoken from a feverish nightmare. Around him were dozens of frightened blood-bags that had retreated to the far corners of their cells, terrified of the Ghost Wolf.

Yuri swayed to his feet, feeling drained. Not only had he lost a lot of blood, most of his energy had been depleted from wielding the Oblivion Claws. He turned and saw that Lena was helping Terias to limp his way into the prison. The knight's eyes were barely cracked open as he looked at his friend. "You have as many white hairs as my grandpa," he jested wearily. "Are you decrepit already?"

The werewolf chuckled, holding his belly in pain. He wasn't laughing at Terias's terrible joke; he was laughing because by some miracle, he'd managed to save his friend and Etaon's last engineer.

Yuri's ears pricked up suddenly, and he looked past Terias and saw that Malyssa was slowly rising from the snow, blood dribbling down her chin. It seemed that they were not safe yet. "What's your name?" he asked the young woman that supported Terias.

"Lena," she replied.

"I need you to take Terias to the southern wing of this encampment. There won't be any vampires there," Yuri said, images from his rampage rushing through his mind. Gripping the wound in his chest, he groaned. "There should be a few mounts there that you can take back to Etaon. I'm sure you know the way. The two of you need to get out of here."

"What about you?" Terias said, watching as the werewolf hobbled past him. "Do you plan to fight Malyssa alone?"

"This is what needs to be done," Yuri said, his eyes on the vampire before him. His hands balled into cracking fists as he ignored the pain that screamed from his body. "Lena is the only known engineer left in all of Escalon. Without her, the werewolves of Horux can't be cured. If I leave with both of you now … Malyssa would only catch up to us and kill us all."

"Then we should all fight—"

"We'll all die!" Yuri shouted, tears glinting in his eyes. He didn't want to do this, to have to fight Malyssa in his weakened state. He knew that without the Oblivion Claws, he would die here. But Yuri had no intention of equipping that cursed treasure again. "This is the only way," he said shakily, nodding to Lena. He watched as the woman pulled Terias away, practically dragging the injured knight.

"Yuri, damn it!" Terias yelled. "I'm not letting you do this. Please, stop! We can figure something out together!"

Yuri exhaled through his nose, blocking out his friend's words as he faced Malyssa, who was now several meters in front of him. The two fighters had sustained a tremendous amount of damage, Yuri more so than Malyssa. His intention was to slow her down, so that she wouldn't be able to catch up to Lena and Terias. Biting his lower lip, he wondered whether or not he would even be able to accomplish that goal.

"Well, aren't you a selfless bastard?" Malyssa cackled, raising her bloodstained hand into the air. Her skin looked even paler than usual, and her chest heaved whenever she breathed. She was clearly in great pain. "A hero, that's what you think you are? But look at what you did to an entire settlement of living beings!" she barked, her gaze filled with burning hatred. She waved her arm, pointing to the corpses buried in the crimson snow. "You're a *monster*."

Yuri said nothing. Under the Oblivion Claw's influence, he'd murdered countless werewolves and vampires with no remorse. He'd felt nothing as he felled his enemies.

Reaching up, he plucked a white hair from his head and held it before his face. A monster? Maybe that's what he'd become. In order to gain the power that he'd needed to save his friend, he'd became the uncontrollable beast that he'd sworn to oppose.

"Thousands of my vampires fell before your vicious rampage," Malyssa roared, charging at the werewolf. She leapt off the ground, her body rotating in the air, driving a kick solidly into Yuri's cheek. "Your death is the first step of my vengeance!"

It felt as if a bomb detonated inside Yuri's head and he grunted, spinning around. Blood spewed from his lips and he nearly collapsed, his body heavy. Planting his feet on the ground, he maintained his balance. His vision was becoming blurry, but he didn't care. *Buy time!* He turned around and slammed his fist into Malyssa's stomach, sinking his knuckles deep into flesh.

The wind exploded from the vampire's lungs as she lurched forward, gasping. Yuri smashed his knee upwards into her forehead, snapping her skull back abruptly. Malyssa swung her entire body into a back flip. The ends of her feet struck Yuri's chin, sending him stumbling back.

Yuri felt as if life were leaving him with every breath he took. Excruciating pain cried out from his numerous wounds and he panted, tears gleaming in his eyes as he struggled to stay conscious. He raised his shaky fists as Malyssa came at him once again. *You can do this.*

The vampire clobbered Yuri across the face, breaking the bones in his nose. An image of Han appeared in his mind. The boy gritted his bloodied teeth as he received another blow to the stomach, knocking the breath from his lungs. He crumpled to his knees, clutching his diaphragm in agony. Bloody drool ran down his chin, dripping onto the snow. *I promised ... that I'd come back and save you.* He raised his head and saw Malyssa swinging her leg at his face. *But first, I need to save the people of Escalon.*

Yuri absorbed Malyssa's kick with his arm, cracking his bone. Ignoring the pain, he pressed one foot deep into the snow and propelled himself upward, smashing his fist into the vampire's chin with a fierce uppercut. *I won't die here!* Striking his opponent, Yuri hoped to at least unsheathe his sword to give himself an advantage. His quavering hand glided to his scabbard.

Malyssa winced at her dislocated jaw, but caught sight of Yuri's hand reaching for his enchanted sword. She hissed and rotated her body in a fluid motion, driving a heavy kick into the side of Yuri's head.

The boy groaned, pain striking through his skull as he fell to the snow. Sputtering blood, his hand quickly reaching for the hilt of his sheathed sword. But Malyssa was already upon him, sitting on his stomach as she struck his face with a barrage of heavy blows. Yuri reached out with his palm, catching her punch in his hand. Wrapping his fingers around her fist, the boy's body morphed its white werewolf form. He jammed his claws into the vampire's chest, lifting her off the ground.

Malyssa's eyes widened painfully as she was thrown against the wall of the blood-bag prison, her body smashing heavily into stone. Collapsing to the ground, she pressed her hand into the snow, spitting salty ichor from her mouth. Her vampiric regenerative powers had healed some of her wounds, but her body couldn't keep up with the damage Yuri had inflicted upon her. The agony was excruciating, unlike anything that she'd felt before.

She bit her lower lip and gasped, feeling the gashes in her skin beginning to seal. Suddenly she turned, but Yuri was already upon her, his weapon flashing through the air. His sword ripped across her torso, the silver blade scorching her flesh. There was no healing from this.

Malyssa screamed shrilly in anguish, smoke rising from the wound in her torso. She bit back her agony as she stared at her triumphant opponent, shock registering on her visage. "Enjoy this petty victory, Ghost Wolf." Her quiet whispers were hardly audible. "It must feel great ... to finally succeed after being accustomed to the harsh taste of defeat."

Yuri narrowed his eyes, listening to the dying vampire's cackle. He raised his sword and delivered the final blow, mercilessly decapitating Malyssa, silencing the wicked vampiric leader.

As he hacked off his opponent's head, a sickening feeling churned in his stomach and his sight become blurry. The corners of his vision blacked out, and his eyes rolled back as he struck the ground. He'd lost far too much blood, and feared there was no way that he would recover from such mortal wounds. Clenching his bloody teeth, he squeezed his chest. It felt as if all of his bones were shattered, his punctured flesh full of wounds from Malyssa's rapier. On top of the excruciating pain, he was freezing, as if he had been dunked in the Lake of Eternity. A shiver ran through his body and he went still, his consciousness fading into an abyss of darkness.

***

An hour later, an emerald glow began to shine next to Yuri's pants. In the snow was the tiny seed that Moriaki had given the boy back in Reidan, coruscating with natural magic.

The wind picked up, creating a whirling vortex around Yuri's body. The seed germinated instantly, and a plant slowly rose from the snow. It grew exponentially over the course of several minutes, eventually becoming a towering tree, taller than any of the buildings in the vampire settlement, shining with an emerald light. Its branches reached towards Yuri, curling around the unconscious boy, dragging him towards the trunk.

The magical tree brought Yuri into a tight embrace, the branches constricting him. A transparent sap oozed from the bark around the werewolf, spilling over Yuri's body until it had

had covered him. It then solidified, trapping him within a translucent pod that softly glowed.

The sound of galloping fused with the howling wind as a horse, bearing two riders, cantered through the corpse-filled streets. The steed halted beside Malyssa's body and Lena dismounted. She had never intended to leave Yuri to his fate, especially after he'd risked so much to save her and Terias. She'd gone to the armory and retrieved pistols for her and Terias so that they could provide support. But it seemed that the battle between the werewolf and vampire had already concluded. Malyssa had been vanquished, her severed head lying several feet from her hemorrhaging body.

But Yuri was trapped in an arcane substance that Lena had never seen before. The apprentice examined the pod that confined the werewolf, rapping it experimentally with her knuckles. It was solid, like layered ice, — tough but not impenetrable. This tree certainly had not been here before. How had it grown in such a short amount of time?

"His wounds," Terias called weakly, still seated on the horse. "Look."

The Ghost Wolf's wounds were closing, the damaged skin kneading together as if an invisible entity were sewing his flesh. This was powerful healing magic.

Lena's foot tapped a silver sword buried under a thin layer of snow. Yuri's weapon. She reached down and picked up the sword, testing its balance in her hands. Gripping the hilt tightly, she swung hard, the blade biting deep into the pod's transparent substance. The material cracked beneath her blow and Terias winced, half-expecting her slash to break through the pod and cut Yuri. "Careful," he warned her.

The woman nodded, knowing that the blow had dealt enough initial damage to the pod. Turning the sword, she began to repeatedly slam its pommel into the cracked substance. Like clay, it shattered beneath her strikes, and the branches that held

Yuri released him, allowing the unconscious boy to fall forward into Lena's arms.

"Think this horse can carry three to Etaon?" Lena grunted as she started to drag Yuri's limp body to Terias and the horse.

The knight shrugged. "What other option do we have? You're the only one that's in any condition to ride." He smiled. "If the worst comes, you'll just have to drag two injured men the rest of the way. No big deal."

Lena groaned as she slumped Yuri's body into Terias's arms, raising an eyebrow at the knight. "You pick the worst times to make jokes."

Second Chance

Archerus was not having the best morning, after spending several hours frantically looking for Yuri. The boy hadn't been in his bed and there was no trace of him anywhere around Etaon. His scent was barely present, meaning that he must've left the gnomish stronghold. To his dismay, he found tracks that belonged to Yuri, leading northwest. He had no idea where his friend went. The boy hadn't traveled in the direction of Malyssa's encampment, and the location of the Phoenix Heart field was east. The only other place he could've gone was the Oblivion Portal.

Archerus scrunched up his nose. *Did that idiot really go off on his own in the middle of the night?*

"Hey, something's approaching from the south!" Noah called, standing atop one of Etaon's outer walls. He held out his palm, creating a telescope in his hand. Using it, he zoomed in on the incoming strangers. "It's Violet! She's mounted on a giant, flying ... bird thing. They're approaching fast!"

A massive bird with feathers the color of fire soared over the fortress walls, descending into the courtyard before Etaon's citadel. Archerus, Lady Amara, and her assistant gathered to greet Horux's princess as she dismounted from the gigantic creature. To Archerus's surprise, the bird transformed, morphing into the renowned druid that he'd seen back in Reidan. Moriaki.

The elf cleared his throat, his nose twitching at the overpowering scent of blood that clung to the fortress grounds. The druid could tell that there had been a fierce battle here, but he said nothing.

"Where's everyone?" Violet asked, meeting Archerus's distraught gaze.

"They're gone," Archerus murmured. "The vampires got here before we did and killed them all. We buried them yesterday."

Violet put her hand to her mouth, exhaling shakily. She closed her eyes, fighting back tears. The princess swallowed her pain, knowing that Senna was amongst the brave warriors that had fallen to the vampires. "What about Yuri? I don't see him here, but he came with you, didn't he?" she let out.

"He's gone missing," Lady Amara said.

"What? How?"

"We don't know," Archerus said, running his hand through his stringy hair. "I believe that he left Etaon in the middle of the night to travel to the Oblivion Portal. Because the gnomish engineers were killed by Malyssa's assault, we planned to fetch the rest of our troops at Lady Amara's fortress and return to Reidan, where we would discuss a new plan to deal with Faelen's werewolves. Perhaps Yuri thought that he needed to complete his accord with Malyios prior to us leaving Lichholme. Though that wouldn't explain why he hasn't returned yet."

"We cannot just wait here for Yuri to return, it's too dangerous," Moriaki said. "I suggest that we follow Archerus's original plan and travel back to Reidan."

Violet was about to protest when Noah suddenly let out a cry. "We have a horse incoming! It's carrying three people. It's a woman and Terias, and — I think that's Yuri!" he exclaimed, looking down at his surprised friends. "He looks different, though."

Archerus tried not to ask what had changed; he wanted to see for himself. The boy had ended up going to Malyssa's encampment after all. But how had he managed to save Terias and this woman alone? Stealth was not an option, especially with vampire sentries surrounding the area. It was impossible to infiltrate Malyssa's settlement without encountering at least a hundred opponents. Archerus would've been surprised if Yuri handled ten on his own. The vampires were extremely apt in battle.

When the horse finally trotted through Etaon's gates, Terias and Yuri practically fell off the exhausted steed, rolling to the ground. Lady Amara and her Frozarian companion quickly rushed to the knight's aid, carrying him to the stronghold to be treated.

Everyone else stared at Yuri, surprised at the sudden change in his hair color. Archerus watched as Violet moved to the werewolf's side, cradling the boy's limp head in her arms. He turned to Moriaki. "Can you do anything to heal him?"

Moriaki shook his head, his arms folded over his chest. "Prior to your departure from Reidan, I gifted him with a Seed of Life. The seed grows into a tree when its holder nears death, and proceeds to heal all of their wounds. However, it does come with a cost. The healed individual falls into a deep slumber of unpredictable length. He may never wake up at all," he said, his expression stern. "He must've sustained an enormous number of wounds for the seed to be activated. But I can sense the seed's magic surrounding him, mending his body even now."

"He's in a coma?" Noah said, jogging into the area after leaving his post at the fortress's outer wall.

"Essentially," the elf replied.

"Take Yuri inside," Archerus commanded and Noah quickly helped Violet carry the unconscious boy towards the fortress. The leader then turned to the stranger, who stiffened. "And who are you?"

"M-My name is Lena! I was an apprentice engineer at Etaon underneath Lord Twinklehart!" the woman exclaimed, her posture straight.

Twinklehart? Archerus smiled slightly. A practitioner of gnomish engineering had survived after all. If she could invent a device that would provide an easy way to deliver the Phoenix Heart antidote into the werewolves, perhaps they hadn't wasted their time and resources in Lichholme after all. "Explain to me what happened from the moment Malyssa's forces infiltrated Etaon until now."

Lena proceeded to tell her tale, explaining in detail what had happened during the incursion of Etaon. Archerus's facial features twitched as the poor woman spoke of her atrocious experience as a blood-bag in Malyssa's encampment. But what she and the other prisoners endured seemed little in comparison to the suffering Terias went through. No wonder he looked so frail.

Then came the description of Yuri, as the Ghost Wolf. Yuri had worn a pair of gloves that had made him lose control, turning him cruel and bloodthirsty. Archerus could hardly believe Lena when she said that he massacred thousands of vampires in only hours and decapitated Malyssa on his own. There was only one place that Yuri could've acquired such a rare item — Oblivion.

"Do you have the gloves with you?" Moriaki asked.

Lena reached into her pockets and pulled out the Oblivion Claws, which hung limply in her hands. Moriaki marveled at the fine cloth, gaping in awe. He could see lines of unholy power surging through every seam of these gloves. The strength to topple empires and quake continents to their very foundations lay within this extraordinary item. "A Sacred Treasure," the druid whispered, taking the gloves from the engineer. "This was taken from the depths of Oblivion. Corrupting magic twists through it. A person who wields this will lose their mind. How did Yuri manage to take these off?"

"He seemed to return to his senses when he saw Terias and me being held hostage," Lena replied.

The elf smiled slightly. The power of this Sacred Treasure should've been enough to completely eradicate Yuri's old self. The druid was surprised that Yuri had managed to retake control of his body at all. "I will hold onto these for now," he said, tucking the gloves into a pocket inside his robes.

"Lena, we've come a long way, seeking the help of a gnomish engineer," Archerus said, gaining the apprentice's attention. "Since you're the last one in Escalon, I was wondering if you could hear us out and help us, if it is within your power."

Lena smiled. "I am forever indebted to Yuri. Any cause that he fights for, I will stand behind him."

Archerus nodded and explained why they had come to Lichholme, telling her every detail of Horux's invasion and the current situation of Escalon.

It didn't take long for Lena to understand the dangerous state of the continent. She tapped her finger to her chin. "Master Twinklehart actually completed the prototype for a device that could combat vampires and, technically, could also kill werewolves as well. It is a pistol that can shoot capsules of melted silver, injecting the metal into the target's bloodstream. It was meant to sear vampires from the inside."

"We aren't looking to kill the werewolves. Our mission is to cure them," Archerus said.

"Yes, yes. It's just that ... I could make some modifications to the prototype so that, instead of the capsules of silver, it could fire the Phoenix Heart antidote. Theoretically, if I extract the liquid from the Phoenix Hearts and put it into the capsules, I could adjust the gun so that instead of firing melted silver at vampires —"

"We could be firing the antidote straight into the bloodstream of the werewolves," Archerus finished, elation sweeping over him. He slapped his forehead, grinning like a child on its birthday. "By the gods, that would work! But we would need to mass produce the weapons."

"Etaon has the resources to make thousands of them," Lena said, pointing at the fortress. "But it would take a lot of time to bring enough Phoenix Hearts back from the fields. It would be even harder to drag the guns back to mainland Escalon."

"Don't worry about that," Noah said, snapping his fingers, summoning his magical sack. "This bag has magical properties. It is practically bottomless and weighs as little as a feather, no matter what I put into it. I can carry the Phoenix Hearts and the guns without a problem."

Moriaki whistled, rubbing the back of his neck. Only moments ago, this quest had seemed doomed. "It would seem that we have a lot of work to do."

Archerus was already dashing into the fortress to get supplies for their journey to the field of Phoenix Hearts. "Then let's get started!"

The Beginning of the End

Long weeks dragged into months, and Archerus grew worried of about the fate of Escalon. Moriaki had assured him that Escalon was safe, because Faelen's accord with Zylon kept him behind the magical wall that Zylon had created. However, Archerus did not like betting the fate of the millions of inhabitants of Escalon purely on Faelen's honor.

Archerus went with Noah and Moriaki to the Phoenix Heart fields to harvest thousands of the plants. The field was located in a lush valley, in the center of a ring of towering mountains. It didn't take long for Archerus's party to find a path to the valley, but they spent a lot of time collecting the Phoenix Hearts.

The valley itself was gorgeous, filled with hundreds of thousands of flowers that blazed like a sea of tiny candles. Even at night, they illuminated the darkness with their natural glow, a sight that Archerus would miss seeing.

The party of three worked hard for weeks, doing their best to collect as many Phoenix Hearts as they possibly could, shoveling piles of the plant into Noah's magical bag. When they were finished, the valley had been nearly cleared of Phoenix Hearts. There were only a few dozen left.

When Archerus and his companions returned to Etaon, they were met with encouraging news. Lena had adjusted Twinklehart's invention so that it would now fire capsules of the liquid antidote present in Phoenix Hearts' stems. She called this ruby substance *Reberna*.

Etaon had now been occupied by several hundred Frozarians, called upon by Lady Amara. The Frost Mistress, like Lena, felt indebted to Yuri because of his victory over Malyssa and her vampires. In all of their centuries of war, the Frozarians had never been able to eliminate Malyssa's settlement. Feeling that she owed Yuri a favor, Lady Amara had her Frozarian warriors defending Etaon from any outside threats, such as undead, trolls, and other foul creatures. In addition, many of her subordinates helped Lena in the mass production of her guns. She named the invention the Phoenix Cannon.

Over the past few weeks, Violet had cared for both Terias and Yuri. Terias had recovered within two weeks. As soon as he was back on his feet, the knight alternated between assisting Violet with monitoring Yuri and helping with Lena's production of Phoenix Cannons.

Two months later, a thousand Phoenix Cannons had been produced, along with a hundred thousand capsules of Reberna. That would be more than enough to retake Horux, assuming that they weren't terrible marksmen and didn't waste ammunition.

Archerus stood at the edge of Yuri's bed, watching the boy as he slept. For two months, Yuri hadn't opened his eyes. Yet, he was alive, and Violet worked to preserve his health. The boy had gotten skinny and frail, but that was to be expected from months of being in a coma.

Archerus turned to Violet, who sat in a chair at Yuri's side. He smiled. There was still hope and love glinting in the princess's eyes as she watched the slumbering werewolf. "Moriaki will fly you and Yuri back to Reidan tonight. He then will proceed to southern Escalon to arm Zylon's forces with the Phoenix Cannons. Horux will soon be ours again, Your Highness."

Violet nodded, smiling. "Thank you, Archerus. For everything."

Archerus bowed his head in reverence to his princess. "Things will get better. You'll see."

"I can only hope so," Violet replied.

Archerus watched the young woman for a moment longer before departing Yuri's room, leaving the two alone. His boots echoed through the silent hallways of Etaon. For the first time in a while, the fortress was not ringing with the sounds of clanging metal or shouting Frozarians. After months of vigorous work, Lena had halted production to give everyone a rest.

The silence was not like the disconcerting quiet of Horux's forests. It was tranquil and serene, like the time he and Yuri had tested their new werewolf skills, trying to catch fish in one of Escalon's rivers.

Archerus's lips curled into a smile. Perhaps this was a sign that peace was finally approaching.

***

For three months, Faelen waited behind Zylon's magical wall, patiently brooding in his confinement. He was calm, confident in Tanya's ability to accomplish the task that he'd given her. He spent every day calming the werewolves, preventing them from trying to tear down Zylon's wall. Faelen wanted to uphold his end of the accord, but with every passing day, he grew more skeptical about Tanya's progress.

Lichholme was certainly a dangerous land, but Faelen was aware Tanya's strengths. He believed her capable of handling the forsaken territory's monstrosities. What was taking her so long?

Perhaps she'd betrayed him. Perhaps Junko appeared and gave her new instructions to dominate Escalon. Perhaps Faelen, if he didn't do anything, would be doomed to eternal incarceration on this accursed peninsula. Just like his imprisonment in Horux's catacombs.

The blood in his veins boiled with ire, his claws shaking at his side. He tried to calm himself, but the more he thought about being trapped behind a wall, the more enraged he became. The werewolves around him sensed his anger and began to howl in response, waiting for his orders. They were nearly sure that he would command them to attack Zylon's wall, but he didn't.

Instead, Faelen closed his eyes and sat on the ground, in the shadow of Zylon's fabricated barrier. Exhaling through his nose, the werewolf looked up, and saw a mystical mist of darkness swirling in a black vortex before him. His fellow werewolves growled at the mysterious entity, sensing a malicious aura radiating from the fog. Faelen recognized the faint magical presence. He squinted his eyes and scoffed. "You've grown weak, Malyios."

"As have you, Faelen," the Titan's voice grumbled. "The humans imprisoned you for centuries and you only butchered the inhabitants of Horux? Is that the extent of your vengeance?"

"I seek a cure for the burden that you've forced upon me," Faelen seethed, his eyes flashing with rage. "Once, I was human. But your promise for power transformed me into this monstrosity. I was shunned by my family and friends, condemned as an abomination by my empire, and confined to a silver cell for no reason other than my appearance as a beast. Revenge upon the human race will not change the monster that you've made me."

"This news will be unfortunate to you then," Malyios said with a snide tone. "You'll never become human again."

"What?" Faelen gnarled, a flash of rage in his eyes. The werewolf rose to his feet, reaching the height of the black mist that drifted before him. He tilted his head slightly. "Why do you say that?"

Images began to shine upon Malyios's misty body, showing Faelen the Titan's memories from within the Oblivion Vault. Faelen watched as Yuri mercilessly murdered Tanya, who had been his final hope for becoming human. The werewolf's eyes widened when Tanya dropped the antidote that could make him human again. He winced when the priceless vial shattered on the ground, cringing at the sound of the breaking glass.

Faelen clenched his teeth as he was forced to stare at Tanya's lifeless corpse. She had done as he had asked. Pushing through Iradia's forces, she'd made her way to Lichholme. She'd managed to find the Oblivion Portal and break into the vault. And when she finally had the antidote that Faelen needed … Yuri had swept in to ruin his plans yet again. That accursed boy hadn't even had a legitimate reason for killing Tanya. He'd just heartlessly murdered her, his gaze as cold as Lichholme's remorseless winter.

Yuri certainly seemed different in the images that Malyios showed Faelen. It wasn't just the boy's hair color that had changed. It was his attitude, his expression, and his indifference towards taking a life. Faelen recognized the apathetic countenance that Yuri had worn when he crushed Tanya's windpipe. It belonged to that of a monster. The humans should be caging that damned murderer!

Faelen quivered with rage. "He'll pay!" he boomed, his fierce voice shaking the ground. Thousands of his werewolves responded to his enraged cry with yowls that echoed in the night. He let out a roar, ordering his beasts to charge Zylon's wall.

Anger burned in his eyes as his horde of monsters charged at the spike wall, beginning to pry off the magical thorns with their claws. Faelen gritted his jaw, dark magic channeling down his forearms into his claws. If there was no way for him to become human anymore, then he didn't care if Escalon was destroyed. Everyone could perish, as long as Yuri was among them.

Faelen swiped his claw outward, sending a rush of demonic magic from his fingertips, slamming into Zylon's wall with enormous force, quaking the earth to its very foundation. Massive fissures split across the ground, but the barrier still held. Faelen expected no less from magic created by the infamous immortal. "Bring it down!" he commanded to his army.

A Taste of Freedom

Zylon extended his quivering hands towards the gigantic wall that trapped Faelen and his werewolves. He gritted his teeth, feeling his magic crumbling beneath the werewolves' unrelenting attacks. The immortal did his best to fortify the wall, sealing whatever cracks it had, to keep the werewolves at bay. But each time Faelen struck out with his dark magic, his power dealt devastating damage that Zylon could not mend in time.

For months, Zylon's army had been stationed at southern Escalon's land bridge, meeting no opposition from Faelen and his werewolves. But suddenly, Zylon was woken in the middle of the night by the sound of heavy banging as Faelen's beasts proceeded to smash the wall's spikes, greatly damaging the barrier.

It was morning now, and the sun shined down on five thousand Iradian knights that stood behind Zylon, their shields and swords raised. Riflemen positioned themselves behind the front lines, their guns trained on the wall, preparing for its collapse.

Zylon felt drained since he'd been rebuilding the wall continuously for hours. The werewolves were relentless; they didn't give him a single moment to rest as they bombarded the barrier. He concentrated a lot of his energy on rebuilding the wall's spikes, knowing that if they weren't present the werewolves would simply clamber over the magical obstacle.

There were still many spikes in place, enough to prevent the werewolves from scaling the wall. Suddenly, a shadow fell over the immortal. He glanced up to find a massive werewolf descending behind him. Faelen.

How did he climb the wall?

The beast hit the ground with such force that a crater formed beneath his feet, clouds of dust sweeping out in all directions. Faelen didn't hesitate for a second as he dashed towards the Iradian forces, his eyes filled with bloodlust. Gunshots rang in the air as bullets sped towards the advancing werewolf, some of them burying into his flesh. But Faelen ignored the searing pain, enduring the damage as if they were toy darts instead of silver bullets.

A single swipe of one claw was enough to rend the front line of Iradian soldiers, shredding their armor and kite shields apart like paper. Faelen didn't stop there, barreling through the ranks of knights like an inexorable bull, sending soldiers scattering in all directions. Hundreds laid slain in his wake, but he didn't bother to infect any of them. He seemed perfectly satisfied with savage murder.

Zylon mashed his teeth together, wincing as Faelen's werewolves continued to attack his wall. He wanted aid his warriors, but he was immobilized while mending the barrier. "Damn it!" he shouted in frustration as Faelen trampled the final defense of Zylon's force.

At least five hundred warriors were slaughtered in only a minute's time. Another three hundred lay injured. The remaining knights hadn't even had a chance to attack Faelen, for he'd moved far too quickly. Already, the werewolf had sprinted into the distance, his body a blur as he darted across Escalon's fields.

Zylon closed his eyes in defeat, knowing that the humans of Escalon were now doomed to infection, if Faelen chose. He grunted, maintaining the barrier that held Faelen's subordinate werewolves back. "We're in trouble now."

***

Moriaki brought Violet and Yuri back to Reidan, allowing them to mount him while he was transformed into a giant bird. When they reached the city the following morning, King Reimos gladly welcomed their arrival.

The druid landed in the courtyard outside of Reidan's citadel, and the Iradian king came out to greet them personally. His hands were outstretched as if he intended to embrace the giant bird. "Welcome back, my heroes," he said, his eyebrows rising when he saw Violet dismounting Moriaki. "Oh my, we were worried about you, Princess Violet. Your parents thought that Lichholme would claim your life when they read the letter that you left behind."

"Well, I'm alive," Violet said, rolling her eyes. "Where are my parents now?"

"They're in Teolan, helping the Horuxians get settled," King Reimos said, concern flashing across his face as his eyes rested on Yuri's unconscious body. "Will their stay in Teolan be long-term?" he asked.

Moriaki changed back into his elf form, lifting Yuri into his arms. He nodded to Noah's magical pouch, dangling from his belt. "The solution to our werewolf problem lies within this bag," he said with a grin. "I just want to make sure that Yuri is taken care of before I depart for southern Escalon, where we'll begin retaking Horux."

Lord Reimos clapped his hands joyously, satisfied with the results of their journey. "I've received word from Zylon that they've stabilized their position in southern Escalon. The werewolves won't be escaping any time soon." He motioned for Moriaki and Violet to walk with him into the castle. "What's happened to Yuri? Why is his hair white?"

"Everyone that ventured to Lichholme has been through a lot," Moriaki muttered, exchanging glances with Violet. "Yuri especially. Most of the adventurers that initially left on the quest have already perished, Kura included." The druid spoke in sepulchral tones, a distinct change from his ordinary mellifluous voice.

A gloomy expression dawned over the distressed king, who shook his head in disbelief. Kura had been one of his greatest warriors, having survived many battles with formidable foes of Iradia. She had always returned to King Reimos as a victorious champion. Hearing of her fall in Lichholme was unexpected. "I can't imagine how dreadful Lichholme must've been," he said as the group ambled through the maze-like corridors of Reidan's royal castle. "Will others be arriving as well? Or are you the only three that survived?"

"There are others," Moriaki said, smiling when he saw the Iradian king sighing with relief. "They're being led by Archerus, traveling on foot. I imagine that they'll arrive two weeks from now. An ally of ours, Lady Amara, will be escorting them out of Lichholme."

King Reimos nodded, leading Moriaki and Violet into the royal infirmary. The room was massive, filled with many empty beds with mattresses more comfortable than most in Escalon. "You may leave Yuri here. I'll have my best doctors look after him. How long has he been unconscious?"

"He's been asleep for a little over two months now," Moriaki said.

"What?" The king's jaw dropped.

The druid indicated to Violet. "She's been watching over him every day since he's fallen into this magical slumber. Don't bother giving him medicines or any special treatments. When he awakens is up to him," he said. "Our job is merely to keep him alive until he does."

The elf set Yuri down gently on an empty bed. He reached into his robes, pulling out the Oblivion Claws that had tormented the boy's mind. The druid turned and handed the gloves to Violet. "If he wakes up, make sure to give him these. He's the only one who truly understands the consequences of using such a dangerous Sacred Treasure," he said. "They should stay in his possession. I trust that you will not put them on."

Violet nodded her head in understanding. "*When* he wakes up, you mean," she corrected.

Moriaki blinked, realizing what he'd said. He chuckled. "That's what I meant. My apologies." The elf reached to his side, digging his hand into Noah's pouch. Pulling out a Phoenix Cannon, he set it on the table beside Yuri's bed. "If he does wake up sooner than expected, I know that he'll want to join us on the front lines. That's just the type of person he is." The druid grinned at Violet. "Isn't he?"

The princess returned his smile. "He is."

Moriaki then departed, waving to Violet and King Reimos as he left the room. As the druid transformed into a raven and took to the sky, he felt a sensation of disconcertion quivering through him. Victory seemed so close — so why did he feel uneasy?

***

A day had gone by since Faelen had finally claimed his freedom. It was wonderful, being able to finally breathe in Escalon's fresh air. He'd dreamed of sprinting across the continent's green fields thousands of times and now he was finally doing it. But he didn't intend to bask in his temporary freedom. If he didn't eradicate the humans, he knew that they would soon strip him of his liberties and lock him away again. Or, even worse, they'd execute him.

Faelen slowed to a stop next to a river, sniffing the air. He turned and saw the faded signs of a bonfire from months ago. The scent of Archerus and Yuri still lingered around this area, though it was faint. The two had set up camp here long ago, when they'd first fled Horux.

The werewolf sat beside the river, touching the stinging wounds that covered his body. Splotches of blood coated his dark fur and he winced, using his claws to painfully pry silver bullets from his body. As long as the silver was in his body, his flesh wouldn't heal. Knowing this, he spent an hour painfully extracting metal from his tender wounds.

When he was finished with the tedious activity, he eased himself over to the river, fully submerging himself beneath the cold surface. The cool water was rejuvenating, cleansing his wounds and slaking his thirst. As he slowly rose from the river, he saw that the rivulet had turned red with his blood. He groaned, cracking his neck to the side.

After only minutes, his deep gashes had already begun to heal. If by some miracle he ever became human again, supernatural healing was something that he would miss. The rest of his prowesses he could easily live without, as long as he could coexist with others again, without being judged or feared.

Faelen raised one his claws before his face, staring pitifully at his monstrous hands. Ever since he'd taken this form, he'd never been able to transform back to a human form. During his confinement in Horux's catacombs, he'd spent every minute of every day searching through every emotion and memory within himself for his trigger. After a century of trying, he gave up. He assumed his trigger was something that was out of his reach. Because his trigger was a mystery, he would never be able to live a normal life. Not when he looked like this ferocious beast.

The werewolf trudged onto the bank of the river, his feet sinking into the moist dirt. He shivered, spraying water off his soaked fur. The only way he could survive on this continent without being treated like a fiend, without being locked away, was if all of his potential jailors were destroyed. Every human had to perish.

Faelen abhorred the idea of living on a continent filled with mindless beasts, but he had no other choice. The image of Tanya perishing by Yuri's hand crept to the front of his mind and he clenched his jaw. *Do you merely exist to foil my plans, Yuri? What are you and your petty friends doing in Lichholme? How did you manage to find the Oblivion Portal?* Realization crossed his face when he remembered the ebony claws on Yuri's hands. Had the boy's transformation and drastic increase in power been because of *that* Sacred Treasure?

The werewolf scowled. "In all of my years, I thought that I was the only being foolish enough to wield the Oblivion Claws," he grumbled, storming in the direction of Reidan. His conquest of Escalon would begin with the toppling of the human capital. From there, the rest of the continent would crumble with ease. "It's time for me to fulfill my end of the accord, Junko."

***

Moriaki was shocked when he soared over Zylon's forces, which were scattered. Dozens of knights were dragging human corpses across the natural land bridge, pulling the dead onto the sand. Hundreds of cadavers were neatly laid out in the afternoon sun. The bodies hadn't been buried yet and it would take a substantial amount of time to dig graves for each deceased warrior.

The druid descended before the front line of Iradian knights, morphing into his elven form. The soldiers gasped, surprised by Moriaki's sudden transformation until they recognized him. The experienced spell caster walked towards Zylon, who looked exhausted. The immortal had been continuously mending his wall, trying to hold back the werewolves on the other side.

"What's happened here?" Moriaki asked, looking over his shoulder at the armed knights, who stood ready for battle.

"Faelen lost his patience and leapt over the wall," Zylon murmured through his teeth, streams of sweat trickling down the sides of his face. "His beasts hunger for freedom. They're relentless, and I'm not sure how much longer I can hold up this wall."

Moriaki winced. He held Noah's bag in his hands and pulled out one of the Phoenix Cannons. "You only need to hold it up for a little longer while I arm your knights." He held Lena's invention high in the air. The sun's rays glinted off the metal and the Iradian warriors all stared at the weapon, unsure of its special function. "This is a Phoenix Cannon!" he shouted. "If you shoot a rampaging werewolf with this, their mind will become human again."

Zylon grinned, lowering his head. "Thank the gods, you guys really did it."

"Ammunition is limited, so don't take a shot unless you know that it'll hit," Moriaki said, beginning to distribute Phoenix Cannons amongst the Iradian riflemen, providing each person with one hundred containers of Reberna. He showed them all how to fire and reload the unique weapons. "With every shot that you land on those werewolves, we gain another ally. The beasts on the other side of this wall were all once human, remember that. If you must slay them to protect yourselves, do so. But I'd like to cure as many of these creatures as possible."

Moriaki walked over to Zylon and pressed a Phoenix Cannon into the immortal's hands. The elf nodded, and Zylon stopped mending the magical wall, watching as the barrier began to suffer critical damage from Faelen's werewolves. "Today," Zylon yelled, turning around to face his force of armed warriors. "We retake the lost city of Horux!"

The druid pulled out the final belt of Reberna ammunition and handed it to Zylon. "I'll pursue Faelen."

The powerful magician nodded and clamped his hand on Moriaki's shoulder. "Go, we can handle the rest here. Thanks for your help."

The immortal watched as the druid morphed into a raven and ascended into the sky. The ground quaked as Zylon's wall fell, pieces of the magical substance tumbling to the earth. A swarm of werewolves pounced over the injured barrier, descending upon Zylon's position. The immortal cocked his Phoenix Cannon and exhaled. "Open fire!"

The Phoenix Cannons fired, sounding like exploding dynamite. Streaks of red followed the projectiles as they buried into the first wave of oncoming werewolves. The beasts toppled over one another, roaring in agony, as if they'd just been struck by silver. But within moments, the fierce countenance faded from their faces, replaced by bewilderment. Some of the werewolves started to speak, as disorientated as if they'd awakened from a deep slumber. Then they collapsed to the ground, exhausted.

Zylon's face lit up with exultation as he extended his hand outward, forcing back the second wave of werewolves with bolts of red magic that burst from his fingertips. The Phoenix Cannons were working! "With these weapons, we can cleanse these beasts of their corruption!" Zylon yelled as the riflemen began to reload their guns, preparing to unleash a second volley. "Fire!"

***

Faelen approached Reidan's walls with frightening speed, the vindictive monster charging towards the unsuspecting city. He could hear the sounds of bells ringing, the alarm that indicated an approaching threat. But it didn't matter. Just as Horux fell, so would this capital.

The werewolf dug the ends of his feet into the earth, obliterating the ground. A crater formed beneath him as he launched high into the air, his arms flailing as he flew towards Reidan. Digging his claws into the hard stone, the beast clambered up the wall effortlessly. He landed on a stone walkway, and three swift bites infected the terrified guards around him. It only took moments for them to transform into his minions, creatures of darkness.

Faelen watched as his three new werewolves howled, still clanking in the armor of Iradian soldiers. They charged into the guard towers, slaughtering and infecting all that stood in their path. The sounds of anguished screams echoed in Faelen's ears. He inhaled through his nose, remembering this familiar scent well. Fear.

Each time a person saw him, terror was the first emotion that radiated from them. The Bount leapt from Reidan's walls onto the city streets, where pedestrians fled in the chaos, screaming at the sight of the relentless beasts. Faelen watched these feeble beings pitifully as they were massacred or transformed into the creatures that they feared. It did not satisfy him, to cause such suffering to these undeserving people. But he knew that this was what needed to be done. Soon, they would all understand what it was like to be him, living behind the skin of an abomination. To be feared by all. This was only the beginning of his conquest of Escalon.

Faelen's nose twitched when he caught a familiar scent. His eyes went wide and a nefarious grin cracked across his lips. Oh, he could not forget this scent. The odor of the white-haired boy, Yuri, had caught his full attention. "You're here?" he snarled, storming through the disarrayed city. "That saves me the time of having to hunt you down myself. I will take great pleasure in eviscerating your corpse, Yuri."

The Soul Within the Shell

Yuri was not sure where he was.

When the boy had first awoken, he'd been in the middle of a forest of gigantic pine trees. The brisk weather was certainly that of a spring morning. The sun's beaming light crept through spaces in the tree canopy, shining down onto the forest floor.

Since then, Yuri had walked to a riverbank near rushing rapids, where the water swept over a line of boulders and then descended into a crashing waterfall. The boy gazed beyond the waterfall and saw that the river flowed through a massive canyon, the sun bathing the rocks in brilliant light, causing them to gleam.

He looked across the river and saw a wolf, with fur as white as snow, sitting on the ground. The beast gnarred, revealing its sharp fangs. Its eyes were violet, glowing like a pair of blazing stars. It pounced forward, landing on a wet rock that jutted from the river. It continued to skip its way from rock to rock, making its way toward the frightened boy.

Yuri was unarmed, and his heart pounded as the creature charged towards him. He pondered whether or not he should run from the wolf. Just from looking at the creature made it quite clear that it wanted to feast on Yuri's flesh. But the elegant motions of the wolf's body mesmerized him into believing that perhaps it had an alternative motive. The beast came closer. One more leap and it would be upon him. An image of his throat being torn open by the wolf appeared in his mind, as fresh as a recently forged memory.

Panicking, the boy spun around and started to flee into the woods. He sprinted, his heart slamming against his ribcage. Panting, he hopped over rocks that lay in his path. *What are you afraid of?* A voice spoke in his mind, but it sounded like his own.

"Death," he responded wearily, stealing a glance over his shoulder as the pale wolf scampered after him. Its speed matched his, as if it were toying with him. He knew that the beast could pounce upon him at any moment and shred him to pieces. Why didn't it?

Do you think that everything in this world wishes to harm you?

Yuri's eyes narrowed, finding that his legs had slowed to a stop on their own. He swallowed, his back facing the wolf for a moment, expecting the beast to tackle him to the ground and rip his chest open. But it didn't.

The boy hesitantly turned. He saw that the wolf had also halted and was watching him, its head cocked to the side as if questioning why Yuri had run. He stared at the creature, and slowly felt himself drawn to the exotic beast. Yuri approached the wolf until he was only a foot away. Surprisingly, the canine didn't attack him.

Yuri gazed into the wolf's eyes and realized that its irises were no longer violet. They were turquoise. Never before had he seen another being with eyes of the same unique color as his own. As he and the wolf stared at each other, he could feel himself peering into the wolf's soul. He saw the beast's selflessness, generosity, bravery, and pain. Beneath the façade of a ferocious animal, he could see the anguished soul of the wolf, who had suffered throughout its life.

Its home, its family, its friends, its very purpose for existence … had all perished at the hands of destiny. And despite the beast's mighty nature, the poor wolf had been powerless as everything it loved crumbled before its eyes. Alone in this cruel world, the creature sojourned through forests, its destination unknown. Surrounded by nature, the wolf waited, hoping that one day, fate would return his purpose.

Purpose.

Yuri watched the wolf with saddened eyes. He understood the excruciating pain that ravaged the beast from the inside.

Initially, looking at the creature, all he'd seen was a savage animal. But now he saw that there was more to this complex wolf.

Reaching out, he stroked the top of the beast's head as if they were old companions. "So accustomed to the feeling of defeat and failure," Yuri whispered softly, remembering the deaths of his family and Asmund, the collapse of Horux, and the lives that he'd been unable to protect during his journey through Lichholme. "I am also tired of its bitter taste."

The wolf looked at him with glistening eyes. A voice spoke in Yuri's mind, sounding like the boy, but in the wolf's words. *You do not acknowledge your recent victory.*

Yuri smiled, knowing that the animal was referring to his battle against Malyssa and her army of vampires. "That was not my victory to claim. I lost sight of myself. There is no reason to feel triumphant when all I did was mercilessly slaughter an entire population."

Then you still have yet to taste victory.

"No more than you."

Do you think that you still have a purpose in this world?

"I don't know," Yuri said, laughing at the absurdity of talking to a wolf. Perhaps he was going insane. It made sense, after he'd wielded the Oblivion Claws.

Do you still have people that you still want to protect?

Yuri thought of Violet, Archerus, and Terias — the list went on. He didn't care only about them; there were countless people that he wanted to protect. He wanted to preserve the population of all of Escalon. "Yes."

Then perhaps your purpose should be to become their protector. After all, they need you. They need us.

Yuri saw that the wolf was staring past him. He glanced over his shoulder to see what the creature was looking at. The trees had somehow parted, revealing the grand city of Reidan. A wicked ambiance exuded from the capital, sending shivers through the young man.

For centuries, a beast was condemned because he was a monstrosity. But beneath the layers of his ebony fur and hardened flesh lay the soul of an innocent human, like you. Tormented for an insurmountable amount of time, frustration and hatred eventually dominated the beast. Finally breaking from the shackles of confinement, the abomination exacted vengeance upon his jailors, reducing the city of Horux to a state of chaos. However, the beast was still not free, for the other humans of Escalon sought to seal him away.

Yuri bit his lower lip, knowing exactly whom the wolf was talking about.

The beast, his thirst for revenge sated, searched for a solution that would allow for the people of Escalon to accept him again. His answer was to find a rare potion, one that was nearly impossible to obtain, which would grant him the humanity that he had lost. He wanted an escape from the curse placed on him centuries ago.

"But I took that from him," Yuri whispered.

Now, enraged, Terrador's first werewolf rampages through Escalon, now seeing the truth. Humans will never accept him, as long as they continue to see him as merely a monstrosity. He intends to fulfill the wish of his master, Junko. He'll eradicate the human race from the face of the continent and replace it with ferocious werewolves, so that he may finally live his life in the company of others like him. He has accepted what he is … a fearful creature of savagery.

Yuri shook his head. "I can't let him do that." He remembered how he had brutally murdered Tanya. Regret swept over him and he clenched his jaw. He understood that he hadn't been in control of himself at the time, but the weight of her death still fell upon his shoulders. Maybe if he'd never allowed Malyios to corrupt him with the Oblivion Claws, Tanya would've brought Faelen the potion that would make him human again. Perhaps then Escalon wouldn't have to deal with the werewolf's wrath. Realization trickled into his mind. "This is my fault."

He remembered the pain that he'd felt when he learned of Etaon's massacre. He felt that it was his responsibility to be there to protect everyone, to make the right decisions. Maybe that was unrealistic, but that was what drove him forward. "I need to go," he said, turning away from the wolf and toward Reidan. "I'm the only one that can stop Faelen."

Why is that?

"Because I understand a bit of what he's feeling," Yuri said, remembering the shocked stares that he'd received when everyone had found out that he was a werewolf. If he'd initially come to Reidan in his beast form, there was no doubt that he would've been imprisoned or even killed. He understood now that it was the nature of terrified humans to judge the unknown by appearance, just as he had when he'd first encountered this ghost-white wolf.

The wolf walked by Yuri's side, conjuring a mystical pool that materialized in front of the young man. Within it was an animated image that showed Horux's marketplace, during the beginning stages of its development. *Before you go, I believe it best if I show you something first.*

Yuri halted. "What will you show me?"

When confronting an opponent such as Faelen, it is best to understand your enemy. I will take you back, three hundred years into the past, to view forgotten memories that have been lost in the strands of time. I will show you the life of Terrador's first werewolf.

***

When Faelen was twenty, he'd never seen anyone more beautiful than the woman that sat on the bench in Horux's marketplace. The plaza was still mostly under construction, for it was early in the city's development. Nevertheless, the marketplace was packed with crowds of people, but the man cared not for any of them. His eyes were upon the tanned woman on the bench, who had silky black hair that curled down to her shoulders. The stranger was enthralled by the words of a book, her attention completely held by whatever tale she was reading.

She didn't even notice Faelen until he cleared his throat and plopped down beside her.

Faelen rubbed his breakfast, a shiny apple, on his shirt and proceeded to eat it nervously as he thought of what to say to the damsel. From the expensive, colorful garments she wore, it was clear that she was of the upper class. As a destitute man from the Lower District, he wondered what he had to offer to a noble. Trying to not think too much of the social gap, Faelen attempted to start a conversation with the woman.

At first, she didn't seem interested in anything that Faelen said. In fact, her countenance made her seem annoyed that her reading session was being interrupted. But Faelen pressed on, and soon the woman found herself as interested in the charming man as she was with her book.

The woman's name was Yazmine, and she was a foreigner from a continent known as Dastia. Her family had traveled to southern Escalon to assist in funding the development of Horux; they were extremely wealthy. She explained that they needed to escape Dastia, since the realm had been made perilous by many raiders and the wars that raged within the chaotic continent. Yazmine had yet to meet anyone in Horux and, to Faelen's surprise, invited him over to dinner.

Faelen accepted the invitation reluctantly, afraid that he was too penniless to afford reasonable attire to attend dinner with such an affluent individual. Nevertheless, he figured that he had nothing to lose. Declining Yazmine's request would only offend the highborn noble.

Returning home to his tiny cottage in the Lower District of Horux, Faelen made dinner for his grandmother that night. The rest of his family had died years ago, on the journey from Iradia to southern Escalon, when new settlers were migrating to Horux. His grandmother was all that he had left.

"I met a beautiful girl today, Gran," Faelen said, setting a bowl of porridge on the table in front of his blind grandma. As his grandma ate, he prattled about Yazmine and how amazing he thought she was from their conversation at the marketplace earlier that day. His grandmother seemed impressed by his description of Yazmine.

"She seems well-read and intelligent," the elderly woman said. "Do you plan on wedding her?"

"One step at a time, Gran." Faelen smirked, carrying his grandma's empty bowl to the sink. He then walked his grandmother to her bed. "I'm having dinner with Yazmine tonight, though. Hopefully things will go well."

And things did go well. At first, Faelen was slightly nervous about impressing Yazmine's family, but her father and mother were very kind and easy to talk to. Enjoying a night of silly banter, hilarious stories, delicious food, and aged wines, Faelen had one of the best nights of his life. Something sparked between Yazmine and Faelen, an unexplainable attraction that made the two want to spend more time together.

Within weeks, Faelen and Yazmine were considered a couple. They went on many dates, and Yazmine's father even managed to get Faelen a job that paid reasonably well. Things seemed to be brightening for the young man. Every morning he would tell his grandma how wonderful his night with Yazmine had been. Gran enjoyed listening to his ramblings, for she loved seeing her grandson happy for once.

On their one-year anniversary, Yazmine went to Faelen's house for dinner. The couple stealthily made love in his bedroom, with his grandmother still in the kitchen, quietly eating her dinner.

The lovers broke a kiss for a moment, gazing into each other's eyes as they pressed their bare bodies together. "Thank you, Yazmine," Faelen whispered, smiling. "I'm glad that you accept the real me for who I am. Even if I'm not the smartest, wealthiest, or handsomest man in town, you're still by my side."

"I love you because you're you, and nothing will change that," Yazmine whispered, planting a gentle kiss on Faelen's lips.

There was a thunderous bang in the next room, and Faelen suddenly pulled away from Yazmine, frowning at the abrupt noise. It had sounded like someone had forced their way into the cottage.

"Faelen, is that you? Are you leaving?" Gran called out, unable to see who had entered the home.

"Who's that?" Faelen rolled out of bed, sliding into his pants. As soon as he opened the door to his bedroom, he was clobbered across the face with a club. He grunted, sharp pain erupting in his head as he collapsed to the floor. His hazy vision shifted about, as if the room were shaking. A piercing noise rang in his ears, and he watched powerlessly as an intruder, dressed in clothing the color of night, stepped over his incapacitated body.

Yazmine screamed as the raider seized her naked body and proceeded to drag her out of the room. "Faelen!" His lover screamed, attempting to pry herself from the invader's stiff grip. Irritated by the woman's defiance, the marauding man viciously struck Yazmine with his fist until she was unconscious.

Watching with shock, Faelen stared at Yazmine's limp body. Fighting against the dizziness that plagued him and the throbbing pain that ravaged his head, the man struggled to stand. His efforts were pointless. The raider rammed his fist into Faelen's cheek, sending him spiraling to the side. His head smashed into a wooden wall, and he was unconscious before he hit the floor.

He awakened minutes later, his lungs filled with smoke. Coughing and sputtering, Faelen lurched forward, realizing that his home was aflame. A blazing fire now engulfed the bed that he'd shared with Yazmine, and it was rapidly spreading throughout the house.

Ignoring his pounding headache, Faelen crawled out of the room, knowing that he had to escape the burning house as soon as possible. Scrambling into his kitchen, he found himself staring at the unmoving body of his grandmother, who was sprawled across the floorboards. The distraught man rushed to Gran's side, pressing his fingers to her neck to try and feel for her pulse. It was faint, but she was alive.

There was a red splotch of blood on the side of Gran's forehead where she'd been struck by one of the invaders. Gritting his teeth, Faelen quickly carried his unconscious grandmother out of the burning cottage, his heart racing.

Stumbling into the cool midnight air, Faelen turned to find that a conflagration had devoured the majority of his street. Dozens of homes were aflame. Horuxian soldiers were throwing buckets of water at the burning structures in an attempt to combat the fires.

Faelen panted and lowered his grandma's body to the ground, catching sight of numerous corpses lying in the road. Many of them he recognized as his neighbors.

A soldier rushed past, carrying a wooden bucket of sloshing water. "What happened here?" Faelen demanded.

"A group of raiders from western Escalon pillaged the Lower District!" the warrior exclaimed, before rushing off to help fend off the blazing inferno.

Faelen had heard of these pillagers before; they called themselves the Hidden Skull. He clenched his jaw tightly, fuming rage coursing through his veins. The bastards kidnapped Yazmine! The man glanced over at his grandma's body, biting his lower lip. It pained him to leave his guardian like this, but he knew that the guards would take care of her. Right now, he needed to save Yazmine. Otherwise, she would end up dead.

That night, Faelen rushed to the stables and stole a steed, departing Horux to pursue the party of raiders. He rode hard, but he knew that it was impossible for him to save Yazmine on his own. He was unarmed and exhausted, his head still throbbing from the blow that he'd received earlier. Alone against the dozens of raiders that had invaded Horux, he stood no chance. Within several hours, his body had become numb and his mount was clearly on the brink of collapse. But he could see the contingent of invaders in the distance, riding off. If he continued at this pace, he could still catch up to them.

Panting, Faelen was about to drive his heels into his horse when a discerning realization swept over him. He was charging straight to his doom. What would he do if he approached the party of pillagers? He couldn't think of any scenario where he successfully defeated the bandits and escaped alive.

Slowing to a stop, Faelen's limp body rolled off his horse. He collapsed to the ground, breathing heavily. Exhausted, the distressed man began to wail to himself. It was a horrible feeling, to see his beloved Yazmine in the distance and realize that he couldn't save her. He felt helpless in the hands of destiny. In his mind, he wished that he were strong enough to save the woman that he loved. For her, he would do anything.

He fell asleep on the dirt road that night. As he slumbered, he writhed about as he endured a terrifying nightmare. Within that horrifying dream, Faelen was approached by a mysterious entity that arose from the earth in the form of a black shadow.

The being called himself Malyios. He promised that he would grant Faelen unlimited power, if Faelen would find a portal to a realm called Oblivion. The portal was located in Northern Escalon, which was surely a grand journey. Nevertheless, Faelen was desperate. In his eyes, any opportunity for omnipotence was worth it. With the strength granted by Malyios, he would never feel weak again. He could save his beloved. "I would do anything for Yazmine," he said to the deceiving god.

In that dream, Malyios struck an accord with Faelen. Inscribing the location of the Oblivion Portal within the desperate man's mind, the god then shattered the nightmare and allowed Faelen to awaken.

Faelen was surprised to see that his horse had stayed by his side throughout the night. He mounted the steed and took off in the direction of Northern Escalon, following the directions that Malyios had burned into his mind.

The man thought he might be insane as he embarked on his journey, for he followed the instructions of an entity that he'd met in a dream. But on his long trek, Faelen had more interactions with Malyios as he slept. Never before had he had such consistent dreams. He began to believe that perhaps he truly was communicating with a divine being.

Months passed as Faelen endured Northern Escalon's frigid weather. He was lucky enough to find refuge in the many human settlements scattered throughout the realm. Without their kind hospitality, the blistering winds and chilling cold would've killed him within days of entering the perilous region.

Eventually, Faelen reached the Oblivion Portal and entered it. He survived the path to the Oblivion Vault, avoiding being crushed to bits by the countless demons, apparitions, and infernal golems that plagued the molten earth of the shadow realm. At that time, there was no door to the Oblivion Vault. Instead, within a massive volcano, there was merely an open room that led to hundreds of thousands of Sacred Treasures.

While Faelen understood that these priceless items could make him rich, he cared not for most of them. He only sought that which would grant him the strength he needed to save Yazmine. Rummaging through the piles of golden treasures, the man searched for a weapon that would make him invincible. Suddenly, he heard a familiar voice in his ear.

"To your right are the Oblivion Claws. They will grant you the power that you seek."

It was Malyios that spoke to him, like a seething whisper in the night.

Faelen slipped on the mysterious gloves without hesitation. After months of interacting with Malyios through dreams, he'd come to trust the Titan. Though he soon regretted his decision.

Corrupt energy rippled in the air around Faelen as the poor man collapsed to his knees, writhing in agony. It was as Malyios had promised; the raw power that channeled through him was unimaginable. But he hadn't expected such a horrific price. His bones elongated, his teeth sharpened, and ebony fur sprouted from his hardened skin. With eyes glowing like one of Oblivion's demons, Faelen let out a howl that echoed through the Oblivion Vault.

Faelen was shocked by the monstrosity that he had become. He trembled, staring at the black hair that now covered his arms and the jagged claws that protruded from the ends of his fingers. "What have I become?" he roared with animosity. "This is not what I wanted!"

Malyios's shadow materialized before the world's first werewolf, examining the creature with profound interest. *"You asked for power and I gave it to you. Now you must fulfill your end of the bargain."*

Faelen tore the Oblivion Claws off and hurled the cursed gloves to the ground, only to find that he didn't revert to a human. He stayed a monster. Enraged, he refused to complete his end of the deal. "I will not free you, deceiver!" he boomed, swiping his hand at Malyios's shadow. "You can stay locked in this forgotten realm for eternity."

Malyios let out a bellowing roar that quaked the vault, watching powerlessly as Faelen left. *"I curse you! The loved one that you seek to save will never accept you as you are! No one will! You have left me in an eternity of solitude and now you shall experience the same!"*

Faelen didn't heed Malyios's words. He'd already been cursed to remain an abomination for the rest of his life. The werewolf left Oblivion and traveled across Escalon, no longer welcomed to any of the human settlements' taverns, as he once was. Whenever a human saw him, they were horrified, even when he insisted that he meant no harm. They all saw him as an appalling monster.

It only took him a few weeks to travel to the base of the Hidden Skull in western Escalon. The werewolf infiltrated the bandits' camp and slaughtered the raiders remorselessly, venting his rage and frustration on the bodies of the helpless raiders. Within minutes, he'd slain every person in the Hidden Skull.

Faelen approached a jail and found Yazmine, locked behind iron bars. Her face was caked in dirt and blood. The noble staggered back at the sight of the abominable creature that towered over her, her eyes wide with fear. "S-Stay back, you beast! P-Please, let me live!" she wailed miserably, putting her head in her hands.

Faelen reached out and ripped the metal bars off, stepping into the cell before the petrified woman. "Yazmine, it's me," he whispered, tears welling up in his eyes. "It's Faelen." He got down on one knee but watched as Yazmine quickly leapt to her feet and struck him across the jaw, running past him.

Wincing, the werewolf turned to find that his beloved had rushed into the hallway. She grabbed one of the torches off the sconces on the stone walls and held it out, pointing the blazing flames at Faelen. "D-Don't come near me!" she shouted, her hand trembling.

Faelen stepped into the jail's corridor, staring at Yazmine. "I know that I look different, Yazmine. But I did this for you, so that I could save you! Didn't you once say that you loved me for who I was and that nothing would change that? My love, this is just my appearance," he said, his voice shaking. "But I'm still me."

Tears trickled down Yazmine's cheeks and she shook her head, stumbling backward. "Y-You never should've come," she whispered. "Not like this ... not as a monster!"

A monster.

Faelen was tired of that word. He heard it shouted every time a human saw him. They didn't care if he could speak. They didn't care if he displayed compassion or emotion. They only cared that he had claws that could flay flesh from bone and sharpened teeth that could bite bodies in half. They only saw his appearance and considered him a vicious instrument of destruction.

The werewolf's hands quivered and he bared his teeth angrily as he stormed towards Yazmine. "Do you know how much I've sacrificed for you, Yazmine?" he barked, the ground quaking beneath him. He stood before the woman he'd once considered his companion, his eyes flashing intensely. "I've endured so much excruciating pain that I've become numb to its bite. I've ventured beyond this world to the realm of the dark gods and cast away my humanity to gain the power needed to save you from confinement! Is that not enough to prove my love for yo—" His eyes widened when Yazmine jammed her flaming torch into his chest.

Faelen swatted the torch from Yazmine's hands, a searing wound burned on his flesh. He glared at his beloved with acrimony, disbelief on his face. "After everything I've done … you still wish me gone, just because of what I've become?" Faelen roared. "I'm still the same man!"

"No," Yazmine said, shivering. "You're not a man, not anymore."

Faelen ripped his claw to the side and mutilated Yazmine's body with a single slash. The woman's corpse crumpled to the floor before the werewolf. He stared apathetically at his beloved.

He understood why Yazmine feared him. If he were human, he would fear werewolves as well. But no one would give him a chance to prove himself, to show that he meant no harm. "You all prematurely judge me," Faelen whispered, hovering over his partner's corpse. "I knew you would be shocked when you first saw me, Yazmine. I just thought you would be different. I believed that you would see past all of this fur and understand the sacrifices that I had to make to ensure your freedom." He stepped over the cadaver, clearing his mind of the grief that now haunted him. "I see now that all humans are the same. If you could not accept me, then how can I expect anyone else to?"

Faelen eventually returned to Horux to see his grandmother, the one person he had left. The beast was attacked the moment he arrived at the city's gates. Thus began the inception of the werewolf race, as Faelen fiercely battled his way through the swarms of Horuxian soldiers, infecting and slaying all of those in his path. Infuriated that everyone only saw him as an atrocity, rage became the fuel that drove Faelen to engage in the savage bloodbath.

The monster returned to his old home in the Lower District, which had been rebuilt. With claws stained with blood, he opened the door to the cottage and stepped into a quiet household.

"Who is that?" a familiar voice called out.

Faelen stood paralyzed in the doorway as tears welled in his demonically glowing eyes. "Gran?" he whispered, his voice shaky. It had been years since he'd seen his guardian. The old woman now sat in a rocking chair, blind and alone in her home. Faelen had left his disabled grandmother to live for years in solitude … he felt as if his heart were about to explode.

"I'd recognize that voice anywhere," his grandmother said, her hand reaching toward Faelen's voice. "Is that you, Faelen?" An elated smile spread across her face. "You're alive? Everyone told me that you ran off after Yazmine and that you'd died! Oh, I'm so glad that you're home."

Faelen fell to his knees, bowing his head slightly as he whimpered. His grandmother didn't know of his horrific transformation, for she could not see him. Now a foul lie twisted in the air, for she believed that things would return to normal. She did not understand how much everything has changed. "I

… I can't stay, Grandma," Faelen said. With every word, he felt as if a dagger was being driven through his heart. He crawled over to his grandmother and took her wrinkled hand in the palm of his paws. "I've changed and become … something hideous."

His grandmother tilted her head to the side, tracing her hand along his palm. She felt the ebony fur on his arm and then touched his face. The elderly woman did not hide her surprise as she mentally pictured Faelen's new transformation. "But you should know that I don't care about any of that. As long as you're the same Faelen that I've known my whole life, I'll accept you. Hideous and all."

Faelen smiled wearily, for he knew that his grandmother didn't care for what he looked like. The outside never mattered to her — for years she'd been unable to see it. What mattered to her was the soul within the shell. Unfortunately, not everyone was like her.

"I know you don't care. But the world does," Faelen said, suddenly embracing his grandmother tightly. He closed his eyes, hearing clanking footsteps at the entrance of the cottage. "I'm so sorry, Grandma. For leaving you alone. I want you to know that I love you so much and that I appreciate everything that you've done for me. I—"

Faelen's eyes widened suddenly as a steel sword was jammed through his back, skewering him and his grandmother in one powerful stroke. Agonizing pain ripped through his body, blood pooling in his mouth. He helplessly watched the pale face of his dying guardian.

His grandmother stared at him, her empty eyes widening with surprise. Her lips quivered and parted as if she wanted to speak, but no words came out. Her eyes closed, and she slumped back in her chair as she exhaled her final breath.

The werewolf gasped as the blade was yanked from his body and he sputtered ichor onto the ground, his hands trembling at his side. Breathing heavily, he glanced at the unmoving corpse of his grandma, squeezing her cold, limp hand in his.

The cruel world had claimed the life of the last person that he'd cared about. At first, sorrow filled him, making him want to bawl and mourn his grandmother's death. But that grief soon turned to ire, burning stronger than the conflagration that had razed his cottage years before.

Faelen clenched his bloody fangs and slowly rose, towering over the squadron of Horuxian warriors that stood in his home. He turned to face the frightened soldiers, his sharp claws itching for the taste of human flesh.

Bloodlust usurped his mind and he rampaged through the streets of Horux, his sole purpose for existence gone. Now all that remained was an insatiable hunger for destruction. Hours passed as Faelen mercilessly slaughtered at least a thousand of Horux's inhabitants. His rage seemed limitless.

Eventually, he was subdued by the squads of Horuxian guards that battled him. As a result, he was locked in a cage of silver while underground catacombs were being built to secure his confinement. Months later, Faelen was moved underneath the city and sealed away for centuries. He never got to bury his grandmother, for the Horuxians cremated her corpse.

And so, the world's first werewolf lay in solitude in the darkness of the underground catacombs of Horux. Behind bars of silver, the beast brooded in his confinement, regretting his decision to leave Horux and pursue the destruction of the Hidden Skull. Now, as his grandmother had for years, he sat in darkness, alone and forgotten.

***

Yuri lifted his gaze from the final images of Faelen's life, now realizing the poor beast's sorrow. He rubbed his moist eyes with the back of his hand, biting his lower lip. "I can't imagine the pain he must've felt," he whispered, lowering his head.

What will you do now?

"Faelen is not a bad person," Yuri said, looking back to the magical pool. He watched as Faelen slumped to the cold stone floor, defeated and depressed. "He is misguided. I plan to set him back on the right path."

How will you do that?

"You'll see when the time comes," Yuri said to the Ghost Wolf, pointing to the animated images that flashed on the pool in front of him. "How are you showing me his memories?"

The Ghost Wolf tilted its head to the side. *I am a manifestation forged by the Oblivion Claws. Thus, I have access to the stream of memories that flow from every wielder of the Sacred Treasure.* The beast watched as Yuri began to walk towards Reidan once again, with more purpose to his stride. *You'll have to fight Faelen if you go back, Yuri. But it's impossible for you to face him alone.*

"But I won't be alone," Yuri called over his shoulder, eying the creature from the corner of his eye. "Isn't that right, Ghost Wolf?"

Survivors of Oblivion

Yuri's eyes slowly opened. His ears pricked up, catching the sounds of anguished and terrified screams in the distance. He felt someone squeeze his hand and turned to find Violet at his bedside, tears gleaming in her eyes. The princess embraced him tightly, relieved that he'd finally awakened. She started to sob thankfully, pressing her face against his chest. The werewolf could feel her rapid heartbeat. Not from fear or exhaustion, but from exultation.

"You're finally awake," she whispered. "Faelen's invaded Reidan. He's started infecting everyone in the Trading District. The king has already evacuated, and we need to get out of here too. I believe that he's come for you."

"I can't run," Yuri said, shaking his head. "I need to face him."

"What? Why?" the princess exclaimed, surprised by the boy's response. It was shocking that Yuri still wanted to fight, having just woken from a coma.

"I can stop this," Yuri said confidently, still hearing the shrill cries of suffering Iradian civilians. He stared at his quavering hands and his stomach knotted. He'd gotten significantly thinner and weaker. "How long have I been unconscious?"

"Two months," Violet replied, giving one of his hands another squeeze.

Yuri winced, surprised by her answer. The last thing he remembered was bleeding out beside Malyssa's corpse. Now he'd somehow awoken in the castle of Reidan, and he didn't have time to wonder about the details. He could sense that someone was approaching the citadel at incredible speed, and he knew exactly who it was.

"I'm sorry," he said to Violet. He leaned forward and gently pressed his forehead against hers, closing his eyes. "I never got the chance to apologize for our quarrel back in Lichholme. I didn't mean to come across as insensitive. I care about you, so much and … I'm glad that you're the first person that I saw when I woke. Thank you for staying by me for all this time." He kissed her tenderly, welcoming the warmth that ignited between them.

Violet broke the kiss, moving back an inch. "You sound like you're saying goodbye."

"Hopefully, I'm not." Yuri bit his lower lip. "But I wanted to tell you that, just in case."

The wall of the infirmary suddenly exploded, and several nurses that had yet to vacate the area screamed in horror as a gigantic beast trudged through a gaping hole in the castle. A cloud of dust swept around the triumphant monster as it loomed over the feeble humans fleeing from him. "There you are, Yuri," the werewolf snarled. "Finally, I get to see the angst in your eyes as I crush the life from you, just as you did to Tanya."

Yuri shoved Violet out of the way as the werewolf pounced upon him, landing on his chest. The bed crashed to the floor and Yuri grunted, feeling Faelen's weight bearing down on him. He gritted his teeth as the werewolf leaned down, baring his fangs inches away from Yuri's face. If he wanted, he could've bitten Yuri's head clean off, but that would've been far too easy.

Yuri launched his fist upward into Faelen's jaw, sending the monster flipping backwards. The Bount landed gracefully on his feet, sliding across the marble floor. He worked his stinging jaw and snarled. "I'll make you pay for the eternal fate that you've condemned me to."

The boy rose from his destroyed bed, brushing his white hair from his turquoise eyes. His body began to morph, elongating and growing to match Faelen's size, his fur the color of snow. Flexing his claws, Yuri cracked his neck, feeling stiff after such a prolonged sleep. An ordinary human wouldn't be able to walk yet, but he wasn't human. "I didn't have control of myself," Yuri said, knowing that the excuse was not enough to justify his actions.

"I know," Faelen said. "At one point, I too sought power from Malyios. The Oblivion Claws granted me that power, but cursed me with the body of a monstrosity. This is the form I'm forced to wear! And now, because of you, I'm stuck like this forever. Your petty excuse will not save you from my wrath," he growled. "I am deemed a threat before I even open my mouth to speak. All of these humans, they all fear me. They don't understand what it's like to be as misjudged, mistreated, and isolated as I am. That's why I'll turn them all into the beasts that terrify them. Then they'll understand what it's like to be an abomination!" He glanced at the princess, on the ground several feet away from Yuri. A nefarious grin cracked across his lips. "And I believe I've found my next victim."

Yuri's body tensed when Faelen dashed across the room. The Ghost Wolf leapt into the werewolf's path, but the Bount knocked him aside with a hard swing of his arm. The white beast slammed heavily into the wall of the infirmary, shaking the castle. Gasping for air, Yuri slid to the floor. Pieces of the marble wall crumbled onto his shoulders.

He watched with horror as Faelen forced Violet to the ground. The monster leaned downward and sank his teeth into the princess's neck, biting her gently. Faelen's fangs could've torn her throat wide open with slightly more pressure, but he controlled his urge to murder the delicate woman. Rising from the hyperventilating princess, the werewolf turned and grinned wickedly at Yuri. "Watch powerlessly as the woman you love is torn from your grasp," he shouted triumphantly. "Feel despair."

Yuri roared, moving with blinding speed across the infirmary. He struck Faelen in the stomach with a heavy blow, sending the werewolf smashing through several walls, rolling out of the castle and onto the grassy courtyard outside. The Ghost

Wolf rushed to Violet's side, morphing back into his human form. He knelt beside the princess, who was writhing in agony. "Violet," he whispered, his hands trembling as he reached for her. Already, he could see that the werewolf's poison was taking hold of her mind. Her eyes had changed from lavender to a beastly orange, and her body convulsed as her bones began elongating.

The boy stared at the suffering princess, shaking his head in disbelief. *This can't be happening. Please ... anyone but you.* He glanced around the room, looking desperately for anything that might help him. He caught sight of a pistol that was lying on the floor beside his destroyed bed. His nose twitched; he could smell that the gun contained the antidote found within Phoenix Hearts. *By the gods, Archerus and the others succeeded!*

Yuri scrambled across the room, snatching the Phoenix Cannon from the floor. Holding the metal contraption in his hand, he sprinted back to Violet's side. The woman's spine was already beginning to twist as her body stretched, her teeth becoming sharp fangs. "P-Please," she gasped, shuddering uncontrollably.

Yuri pressed the barrel of the Phoenix Cannon to Violet's fresh bite wound in her neck. He could only hope the gun would actually work. Fighting Violet was probably the last thing he wanted to do.

Pulling the trigger, he heard a click, then a hiss. A dart shot from the Phoenix Cannon and buried itself in Violet's flesh, injecting the ruby-colored liquid into her bloodstream. Within moments, the princess's pain had subsided and she stopped shivering.

Violet gazed up at Yuri wearily, her eyes returning to their normal color. She smiled, exhausted. "Thank you," she said softly. Her body currently looked human, but Yuri knew that she'd become a werewolf. At least she wouldn't be mindless, like the savage beasts that now plagued Reidan and Horux. She reached up and brushed some of Yuri's hair from his eyes. "I don't mind your change, so hopefully you don't mind mine."

Yuri laughed, planting a kiss on her forehead. "Nothing will change the way that I feel about you," he said, slowly rising to his feet. "Now, stay here. The antidote will take some time to settle into your body, so it's best for you to rest. I'll be back once I deal with Faelen," he said, morphing back into his werewolf form.

Yuri spotted the Oblivion Claws lying on the ground beside Violet. She'd been holding onto them? The Ghost Wolf reached down and picked up the Sacred Treasure, staring at the powerful artifact. *I can't leave this here.* Sliding the Oblivion Claws into his pockets, he turned to the gaping hole in the infirmary wall.

"A contraption that can inject the Phoenix Heart's agent straight into a werewolf's bloodstream. Your lot has certainly been busy," Faelen said as Yuri stormed out into the castle's courtyard. "But you can't cure every werewolf in Reidan. Your ammunition is limited."

"Indeed," Yuri said, knowing that with every passing second, more Iradians were being infected by Faelen's minions. If too many became infected, there wouldn't be enough antidotes to cure all of the werewolves. He needed to defeat Faelen swiftly.

Since wielding the Oblivion Claws, Yuri had gotten taller and stronger in his werewolf form. In terms of physical ability, he would've been equal to Faelen, had he not been weakened by the coma.

He remembered the magical attacks that Faelen had used to destroy entire buildings back in Horux. A swipe from Faelen's claws could send forth a projectile of black energy in the form of a crescent slash. It was similar to the ability that Yuri had used when he wielded the Oblivion Claws. Could it be that Faelen somehow could still harness the same power that he'd had when using the Oblivion Claws?

Yuri let out a howl loud enough that it reached the ears of every being in Reidan. The werewolves of the city returned the cry, and Faelen's eyes widened as the beasts all started to rush towards the castle's courtyard. The infected monstrosities ignored the fleeing humans of Reidan and sprinted in the direction of the Ghost Wolf's summon.

"Why are they responding to your call?" Faelen growled, watching as dozens of werewolves scampered into the courtyard. Iradian guards, clearly overwhelmed, ran at the sight of the ferocious beasts. But the creatures posed no threat to the guards. Instead, the army of beasts crowded around Faelen and Yuri, forming a circle around the two werewolves.

"Werewolves look to their strongest as their leader," Yuri said, tilting his head back as he grinned. "As a Ghost Wolf, they deem me on equal footing with you." He indicated the patiently waiting werewolves that surrounded them. "Our battle will decide who becomes their leader."

"That's preposterous! I'm the one who turned them into werewolves in the first place!" Faelen barked, snarling at the beasts. "Obey me!" But they did not heed his command; they stared at him and retreated several steps from the enraged Bount. The dark monster glared at Yuri, his face contorted into an angry scowl. "I have to rip you to shreds in front of these mongrels for them to acknowledge me as their ruler? So be it."

At least the first part of his plan had worked; he'd managed to stop the werewolves from massacring and infecting the rest of Reidan's citizens. Now Yuri just had to prove that he was stronger than Faelen so they would obey him. Though that was much easier said than done.

Faelen charged towards him, moving as fast as lightning, his image barely visible. The Ghost Wolf grunted as he was tackled backwards, slamming heavily onto the grass. Dirt kicked up into the air as the two creatures struggled for domination, rapidly clawing at each other. Yuri finally managed to drive his legs into Faelen's chest, propelling the Bount high into the air.

Faelen smashed into the earth, rolling back to his feet. The crowd of werewolves had separated, giving the two potential leaders more room to battle. There was nothing but scorching rage flaring from Faelen, as if he were a roaring conflagration of hate. "You've interfered with my plans enough!" he boomed, dashing at his opponent once more.

Yuri swung himself to his feet, raising his fists before him. He jabbed at the werewolf's face, but the Bount moved his head slightly, narrowly avoiding the fast blow. Faelen sank a punch solidly into Yuri's stomach, drastically damaging his diaphragm. Another blow met his face, sending him sprawling onto the ground.

Yuri clenched his bloodied teeth, rubbing his aching jaw. Pressing his palms on the ground, he could feel Faelen's overwhelming presence looming over him. *Wouldn't it be nice if I could just stay down?*

He let out a ferocious roar as he swung around, dragging his claws across Faelen's chest. Blood splattered onto the ground and the Bount let out an agonizing scream, falling to one knee. Yuri rushed at Faelen, taking advantage of the werewolf's weakened state.

But I can't. All of the battles that I've endured have led to this final fight.

Faelen's fist flashed upward with blinding speed, slamming into Yuri's jaw. The Ghost Wolf flipped backward and slammed onto his back, gasping. The metallic taste of blood filled his mouth and his ears rang with pain.

The fate of Escalon rests in my hands.

Yuri felt nails digging into the flesh around his ankle and he gritted his teeth, biting back pain. Faelen squeezed Yuri's leg, rotating his body as he used his titanic strength to swing the Ghost Wolf hundreds of feet into the sky.

Yuri screamed, his arms flailing as he spiraled wildly through the air. The blustering wind rushed into his face, pulling back his cheeks. He grunted as he hit the rooftop of a building, crashing into an abandoned general store. His body rolled off the counter, knocking an amalgam of tools to the floor. Sharp pain erupted through his back and he groaned, dazed, blinking his eyes to clear his vision.

His ears pricked up, hearing werewolves scampering about outside. That meant that Faelen was nearby as well. There was no time to rest.

The door to the shop was ripped off its hinges, and Faelen stormed into the empty store, frowning when he saw that the building was empty. He knew that Yuri had fallen here; there was a gaping hole in the roof to prove it. "Where are you hiding?" he barked, sniffing the air. There was a loud bang as Faelen was struck on the head with a silver pan.

Yuri had popped up from behind the counter, gripping the silver pan tightly by its leather grip. The silver had a harsh effect on Faelen; the werewolf's flesh sizzled as if he had just been hit by a flaming rock instead of a kitchen utensil. Unfortunately, this was the only silver item in the store that had an actual grip on it, and it didn't deal enough damage to incapacitate or injure the Bount. If only Yuri had his enchanted sword.

Faelen swung around, jamming his fist into Yuri's stomach. The Ghost Wolf gasped, lurching forward, feeling as if he would retch. The breath choked out of his lungs and he crumpled to his knees, grabbing his aching stomach. "I find it intriguing that you're risking your life for the pathetic humans of Escalon," Faelen growled, rotating and striking Yuri in the face with a powerful kick that sent the beast crashing into a shelf of kitchen appliances. "To them, we're monsters. Right now, they come to you for help out of desperation, fearing for their survival. But once they no longer have a use for you, you won't be hailed as a hero. You'll be cast out as a freak."

Yuri wheezed, staggering to his feet. He wiped a stream of blood from his nose and yelled as he hurled himself at Faelen. The Bount sliced his arm in an uppercut, striking the white werewolf in the jaw, sending him flipping across the store.

"Everyone will toss you aside like unwanted trash," Faelen shouted, watching as Yuri rose to his feet once more, his body swaying. "Before long, they'll lock you behind silver bars and you'll waste away decades, maybe even centuries, brooding in the claustrophobic isolation of a cell. You want to save a race of arrogant humans that believe that they are the *center* of the universe! They look down on all other creatures and reject them as outsiders. They judged me without even listening to a word that I had to say! Beings that blindly think they know who someone is merely from their appearance deserve to be turned into the monstrosities that they condemn. There is no room in my heart for mercy for fools."

Yuri spat blood onto the ground, raising his fists in front of him. "You want to be accepted, right? Well, murdering and infecting the humans of Escalon is not the right path! You need to show them that you deserve their companionship!"

Faelen guffawed, shaking his head at Yuri's words. "That I deserve their companionship? No human deserves to even stand on the same soil as me. They're arrogant and cursed by ignorance, never considering the possibility that they're not this world's superior race." He flitted across the store, his claws rending the air at Yuri's face. "They need to open their eyes to reality!"

The Ghost Wolf ducked the slash and jabbed two quick punches into Faelen's snout, causing the Bount to stagger back several steps. He twisted his body and focused his power into his left arm as he rocketed a blow straight into Faelen's cheek, sending the werewolf spinning to the ground. "Not all humans are like that," Yuri gnarred, flipping into the air as he came crashing down, eager to smash Faelen's body with a finishing blow.

The ebony werewolf rolled away at the last moment and Yuri's fist smashed into the store's floorboards, breaking straight through the wood. He grunted as he pried his claw from the floor and launched his other arm at Faelen, knowing that he needed to maintain momentum in this fight. His eyes widened when his punch was abruptly halted by Faelen's palm.

Faelen grinned nefariously, his nails digging into the flesh in Yuri's hand. "But most of them are." He swiped upwards, unleashing a magical shockwave at the Ghost Wolf that was shaped like an ebon crescent and detonated upon impact. The general store exploded as if it had been full of dynamite, swallowed by a cloud of darkness. Werewolves scattered in an attempt to avoid the flaming debris that rained from the sky.

The weight of collapsed wreckage bore down upon Yuri, whose chest was now seared with a raw wound, his flesh burned from Faelen's corrupted magic. The Ghost Wolf grunted, squeezing out the remainder of his strength to haul the detritus off his chest. Coughing, he squinted through the cloud of dust that engulfed him. Catching sight of an approaching silhouette, he gritted his teeth, knowing that he was immobilized with half of his body still buried beneath rubble.

Faelen appeared, driving a relentless kick into Yuri's cheek. The Ghost Wolf's body twisted as he was propelled from the destroyed shop's ruins and launched into Reidan's abandoned streets. Flipping wildly, the werewolf hit the ground hard.

Lying on his stomach, Yuri clenched his jaw tightly, his teeth bloody. He tried to move, but many of his bones were broken. It was a miracle that he was still alive. Rivulets of blood streamed down his face, soaking his white fur with the pungent scent of ichor. He could barely open his swollen right eye.

He should've been terrified when he felt Faelen's exultant shadow looming over him. But everything, including his emotions, was numb. Yuri accepted death, knowing that he was currently too weak to defeat Faelen alone.

"So weak," Faelen said, grabbing Yuri by his skull as he lifted the white werewolf off the ground by his head. The Bount squeezed, feeling the Ghost Wolf writhe in pain before his incredible strength. But instead of crushing Yuri's cranium, he hurled his enemy across the street, slamming him into the wall of an empty cottage. "How is it that you've managed to travel so far in your efforts if you're this delicate? Are a few attacks all that you can endure? You're a mouse in lion's skin, acting all high and mighty, when you're really just a powerless weakling, accustomed to the taste of failure."

Yuri groaned, blood dribbling from his lips onto the dirt. He pried himself from the wooden wall of the building, staggering forward. His legs wobbled, barely able to stabilize his body. But he wasn't standing for long. A backhanded swing from Faelen's hand sent the Ghost Wolf spinning back to the ground. Wheezing, he pressed his bloody palms into the cracked tiles of the street.

The werewolves gathered around the area, perching themselves on nearby roofs and gathering inside alleyways to witness Yuri's torment. Most of them had already decided to pledge their allegiance to Faelen, who clearly seemed to be the stronger of the two werewolves. But they stayed, eager to watch the battle's conclusion.

"I'd think, considering your suffering, that you would strive to obtain more power. When Malyios showed me a vision of you in Oblivion, wearing that apathetic gaze and confident posture as you murdered Tanya, I thought that you were different from our initial meeting in Horux. But you haven't changed at all, have you? You're still groveling at my feet, like a servant in the presence of a god," Faelen said, stomping before Yuri. He watched as the Ghost Wolf's form reverted back to his human state. "It's disheartening to see that the bastard that ruined my chance to be normal again is nothing but a frail boy."

"I didn't mean … to kill her, or to stop you from becoming human," Yuri rasped. "I just couldn't—"

Faelen silenced Yuri with a hard kick to the boy's face, smirking. "You're right, it wasn't your fault. The Oblivion Claws' corruptive energies manipulated you," he said, squatting down as he reached into Yuri's pockets and pulled out the Sacred Treasure, dangling the gloves before the boy's face. "In that case, perhaps I should bring out the real monster that foiled my plans and kill him instead."

Yuri stared at the Oblivion Claws with dismay. He couldn't wield that type of power again. It was corrupt and uncontrollable. His hands curled into clenched fists, his body quivering. If he had the power to defeat Faelen on his own, he wouldn't be in this position.

"You look frustrated," Faelen asked, bringing his foot down on Yuri's right leg, breaking it with a clean strike. The werewolf listened to the boy's anguished scream, sadistically grinning. To hear the one he hated suffering so was like listening to harmonious music. "Good." He broke the boy's other leg with another stomp. "Now you shouldn't be able to move."

Tears trickled down Yuri's cheeks and he sobbed, unable to believe the excruciating pain that he was in. He watched with horror as Faelen started to slip the Oblivion Claws onto his hands. *Don't do this … I won't be able to control myself!* "Stop! You don't understand—"

"Oh, I understand perfectly," Faelen said, sliding the gloves onto Yuri's hands. A wicked grin stretched across his face when an eruption of magical power shot through Yuri's veins, causing the boy to let out a tormented cry. "Show me the monster that I've been waiting to slay. This is the beginning of my new vengeance!"

Yuri felt cold, as if he'd been dipped in the waters of the Lake of Eternity. The Oblivion Claws fused with his flesh, turning his hands the color of night, as sharp, dagger-like ends protruded from his nails. He recognized this invincible feeling, this smug sensation that he could obliterate everything. With eyes gleaming violet, he slowly rose to his feet. As soon as Yuri merged with the Oblivion Claws, his body's regeneration increased drastically. His bones snapped back into place while his flesh mended. Within moments, his wounds had vanished and he looked unscathed.

The moment that the gloves slipped onto his hands, Yuri could feel himself being cast into the back of his mind, as a new malicious entity took over. Like a forgotten ghost, he faded from existence, his body controlled by a new ruler.

Faelen narrowed his eyes as he watched his opponent. The werewolf's maleficent aura surely did not belong to the boy. Centuries ago, when the Bount had wielded the Oblivion Claws, increased regenerative powers was not among one of the enhanced attributes he'd experienced. "It would seem that the Sacred Treasure reacts differently when it finds a new master," he grumbled, digging his feet into the ground. He burst forward, practically teleporting in front of Yuri, his right hand tearing at the boy's face.

Yuri reached out and grabbed Faelen's wrist, halting the Bount's powerful attack effortlessly. He smirked arrogantly, using his grip on Faelen to swing the werewolf to the ground with immense force, creating an explosion that shuddered the city.

The spectating werewolves, surprised at the sudden change in Yuri's power, attempted to steer clear of the blast. Still intent on watching, they distanced themselves from the battle to stay out of the crossfire between the two formidable fighters.

Yuri released Faelen's arm, watching as it slumped to the ground. He swung his arm to the side, slicing the air. The cloud of dust that obscured his vision cleared instantly, and he raised his eyebrows when he saw that the Bount was not on the ground in front of him.

There was a thump behind the Ghost Wolf, and the he stole a glance over his shoulder, catching sight of Faelen from the corner of his eye. "What happened to all of that confidence?" the boy called snidely, flexing his right claw inches from his face. "I'm the one that shattered your dream of becoming human. Come and claim your revenge."

The True King

Faelen panted heavily, feeling a twinge of pain in his wrist and shoulder. He hadn't expected that Yuri's reflexes, speed, and strength would be enhanced *this* much. The boy's aura was overwhelming, creating a dark, evil atmosphere that covered the entire city of Reidan. Every living being in the area could feel Yuri's daunting presence. Flocks of terrified birds flew away, the surviving humans fled from the scene, and even the werewolves seemed to shift nervously as they stared at Yuri.

Faelen worked his jaw as Yuri faced him. Other werewolves had always regarded him with respect, viewing him as a leader. But Faelen could clearly sense quivering fear emanating from the beasts with clarity. They were terrified of the Ghost Wolf. *Why are the Oblivion Claws making you this powerful?* Faelen clenched his jaw so tightly that he thought his teeth might shatter. *It's like you've become a different person!*

He let out a furious roar as he charged forward, digging his claws into the ground as he launched himself at his opponent. But Yuri simply stepped to the side, easily avoiding the assault. Faelen jammed his feet into the cracked ground, skidding to a stop. Whirling around, he unleashed a barrage of fierce slashes at the Ghost Wolf, his irate gaze filled with murderous intent.

But everything seemed to be moving in slow motion for Yuri. He had more than enough time to avoid Faelen's attacks. Every swipe met open air as the composed boy ducked, flipped, rolled, and stepped out of the path of the Bount's strikes.

"Not bad," Yuri said, spinning around Faelen's final attack. He rotated his body and kicked Faelen straight in the chest, sending the werewolf rolling down the street. Dark energy, drawn from his core, channeled through his forearms and into the Oblivion Claws. The ground began to quake as his hands emitted black and purple light, shining like two bright suns. Yuri grinned. "Recognize this?"

The Bount flipped to his feet, his eyes widening at the sight of Yuri's glowing claws. Demonic energy that belonged to Oblivion poured into the boy's Sacred Treasure. This was the same ability that Faelen was capable of using, and he knew of its destructive strength.

Faelen squatted down and launched himself into the sky, jumping a hundred feet into the air just as Yuri slashed his claws outward. A massive crescent of corrupted magic swept forth and ravaged the streets, practically ripping the area apart. Buildings ignited and crumbled, collapsing beneath Yuri's devastating power. A whirlwind of dust consumed the destruction, engulfing the Ghost Wolf for only a moment. Bursting from the top of the cloud, Yuri propelled himself after Faelen.

Yuri transformed into his werewolf form just before he struck Faelen, tackling the Bount, sending them both smashing through a gigantic tower, piercing the structure like an unstoppable arrow. Bursting from the wall of the crumbling building, the combatants fell toward the city streets, biting and clawing at each other.

Faelen cried out as Yuri jammed his claws into the Bount's flesh and hurled the werewolf down towards the city. The beast smashed into the earth with tremendous force, cracking the street pavement. Faelen gritted his teeth, struggling to get back to his feet. A powerful tremor vibrated beneath him, indicating that Yuri had just landed in front of him.

Faelen could only see a silhouette of the Ghost Wolf through the thick screen of dust that obscured his vision.

Corrupt energy flooded from Faelen's chest and surged toward his claws, temporarily empowering him. Dark magic swirled around his forearm, taking the form of an ebon mist. The

Bount's arms quivered at the enormous amount of concentration that it took to amass this much foul energy.

Faelen let out a fierce roar as he slashed his claws upward, releasing two projectiles of dark crescents that rushed forward, slicing through the smokescreen of dust, revealing Yuri.

The Ghost Wolf's eyes widened as he stared at the deluge of magic darting towards him. There was a massive explosion when the crescents struck him. Yuri lost his foothold and was sent flipping backwards through the air, smashing through entire rows of buildings. A dozen streets were annihilated by the wave Faelen's dark magic.

Faelen panted, collapsing onto his knees, drained by unleashing so much energy. Quavering, he looked forward at the scorched earth before him. What had once been a road of intact structures was now only smoldering ashes. The Bount smirked slightly. There was no way that Yuri could've survived.

The Ghost Wolf was lodged in the outer wall of Reidan, his arms and legs outstretched. Pieces of rubble crumbled from his body as Yuri groaned, prying himself from the cracked stone. He fell from the wall, falling a hundred feet to the ground. Smashing to the earth, the white werewolf reverted to his human form. A rivulet of blood trickled from his lip to his chin, dripping droplets onto the charred earth.

Yuri pressed his palms into the ground and rose to his feet, wiping the blood from his mouth. His gaze followed the path of destruction to Faelen, who was at least five miles away. "An impressive display," Yuri shouted, flexing his claws at his side. "But your borrowed power from Oblivion is nothing compared to the real thing."

Faelen blinked, and Yuri had disappeared. His heart skipped a beat when he sensed the corrupt presence of the boy behind him. A hand clamped onto the back of Faelen's head and forced him downwards, cracking the street with the werewolf's skull. Yuri had practically teleported behind Faelen, traveling multiple miles in only a millisecond. Such speed and power … it exceeded even that of gods.

"How does it feel to finally meet your match?" Yuri seethed, rotating his body as he hurled Faelen through a cottage behind him. The beast smashed through the wooden structure and rolled into an empty plaza, cracking his head painfully on the edge of a large marble fountain in the center of one of Reidan's marketplaces.

An agonizing headache ravaged Faelen's cranium and he groaned, massaging his head with his hand. He glanced up to see Yuri sauntering over the crumbling debris of the collapsed cottage. The boy stepped into the empty plaza and examined the area, smiling slightly to himself. "After using most of your magic to hurl those projectiles, you hardly managed to scratch me. What's your plan now? Will you slash and bite me to death?"

Faelen spat blood on the ground, swaying to his feet. He held his fists out, clenching his teeth angrily. He bit back the temptation to charge at the Ghost Wolf, for he knew that would only result in his defeat. He needed to use his experience and skill to his advantage. Even if Yuri had many of his physical attributes augmented by the Oblivion Claws, Faelen could hopefully still beat him in a contest of aptitude.

Yuri ambled forward, grinning wickedly at the injured werewolf. "While I do think you are physically weak, Faelen, I must say that I still respect you. To spend centuries confined behind bars, wasting precious time in the cruel silence of isolation, must take a toll on your mental health. To think that you're still stable after what could've been eons underneath the city of Horux — why, I don't even think that I would last."

Faelen slammed his foot into the tiled ground and launched a fast jab at Yuri's face. "What would you know about confinement, huh?" he barked in frustration, watching as the Ghost Wolf stepped around his strike. He unleashed a flurry of punches, slashes, and kicks in a futile attempt to hit his nimble opponent.

Yuri swiftly ducked a sweeping punch and countered with a clobbering blow across Faelen's face. The beast spiraled through the air and crashed into the fountain, splashing water at Yuri's feet. The fountain's clear liquid ran red with Faelen's blood as the water poured onto the werewolf's soaked fur.

The wounded creature wheezed, his entire body aching. "You think you know suffering, but you've only experienced a fraction of anguish that I've endured. I was tortured for centuries by the chosen wardens of Horux's Wolf Noble House. Each keeper tormented me differently. I've suffered so much pain that I've become numb to its sting."

Yuri watched Faelen apathetically. *Becoming numb to pain.* An image of Han flashed through his mind and he winced, feeling something pricking at his mind.

"Because I once wielded the Oblivion Claws, corrupted energy from that forsaken land fills me, keeping my body from aging. I've been caged for the length of multiple human lifetimes. You can't begin to imagine the misery that I've been through. And yet, you have the audacity to call me *weak?*" Faelen roared, quaking the ground with his irate voice. "All of your power stems from the gloves on your hands; it isn't even your own! You're the one that's feeble and wea—"

Yuri ended Faelen's sentence by slamming a heavy kick into the werewolf's stomach, sending the beast flying through the plaza and through the wall of a warehouse. "You'll regret denying my power."

Faelen was sprawled on the wooden floor of the empty warehouse, clutching his diaphragm. His right ankle was twisted in an unnatural position and a tiny pool of blood had formed underneath his injured body. He clenched his bloody teeth as he watched Yuri step through the hole in the building's wall.

"I will acknowledge that you are indeed stronger than Tanya and Malyssa," Yuri said, hovering over the incapacitated werewolf. "Your dark magic has enough destructive power to incinerate most beings in this world."

"It should've vaporized you too," Faelen snarled. "But you're a monster."

The smile faded from Yuri's lips as his eyes narrowed. "It didn't, because I am superior," the Ghost Wolf said haughtily, malice gleaming in his eyes. He watched as Faelen lashed out at him with both claws, attempting to skewer the arrogant boy. But Yuri simply reached out, grabbing both of Faelen's wrists before the werewolf reached him. A bit of pressure snapped the Bount's bones like twigs.

Faelen dropped to the ground, his eyes wide with excruciating pain. "Gah ... you filthy—"

"You look frustrated," Yuri said, mirroring the Bount's words from earlier. The boy ambled around the werewolf, calmly halting at the werewolf's legs. "Good." Mercilessly, he slashed his claws across Faelen's legs, lacerating them so deeply that he couldn't stand.

Disregarding Faelen's screams of agony, Yuri's eyebrows knit together as he frowned. He'd been ignoring a distant voice that echoed in his head, but now it was growing louder. Much louder.

Stop this!

Yuri scowled, aggravated at whoever was trying to command him. He listened to no one.

This is not me.

Yuri grabbed Faelen by his skull, the tips of his claws barely digging into the werewolf's flesh. Streams of blood oozed from the cuts and trickled down the suffering beast's face. Rage seized the Ghost Wolf and his arm quivered. It would be so easy to just smash Faelen's head. To end the villain's life, just as he had with Tanya and her werewolves, just as he had done to the hordes of vampires in Malyssa's encampment! These claws have already felled thousands. What was adding one more to the list of dead? A harsh tempest of angry memories churned within him. "This isn't me? Then what is?" he boomed, his voice reverberating in the empty warehouse. "Mother, Han, Asmund, Beo — all of Horux suffered at the hands of this disgusting mongrel! What madman would spare a monstrosity like this?" He shook Faelen's limp body in his hand.

That was when a translucent wolf with white fur materialized before Yuri. The corrupted boy stared at the spectral being, wondering if it was a ghost or a figment of his imagination. He ground his teeth, his eyes narrowing. "You're the one speaking in my head?"

The wolf nodded. *I am the real Yuri.*

"I don't know what the hell that means," Yuri snarled, his eyes burning with impatience. "All I know is that you're pathetic. I can't believe that you would even think about sparing this wretched cur. Memories," he grumbled, remembering all the companions that he'd lost in the past year. "Every memory I have has been corrupted by this filth! If you really are a part of me, then you understand that he's harmed every person that we've ever loved."

So, you kill him. Then what? Your hatred will not be sated by the death of just one.

Yuri averted his gaze from the Ghost Wolf.

You will continue massacring others until there is no one left. Faelen, like us, has also suffered immensely. For centuries, he's searched for acceptance. But the humans deny him. They treat him like a monster, although all he wanted was their companionship. Horux's massacre was a tragedy. We lost many loved ones on that day. The wolf met Yuri's gaze. *But if we were locked up for hundreds of years, I know we would understand his rage.*

Yuri clenched his jaw, incapable of believing this mirage that was speaking to him. Why the hell should he listen to a hallucination?

The Ghost Wolf heard a crunch, and glanced up see Violet walking through the hole in the warehouse wall.

"Yuri?" she whispered, slowly walking forward. "What are you—

"Stay back!" Yuri snarled, raising his claw, prepared to execute Faelen.

It is time that you return control to me.

The voice spoke in Yuri's mind once again and he trembled with fury, the wolf's words echoing in his head. Over and over again, he heard the real Yuri speak the same phrase. But to spare Faelen … to be merciful was to show weakness. He was anything but that — the Oblivion Claws had granted him the power of a god! "For so long, we've sought power," Yuri growled. His voice rose to an infuriated shout. "So why is it that when we finally have obtained the strength to defeat any enemy, you want to cast it away, huh? *I am true strength.* Without me, we're nothing but frail weaklings that die at the hands of wretched beasts like Faelen and Malyssa!"

Yuri sensed a flicker of movement in front of him and instinctively slashed outward. Blood splattered onto his face, and his eyes widened as he saw Violet fall, clutching her eye. The princess struck the ground, gasping in agony as crimson liquid oozed through the cracks of her fingers.

The rage drained from Yuri, replaced by disbelief of what he had done. He'd harmed the woman that he loved, the woman that had cared for him even when things seemed hopeless. They'd made sacrifices for each other, and Yuri had betrayed her.

For that moment, Yuri no longer cared for power, and without that hunger, the Oblivion Claws reverted to their original form of ebony gloves. The boy's eyes returned to their turquoise color, gleaming with tears. Releasing Faelen, he fiercely tore off the Sacred Treasure and threw the gloves to the floor, quickly rushing to Violet's side.

"No, no, no, no! I … didn't mean for this to happen," he whispered, holding the princess's limp body in his arms. She was unconscious, blood gushing from her eye. The Ghost Wolf's lips quivered as he desperately looked around for something to bandage her with. He needed to stop the bleeding!

The warehouse was empty of all but the unmoving body of Faelen. It reminded him of the last time he'd been in an empty warehouse, just like this one, back in Horux. In both instances, he'd lost control.

Biting his lip, he reached to pick Violet up in his arms and carry her away. He knew that it was foolish to leave a threat like Faelen alone, but he didn't care. Violet needed to be treated immediately.

A black raven dove through the hole in the warehouse, swiftly landing beside Violet's body, startling Yuri. He cringed as the animal transformed into a tall humanoid. Moriaki.

The druid said nothing as he knelt beside the injured princess's body, extending his hand over the hemorrhaging wound ripped across the right side of her face. The elf's hand glowed with green energy, emitting healing magic. The deep gash sealed itself within seconds, and the blood stopped flowing, but there was a stretching scar that traveled from Violet's lower cheekbone, across her eye, and up to the top of her forehead.

Yuri was relieved that Violet was healed, but felt an overwhelming sense of guilt as he stared at the mutilated face of his love. He'd done that; he'd been the one to disfigure her. He closed his eyes, devoured by grief.

Moriaki looked at the Oblivion Claws, which lay on the floor. "She'll be blind in her right eye, and she'll have a nasty scar," he said. "But she'll live." The elf stood, nodding to Faelen's unconscious body. "I'm surprised that you managed to halt Faelen's invasion all on your own. You defeated a Bount, and there's an army of obedient werewolves just outside this warehouse, awaiting your commands. You've saved Escalon, Yuri. You halted the infection before it became inexorable. That's a true feat."

Yuri lowered his head, his lower lip quivering. He felt like bawling like a child. "I didn't do it on my own," he murmured, his gaze wandering to the cursed gloves on the floor. His hands quavered, curling into clenched fists. "Without the Oblivion Claws, Faelen would've killed me long ago."

Moriaki nodded, looking at the scar on Violet's face, now realizing what had happened. "That Sacred Treasure warps the mind, granting its wielder immeasurable power at a terrible price," he said, reassuringly placing his hand on Yuri's shoulder. "I know that you won't believe me, but you ought to know that Violet's injury isn't your fault."

Tears now streaked freely down Yuri's cheeks and he sniffed, bowing his head. That's what everyone kept saying — that it wasn't his fault, that the outcome was unchangeable. But he didn't believe that. There was always something that he could've done differently with each action that he'd chosen. Unfortunately, he'd made mistake after mistake. His blunders had caused many people to suffer.

The boy's eyes widened as the old druid embraced him tightly, surprised by the warmth he felt from the elf. "It's okay to be distraught. There's no point in hiding it," Moriaki said gently. "But know this. Zylon and his forces are successfully retaking Horux as we speak. None of this would've been possible without you. You helped the Iradian party get through Lichholme, and you saved Escalon's last practitioner in gnomish engineering from Malyssa's army of vampires. We never would've been able to create the Phoenix Cannons without you. And now you've stopped Faelen, the werewolf that threatened the wellbeing of everyone in Escalon." The elf grinned, the first time that he'd smiled so broadly in centuries. "Regardless of what you think of yourself, Yuri, you've saved millions. You're a hero. Never forget that."

Yuri leaned forward and pressed his face against the druid's robe, sobbing freely. He released all of his frustration, sorrow, and regret, crying harder than he had since his family's death. Moriaki held Yuri as tightly as a father would his son, patting the boy's back to comfort him.

"When you're ready, I'll take you home," Moriaki said, pulling back from the embrace as he looked at Violet. "Both of you."

The King of Horux

Yuri walked out of the warehouse with Violet in his arms, standing tall before an army of obedient werewolves. Behind him was Moriaki, whose gaze shifted nervously at the myriad of beasts, unused to seeing so many of them as allies.

Yuri's body shifted into its gigantic werewolf form, towering over his subordinate creatures. The beasts gave obeisance to their new leader, bowing their heads to the ground, pledging fealty to the strongest werewolf. The Ghost Wolf stole a glance at Faelen, who was now awake. The Bount, with most of his bones broken, was still unable to move.

A simple nod from Yuri was enough to command three werewolves to rush into the warehouse and lift up Faelen, bringing the injured beast with the Ghost Wolf as he walked.

"You're not going to kill me?" Faelen said, his eyes filled with shock. He bared his fangs at Yuri, who didn't even look at him. "I caused you so much suffering! How could you just let me live? I am responsible for the death of your family and your best friend, and the destruction of your city! Do you not realize—"

"I know," Yuri said, his words filled with such power that the Faelen was silenced immediately. "But I understand why you were angry. To feel neglected by everyone in the world, to be treated like an outcast and abomination, that's something that no one wants to feel. That's why I'm taking you to Horux, a city reborn."

"What do you mean?" the Bount said, frowning.

"Most of the werewolves in Horux will be cleansed," Yuri explained as he strolled through the destroyed streets of Reidan, trailed by his army of beasts. "They'll be rational, like you and I.

And I would welcome you there, where you will be surrounded by a community of beings that will finally accept you. They will not jail you as the founders of Horux did. They will not condemn, disrespect, punish, or scorn you for your appearance. This is a second chance for you, Faelen. Will you accept it?"

Faelen stared at Yuri, disbelieving the nonsense that he was hearing. This boy was willing to trust him, after all he'd done? "How do you know that I won't try and wreak havoc as I've done here?"

"I don't," Yuri said honestly. "But you don't have a reason to. After all, this is your wish, isn't it? To live amongst others like you?"

The Bount lowered his gaze, his injured limbs drooping as Yuri's werewolves carried him through the streets. Faelen had never met anyone as genuinely compassionate as this. A weary smile appeared upon his lips and he bowed his head in defeat. "You really are something," he murmured. "Why are you doing this?"

"I would like to say that it's from the goodness of my heart," the Ghost Wolf said with a chuckle. "But in reality, I feel guilty that I heartlessly murdered Tanya and stole your one chance to become human again. I don't think you're nefarious, Faelen. You're just misled. Perhaps an era of harmony will set you on the right path again, as you once were with Yazmine and your grandmother."

Faelen's eyes widened at the mention of the two people he'd loved most. He'd cast them into the back of his mind, locking his memories of them away in a mental vault. Lowering his head, he remembered.

Recollections of times that he'd spent with his beloved Yazmine and occasions when he'd stay up all night to talk to his grandmother flooded into his mind. His eyes filled with fresh tears. Suddenly, his arms and legs began to shorten, his body altering and condensing in size. His fangs became ordinary teeth, and his blazing red eyes became cerulean. For the first time in centuries, since Malyios had condemned him to an eternity as a monstrosity, he took the form of a human.

The man stared down at his broken limbs, not caring about how hideously injured he was. He could finally see past his ebony hair. He had a beard and normal teeth. His fingernails weren't claws honed to rip victims in half, and he was no longer hunched by his arched, werewolf spine. "I ... how?" he whispered, his lips twitching with incredulity. "For so long, I've searched for a way to change forms. I thought that I'd rummaged through my entire mind for my trigger. Why now?"

"Love and acceptance," Yuri said, grinning at Faelen. "Those feelings that you sealed away hundreds of years ago. Together they are your trigger."

Faelen bit his lower lip, recalling the wonderful times that he'd spent with Yazmine and his grandmother. He wept, realizing how much he missed them. To avoid affliction, he'd forcefully forgotten them. Since he'd become a werewolf, all that he'd felt was rage, frustration, and hatred. This throbbing feeling in his heart, the tingling sensations of love and acceptance — it had been centuries since he'd felt like this. The man's tears dripped onto the fur of the werewolves that carried him, but the beasts did not react. A grateful smile spread across his lips as he sniffed. "Thank you."

***

By the time Yuri led his army of beasts to Horux, Zylon's troops had already conquered the city. Most of the werewolves that had been under Faelen's command were cured of their bestial ways. Only a handful had been killed.

Upon their arrival, the Ghost Wolf ordered his werewolves to stay calm in the presence of the Iradian army, and they obeyed. All of them were then injected with antidotes fired from the

Phoenix Cannons, restoring their rational minds. Underneath Yuri, Zylon, and Moriaki's supervision, the cured werewolves began to rebuild their wounded city.

A day after Yuri's return, the legendary Ghost Wolf stood outside of the great walls of Horux. Behind him stood Moriaki. Zylon was in the city, monitoring Faelen closely as the werewolf assisted with reconstructing the wounded city.

The immortal, along with many Iradians, had been against Yuri's decision to spare the old Bount. Zylon was even more surprised when the Ghost Wolf requested that Moriaki mend Faelen's shattered bones. However, out of respect for Yuri, the magician honored the young man's decision. Though he decided to keep a close watch on Faelen for the time being.

"Faelen and I made an accord," Yuri said to Moriaki as the two heroes stood alone on the soft dirt outside of the city, watching the empty road. "I believe that he will stay true to his word."

"His emotions clouded his judgment when he broke the accord that he'd made with Zylon. That is why Zylon is so worried that Faelen might do the same to you," Moriaki said with a slight smile. "Though I agree with you. I no longer sense such senseless rage dominating him. He seems to get along with the other werewolves so far, but perhaps it's too early to tell."

"Perhaps," Yuri said, reaching into the pockets of his black cloak. He pulled out the Oblivion Claws. "Moriaki, I know that you've done many favors for me already, and I don't want to ask any more of you. But I was wondering—"

"You need not feel guilty about asking favors," the druid said with a hearty chuckle.

Yuri grinned and respectfully bowed to the elf, holding out the cursed gloves. "As the Druid of the North, I hoped you would be willing to safeguard this Sacred Treasure. I fear that its terrible power might one day fall into the wrong hands. It cannot stay in Horux."

The druid nodded in agreement. "That it cannot." He reached out and grasped the gloves in one hand, gripping his staff in the other. "I will hold onto the Oblivion Claws until you are ready to wield them."

The young man blinked. "I don't believe I will ever be ready," he admitted. "The Oblivion Claws feed off its wielder's desire for power. No matter what, I feel that I will always subconsciously hunger for more strength." He smirked at the elf. "But maybe there will come a day when I truly am worthy of wielding it."

Moriaki tucked the gloves into his robe, patting Yuri on the shoulder. "I believe that day will come a lot sooner than you think," he said, nodding towards the road. "Ah, our friends are finally here."

Yuri turned, spotting them. A large group of Horuxian refugees from Teolan were being led down the road by a handful of cloaked riders. Archerus rode in the lead, a broad smile upon his face as he gazed upon his old home. The warrior waved to Yuri.

Noah rode to the leader's left, his attention focused on a massive tome. The magician glanced up and saw Yuri, smiling slightly. He adjusted his glasses with a poke and then gave a nod of acknowledgement before returning to his reading.

To Archerus's right was Lena and Terias. The knight and engineer were discussing something, so deep in conversation that they hardly noticed they were approaching Horux.

The group halted before Horux's champion, and Archerus dismounted his horse first, followed by Lena, Terias, and Noah. "We heard about what you did with Faelen," Archerus said with a smile. He reached out and clamped his hand on Yuri's shoulder. "No matter what anyone says, I support you. I know you have your reasons."

"Thank you." Yuri smiled, embracing his friend tightly. He flinched when he felt a heavy thud on his back. Turning, he saw that Terias had wrapped an arm around his shoulder. "Eh?"

"They're calling you the Ghost Wolf of Terrador now! Hero of Escalon and Champion of Horux!" Terias said with smirk. "Word travels fast, and it's only been a couple days since you saved Escalon."

"*We* saved Escalon," Yuri corrected, rubbing the back of his neck, slightly embarrassed. "Though I didn't know that people were calling me that."

"They are," Moriaki confirmed, trying to hide his words with a cough.

"How'd you manage to defeat the great Faelen? If he got past my father, then he must be very powerful," Noah said, lowering his book.

"Yeah, I want to hear this!" Lena exclaimed, sounding like an excited child.

Yuri blinked, feeling overwhelmed for a moment. Then he smiled, looking past his friends to the sea of refugees. People craned their necks to get a glimpse of the man that had halted the werewolf infection. He waved for his friends to follow him through the gates of Horux. "You all must be exhausted from your travels. Let's get everyone settled in, and then we will share tales. I want to hear all about yours as well."

***

The Horuxian refugees were initially terrified of living amongst werewolves. But after several days, they began to realize that the beasts were really no different than other humans. They even came to accept Faelen. The werewolf worked hard to rebuild homes and perform favors for anyone in need, trying to redeem himself in the eyes of the people. And it was working.

As the months went by, Horux developed further. Archerus started a class in Horux to teach new werewolves how to control their enhanced senses and abilities. Lena, Noah, Terias, Faelen, Zylon, and thousands of civilians worked together to mend the city's infrastructure. Moriaki had returned to his home in the woods, now that balance had been restored within Escalon.

When Yuri wasn't helping to rebuild the city, he was at Violet's bedside as she recovered. He hadn't been able to forgive himself for hurting the one he loved. The scar across the right side of the princess's face constantly reminded him of his crime. Even when Violet told him that she forgave him, and that she only wanted to move forward, he didn't feel any better. There was still a knot in his stomach, twisting painfully at the thought of the pain that he'd caused.

The Ghost Wolf and Horux's princess stood on the balcony of Violet's royal chamber, overlooking the healing city in the distance. More homes were being built in the Noble District, housing for the Iradians that were forced to leave their home once they became werewolves. Because they were no longer human, they knew that they had to migrate to a place where there were others like them. A place like Horux.

Yuri still wore the red scarf that Violet had given him at the beginning of their journey, fingering the cloth with one hand, his other hand on the marble railing. He felt soft fingers interlacing with his and turned to his dearly loved partner. She smiled at him and squeezed his hand, and together they gazed upon a monumental statue of the Ghost Wolf that had been built in his honor. Two other statues were built in the city. In the trade district was one of Zylon, the immortal who bravely led the Iradian forces to retake Horux. In the Lower District was one of Archerus, who facilitated the creation of the Phoenix Cannons that had saved the werewolves from their bestial ways.

"Things are changing," Yuri said, gently kissing Violet's forehead. "I wonder what's in store for the future of this city."

The king and queen of Horux had returned to their thrones upon their return from Teolan. They seemed unsure of how they should lead a city of both werewolves and humans. Often, they consulted Yuri and Archerus, since they understood the people, both human and beast.

There was a knock, and Yuri turned as Terias opened the door to the chambers for the king and queen of Horux. The royal pair ambled into the room and Yuri immediately gave obeisance, in reverence to his lords. "I-I was not expecting you," he said, blushing slightly. He'd never kissed Violet in front of her parents before, and he knew that they'd seen him.

Terias smirked at his friend but said nothing.

"Oh, set aside the formalities. You're practically family," the king said, grinning.

"He will be, when he finally decides to wed Violet," the queen teased.

Now Yuri could feel the heat rushing to his face as he straightened his back, hearing the princess giggle beside him. He smiled at the king and queen. "What can I do for you?"

"We've come to you asking for something that you might find ... surprising, at first." The king shrugged. "But I'm sure you will understand the reasoning for our decision. We're offering to pass our royal power to you and Violet."

The young man blinked, as surprised as his lord had predicted. Such an offer had never been made in the history of Horux. He knew why the king had approached him, though. He already had the peoples' love and loyalty; the monument that the civilians had built for him was proof of that. The royal pair did not understand werewolves, and Yuri didn't expect them to. For them, ruling Horux was like a couple of rabbits trying to govern a society of lions. The two races were extremely different and, should the werewolves choose, they could easily overthrow the human king and queen.

Yuri and Violet were both werewolves, and the Ghost Wolf was easily the strongest in the city, other than Faelen. There had been no threat of a coup for the citizens of Horux trusted him, as did the king and queen. He had already advised the royal family on many of their decisions, so they knew that he was capable of making wise choices. "Wouldn't Archerus be better suited for the position than I?" Yuri suggested.

Archerus was a great leader, having shared the reins of the expedition through Lichholme with Kura. He'd taken over after she'd been killed, and had managed to complete the quest even though Yuri had been in a coma. Without Archerus, Yuri knew that he would've perished a long time ago. He owed the man a great deal.

"Archerus was actually the one who recommended that the kingship be passed onto you," the king said, beaming, catching Yuri off-guard once again. "You have recommendations from many of your friends as well. Even the immortal, Zylon, believes that you would make a great king, considering the contributions that you've made since your return to Horux."

"So, what do you say?" the queen purred. "Violet, we also await your answer."

"I'll take the role if Yuri does," Violet said, hugging the hero's arm. She nuzzled her cheek against his shoulder. "I wouldn't want anyone else as my king but him."

Yuri smiled amiably, feeling the gazes of the royal family and Terias upon him. To become king was an enormous responsibility. He never thought that he would ever be in a position of power, having lived in the slums for most of his life. Yet, here was his chance to become a lord, and the first werewolf king in Terrador's history. It would be a stressful duty, but Yuri knew that with his friends helping him, he could steer Horux in the right path.

The young man met Violet's gaze, his heart fluttering. *And there's no one else that I'd rather have as my queen.*

"I'll do it."

***

Time flew by after Yuri took Horux's throne. After several months, he'd married Violet, the one person that he wanted to spend an eternity with. The city had been rebuilt and even improved. The economy prospered, with open trade routes to Iradia, established by Commander Terias and his army of werewolf knights.

Archerus continued to teach the new werewolves, including Queen Violet, how to control their new abilities. His real duty, however, was functioning as Yuri's right-hand man. The king never made a decision without first consulting with Archerus and Violet; the three practically ruled the city together. Meanwhile, Violet's parents enjoyed their retirement in a luxurious home in the Noble District.

A year had passed since Yuri had taken the crown. The Ghost Wolf walked with Zylon past a recently built statue of Senna that was positioned outside the barracks in the Noble District. "Much has changed," Zylon said with a grin. "You've done well for this city, Yuri. Much better than the tyrannical kings I've met over my lifetime."

"Thank you." Yuri replied. "I appreciate you staying for the past year to help with the rebuilding of Horux."

"I've actually called you here today to tell you that I'll be leaving. And I think that you should come with me," the immortal said, causing the king to halt. Zylon smiled, expecting the surprised reaction from the Ghost Wolf. "Junko is still out there, corrupting others like Faelen and Tanya, using their weaknesses to manipulate good people. As long as he remains in this world, no one is safe. The Bount organization's goal is the domination of Terrador. Eventually he will return to Escalon. Horux will not be safe forever, you know that."

Yuri nodded. He'd been thinking about Junko, about where the cloaked man might be hiding and what his next move would be. His knuckles cracked at his side as he clenched his fists. "Junko preys upon those enraged at the world and drags them to his side," he murmured. "He was the true mastermind behind Horux's massacre. The blood of thousands stains his hands."

"I've located him, on a faraway continent to the south that is inhabited only by humans," Zylon said. "No werewolves, no vampires, no undead—"

"No creatures that will want to gobble me whole?"

"I can't promise that."

"And you want me to come with you to this foreign continent," Yuri said, raising an eyebrow at the magician. "To oppose Junko and his Bounts."

"You've saved Horux and Escalon from destruction," Zylon said, patting the werewolf on the shoulder. "But now it is the world that needs saving. The Bounts are amassing an enormous amount of power. I believe that they plan to awaken a being so strong that he will make Faelen seem like a child in comparison."

Yuri winced at the sound of that. "I am the leader of a settlement of people now, Zylon. I cannot just abandon my duties as king and—"

"I've already talked to Archerus. He said that he was willing to fill your seat if you came with me on this expedition to put an end to the threat of darkness that plagues Terrador. Together, Archerus and Violet will be able to keep Horux on its feet in your absence," Zylon said. "Noah and I have created a force of our own to combat the Bounts — an army of magical assassins that will be specially trained to hunt Junko and his accomplices. It is your choice, but know that we could use more help. Noah, Lena, and I leave tomorrow morning."

Yuri pondered the offer for a moment. He knew that he didn't have to go. No one would judge him badly if he decided to stay here and lead the citizens of Horux. He could live a happy life with Violet and enjoy the peace, while it lasted. But if Zylon and his allies were unable to stop Junko, then he would surely have to fight in the future. The Ghost Wolf didn't want events like the massacre of Horux to happen again. If he helped to stop Junko, then the Bounts would never be able to cause any more atrocities. This was his chance to save countless lives.

"Junko is responsible for the hardship that Escalon suffered a year ago," Yuri said, sighing. "I agree that he needs to be stopped. It's just that—" He stopped speaking, biting his lower lip. He was afraid of the dangers that lay ahead. If there were going to be foes that were stronger than Faelen … what were the chances that he would return home in one piece?

"You have until tomorrow morning to think about it," Zylon said with an understanding nod. The immortal bowed respectfully to the king before walking towards the Lower District, where he was meeting Lena and Noah about their departure plans. "We leave at sunrise."

Yuri watched the esteemed magician as he strolled off. He bit his lower lip, thinking about his last encounter with Junko at Lady Amara's fortress, where he'd been humiliated. He remembered Junko's violet eyes burning with true malice. To leave on this journey would be risking all the happiness that he'd fought to secure over the past two years. He would encounter powerful opponents. But something within him knew that he couldn't just let a madman like Junko roam free. The nefarious Bount must be brought to justice; his crimes could not go unpunished.

The Ghost Wolf would accept this precarious quest.

***

As expected, when Yuri broke the news to Violet, she was distraught. The thought of Yuri thrusting himself back into harm's way was worrying, but he promised that he would return. It was an assurance that seemed to put Horux's queen as ease, as if the promise could immunize her husband against the cold grip of death.

The two lovers spent the night in each other's arms, cherishing what could be their final moments together. The king watched his beautiful wife as she lay asleep beside him, still gripping his hand tightly.

Yuri slowly slipped away from Violet and rose from his bed, sweeping his black cloak over his body. He snatched a leather bag that lay beside his door, slinging it over his shoulder, and slipped his feet into a pair of leather boots.

The Ghost Wolf went to his balcony, welcoming the chilling breeze that blew the hair from his face. He pressed his clammy palms against the railing of the terrace and exhaled shakily. The moon shined its luminous light on him as he looked at the grand statue of himself that stood triumphantly in the castle's courtyard.

What was this uneasy feeling in his chest? Just thinking of the dangerous journey ahead made him feel queasy. Was he afraid of death? A year ago, he hadn't been. The young man glanced over his shoulder at Violet, who slept soundlessly. "It's you, isn't it?" he whispered. "I don't want to hurt you." He feared that it would stab his beloved through the heart if he failed to fulfill his promise. The very thought of hurting her, of leaving her, made his chest ache.

For a moment, Yuri's mind called him back to the bed, where he could entwine himself in the warm blankets and forget all of his fears. No one would condemn him for wanting to stay in Horux. He'd already done Escalon a great service. But then the world called to him, crying desperately for help. The imaginary voices of the millions that would suffer from Junko's wrath echoed in his mind, fusing together in a cacophony of pleas.

Yuri glanced across the room at the red scarf that Violet had given him years ago, lying upon his bedside table. He thought about going to it, but didn't. Instead, he turned and leapt off the balcony and dashed off into the night. A small smile formed on his lips. He knew that he didn't need a memento to remember the woman that he loved.

Earlier in the day, he'd said goodbye to many of his close friends. But there was someone that he'd forgotten to speak to before he departed Horux.

As the king walked through the empty streets of the sleeping city, he wandered into the trade district. The marketplace was practically empty, except for a man sitting on a wooden bench, his attention transfixed by Zylon's statue in the center of the plaza. Yuri walked closer to the man, blinking when he realized that it was Faelen.

"Greetings, my liege," Faelen said with a polite bow of his head.

Yuri hadn't seen the werewolf in months. But he'd heard only praise of Faelen, which made him believe that the ex-Bount was honestly working hard to turn over a new leaf. "What brings you here so late?"

"It is morning," Faelen corrected, leaning back into the bench. "I wake up early so that I can see the sunrise. It's a magnificent sight that I never got to see when I was jailed. Seeing the warm, beautiful rays of light fill me with hope that each day will be a good one." He tapped the wood of the bench, smiling. "This was also where I first met Yazmine, the light of my life."

Yuri smiled at him. "You've come a long way. You've done more than uphold our accord. I've heard of your gracious contributions to Horux's growth."

"Only because you saw past my vicious image and gave me a second chance," Faelen said. "I was misled and wrathful. Because of my lack of control, I've injured this wonderful city and its people. I do whatever I can to make up for my wrongdoing, but it never seems to be enough."

Yuri averted his gaze, now staring at his feet. He'd felt the same way after he'd scarred Violet.

"You're going somewhere?" Faelen asked, nodding to the bag on Yuri's shoulder.

"I depart today to join Zylon's hunt of the Bount organization," Yuri said, watching as Faelen's eyes went wide with surprise. "Junko is malevolent and poses a danger to Terrador. He must be stopped. The city will be governed by Archerus and Queen Violet. I expect that you'll behave in my temporary absence."

"Temporary," Faelen murmured, crossing one leg over the other. He thrummed his index finger against the bench's arm, as if he were impatient. "Milord, I cannot stress the amount of danger that lies ahead in this quest that you pursue. Junko is a master of manipulation. He may not physically fight many of his battles, but the allies that he gathers will surely be fearsome. Even I wouldn't stand a chance against them."

"Danger cannot deter me from this path," Yuri said. "The Bounts almost drove you to destroy Escalon. If we had not stopped you and Junko's sick plan, then this continent would be in ruins and millions would be dead. What if they do the same thing elsewhere … and there aren't courageous warriors powerful enough to stand against the Bounts? Then what?"

Faelen was silent. He knew the answer; the weak would perish.

"With every continent that falls beneath the Bounts' influence, their strength grows," Yuri said. "They want to conquer the world, and that means that the security of Horux and Escalon is also at stake. I don't want anyone else to have to go through the hell that the citizens of Horux have endured." He straightened his back, his countenance gleaming with confidence. "That's why I'll help bring Junko and his organization crashing down, no matter what it takes."

Faelen smirked, recognizing the Ghost Wolf's look. "You're stubborn. Once you set your mind to something, you're impossible to convince." Standing up, Faelen walked over to the king. He patted Yuri's shoulder and led him out of the trade district. "I don't know when I'll see you next," he said, his body morphing into a werewolf. "That's why I'd love to watch the sunrise with you on this fine morning. Come with me." The beast took off into the empty streets, sprinting towards the outer walls of Horux.

Yuri watched Faelen for a moment, smiling. He swiftly transformed into the white werewolf and charged forth with incredible speed, following the ebony beast. The two creatures scaled the side of Horux's wall with ease, landing gracefully on the walkway at the top.

From there, Yuri could see ribbons of warm colors creeping over the horizon, stretching outward as the sun slowly began to rise. Light expanded from the awakening star, sending vibrant light streaming across the sky. A sea of clouds held the radiant light as the sun ascended.

The king found himself grinning, extending his hand outward, watching as trickles of light streamed through his fingers. He closed his hand into a tight fist, the perimeter of his hand glowing gold from the sun's luminous rays. The Ghost Wolf put his hand on Faelen's shoulder, finally considering the werewolf as a companion. "The world and its inhabitants are always changing for better or for worse," Yuri said, still watching the horizon in awe. "But the sun will always be this beautiful."

"That it will," Faelen said warmly, pointing down to Zylon, Lena, and Noah, standing at the gates of Horux. The three were preparing to leave and hadn't yet noticed the Ghost Wolf. "A grand quest lies ahead of you, Lord Yuri, one that will be even more treacherous than your last. But something tells me that you will endure. You somehow always do." He struck his chest as a soldier would and bowed in deep reverence to his king. "I wish you a safe return, my king."

Yuri watched the werewolf for a moment, shifting back into his human form. He smiled and gave Faelen a gracious nod. Exhaling, the young man leapt off the wall, landing on the ground beside Lena and Noah. The two jumped in surprise at the lord's abrupt arrival.

"So, you came," Zylon said, smiling. The immortal adjusted a giant bag on his back. "You are doing Terrador a great service, Yuri."

The Ghost Wolf brushed his white hair from his eyes. "Nonsense. We should all contribute to the preservation of this great world." He grinned. "I'm just doing my part."

The End

Continue reading of Yuri's journey in the *Age of Darkness* series!